Hart Turns Cole

Book Two Of Lucien's Hart Saga

Anthony Blodgett

BLODGETT VENTURES

Published in the United States by Blodgett Ventures LLC

First edition, December 2025

Cover design, formatting, and layout by Anthony Blodgett

Typography and layout prepared with precision and intentionality to preserve the integrity of the story and reading experience.

For permissions or rights inquiries, contact:

blodgettventures@gmail.com

Before You Step Back In

You made it through the first story, so you already know the rules of this world.

Love cuts deeper than knives.

Loyalty bends until it breaks.

Mercy is a debt paid in blood.

But what you saw before was only the spark.

This time the fire isn't personal.

It's structural.

It's citywide.

It's the beginning of a war no one can contain.

What began as a collision between two people

is becoming something else now.

Something larger than either of them.

A reckoning.

A second descent.

Some answers arrive late.

Some arrive burning.

Some break things you thought were already broken.

And everyone who thought they escaped the fire

is about to learn what it means to burn twice.

If you're ready, open the door.

If not, walk away now.

But don't say I didn't warn you.

Anthony Blodgett

Authors Note

I always knew this story had a long road.
    But I didn't expect it to return the way it did.
    Not like a plan, but like a pulse.
    Like something unfinished that refused to stay quiet.
    Some worlds don't wait for permission to continue.
    Some characters keep walking with you long after the page turns.
    Lucien and Lena did that.
    They never stopped.
    They never could.
    This book cost more.
    It burned slower.
    It carved deeper.
    I wrote it with steadier hands and a heavier heart.
    Not to outdo the first,
    but to understand it.
    To understand love under pressure.
    To understand power after consequence.
    To understand what a man becomes when he turns toward the fire instead
of away from it.
    If you're holding this, thank you for coming back.
    Thank you for stepping into the heat with me again.
    The fire didn't die.
    It just changed shape.
    This is Hart Turns Cole.
    And this time, it's fucking war.
    Anthony Blodgett

Prologue

They say there's nothing after death.

That's when the heart stops, the story ends.

They're wrong. Because I died. Not in metaphor. Not in spirit.

I flatlined. Everything faded. The sounds. The pain. The fight... gone.

And for a moment, I felt nothing.

Not peace. Not light. Not fire. Oblivion.

And the oblivion was real.

But here's the secret they never tell you:

Oblivion isn't empty. It's full.

Full of every choice you ever made.

Every name you whispered. Every hand you crushed. Every love you broke.

It holds them like weapons, and it waits.

I stood there, weightless in the dark,

watching the man I was get torn apart by the man I could've been.

And then I chose. Not to return. To rise.

Because when the devil dies, he doesn't beg for heaven.

He doesn't knock on the gates.

He kicks open the door to something older than God,

and walks back into the world as something the sky never planned for.

I didn't survive. I became. Not a man. Not a monster. Something in between.

Something holy enough to protect what I love,

and violent enough to burn the rest to ash.

So let the world brace. Let them pray.

Because I crawled out of that bed with fire in my lungs and thunder in my blood.

And now I remember who I am.

Not the king. Not the criminal. Not the ghost. **I am the reckoning.**

Contents

CHAPTER ONE

AFTERLIGHT

They said Lucien Cole died that day.

They said the bullets were too close, the damage too deep.

Because even monsters bleed when you stand close enough to aim.

The city mourned him the way it mourns all fallen kings, in whispers, graffiti, and silent shrines that weathered beneath streetlights.

Enigma's doors were chained shut. Heaven on Fifth was boarded again, taped off like a tomb, still waiting for a debut that never came. Every shadow of the empire he'd built went dark overnight.

And then the city showed its teeth.

Men who had bowed to his name began testing locked doors. Debts were called. Old insults resurfaced. The city did not grieve him cleanly. It sharpened itself on the rumor of his death.

In alleyways and penthouses alike, whispers grew into questions. Scumbags and kingpins, hustlers and killers wanted to know who had crossed his shadow and come out breathing.

Animals crawled from their darkest holes, daring to claim a throne they never could have touched while Lucien Cole still breathed.

They circled his territory like vultures, fighting over scraps of power, blind to the truth waiting silently in the dark.

A throne isn't empty just because the king has vanished.

And absence doesn't always mean death.

Sometimes the throne is bait.

The media couldn't resist the story.

They spun it like wildfire, calling it a cautionary tale, a criminal's downfall, a silent victory for law and order.

But that was their mistake.

Because the more they talked, the more the city listened.

The underground was no longer rumor. It was televised. Hashtagged.

People flooded social media with grainy footage, wilder theories, and whispered confessions from bartenders and bodyguards who swore they'd brushed shoulders with the devil.

Lucien Cole became a memory, one of those names you weren't sure had ever truly existed, yet felt like he'd always been there, watching.

A man whose name was spoken in the same breath as violence and seduction.

A ghost carved from shadow.

And now the city couldn't forget what it had seen.

It became aware.

Aware of the closed-door deals, the blood-soaked alleyways, the empires hidden behind neon lights and clean suits, and what moved beneath their feet.

But somewhere beyond the noise, past the headlines, the hunger for blood, one light still burned for him.

Inside the estate across the Hudson, perched above the quiet black water, Lena Hart didn't mourn him.

She refused to.

She had seen the flatline, watched the monitor count his pulse down to silence, felt the last trace of warmth leave his fingertips.

Then the line surged.

His voice followed, raw and impossible, cutting through the void.

"Will you marry me?"

She said yes with blood and iodine in the air. Then the light in his eyes dimmed again.

The monitors screamed. Nurses stormed through the room, terrified of losing him twice, hands flying across his chest as oxygen masks dropped and orders cut through the room. Lena was pushed back, her palms pressed to her heart, a voice at her ear.

"He needs space. Time. Oxygen."

He didn't die again. Not officially.

But the man she loved vanished behind blackout curtains and white corridors that swallowed him whole.

Private security took their posts outside the door, as if she were just another visitor. As if love carried no clearance.

The transfer came twelve hours later, Alexander at the helm, Victor beside him, silent.

A private ambulance waited in a loading bay no one had cleared. No sirens. No paperwork. No trail the city could follow.

Lena sat in the front seat of a black SUV, clutching the black book as if letting go would undo everything.

It was the one he always carried, the one she opened at his bedside when she thought he was gone.

The leather lay cool beneath her palms. Not a relic. A record. Proof he had bled. Proof he had risen.

The pages stayed sealed, silent and waiting. Now it felt less like something he owned and more like something that had carried him.

They arrived at the estate just before sunrise.

Lucien was alive somewhere deep in the house, surrounded by doctors she wasn't allowed to question and guarded by strangers who watched but never spoke.

The estate had become a vault, and Lena was the ghost trapped inside it.

Everyone moved around her with purpose. Doctors. Guards. Alexander. Victor. All of them carrying pieces of a truth no one would place in her hands.

On nights like this, she paced the hallways barefoot, wrapped in one of his shirts.

Her mind replayed every moment they'd had together.

It hadn't been long, just a few months, if time meant anything at all.

But what they had wasn't measured in days. It was measured in scars, in breathless silences, in nights that never truly ended. The way they moved, fought, burned, it felt like a lifetime in each other's orbit.

Tonight felt different.

The air felt heavier tonight, making each breath harder than the last, as she moved slowly down the hall with her arms wrapped tight across her chest. Cold crept up her legs from the stone floor.

She had told herself she wouldn't come here again. Not tonight. Maybe not ever.

Not because she didn't love him, but because standing outside that door, night after night, being ignored, being forgotten, was starting to feel almost worse than losing him.

At the end of the corridor stood the double doors to Lucien's private wing, guarded by two men who said nothing.

Lena didn't stop until she was directly in front of them.

"Let me through," she said, her voice steady and close to breaking.

The taller guard shook his head. "We have orders. No entry."

"Orders from who?" she asked, the words trembling loose.

"Lucien is,"

From inside, footsteps approached.

The doors swung open without a sound, cutting her off.

Alexander Cole stepped through, framed by shadow, his suit immaculate, his expression carefully controlled. Yet in his eyes lay a quiet exhaustion, one that mirrored Lena's own.

"It's all right," Alexander said, waving a dismissive hand toward the guards. They nodded, stepping aside instantly.

Lena swallowed, her heart hammering against the ache of being cast aside.

"You're keeping me away from him," she whispered. "Why?"

Alexander regarded her for a moment.

When he finally spoke, the words were slow, measured, and achingly human.

"Right now, Lena, love won't save him. Not the way you want it to."

"What's fighting its way back to life in that room is not the man you remember. Not yet. It's every wound he's ever survived, every ghost he's ever buried. And if you reach for him too soon, you'll pull him under with you."

Her fists trembled at her sides.

"So what am I supposed to do?" she whispered. "Just stand here and wait?"

Alexander stepped closer.

"Stand," he said simply. "Be the one thing that doesn't fall apart.

He'll crawl through fire to reach you when he's ready, because that's who he is.

And when that moment comes, nothing in this world, no man, no god, no heaven or hell, will stop him from coming back to you."

His hand rested briefly on her shoulder, a weight meant to steady her, not comfort her.

"You haven't lost him. Not yet. But if you open that door now, you will. Let him find the way back to you without dragging you into the dark with him."

Lena didn't move. Alexander's words hung in the hallway long after the door whispered shut.

Stand. Be the one thing that doesn't fall apart.

Her fists unclenched slowly, blood rushing back into her fingers. She wanted to scream, pound against the door until it splintered, until someone dragged her away. But the weight of his warning rooted her in place.

She pressed her forehead against the cool wood, breath fogging the dark grain. Somewhere in that darkness, Lucien was breathing.

Minutes bled into each other. A floorboard creaked behind her, one of the guards shifting his stance, but her focus narrowed to the faint hum she thought she heard beyond the door. Machinery. A monitor's soft beep.

Then, fainter still, a sound she almost missed. A drag of breath, rough and uneven.

Her heart lurched. "Lucien?"

Silence.

Then something else. Not a voice, but a faint scrape. Fingertips dragging slow against wood, right beneath her hand.

Lena froze. Her breath locked in her throat. She pressed her palm harder to the door, as if skin alone could close the distance.

"I'm here," she whispered, her voice breaking. "Do you hear me?"

The scrape stopped. A heartbeat passed.

Then one soft knock, hollow and measured, from the other side.

Maybe her mind, starved and unraveling, had built the sound just to survive it. Still, she didn't move. Her forehead rested against the wood. She let the quiet move through her ribs.

Because truth or dream, it no longer mattered. Some things were true before they were proven.

In her bones, she knew: the dead didn't reach back.

Lucien Cole did.

CHAPTER TWO

LIMBO ONE: THE SILENCE

Lucien opened his eyes to nothing.

Not darkness. Just the flat, blanched absence of it. A sky without color. A horizon without end.

The ground beneath him was cold and wrong, grit grinding into his shoulders like broken glass. He lay on his back, staring up at a sky that neither moved nor breathed. No clouds. No sun. No source for the light.

When he sat up, the world felt unnaturally still. The silence pressed against his skull with weight.

The first thing he noticed was what was missing. No wind. No birds. No hum of power lines.

He stood on a road that went nowhere, asphalt split and buckled, its white lines fading into dust. On either side, trees rose in skeletal ranks, branches brittle, leaves long dead. Bark flaked beneath a sky drained of color, as if the world itself had been bled dry.

Each breath left his lungs too slowly. The air was flat and tasteless. His footsteps sounded wrong, too sharp in the stillness. They echoed like gunshots in an empty cathedral.

Behind him, the horizon shifted. Not clouds. Not a storm. A wall of darkness moved forward in slow, silent waves. It did not blot out the light so much as swallow it, taking the dead forest one jagged treetop at a time.

He did not know why he started walking. There was no destination. No plan. Only forward.

Move, or you disappear.

The ground cracked under his boots. Dust lifted in pale plumes. The air thinned with each step. The sky shifted from dull silver to a muted gray that pressed low and heavy.

Then he saw it.

Color. Real color. Cutting through the monochrome world like a wound. A single red rose, its stem impossibly green, blooming from a crack in the dead earth. Beside it lay a woman's wedding band, its diamond catching the dim light in a way nothing else could.

He crouched, fingers brushing the petals. Soft. Alive in a place that was not.

He reached for the ring next. The metal was cold in his palm.

A thorn bit into his skin.

The pain was sharp. No blood came.

He did not know why they were there. Or why he kept them. But his hand closed over them as if they were proof. Of what, he could not say.

And he kept moving.

The darkness stayed behind him. Closer now. Close enough that when he glanced back, it seemed taller. More deliberate.

It did not rush. It did not need to.

Forward.

The road narrowed into gravel. The light dimmed until he realized it had no source. No sun. No moon. Just a diffuse glow from everywhere and nowhere, weaker now than when he first opened his eyes.

The rose stem pressed into his palm. The band sat cold against his skin.

He did not look back again. Instinct had taken hold.

And instinct said: Keep moving, Cole.

CHAPTER THREE

THE RESURRECTION SIGNAL

Lena hadn't slept. She had tried.

She paced the hallway until her calves ached, then turned and paced it again. At night, the estate felt longer. Wider.

She was still wrapped in one of Lucien's shirts, the cotton worn soft, his scent fading faster than she could bear. Her eyes kept drifting to the thin strip of light beneath his door.

Sleep never came. Only the knock. Soft. Hollow. Imagined or not, it echoed in her skull long after the sound itself had faded.

If she imagined it, then some broken part of her had chosen mercy.

By dawn she felt hollowed out, scraped raw from the inside, every heartbeat too loud for the quiet. Pale gold spilled across the horizon, sliding over the Hudson and catching on the stone railings. The river moved slow and indifferent, the world beyond the estate almost peaceful, as if it hadn't ended the night Lucien fell.

An engine broke the quiet. Gravel crunched at the gates.

She didn't think. She moved. Barefoot, cold biting into her skin, she stepped outside as a black sedan rolled to a halt.

Victor Dresnik climbed out in a pressed shirt, sleeves rolled, tie loosened just enough to show fatigue, not defeat. He struck a match, cupped it against the wind, and lit his cigarette with precise ease.

Lena descended the stairs, her throat tightening without warning.

"Victor."

Her eyes were bright.

His gaze lifted, the edge in his features softening.

"What's wrong, sweetheart?"

She let out a brittle laugh.

"I don't know what's real anymore."

She swallowed.

"Give me one."

A brow rose.

"You smoke now?"

"Not until tonight."

Her voice held steady. Nothing else did.

"Sometimes you want something that burns slower than your life does."

He studied her, then placed a cigarette in her hand. The match flared, lighting her tear-tracked face in amber. Unyielding.

They sat on the cold stone steps, shoulders almost touching, watching the city wake in the distance.

Victor glanced at her.

"At least he's alive."

"I know." She took another drag. The smoke scraped her throat raw. It steadied her.

"But alive isn't the same as back."

He said nothing.

Lena kept her eyes on the horizon.

"I feel like I'm standing outside myself. Like I'm watching everything happen and I can't step back in."

"These moments get under your skin. They remind you how easy it is to lose everything. One phone call. One bad breath."

"It's insane how normal everything feels until it doesn't. Until the floor drops out and you realize none of it was promised."

She swallowed.

"I never held anyone the way I held him. I was always scared. Anything I loved too much, I thought I'd lose. So I let go first."

Victor looked at her then.

"And now?"

She exhaled slowly.

"Now I know that was the lie. Fragile doesn't mean pointless. It means it matters. Every breath counts. Every touch counts."

Victor stood, crushing his cigarette against the stone.

"He's still fighting. So we don't stop."

The shrill ring of the phone shattered the morning quiet. Lena had barely stepped back inside, the bitter taste of Victor's cigarette still clinging to her tongue, when Victoria's name flashed across the screen. She answered on the first ring.

"Vic?"

"Turn on the TV," Victoria's voice snapped, tight, urgent. "Channel six. Now."

"What?"

"Just do it!"

Lena fumbled for the remote, nearly knocking it off the table. Her pulse hammered so hard she could hear it. The television crackled to life in a flare of static and light.

And then she saw it.

Lucien.

Shaky cellphone footage under blurred night lights. A stretcher shoved toward an unmarked ambulance, flanked by silent men with rifles.

A voice murmured, urgent but low,

"Cole's alive."

The mic caught the scrape of boots on asphalt, the rush of gurney wheels, then a flash of Lucien's face, pale as marble, an oxygen mask fogging with the faintest breath, before the paramedics slammed the doors shut and the screen cut to black.

Then bold white text flashed across the screen: COLE ALIVE?

"And this just in. Mayor-elect Roland Lansing has issued a statement on the leaked footage. He called the video a dangerous hoax and told New Yorkers that any administration he leads will purge the underground power structure that has held this city hostage. His exact words: 'We will not bow to ghosts.'"

The anchors' voices tangled over each other:

"Exclusive footage leaked overnight."

"What does this mean for the Cole empire?"

Lena stumbled back a step, phone still pressed to her ear.

"Oh my God."

"Yeah," Victoria breathed. "Keep watching."

The broadcast broke into split-screen chaos across the city:

Lieutenants' bodies dragged from a gutted warehouse, headlines screaming GANG LAND MASSACRE, RETALIATION?

FBI and NYPD closing in on Cole. Clubs, offices, safehouses hit in a single strike. Black SUVs jamming the streets. Agents moving with military precision.

Graffiti sprayed across boarded club doors in dripping red: COLE LIVES

Enigma's chained doors hung open for the first time since his "death." Candles flickered outside. Black roses lay at the threshold like offerings to a ghost king.

Lena's hands trembled as panic ripped through her chest.

"Victor!"

Her voice broke against the walls.

Footsteps thundered in the hall.

Victor appeared first, eyes sharp, gun visible at his hip. Alexander followed, buttoning his jacket as if preparing for war. Both men froze at the sight of the screen.

The anchors droned on: "Federal task forces are mobilizing. Sources claim the underworld is already fracturing as rumors spread of Cole's survival."

Then the tone shifted, cutting to a new anchor, voice more composed but charged with urgency.

"In a breaking development, an internal memo was accidentally leaked by a federal intelligence liaison closely tied to Cole investigations.

The memo suggests Lucien Cole may have been more than just a whistleblower, alleging he orchestrated violent purges within criminal networks and quietly benefitted from their collapse.

Though officials have yet to confirm the leak's authenticity, early reports indicate the Department of Justice is under pressure to revisit immunity deals granted during the investigation's final phase.

"No formal charges have been filed, but behind closed doors, high-level sources admit: Cole may not have just brought empires down.

He may have been shielded by what came after."

Victor rubbed his mouth once.

"Agent fucking Hall."

Alexander's head turned slowly toward him.

"The same agent who handled you and Lucien during Royce?"

Victor didn't answer at first.

"Only one who knew enough to accidentally leak a memo and make sure it burned."

Alexander's gaze narrowed. "Then we have a bigger problem than headlines."

The leak wasn't just a breach. It was a countdown.

Someone had started the clock on purpose.

Lena's voice cracked as she turned toward them, still clutching the phone. "They know."

Alexander didn't answer. He stepped forward and lowered the volume without taking his eyes off the footage looping again and again.

The quiet window was gone. Now everything would happen in the open. The world had found the door.

"Vic, I'll call you back," Lena said quickly, eyes still locked on the screen. "I've gotta go."

She hung up without waiting for an answer.

Alexander's voice cut through the silence, low but edged with urgency.

"We have to get him out of here. Now."

Victor's head snapped toward him.

"Move him? He's barely breathing on his own."

"We can't risk it."

Alexander's gaze stayed locked on the screen, watching Lucien's pale face flash between ambulance doors on an endless loop.

"The second they confirm he's alive, every enemy he's ever made will start circling. Cops. Feds. Doesn't matter. They'll all come."

Lena barely heard them.

The footage was everywhere.

Dozens of posts were already taking off, shaky clips reposted with captions screaming:

COLE'S NOT DEAD

DEVIL WALKS AGAIN

#COLELIVES trending in under an hour.

Comments flooded beneath each upload: conspiracy theories, prayers, death threats, emojis of black roses and fire, threads speculating who would strike first. Some celebrating. Some terrified.

Lena's stomach turned. The entire world was watching, and she was standing in the middle of it, barefoot, trembling, smoke still ghosting the back of her throat.

"Lena." Alexander's voice pulled her back.

She looked up to find both men watching her, Victor tense, Alexander unreadable.

"We're moving him. Before anyone else tries to."

"Where?" Victor asked.

Alexander didn't hesitate. "The Glass Chapel."

Lena blinked. "What the hell is that?"

"Decades ago, our family bought an old monastery deep in the north mountains. No roads. No cameras. We turned it into a sanctuary long before Lucien ever needed one, a place to hide people, protect assets, disappear from the wrong eyes. When the time came, we refitted it for this."

"Why didn't we take him there earlier?" Lena asked.

"Because we didn't know if he'd survive. We needed proximity. Surgeons. Machines. The moment he was stable, we started preparing it."

"And now?"

"Now he's breathing on his own. Just barely. And the whole world knows he is."

Victor exhaled, already reaching for his phone.

"We'll need three vehicles. No plates. Diversion routes."

Alexander nodded. "Get Ghost on the line. Tell him we activate the sanctuary."

He turned back to Lena, his gaze cold but not unkind.

"It's the only place Lucien ever said the world went quiet."

For Lena, that was the first thing about the place that made sense.

Alexander's eyes hardened.

"Pack. We leave before the hour turns."

Lena looked down at her phone again.

#COLELIVES

312K SHARES

Then she looked up at the screen, Lucien's face flashing on an endless loop.

This time, she didn't flinch.

Chapter Four

THE KINGS EXODUS

The hours after dawn passed under a hush too heavy for morning. Lena stood at the edge of the estate's grand hallway as Victor pulled folded maps from a leather satchel and spread them across the long oak table. A single desk lamp cast stark light over the routes marked in red. Arterial roads. Known checkpoints. Old smuggling paths curving like veins toward the mountains.

Outside, weak late-fall light fractured through tall windows, sharp against chilled glass. The house, once a fortress, now felt like a grave.

"He's stable," a voice muttered behind her.

She turned. A doctor, young and exhausted, hands still gloved, nodded once as he slipped past.

"Vitals stable. Deep sedation. Brainstem intact. No higher cortical response."

Lena didn't answer. She could barely breathe.

Across the room, Victor straightened, tapping the map twice.

"That's the primary," he said, pointing to the winding stretch of blacktop disappearing into the northern range. "No digital markers. Cell dead zones. Ghost gives us three hours before the Feds sweep again."

Alexander stood a few feet away, arms crossed, unreadable. He hadn't spoken since the broadcast.

This wasn't a meeting.

It was a mobilization.

This was what grief became here: maps, engines, weapons.

"We run three vehicles," Victor continued, glancing at Lena.

"Two decoys, one transport. No plates. We rotate between civilian and private access roads, no pattern."

"And Ghost?" Alexander asked.

"In position," Victor confirmed. "Satellite uplinks. Infrared sweeps. He'll have eyes the whole way."

Lena finally spoke. "I'm going with him."

"No." Alexander didn't raise his voice.

Lena stepped forward. "He's not cargo. I'm not leaving him."

"It's not about leaving," Alexander said. "It's about exposure. If that transport gets hit,"

"Then let it hit me too. I'm not staying behind while the fucking world decides if it gets to keep him."

Victor said nothing. He looked between them, calculating, then nodded once.

Alexander exhaled through his nose.

"Then don't flinch when the gunfire starts."

No one moved.

Then Alexander turned back to the map.

"We roll out in twenty."

Hallway lights dimmed.

Medical gear packed.

Surveillance feeds flickered.

The estate wasn't home anymore. It was a staging ground.

Lucien's stretcher was wheeled down the west corridor in silence, flanked by two guards and a doctor adjusting IVs with gloved precision. His face was still, drained of color, surgical dressings clean against his skin. But the steady rise and fall of his chest told them one thing. He was still here.

Lena stood beside Alexander, dressed in black from head to toe, hair pulled back, jaw set. She said nothing. Her body had already given itself to motion. Fear had nowhere to sit.

Victor signaled one of the drivers stationed at the side gate. "Vehicles are in position. Diversion cars are moving into a two-mile perimeter."

Alexander didn't look away from the stretcher. "Good."

The three-vehicle convoy moved fast. No lights. No sirens. Just low engines and precision. Ghost's encrypted comms fed in updates: thermal readings, roadblocks, patrol shifts, drone recon. Every stretch of road was covered. Anything moved, he'd see it. As the gates opened, morning light cut across the courtyard, sharp and winter-cold. They rolled out.

The estate blurred behind them as the mountain road stretched ahead, tense and waiting. From the rear window, Lena caught one last glimpse of the skyline's distant crowns, slivers of steel and light dissolving into pale blue. The forest had already claimed everything else. Pines flanked the road in both directions, dense and unbroken, their spines stiff with frost. With every mile, the world grew quieter. Roads narrowed. Cell towers vanished. Civilization was left behind.

In the middle SUV, Lena sat between Lucien and radio static. The signal-jammer thrummed beneath her seat. Her hands stayed locked in her lap, knuckles pale, spine rigid, but her eyes hadn't left Lucien once. He lay on a stretcher bolted to the reinforced floor. Blanketed in black. Monitors dark by design, no beeping, no traceable signal. Only a faint green pulse on a shielded screen and the steady rise and fall of his chest. Enough.

Victor drove with one hand on the wheel and a burner phone to his ear.

"Five out from first checkpoint. Traffic's clean."

Ghost's voice came through the encrypted line.

"Diversion cars in place. No heat on your tail. Keep it tight."

Victor's eyes stayed forward, scanning the empty two-lane road.

"If anything shifts, we drop the route and kill the signal."

The third vehicle trailed behind, carrying the surgical team and extra guns.

Up ahead, Alexander rode in the lead car, his silhouette sharp against the glare of morning.

Every few minutes, updates pinged through the comms:

"Highway's clear."

"Bridge sweep negative."

"No heat signatures at checkpoint."

Still, no one relaxed.

Lena's eyes flicked to Lucien, his lashes still, his lips parting in a shallow rhythm, a shadow of bruising carved along his temple. Beneath the thermal blanket, his chest lifted faintly, each breath barely disturbing the fabric. Every mile should have made her feel safer. Instead, it felt like watching him fade behind glass, close enough to see and too far to touch. Victor met her eyes in the mirror, unreadable, then looked away.

She remembered Lucien's eyes opening that first time. Wild. Terrified. Human. Not reborn. Dragged back.

"You look like hell," she whispered, almost to herself.

Victor's voice cut through the silence.

"He'll walk again."

Lena looked up.

Victor didn't turn.

"Maybe not soon. Maybe not clean. But he will."

"How do you know?" she asked, her voice barely above the hum of tires on asphalt.

Victor reached into his coat, pulled out a cigarette, then stopped, remembering the sealed cabin.

"Because I've seen what happens when men like him stay down."

Silence stretched.

"What happens?"

Victor's eyes moved to Lucien's still form, then back to the road.

"The wrong people stop being afraid."

They drove deeper into the trees. Signs disappeared. The asphalt cracked. The path narrowed into an old service trail carved through the mountain like a forgotten scar.

Lena's breath fogged the window. She felt the shift. Not distance, but threshold. And somewhere between gear shifts and static, Lucien's fingers twitched.

Chapter Five

SANCTUARY

The road fractured into gravel long before the first gate appeared. Steel and stone rose from the treeline, layer after layer, as if the mountain had been carved to keep the world away.

Ghost's voice crackled once in Victor's earpiece.

"Perimeter's clean. No heat signatures. No signs of intrusion."

After that, silence. No guards. No movement. Only the grind of tires and a low hum in the ridges, steady and too precise to be wind.

Lena leaned forward, palms braced on her knees, eyes fixed on the climb ahead. She'd never been this far north. The mountains were stripped bare by late fall, their faces dusted in frost, the sun already sinking into long shadows.

The first gate groaned as it opened, slow, mechanical, as if the hinges hadn't been touched in years.

Something shifted behind the treeline, not sound, not movement, just pressure, like the mountain had turned toward them.

Beyond, the gravel narrowed into switchbacks. The cliff edge dropped into shadow, each turn stealing a little more light.

Victor caught her staring.

"Apparently this place doesn't exist," he said. "Not on paper. Not on maps."

Her gaze traced the ridgeline.

"Then what is it?"

He hesitated.

"Alexander called it a sanctuary. That's all I know."

Birch replaced cedar, their white limbs rattling in the wind like bones strung together. The air thinned. Even the sound of the convoy seemed swallowed whole, as if the mountain were deciding whether to let them through.

At last, the slope broke into a plateau.

The Glass Chapel rose from the cliffside, iron and dark glass fused to the bones of an old monastery. Arches scarred by centuries framed bands of steel reinforcement. The sacred and the brutal welded into something permanent.

The panes caught the sun in fractured gold, scattering shards of light across frost-slick stone. Annexes clung to the slope like outgrowths, half swallowed in shadow, thick enough to survive siege or silence.

It wasn't grand like Lucien's Palisades estate. It was sharper. Colder. Built to last, not impress.

The reinforcements didn't look new. They looked like they'd been waiting.

Victor eased the SUV into the courtyard. Gravel snapped beneath the tires. The other vehicles fanned into place without a word.

Lena's eyes caught on a balcony jutting over the abyss like the prow of a ship. She imagined standing there at night, the valley erased beneath her, no roads, no lights. Nothing.

A door on the last SUV opened. A man in a dark field jacket stepped out, unarmed, but built like someone who didn't need weapons. His eyes swept the convoy, settling on the stretcher.

"East wing's sealed."

His voice was low, steady.

"Medical's inbound."

The words barely landed before the ground began to tremble. A low thrum rolled over the courtyard, growing into a steady shake as a helicopter cut across the ridge and descended toward the landing pad carved into the cliffside.

Lena shielded her face from the blast of wind and frost.

Victor didn't flinch.

Alexander didn't move at all.

The helicopter touched down in a storm of dust and rotor wash. A medical team stepped out fast, bags slung across their shoulders, coats snapping in the wind.

"Move him," Victor said.

The medical team reached the stretcher with practiced precision, locking restraints, checking vitals, preparing the lift as if they'd rehearsed it for years. Lena followed close, her steps quickening whenever the blanket shifted enough to reveal a fragment of Lucien's face.

Inside, the air carried warmth without welcome.

Stone walls. Vaulted ceilings. Corridors washed in muted amber. No family photos, no clutter. Only the machinery of survival.

They crossed the main hall toward reinforced glass doors. A medic keyed a code. The lock hissed open.

Inside, the hum deepened, low and even, almost comforting. The machines blinked in rhythm with his heart.

Crossing the threshold, Lena felt it, a subtle shift, as if the air itself sealed shut behind them.

Not a door closing. A boundary forming.

Alexander's voice cut from behind.

"This is where he stays until I say otherwise."

Not heals. Stays.

Lena froze. The temperature seemed to drop, the air too clean. Stone gave way to glass, the surfaces hiding something older beneath. Not designed for healing. Designed for containment.

A faint rhythm pulsed below hearing, impossible to ignore once she caught it.

The room felt tuned, as if it were listening.

The gurney wheeled forward. Lucien didn't stir. The medics checked vitals in silence, machines whispering diagnostics.

"How long do you keep him locked away like this?" Lena asked.

Alexander didn't glance up.

"As long as it takes."

"Containment isn't the same as safety."

His gaze cut sharp.

"It will keep him alive."

The words hit, but she didn't flinch. She watched Lucien vanish behind sliding glass etched with security seals. A lock engaged with a clean click.

"Can I stay?" she asked quietly.

Alexander studied her, not disdain, not warmth. Calculation. Then he inclined his head toward the observation corridor.

"You'll have access to the outer wing. That's as far as it goes."

Lena pressed her hand to the glass, eyes fixed on the figure inside. He looked asleep. But she knew better. Whatever dream held him was no mercy. It was something he would have to claw his way through.

For a moment, the glass didn't shine. It pulsed faintly, like breath behind it.

Outside, the wind tore at the cliffs. Deeper in the mountain, machinery rumbled awake.

Sanctuary, Victor had called it. But sanctuaries are built by someone.

As the locks sealed, it felt less like a haven and more like a tomb.

Deep in the mountain, something stirred.

Chapter Six

THE WATCHERS

On the first night at the Glass Chapel, the silence still felt borrowed.

Light vanished behind the peaks as if it were fleeing. Shadows climbed the walls in slow, deliberate folds. Outside, the wind stirred the trees.

Inside the iron-and-glass heart, the quiet shifted around her, matching her pace too closely to ignore.

Lena sat on the edge of a narrow cot in the outer wing, her fingers working the hem of her sleeve in a rhythm she couldn't stop.

The room had been made for waiting, not living. A folded blanket. A narrow desk bolted to stone. Enough to keep a body there. Nothing soft enough to comfort one.

No TV.

No signal.

Just an internal satellite feed rigged for Ghost to cycle coded transmissions. Everything else from the outside world was sealed.

Lucien was alive. Locked behind glass and machines. The medical team moved like ghosts, efficient, silent, gone before she could ask anything.

She hadn't spoken since Alexander left.

He had disappeared down a corridor with Victor. She didn't ask where.

Now Lena stood alone in the quiet, and it felt chosen for her.

The hallway met her with a dry, sterile chill that sank past skin and settled in her bones. Somewhere in the walls, the systems whispered. She passed the sealed door to Lucien's chamber without pausing. Not yet. She needed air.

The glass doors at the end of the corridor led outside. She keyed in the temporary code Alexander had granted her. A soft chime, then a mechanical hiss.

She stepped into the courtyard. Stone walls rose around her. Beyond the open edge, the valley had vanished into a star-filled void, a darkness that swallowed everything below. She didn't remember the cliff feeling this close when they'd arrived.

Cold hit her throat first. Then her chest.

The sky above was infinite. Stars sharp as pinpricks. The moon hung pale and distant. With no light pollution for a hundred miles, the heavens opened wide.

Distant galaxies shimmered in impossible hues, violet and silver streaked with blood-red across the black.

For a moment she thought she heard the same low hum she'd felt inside, carried through stone, beneath the wind. But when she held her breath, it was gone.

She remembered that night on the beach in Miami. Warm salt wind. The hush of waves against sand. Lucien beside her, eyes fixed upward as if searching for something not built by human hands.

He'd asked who made all this. Not the buildings. Not the empires. The stars. The gravity. The order behind every breath.

Now that same man lay behind a vault door, unconscious beneath glass and steel, hidden in the mountains while half the world waited for proof he was still real.

Then a sound.

Low and long, carried on the wind.

A howl.

She froze.

Another followed, higher, sharper, answering the first. Then a third, closer. A full chorus somewhere down in the woods.

Wolves.

A whole pack moving through the forest below, hunting, claiming ground.

Lena closed her eyes, her breath fogging in the cold.

The door opened behind her.

Boots scraped softly against stone. A thread of sulfur drifted through the wind as Victor struck a match.

He came to stand beside her, not close, not far, just near enough for his warmth to register.

The flame caught. He held the cigarette without smoking, letting it burn between his fingers as if he were waiting for something worth saying.

"They move different up here."

Lena turned slightly. "The wolves?"

Victor watched the tree line. "No fences. No people. They're free. That's when predators are worst."

She watched him in profile, his face harder in the dark, shadows settling into old scars.

"They sound like they own the world," she murmured.

Victor exhaled smoke through his nose. "Tonight, maybe they do."

Silence settled again, deeper this time.

She looked out into the endless black.

"You think he's dreaming?"

Victor didn't answer at first. He just stared into the dark beside her.

"I think he's fighting."

The answer hurt because it sounded true.

Her throat tightened. "Still?"

"He's not built to rest, Lena."

"Sometimes when the machines shift, it sounds like breathing. Like something here is listening for him."

Her arms folded tighter around herself.

"I was with him that second time. Right after he asked me to marry him. He looked at me like he knew he wasn't staying. Like he just needed to hear my yes before he slipped away again."

Victor didn't move.

She glanced at the cigarette in his hand, burning slow and clean.

"I used to hate you," she said. "For about five hours."

Victor let out a dry chuckle, smoke riding it. "Would've been worried if you didn't."

Lena smiled despite herself. Small and quick, gone as soon as it came.

"I couldn't understand how Lucien partnered with the man who had just threatened to kill him. It felt backwards. Reckless. I asked him why."

"He said, 'It was dominance masked as forgiveness.'"

Victor's gaze flicked her way, sharp and unreadable, but he said nothing.

She looked out over the ridgeline. "Whatever it was, I'm glad he made that call. When everything else fell away, you were still there."

Victor took another drag, as if there were nowhere else he needed to be. The ember glowed between his fingers.

"Doesn't matter what we say. The only thing that counts is who stays when the fire hits."

Lena turned toward him. "You stayed."

Victor looked down for a second. "So did you."

His eyes held hers. "And now?"

She swallowed. "Now I understand."

No smugness. Only gravity.

"Took me a long time too."

Smoke drifted between them.

"But understanding's only the first step." His gaze went to the horizon, hard and distant. "Now we hold the line."

She stared at him, the wolves still crying below.

"Do you believe in fate?"

Victor took another drag.

"I believe in patterns. Cycles that don't break on their own."

He let the smoke roll out between his teeth.

"And I believe the devil always gets a second wind when people think the war is over."

Lena turned toward the drop again, her voice quieter now.

"When I met him, I thought I was getting away from my old life. From pain. From fear. I thought he was the end of the story."

She blinked, lashes wet.

"But he's not. He's the next chapter. And I don't think it ends."

Victor held her gaze.

"Then make sure it doesn't."

She glanced at him. "End?"

He met her eyes.

"Break you."

Then he flicked the cigarette into the abyss.

It vanished into the forest below without a sound.

The howling had stopped. Only the wind remained.

They stood there a moment longer, side by side, staring into the black.

Behind them, Sanctuary pulsed with low, steady light.

Waiting.

CHAPTER SEVEN

LIMBO TWO: THE CLIMB

The ground had changed.

No broken road. No skeletal treeline. Only jagged slopes biting at his boots, black rock veined with pale fractures catching the last of the dying light.

Lucien walked.

Each step grated stone, the ground shifting under his weight. His balance slipped, caught, then slipped again. The climb tore at him, slow and merciless.

The air thinned as he moved higher, dry and metallic in his throat, tasting like rust.

Above him, the sky darkened and sagged lower. Not night. Not storm. A heaviness, as if the light itself had grown too tired to hold itself up.

The rose was still in his hand, the wedding band looped around its stem. One petal was gone, torn away somewhere behind him. The stem bent and bruised, as if the climb had wounded it too.

He turned it once in his grip, thumb brushing the torn edge.

Then he kept moving.

The darkness was closer now. No longer a wall but a tide, silent and black, swallowing stone and shadow. No roar. No wind. Only motion.

Something in it watched him.

Not eyes. Not faces. Attention.

Cold in the marrow.

He looked forward and climbed.

The slope grew steeper, but the strain felt wrong. His muscles burned, yet no sweat rose on his skin. No breath caught in his throat. His body labored, but the fatigue felt older than flesh.

This was not exhaustion.

This was weight.

Not the weight of a king.

Not the ledger of a criminal.

Not even the shadow of an empire.

Older. Deeper.

Not the crown or the ghost, but the boy.

The boy who learned no one was coming.

The boy who became dangerous because of it.

His grip on the rose tightened until the band bit into his palm.

Movement stirred behind him.

Figures in the fog. Shapes that dissolved when he tried to focus. Some tall. Some small. All faceless.

Whispers sifted through the thin air. Close enough to graze his ear. Too distant to understand.

Then one broke through, sharp as glass. Another followed, low and mocking. Another came sweet before it turned.

They tangled and rose until the words blurred, but the knives of them still found him.

He pushed forward. He kept moving.

The mountain above sharpened, its ridgeline carved into impossible angles. Architecture, not nature. A crown cut from stone, a throne set into the peak.

It wasn't calling him. It was dragging him.

Déjà vu sank its teeth into his mind. He had been here before, or somewhere that remembered him.

The whispers swelled. Faceless silhouettes thickened in the fog. Shapes closing in. Men he had killed. Boys he had beaten. Lovers he had lost.

The darkness surged again behind him. Faster now. Not only rising but reaching.

The band dug deeper into his palm. He looked down. Another petal gone. The rose bending lower.

The slope cracked beneath him.

For a moment the ground turned from stone to ledger paper.

Thin. Fragile.

Names inked across it, names he remembered, names he had buried.

The tide licked at the edges, swallowing them line by line.

For a fraction of a second, the air changed.

Not cold stone. Not fog.

Clean. Sharp. Antiseptic.

Then a single flat beep cut through the void.

Thin. Electronic.

Wrong in a world with no machines.

He staggered forward, tearing through the paper as it bled back into rock.

The whispers turned to shouts. A thousand voices. No faces. All hunger.

The ridgeline loomed closer, its angles cut sharper now, the crown shape coming into focus.

Every step forward felt like a verdict.

The darkness surged again. Reached. Brushed cold against his heel.

Still he climbed.

A voice threaded through the noise.

Older. Softer. Fractured like static.

His mother. Evelyn.

Not warning. Not command.

Just a fragment, as if pulled from a place where thought was slipping.

"I forget things sometimes. But never you."

It hit harder than any accusation. Not a voice from memory, but from decline.

He stopped with one foot on paper and one on stone.

The rose bent lower in his grip, petals trembling.

He slid the band from the stem and set the flower on the ledger, as if laying her name back where he found it.

Petals shivered.

The paper held.

He closed his fist around the ring until it pressed a circle into flesh, pain bright and exact.

The mark burned like a seal.

Proof he was not walking toward judgment. He was carrying it.

The tide brushed his heel again. Cold. Insistent. It wanted to claim him as one of the faceless.

He looked up at the jagged crown carved into stone.

Not for kings.

Not for ghosts.

For the boy who survived.

And he climbed.

Each step took back a yard of darkness.

A decision didn't redraw the map. It burned the old one.

The whispers faltered. Thinned.

One voice rose above the rest. His own. Younger. Raw.

"No one is coming."

The mantra that kept him alive.

The child in him still believed it.

The weight of it pulled at his ribs.

He didn't argue. He answered.

"I am."

Not waiting. Not pleading.

The dark surged once more and stopped, as if it had struck glass.

The dark couldn't enter what he refused to surrender.

Above him, the stone crown waited. Not for worship. For confession.

He kept the ring tight in his fist. The stone waited for him to kneel, to surrender, to let the weight define him.

He did not.

"Honest," he said, breath fogging in the cold. Not right. Not clean. Honest.

Truth over absolution.

The silence around him shifted. It was no longer empty. It was listening now.

So he climbed, carrying the ring, the weight, the wound, and the boy he had been.

The dark pressed close but could not take him.

The fight stretched on without end.

But he did too.

CHAPTER EIGHT

TWO MINUTES

Two weeks into Sanctuary, the doctors finally started pulling him back toward the surface.

Grey light slid down the tall glass, pooling in dim bands across the floor.

Somewhere deep in the structure, ductwork whispered, dry, recycled air moving with a steady rhythm. A tone too constant to be entirely mechanical.

Sanctuary held itself still. Not with reverence. Like a vault that had already decided what was worth keeping inside.

Lena stood just outside the inner wing, holding her breath without realizing it.

The reinforced glass door vibrated faintly in its frame.

A doctor in a dark sweater scanned the chart before speaking.

"We'll start reducing sedation in intervals," he said. "Could trigger disorientation. Agitation. Maybe clarity. Don't expect consistency."

He hesitated before the last word, like "consistency" was a promise he couldn't make.

Her hands tightened on the lapels of her coat. "And if he wakes?"

He looked up, meeting her eyes. "He may know you. He may not. There are no guarantees."

The door behind her hissed open. Alexander stepped through, his shadow stretching long in the angled light.

"You'll have two minutes," he said. "Twice a day. Inner door only. Full sterile protocol."

"That's nothing," she said.

"It's what he gets until I decide otherwise." His tone carried no cruelty, only weight.

Lena's pulse spiked. "He needs,"

"What he needs," Alexander cut in, "is to find his own footing. Without anyone pressing the world into his hands before he's ready to hold it."

The inner wing lock disengaged with a solid click. Beyond the glass, the machinery shifted tone, like the slow draw of an inhale.

Alexander moved aside. "You want those two minutes? Take them, Lena."

The doctor was already offering her a sterile gown and gloves. She pulled them on without looking away from the door. The gloves sealed tight at her wrists.

The second lock released. A seam of chilled, filtered air slid past her as the seal broke.

Inside, the room was pared down to essentials. A narrow bed. Shielded monitors. Tubes feeding into silence. Everything arranged with the cold precision of a place built to keep a body alive, not bring a man home.

Numbers shifted in quiet pulses. Lucien lay motionless, turned slightly toward the high window. Washed-out light traced the line of his jaw and throat.

For a moment Lena only stood there, trying to breathe.

Then she crossed to the bedside.

She didn't speak. Instead, she reached for the water bowl and cloth the staff had left for sterile care, dipping the fabric and wringing it out until it dripped once, then stilled.

Her hand trembled as she brushed the cool cloth across his wrist, over the faint dents left by IV tape. The water left a sheen on his skin that almost looked like warmth.

It felt obscene to be allowed only cloth and water when what she wanted was his pulse beneath her palm.

She moved the cloth up his forearm, over the line of his knuckles. Slow. Careful.

The monitors answered with a faint change in pitch, as if the room registered the touch.

His fingers twitched at the contact, faint but real. The monitor ticked upward, almost imperceptible.

Not memory. Not yet. But response.

Her chest clenched. "Lucien,"

The doctor's voice cut in from the doorway, controlled but firm. "That's enough for now."

She set the cloth back into the bowl, her hands steady only because she forced them to be.

The seal whispered shut behind her.

The glass split her reflection in two. She left her palm against it, watching his breath gather and fade in a fragile cloud on the other side.

When she finally turned away, the corridor felt longer than it had minutes before.

A faint strip of illumination ran along the baseboards, casting thin shadows across the floor. At the far bend, steel and stone replaced the view. No windows. Only walls that seemed to lean inward.

Her quarters were halfway down. She keyed in and stepped into the narrow space, peeling off the gloves.

Red marks circled her wrists. Her skin tingled where the seal had pressed.

From the doorway came the sound of knuckles rapping once against the frame.

Victor stepped in without waiting for an answer, his coat still carrying the frost of the mountain air. "He moved?"

She nodded once. "Fingers."

He closed the door behind him and crossed to the small desk. From his coat he pulled a folded thermal printout, Lucien's vitals stacked in narrow columns, and set it in front of her.

"Saw this coming off the monitors. Not much, but not nothing."

Her eyes moved over the paper, tracking the shift in numbers. The subtle uptick in stability.

"Why are you showing me this?"

"Because tomorrow, if it happens again, I'll need you to tell me if it feels different." He leaned closer, lowering his voice. "Patterns matter now. And you should know, Alexander isn't the only one watching these numbers."

Something in his tone told her he wasn't talking about doctors.

She stilled. "What do you mean?"

He shook his head, already turning for the door. "Just keep your eyes open. I have a feeling not every set of eyes on those numbers is hoping for the same outcome."

The warning stayed in the room after he moved.

At the threshold he paused, one hand on the frame. "Eat something. You'll miss details if you start running on fumes."

Then he was gone, boots fading into the stone hall.

Lena stayed seated, the printout still in her hand. Her gaze fixed on the faint rise in a single column of numbers. Small. Fragile. Enough to keep her breathing with it.

Somewhere behind the walls, the steady hum returned. Soft. Almost merciful.

She didn't notice when her breathing fell into its rhythm.

Chapter Nine

TELEMETRY

The corridor held a night of its own.

By the fourth week, waiting had become a skill. Lena hated how good she'd gotten at it.

Low strips of light ran along the baseboards, each diode pulsing in quiet sequence. The glass of the inner wing reflected her every time she shifted, hollow-eyed, her coat still clinging to her shoulders as if she'd forgotten it was there. Air moved through the ducts in a dry, steady drag, turning the silence into something counted.

Somewhere inside that rhythm, a lower note pulsed under everything.

She traced invisible lines across her knee to keep time with it. Up. Down. Proof her hands still obeyed.

Beyond the door, the sealed wing glowed with the sterile dusk of machines. Monitors breathed their numbers in silent pulses. Somewhere behind those panes, a man existed only in measurements, oxygen, pressure, rhythm. She had a name for him. The building had values.

Two doctors passed in quick succession, neither looking at her.

Lucien had moved. A twitch. Something turning. She felt it more than saw it, the way you feel thunder before the sound arrives. It woke something she couldn't put down again.

Footsteps clicked, unhurried, then stopped just short of her toes.

"Coffee?"

Victor held it without ceremony, a paper cup gone cool, the lid dented beneath his thumb. He didn't sit. He leaned against the wall, eyes fixed on the door as if it might move first.

"It's cold," she said.

"Most things are up here." He tilted his head toward the glass. "How long have you been timing your breathing to the ductwork?"

She tried to laugh. The air refused. The rhythm owned more of her than she wanted to admit.

"Since they took him off one of the drips. Long enough."

He slid a folded strip of thermal paper from his pocket and placed it in her hands.

"Telemetry from fifteen minutes ago. Micro-variability. Not much. Not nothing."

The slip looked like a city skyline. Small differences. A lift here. An easing there. If you didn't know the man the line belonged to, you'd miss it.

"What am I supposed to see?"

"Remember how it felt when he moved. Map your body to the line."

His tone offered instruction, never comfort.

"If it happens again, I want what you feel. Not what they measure."

"Because?"

"Because the doctors report to Alexander. You report to no one."

"Except you?"

"On this, yes."

She angled the paper. Tiny variations caught the light. "You think it means something?"

"The rhythm matters. Watch for the wrong ones. A spike. A stall. Anything that doesn't belong."

Before she could answer, the air changed.

It always did when Alexander arrived. The corridor narrowed, the lights steadied, the corners sharpened.

He came alone, hands bare, coat undone. His gaze moved over Lena first, then Victor, then the door.

"How long," he asked Lena, "did you watch his chest?"

"Until mine followed it."

"Then leave the wing tonight," he said. "What anchors you to him can drown you before he wakes. I won't lose you to that."

"You think I'll drown?" The paper crackled in her fist.

"I think you love him enough to forget yourself." He looked to Victor. "You don't need to stand here."

"I'm not standing," Victor said. "I'm counting."

"And what have you counted?"

"A new rhythm," Victor answered. "Small, but his."

"The doctors noted it," Alexander said.

"They don't feel it," Victor replied. "We do."

"Then keep counting."

Victor's mouth cut a brief smile. "Always."

"Two minutes. Twice a day. If he shifts into agitation, they go away."

36

"I know. If he wakes and doesn't know me?"

Alexander met her eyes fully now.

"Then he learns. Or he doesn't. Either way, you are not going anywhere."

"What is my job?"

"To hold steady for him," he said. Then, softer, "And for yourself."

He paused.

"Glass gives distance for a reason. It keeps what matters intact."

When he left, the silence felt less like absence and more like something held in place.

Lena stared at the cup, thumb in the dent Victor had made. She slid the printout back toward him, but he didn't take it.

"Keep it," he said. "Tape it somewhere you'll see it when you're too tired to think. You'll know if the next one is wrong."

"Wrong how?"

"Spikes are loud. Stalls are quiet. I'm less worried about loud."

He nodded toward the kitchen. "Eat. Exhaustion makes ghosts out of things that aren't there."

He left her with the cup, the paper, and the silence she had begun treating as a clock.

She heated broth she didn't want and drank it standing. Outside the slit window, the mountain's profile cut a silver edge against the night. Snow sifted like powder. Far below, the river showed itself only where moonlight caught the ice, a dull pewter vein through the forest.

Her quarters greeted her with the same starkness as the corridor. She taped Victor's strip to the wall above the desk lamp and stepped back. From a distance it looked like a seismograph of a polite earthquake, all tremor, no break.

She lay down without taking off her boots and turned her face to the wall. Rest came like fog, by degrees too small to notice until she couldn't see.

Something pulled her up out of it.

Not a sound at first. A pressure.

The building shifted half a breath. A note beneath the note. Wrong.

She held her breath and listened.

There. A thinner thread woven through the metal.

Not mechanical.

Not entirely human.

A rasp beneath the current.

"Lena."

She froze.

The rhythm smoothed back into order. Exact. Measured.

But the word lingered inside it, not spoken, not heard, only shaped.

As if somewhere in the sealed wing, beyond the glass, his breath had learned her name before his mouth could.

Grief could do that. Bend air into memory.

The inner wing stood where she'd left it. Immaculate. Impenetrable. A cathedral of numbers.

Beyond the glass, the room that held him kept its own slow weather. Monitors pulsed their quiet light. The window over the bed was nothing but a darker shadow, a square of night suspended inside the room.

She pressed her palm to the door as if the glass belonged to her hand. It took her heat and gave none back.

"Lucien?" Quiet. Almost unwilling to disturb the air.

Nothing moved.

She waited for nothing to answer.

Then, not motion. Almost.

The sheet seemed to consider shifting.

A line on a monitor stuttered, then steadied.

Her shoulders locked until they ached.

A diode blinked. Once. Twice. A pause.

"If you can hear me," she whispered, "I'm here."

The word here touched the glass and thinned. There, then gone.

She leaned her forehead against the pane and closed her eyes. Not to pray. To remember the weight of him. His mouth against hers. The palm at her back. The hidden gentleness beneath the violence he showed the world.

The body beyond the glass carried those maps. Somewhere, he was walking back into them.

"Keep moving," she whispered.

She didn't know if she meant it for him or herself.

The hum lifted half a pitch, answering like breath through teeth.

The diode blinked again. Hesitant. Almost human.

Her hand slid down the glass to the seam of the frame.

Nothing changed.

The monitors told her only what she already knew. Alive. Alive. Alive.

Back on the bench, she lifted Victor's strip to the corridor light. Tiny lifts. Tiny shifts. Her body filled in the rest.

The hum steadied. She matched it.

Her eyes burned with sleeplessness, but they refused to close. What she carried was harder to bear. The memory of his fingers curling against linen. Her body replaying it in case the world tried to take it away.

When the baseboard lights dimmed to their false dawn, she stood and stretched, aching from having held still too long. The door to the inner wing wore her handprint like a secret no one else would read.

Behind the glass, numbers kept their promises.

"Let them keep their promises," she told herself. "He's still ours."

It wasn't bravado. It was the only sentence that let her stay upright.

Two minutes would come. Two minutes would go. The man beyond the glass would twitch or not.

Lena lifted her chin, as if sight itself were a weapon, and stared through the distance holding him.

Chapter Ten

LIMBO THREE: THE RECKONING

The climb ended at the edge of the mountain.

Not a summit, only a blade of stone dropping into nothing.

Below, the world had been erased. No valleys. No forests. No horizon. Only a tide of black, swelling and folding like smoke and water, swallowing the last veins of earth. It breathed, a soundless exhale that chilled the back of his neck.

The dark began to take shape.

Hands pressed outward, dozens, then hundreds, pale and weightless, bending the air toward him. Fingers clawed. Palms spread. They dragged at him without ever touching him.

Faces followed.

Some he knew instantly.

Others blurred by time and blood. Men who had stood across from him, guns raised. Men who had stood beside him until they didn't. Strangers caught in the wrong place when he chose not to stop. Innocents. Enemies.

All the same now.

Every face was drained of warmth, but their eyes found him.

They whispered without moving their mouths.

Accusations. Bargains. Names.

Some called him killer.

Some called him king.

Some called him nothing at all.

The rose trembled in his fist. His heels edged the brink. One more step and the stone would vanish beneath him.

The stem snapped. Silent. Clean.

The rose withered in an instant, petals collapsing to ash that lifted from his hand, leaving only the dull band sliding loose against his skin.

The tide surged. Hands reached for his chest, his throat, his eyes. Faces leaned close enough for him to feel their breath.

He did not retreat.

Did not beg.

He stood.

The tide came anyway.

Something cut through.

Not light. Not sound. Something finer. A thread.

It tugged at his wrist, gentle, insistent. His head turned toward it, toward the ridge where the fog broke.

For an instant, through the blur, he saw her.

Lena.

Not whole, not solid, but a shape made of light. Her face half hidden in haze, her hand outstretched. Her voice jagged, broken, like static splitting silence, but his name carved through it.

Lucien.

The sound burned. It branded.

His hand moved before thought could stop it.

The tide screamed behind him. Faceless mouths open with hunger. Hands dragged lower, pulling him toward the brink. But hers pulled higher, sharper, burning like iron through his wrist.

A sound cracked the void.

Not thunder. Not gunfire. A resonant call, vast and deep, splitting the silence open. It carried through the cliff, through the mountain, into the marrow of his bones.

He looked up.

The sky was breaking.

Not with light. There was no light here. But with motion, violent and infinite, as if something above the clouds had turned to notice him at last. The dark ceiling tore in spirals, edges splitting like fabric ripped from seam to seam.

The pull came from above. Sharp. Sudden. Absolute.

His body tore upward.

Hands slipped away. Faces dissolved into static, mouths open but voiceless. Whispers unraveled into wind.

The mountain shrank below. The tide folded in on itself, devouring its own shadow. The cliff where he had stood thinned, cracked, and vanished.

The rose was gone. The band too. But the pressure in his palm lingered, seared into him as proof.

The void collapsed.

Glass.

He felt it before he saw it. Smooth. Cold. A barrier pressed to his back. His chest heaved, and the air this time caught in his lungs, not metallic, not weightless, but real. Machines droned low, steady as distant thunder.

The darkness didn't follow. It stayed behind.

His body lay beneath him like a reflection on a pane of water, still and pale, his face tilted toward the faint light of a high window. Tubes glinted. Numbers pulsed. His chest lifted in shallow rhythm.

The two halves folded into each other. The man climbing through void. The man lying in glass.

Impact.

Weight crashed back into him. Limbs. Breath. Veins aching as they were forced to move again.

His hand twitched. Once. Then again. A curl of fingers against linen.

Gray light pressed closer, cold, unrelenting.

And then he heard her.

CHAPTER ELEVEN

THE AWAKENING

Five weeks in, Alexander stopped calling it recovery and started calling it return.

Sanctuary had taught her silence. Not peace, but weight.

The sigh of vents. The tick of distant pipes. Even the pulse in her throat when the glass gave her nothing back. She heard everything now.

She had stood there so long her breath filmed the pane, then vanished into the chill. Machines never wavered. Beyond the glass, his chest rose and fell in that uneven cadence she had memorized, each breath a coin tossed to fate.

At some point, her body betrayed her.

Her knees buckled. Her chin dropped to her chest. Exhaustion dragged her under. She fought it, even in sleep. Her spine curled against the bench as if she could keep watch in her bones.

It was not the mountain's silence that woke her. It was a hand on her shoulder.

Her head snapped up, throat raw, vision fractured by light. Sanctuary's false morning pressed thin across the floor. Alexander stood above her, not looming, not cruel, simply immovable. He looked like he had already decided how this day ended.

"You can't keep this schedule." His voice was level, stripped of any human edge. "Nights watching. Days collapsing where you sit. It's unsustainable."

Her voice cracked. "If I stop, I might miss something."

"What you'll miss will not be measured in minutes." His eyes flicked toward the sealed wing, toward the narrow bed where Lucien lay.

"Then why now? Why wake me?"

Alexander's pause was long enough to change the air. "Because there's movement."

Her heart stuttered. She pushed half to her feet, but his hand pressed down, not harsh, just unyielding.

"Doctors are with him," Alexander said. "They'll measure what they can, breath, rhythm, blood. What matters to you is something else entirely. And if you go in now," he shook his head once, "you'll confuse what's happening. For him. For you."

Her lips trembled. "He's awake?"

"He's surfacing," Alexander said, though it sounded less like relief and more like observation.

"That doesn't make him yours yet. Or mine. Or anyone's."

Through the glass, the room stirred. Shadows bent around a body that had been too still for too long. Doctors moved in arcs of efficiency, their murmurs stripped of emotion. A hand twitched against linen. A tremor cut across the ribs.

A sound followed. Not mechanical this time. Not routine. Raw. Human. A scrape in the throat like steel dragged over stone.

"Lena."

Everything in her stopped. For one sick heartbeat she thought it was hallucination, the cruelest trick, but his lips had moved. Clumsy. Parched. Shaping her name like it cost him blood.

The room erupted. Chairs scraped. Orders cracked sharp. Monitors spiked in alarm.

Lena slammed her palms to the glass. "He said my name." Her voice broke. She struck once, as though sheer force might shatter the barrier.

Inside, Lucien's eyes dragged themselves open through stormlight and sedation. Not steady. Not certain. But open.

"Lena." The sound was more breath than voice, but it split her in two.

Alexander was already at the seal, arms a wall across the door. "If you go in now, you drown him in noise. Let the doctors,"

"Move!" Her voice broke on the edge between prayer and threat. "You don't get to tell me not to answer when he calls me."

Victor's steps sounded behind her, boots grinding frost from outside. His coat was streaked white, breath rising in smoke. No smirk. No shield. Just his face cut hard, eyes narrowed against something he couldn't stop.

The lock disengaged with a hiss. Lena didn't wait.

She crossed the sterile space in three strides, knees hitting the bed frame. Her hands found him. Clammy skin, but alive. Heat. Pulse. Life. His storm-battered gaze found her like a compass dragged to true north.

"It's me," she whispered, breaking apart. "I'm here. You came back to me."

His mouth fought around a sound, wrecked and unrelenting.

"Mine."

Barely a word. Still a vow.

She folded over him like her body finally remembered how to breathe.

The sob tore from her against his chest.

She had imagined this moment a thousand ways. Prayed for it until her knees bruised. Nothing had prepared her for the brutal truth of him alive beneath her.

She wanted to tear every wire free. Climb in beside him. Anchor him there until he remembered.

She forced herself still.

Her hand clamped to his until the doctors tried to pry her back.

Alexander stood with arms crossed, jaw stone, silent. Even he knew no command could compete with this.

Victor lingered in the doorway. "Storm's back on the horizon."

Tears streaked down Lena's face. She bent closer, words breaking into salt. "You don't get to leave me. Not again. Do you hear me?"

His hand twitched, weak but intentional, until his fingers tangled with hers. Even half-shattered, his grip carried command, not a plea but a claim.

"Always," he rasped.

Machines wailed. Doctors adjusted. The mountain groaned under winter wind. But the world had already tilted.

Life had clawed its way back into the man she had refused to mourn.

He was awake.

And the silence that had ruled these halls was broken forever.

Somewhere in the walls, the hum faltered, like the mountain itself forgot its rhythm.

Chapter Twelve

THE HORIZON BURNS

The air had changed.

Not temperature or pressure. Sanctuary kept those constant as commandments. Gravity had changed, a heaviness that bent sound before it reached her.

He was awake. That changed everything.

Not because he could stand. Because everyone else would start moving.

Over the next ten days, lucidity came in waves. Lena stood outside the glass, the gown half-tied, gloves limp in her fist. The first rupture had already come. His voice had torn her name out of the dark. Now the world moved like survivors after a flood. Cautious. Disoriented. Pretending the tide had not redrawn everything.

Inside, the medical team worked in quiet arcs around the bed. Numbers pulsed. Soft light breathed against stone. Alexander held his station at the threshold, neither in nor out. His posture said he owned the hinge.

"You know your window," he said.

Lena did not answer. If she spoke, it would be a plea, and she was done pleading with doors.

"Low stimulus," the doctor said. "No sudden touch. If he tires, we stop."

"I know what to do." Lena tied the gown and sealed the gloves. "Open."

The seal released. Cold, filtered air took her heat like a tithe.

Lucien's eyes were partly open. A sliver of storm. Unfocused but hunting. A drop crawled down the IV tube, slow as sand in an hourglass. His body was not still anymore. Tension flickered at the edges, a jaw remembering how to set, a hand remembering how to clench.

"Lucien," the doctor said, low and even. "If you can hear me, squeeze Lena's hand once."

She reached. His fingers found hers, as if navigating by her shape alone. Weak. Still absolute.

"One. Good. Where are you?"

Lucien's brow creased. The answer did not come.

"Cold," he said at last.

"Do you know your name?"

No answer. His eyes tracked to Lena as if the body were remembering who had called it back from nothing.

"Water," he rasped.

She brought the cup before the word finished. "Small sip," the doctor said.

She slipped the straw to his mouth. His lips were split. He swallowed, breath hitching around the effort, eyes closing, then opening again with a slow, stubborn lift.

"Where," he tried, softer, "are we?"

"The Glass Chapel," Alexander said from the doorway. "You're safe."

Lucien's gaze slid past Lena and found Alexander. It held there. Something old moved between them, history and refusal braided together. His fingers tightened around Lena's.

"Time," the doctor warned. "Thirty seconds."

Lena leaned in until her breath warmed his cheek. "It's me," she said. A secret. A dare. "I'm here. I'm not leaving."

His mouth shaped the smallest ghost of a smile. "You said that," he murmured. "You never leave."

Her vision blurred. She forced him back into focus.

"How long?" he asked.

The question hung like wire.

Alexander's reply held no comfort. "Long enough for people to make plans without you."

"Time," the doctor said, firmer. "We stop now."

Lena didn't barter. She took what was given. A final press of her fingertips into his wrist, mapping him in secret, then she let go. Not because she wanted to, but because she intended to take it back.

The airlock sighed behind her as she stepped into the corridor. Victor waited against the glass, cigarette unlit. He glanced at her without turning his head.

"Coherence?" he asked.

"Enough to hurt."

"That's coherence."

He tapped the cigarette once against his knuckle.

"They'll cut sedation at night. He'll be clearer. Angrier. Don't mistake one for the other."

"I won't."

When she returned, Alexander was gone. The doctor was making notes in a clean, narrow hand, and Lucien slept with his eyes half-open, ready to return to the fight without the courtesy of waking fully.

"Second window at nineteen hundred," the doctor said. "He'll tolerate more. He'll also tolerate less."

"I know what more feels like," Lena said. "I know what less is."

The doctor paused, nearly human, then went back to the chart. "Then you know when to stop."

At nineteen hundred, Lucien's eyes opened before she reached him. No confusion this time. No drag through sedation. The storm had found a center. He tracked her in as if she were the motion he expected.

"Lena," he said, voice low, still rough but his.

She had learned restraint the hard way. She practiced it now.

"Hey," she whispered. Greeting and apology in the same breath.

Her hand hovered, then settled lightly over the inside of his wrist.

"Can I?"

His eyes dipped to her fingers and back. Permission. Claim. It did not matter which.

The doctor ran quiet checks. Pupils. Reflex. A light passed across Lucien's eyes, catching the edge of something violent before moving on.

"Time. Place. Name."

"Later," Lucien said. Soft. Final.

He never looked away from Lena.

"Did it change while I was gone?"

She frowned. "What?"

"The world," he said. "Or just us."

A beat.

"Both."

"You stayed."

She didn't hesitate.

"Where else would I be?"

"You look," he began, stopped, corrected himself. "Worn."

"Good." A ghost of heat. "Means I was here to feel it."

"Minute left," the doctor said.

"Alexander." His voice went flat. Colder. He never glanced at the door. He did not have to.

"He's here."

"Of course he is." Lucien closed his eyes once, opened them steady. "Tell him I've heard the rules. I'll break none until I have to."

"Tell him yourself."

"I will." A single cough. Controlled. Irritatingly so. "After."

"After what?" the doctor asked.

Lucien looked at Lena like the answer had always lived there.

"After I know what it cost."

Lena understood then that he was not asking about pain.

She didn't look away.

"Everything. But the debt is paid. You're here."

"Time," the doctor said, softer. "We stop now if we want him strong enough to go on."

Lena eased her hand away. The seal kissed shut behind her, habit turning into law again. She did not go far. Victor took her place like they had rehearsed it, a switch in a relay neither of them had agreed to run but both were running anyway.

"He's calculating," Victor said, low. "You can hear the ledger moving."

"He's alive. The rest is solvable."

"No," Victor said, almost tender in the refusal. "The rest is what comes for us."

Night settled on the mountain. Lucien slept again, but it was not the sleep he'd worn for weeks. It held tension now. Decisions moving under the surface. His breath caught and released like a man testing a weapon's weight in the dark.

Lena stood at the glass until the numbers steadied, until the room remembered how to pretend nothing had changed.

She knew better.

Sanctuary had been built to contain damage. To quiet storms. To smooth men into manageable shapes.

It was already failing.

Beneath the floor, the hum shifted and didn't settle back into place. Not louder. Not broken. Just wrong, like a pattern interrupted mid-cycle. Alexander felt it too. She saw it when he let the monitors spike without stepping in, and when he stayed still as Lucien's pulse climbed instead of calling the sedation back.

Lucien had crossed back carrying something with him.

Not peace.

Momentum.

And whatever came next would not happen behind glass.

CHAPTER THIRTEEN

MONSTERS MADE

Weeks bled through stone and silence.

The mountain never changed, but Lucien did.

He learned to sit without swaying, to stretch his arms like a man reaching back into himself. He held his own weight for seconds, then for minutes, as though strength remembered him reluctantly but could not refuse forever.

He already knew the shape of the world he had woken into. Victor and Alexander had given him the truth in pieces, quiet and unvarnished, while he fought to stand on his own legs again.

When pain arrived, he treated it like currency. Gritted teeth. Long exhales. Nothing wasted.

They thought the world would settle when the snow did. Frenzy, like any fire, ought to choke on its own smoke. But news had no doors into Sanctuary. It came only when Ghost chose to let it in. One encrypted thread fed into the living-quarters screen, rationed like contraband.

Through that narrow drip of connection, Lena watched new myths take root where facts had died.

Lucien Cole seen in six countries.

Lucien Cole walking underground tunnels.

Lucien Cole in a senator's conspiracy chart.

Lucien Cole as resurrection.

Lucien Cole as corruption.

The candles were gone now, melted and swept away, replaced by graffiti.

WE SAW HIM sprayed in hurried red strokes.

FAKE FOOTAGE slapped over it in thick black letters.

The city split between believers and doubters, each certain the other was blind.

Lena carried it all like extra weight in her bones.

Sometimes she cut the feed mid-sentence and stood with her forehead pressed to the observation glass, the cold pressing one honest truth into her skin.

He was here.

Breathing. Existing.

The lie and the truth didn't cancel each other out. They lived side by side, and the world seemed content to believe both.

The city roared, speculated, painted walls with his name. All the while he slept a few feet away, unreachable, unseen.

For weeks he had lived behind clear walls, monitors glowing, voices muted through sterile glass. She had memorized the drone of the machines, the staccato print of his vitals, the way her own reflection haunted her more than his.

But this morning, the protocol shifted.

Lucien had been moved. No longer caged in the medical wing. A regular room now. Less watched. More human.

The walls were plaster and wood, not sealed glass.

No locks spoke between them now.

She stood at his door, a brass knob cool beneath her palm. Her pulse thundered so violently she swore it might rattle the hinges.

She pressed her forehead against the wood and whispered once to herself. "Open it."

Then she turned it.

A soft click. Delicate. Deafening.

The door eased inward. A thin line of morning light crossed the floor, gold dividing the room without force and pushing the dark back into its corners.

She saw him.

Lucien lay half turned toward the window, pale as cut stone. His features were softened by exhaustion, framed by a stillness that made him seem carved instead of born.

For a moment she could not breathe. Relief and terror crashed together until neither made sense.

His eyelashes fluttered, slow and uncertain, as if the world behind them had been oceans deep and he was not sure this one was real.

He looked like a man waking from distant shores, dragged across impossible waters to arrive here, in her light.

Lena moved before she realized she could.

Across the room. Unsteady. Floating.

She reached his bedside like gravity had finally claimed her.

His eyes found hers.

The world steadied.

"I was gone, Lena." His voice rasped, broken and dragged from somewhere deep.

"I know."

He shook his head faintly, the motion cutting pain across his face. "No. Not gone like that. Gone. Beyond gone."

Her breath froze.

"There were faces," he whispered. "Shapes. Hands pulling me down into the endless dark. No names. No voices. Just emptiness trying to keep me."

His gaze drifted past her, unfocused.

"They dragged at me. They wanted me quiet."

When he said dark, something shifted behind his eyes, a shadow that didn't belong to this room.

Lena's hand trembled as it found his.

"But beyond them, past the dark, there was light. And in the middle of it was you." His voice cracked. "Your voice reached me first, calling my name like it belonged to you. Then your hand around my wrist, pulling me back."

His throat worked. "Dragging me home."

She believed him before she understood him.

Her eyes blurred. "I wasn't going to let you go."

"You didn't." His gaze sharpened faintly, grief and gratitude tangled. "That is why I am here."

The doctor had stopped pretending to take notes. Whatever this was, medicine had no name for it.

Sunlight shifted across the sheets, climbing his chest like a slow coronation.

Then Lucien's expression changed. Harder. Clearer.

"This life." He paused, breath thin. "We tell ourselves it is real because there is pain. We bleed. We love. We break. We believe it matters. We fight. We build. We pretend we can control it. But the truth is, we are ghosts pretending to be alive."

"Then haunt this life with me," she whispered. "We will take back the plans we once made. Leave behind the blood, the darkness, everything that tried to claim you."

His eyes stayed on hers, but sorrow lingered at the edges. "That might be your road, Lena. But it was never mine."

Her breath stilled. "What do you mean?"

Lucien looked past her, toward the window and the frozen mountain sky.

"I don't know who holds the scales of this world. God. Fate. Something worse. But I know this. They never meant for me to stop being the monster.

The moment I tried, the bullets came. They always would. This time, they didn't miss."

Lena's chest ached. "Don't say that."

"No." His voice cut sharp but not cruel. "If there is balance, then it demands both sides. Angels and demons. Light and shadow. Pain and peace. One cannot outweigh the other."

His eyes burned now, fevered clarity returning.

"When one of us crosses into something we were never meant to be, the balance snaps back. It does not forgive. It retaliates."

Silence crushed the room.

His hand twitched against hers, faint strength flexing. His voice steadied, low as a vow.

"I came back for more than one reason."

Her breath caught. "For what?"

His gaze dragged back to her, raw and unguarded.

"For you. Because there was no world worth clawing back to without you in it."

The silence held, fierce and trembling.

Then he looked past her, past the mountain, into the world waiting with sharpened teeth.

"And because there is work unfinished. The scales are off. And I will not rest until they are even."

The sunlight burned brighter, catching in his eyes like fire held behind stone.

"I'm cleaning house."

CHAPTER FOURTEEN

THE THAW

Winter died in pieces.

First the icicles along the eaves loosened and fell like dropped daggers. Then the snowpack gave way, seeping down the cliff's black ribs in silver threads.

By the third month the mountain wore green again. Pines flashed wet, the ground steamed where the sun found it, and wolves that once howled at the gates now moved unseen through thicker cover. The wind changed its voice, less a keening, more a low, steady draw, like something vast taking its first deep breath of the season.

Sanctuary no longer felt like a tomb. It felt like a fortress that had finished its vigil and was ready to release its charge.

In the weeks that bridged the thaw, the rooms learned a new rhythm because he did. The corridors picked up the cadence of recovery: the careful turn against the wall, the slow push from sitting to standing, the breath held before a stretch reached its limit and demanded more. Bruises faded. Sutures dissolved. Scars stayed, pale lines carved into him like maps only he could read.

He grew quieter. Not the blank silence of sedation, but the sharpened hush of a man counting. Pain came and he treated it like a tax, paid in full, without complaint, collecting his due in return: another step, another inch, another breath unbroken.

Sometimes, before dawn, Lena found him in the makeshift training corridor Victor had bullied into existence. Mats down. A single bag hung from a beam. No gloves. No theatrics. Lucien moved as if teaching his body its alphabet again: jab, step, breath, brace, pausing when rebuilt lines protested, waiting, then starting again.

Victor had made him keep it small, economy over spectacle, warning him that the big moves would charge interest. Lucien took it the way he took everything now, with focus, sweat, and patience. He didn't chase triumph. He chased function.

The mountain taught humility even to kings.

Spring reached them before they reached it. The air warmed by degrees. Real dawn replaced the baseboard lights, sunlight climbed the high windows and drew pale ladders on the stone floors. The smell shifted from antiseptic to thawed earth and damp cedar. Sanctuary was no longer holding him. It was opening.

This morning made that truth final.

Lucien stood at the great glass doors facing south. He had abandoned the crutch two weeks ago. The rib brace came off last night. The doctor in the dark sweater said nothing about either choice, which was his version of acceptance. Scars remained, pale and hard, pulling when he stretched.

The mountain wind hit his chest like a dare.

Behind him, Lena braced on the doorframe, steady in the way only someone who had learned how to keep a world together could be. Three months of corridors, recirculated air, and quiet wars fought behind glass. Three months of watching him claw back into himself, relentless as spring.

"You're not the man who came here," she said.

"No," Lucien answered, eyes on the widening cut of the valley. "That man died."

She saw the truth in his reflection. Not a devil from the city. Not the broken man winter delivered. Something forged. Held. Scarred clean.

Victor appeared down the corridor with unhurried steps.

"Car's ready. Route's clean."

Farther back, Alexander stood still. He had treated every doorway in this place as if doors were courtesy. Today he chose open ground instead. His hands were empty. His attention was not.

Lucien tapped his knuckles once against the glass, testing whether it was still a barrier or only a memory.

Lena reached for him. No hesitation this time. Fingers locked, scar to softness. Current, not comfort. Some rooms made vows without words.

"Ready?" she asked.

"No," he said, honest as a cut vein. "But I'm going."

"Then I am, too."

Victor exhaled a laugh without humor. "That's the problem with thresholds. You cross them and they stop being metaphors."

"Your poetry's tragic."

"Tragic pays better." He turned toward the stairs.

The doctor appeared with a clipboard he didn't bother to read. "Mind the pain, or it'll mind you. Short stints. Long rests. No adrenaline games."

"You say that like I play games."

"I've had you over ninety days. I've learned to use small words around liars."

"Good. Means I'm not dead."

The corner of the doctor's mouth tipped; on some other planet it might have been a grin. He offered his hand; Lucien took it, and pride passed between them, clean and simple.

The overhead speaker crackled to life, dust trembling in the grille. Ghost's voice came through, low and unmistakable.

"Two notes. One public, one private."

Alexander cut the air with one word. "Public."

"Mayor Lansing. Barely two months in and already swinging the hammer. Promising to 'disengage the underground empires strangling this city.' Transparency, arrests, a week of action. Same script, different actor."

"There's always a week of something," Victor murmured.

"Private," Lucien said.

"Your mother's been trying to get through," Ghost added. "Connection keeps cutting. I'll keep the line open as far as the mountain lets me."

Something in Alexander's gaze tightened, then smoothed as if smoothing were simply another discipline. He didn't look at Lucien. He didn't need to.

Lucien set his palm to the seal plate. The doors answered with a low surrender, hydraulics relaxing their hold. Spring rushed in: pine, wet stone, sunlight so bright it almost hurt. The air changed temperature and name.

Lena glanced at him, knowing the world thought him buried, vanished, erased. He looked at the doors like they'd been bars all along.

"Time to go," he said.

No triumph. No speech. Just the end of one captivity and the beginning of another war.

They stepped through together.

The mountain did not applaud. It simply allowed.

The path along the cliff had shed its frozen armor, water slicking the stone where ice had ruled for months. Below, the pines stood in disciplined rows, their tips burnished by new sun. Farther out, the valley opened wide, not welcoming, just vast. The river cut through it, a vein of steel and light, moving with the kind of patience that outlasts men and walls.

A convoy idled by the lower doors where rock met road. No spectacle, just function. Sanctuary didn't decorate its exits. Two matte SUVs bracketed a larger vehicle built heavier than it looked, its paint hiding angles that didn't belong on anything ordinary.

Victor went first, scanning the treeline out of habit. The new guard, men and women hired because reputation was a uniform, moved smart without noise. Door, step, door. Habits stacking on habits.

"Last chance to trade the crown for a halo," Lena said, voice edged in smoke.

Lucien almost smiled. "Halos don't fit."

Victor grunted. "Neither do crowns, if we're being honest."

Lena's eyes stayed on Lucien. "Some things are worth the weight."

Alexander descended last, deliberate as always. He stopped where his voice would carry and sentiment wouldn't. Whatever he thought about the waiting convoy, he left unsaid.

The doctor lifted a hand. "If you get dizzy, sit. If your vision goes, lie down. If you can't breathe, stop. There's no honor in passing out."

"Honor's overrated," Victor said.

"Health isn't," the doctor replied, and the subject died of natural causes.

They loaded clean. Lena slid across leather and reached without looking; Lucien's hand found hers before it fully arrived. He didn't squeeze. He didn't need to. Contact sealed the moment and still left it dangerous.

The convoy rolled out from the mountain's shadow. Tires hissed through meltwater. Trees blurred past, their wet bark flashing in the light. A hawk wheeled above the ridge, patient, unbothered. The road wound down in sharp switchbacks, the valley rising to meet them.

"No chatter," Victor said, not as a rule so much as a mood. "We're safest when we're boring."

No one spoke.

Silence wasn't empty; it was a different kind of noise. Through it, Lena heard small things: seat leather breathing, Lucien's inhale steadying after the long stretch, the faint electronics in the dash whispering into the quiet. Through her open window, water worked its way downhill, quiet and relentless.

Signal bars climbed a notch, then another. Phones woke ravenous, buzzing, flashing, vomiting months of backlog. A push alert lit her lock screen; she meant to swipe it away but her thumb slipped. The feed opened before she could stop it.

Mayor Lansing stood at a podium draped in flags, voice practiced, eyes bright with the kind of conviction that bought headlines.

"A week of action," Lansing promised. "We will disengage the underground empires strangling this city. We will bring names into the light. No one is beyond the law."

Lucien's reflection ghosted over the screen, watching a man speak about his world like it was already gone.

"He thinks he's declaring war."

Victor looked back from the passenger seat. "No. He's auditioning for it."

The feed stuttered back to the podium. Lucien's face still seemed to hover there in memory.

"Viral worship," Victor said. "Useful and rotten in the same mouthful."

Lena didn't trust her voice. She felt Lucien turn to the glass, then to her. He didn't remark. He didn't need to. The world had already built something out of him that humans were bad at dismantling.

Ghost's voice cracked through the dash speakers, dragged thin by the mountain.

"Lansing's not stopping at speeches. He's calling a closed council tonight, governor, feds, three bankers I don't like the look of. No cameras. No transcripts. Just war prep behind curtains."

Victor's mouth tightened. "So the podium was the audition."

"And this," Ghost said, "is rehearsal for the blood."

Lucien looked out at the road. "Good. Now we know the play."

Static threaded Ghost's next words.

"As far as the world knows, you're gone, buried or vanished in spirit. That silence is your camo. Lansing's preaching to a crowd that thinks you're myth, not man."

"But myths don't bleed. Once they catch a scent,"

"Exactly," Ghost cut in. "The moment you make noise, the wind shifts. Lions smell it, and they'll follow straight to you. Because you're the reason this storm started moving in the first place."

Lucien's reflection lingered in the glass, storm-eyed and steady. "Then let them smell it. I want them to."

"Your funeral's stretched long enough to make a calendar," Victor said. "He'll try to end it on his terms."

"He'll learn the terms aren't his," Lena answered.

"Teach him quick," Ghost said, and severed the line before the mountain's static swallowed it.

The road leveled. The convoy held formation. The valley spread its map, water and road crossing through distance, no towns yet, just the suggestion of return. Far off, a pale streak of highway promised speed.

"You know, you could still stay," Lena said, not because it was true, but because love sometimes asks on principle.

"Where?" he asked, turning her question into the map it had always been.

She faced forward. Where was never the problem. When always was.

Alexander didn't ride with them. He took his own car. Some distances even fathers don't close without a reason better than sentiment.

On the two-lane, the vehicles drew level for a moment. Through beveled glass, two profiles regarded each other not as men but as sums: cost, worth, risk, weight. Alexander's hand lay flat on the wheel. His other hand touched his chest pocket, then dropped. Nothing, and everything.

Lucien inclined his head. Alexander returned just enough to call it acknowledgment and not one atom more.

Traffic thickened. Trucks with timber. A bus with no children yet. A sedan with a cracked windshield and a mother gripping her temple at a light as if that might hold the day together. The ordinary suffered and kept moving.

"You okay?" Lucien asked.

She nodded. Then told the truth. "No. But I'm still going where you go."

"Good," he said. "It's the only rule that matters."

They hit the long straight where the mountain gave way to lowland. Behind them, stone rose and folded into sky. Ahead, the road ran through farms, then repairs, then the kind of outskirts that couldn't decide whether they belonged to city or country.

Lena rested her head against his shoulder for a breath. His hand tightened around hers, not to claim or console, but to answer. Here. Here. Here.

Outside, spring kept its promise. Buds broke through bark, fields drank what the thaw left behind.

Inside the car, the future narrowed to a point so sharp she could almost see it. Somewhere ahead, a mayor rehearsed a sentence he thought would taste like history. Somewhere else, a ring she didn't yet know about was already waiting.

The mountains receded, but the lesson stayed with her. Lena breathed with it one last time and held on to what it had taught her: stay close; don't look away; keep moving.

She opened her eyes and found the horizon where she'd left it, burning even under all that new blue.

They were done hiding.

The road unfolded.

Chapter Fifteen

THE LEDGER

The convoy had gone silent miles ago.

No music. No chatter. Just the low vibration of engines eating distance.

Lena wasn't watching the road.

Her eyes stayed on him, on the way the light carved across his face, no longer the pale stone of Sanctuary but something sharper. Alive. Awake. Dangerous enough to make her blood thrum.

He hadn't spoken since Lansing's speech.

Since Ghost's warning.

Since the talk of myths bleeding.

The world thought him dead.

But he sat there steady, like a loaded weapon that hadn't decided where to aim yet.

Finally, Lena broke.

"You said something," she murmured, voice low enough the tires almost swallowed it. "Back in the Glass Chapel. You told me, 'I'm cleaning house.'"

He turned toward her, storm-colored eyes locking on hers.

"What did you mean?" she asked. "Who are you coming for first?"

He looked past her, out toward the horizon where the city waited, steel and glass hiding rot and empire.

"There are men," he said. "Men who were meant to protect what I cherished most. Instead, they laid it at my enemy's feet."

His voice lost its warmth.

"They didn't just fail me, Lena. They invited the knife in."

He didn't need to say the name.

The Corsinis hung between them, betrayal left too long, now stirring again and ready for blood.

Lucien leaned closer. "When I said I'm cleaning house, that wasn't poetry. That was promise. Every man who traded my blood for favor will pay it back with his."

He looked ahead.

"They opened the door for Royce. They looped the feeds. They handed you over. And the fact that Royce is gone doesn't erase that. It just means they're next.

"This isn't rage born from a hospital bed. This was written before the bullets found me. It followed me into the dark and waited there, patient. Unfinished. Death didn't change it. Coming back didn't either."

He looked at her, cold.

"Some debts outlive the men who owe them."

The SUV hit a rut. The jolt landed like punctuation.

Victor's gaze lifted in the mirror, but he said nothing.

Ghost's voice stayed dead in the speakers.

The car held the kind of silence only men planning violence knew how to respect.

Lena's pulse hammered, half dread, half devotion.

She tightened her grip on his hand. "And Lansing?" she whispered. "He's already moving."

Lucien almost smiled. "Lansing wants empires to burn? Good. Let him look this way."

He paused, and the silence settled like a decision.

"He'll see fire. But first," his eyes darkened, "I settle the debt that waited for me on both sides of the grave."

By the time they reached the safe house, an anonymous tower wrapped in scaffolding, its top floors gutted and rebuilt clean, the press conference had already turned into a feeding frenzy. Reporters shouted names. Hashtags crawled. Lansing grinned like a man convinced he had history by the throat.

Victor opened the door for Lena. "Inside. Quick."

The lobby was bare, concrete, steel, nothing soft. The kind of place you could trust to hold secrets because it never pretended to be anything else.

Lucien stepped out last. He didn't look for cameras that weren't there. He looked at the skyline through a gap in the scaffolding, silent, measuring, already choosing where the fire would start.

The safe house smelled of paint and plaster, too new, too clean. It hadn't earned its scars yet. Victor had picked it for function, not comfort: two exits, blacked-out windows, space for a war council and nothing that looked like home.

A single television was already on in the corner, Lansing's speech looping, flags stacked like threats. Lena muted it before Lucien even looked.

Victor stood by the door, coat still on, phone buzzing in his pocket.

"I've got something to handle in the city," he said. "Back by sundown."

Lena straightened. "Now? With Lansing stirring the city and Lucien barely standing?"

He met her stare, unbothered. "Now. The board's already moving, and I don't wait to be cornered."

Lucien nodded. "Go."

Victor left without ceremony. The silence closed behind him. Lucien stayed standing at the center of the room, eyes on nothing and everything, as if the city had followed him inside.

Then he lowered himself into the chair, too plain for thrones, too solid to be disposable.

His elbows braced on the arms. His gaze locked on her.

Lena froze for a breath she hadn't meant to hold. The air between them charged, like the moment before a storm.

She'd waited months for this, for him, and now the distance across the room felt more brutal than the months without him.

"Come here."

The words weren't loud, but they left no ground between them.

Lena's pulse climbed, traitorous, ravenous.

She moved as though pulled, knees brushing the cold edge of the chair as she straddled him, thighs caging him in.

She hovered, spine straight, chin lifted, like she'd make him work for every inch.

But when his hands rose and threaded through her hair, she folded.

"I thought I lost you," she whispered.

The admission cracked against the quiet.

"You did," he said, cruel in honesty. His thumb traced her jaw, cataloguing the fracture.

"But you dragged me back."

Her mouth found his before the ache in her chest could finish tearing.

The kiss was jagged at first, blood, hunger, grief, all wrapped in teeth.

Then it softened, dangerous in a different way, as if worship could wound differently than violence.

Lucien's hands slid down, gripping her hips, pulling her flush against him.

Hard already, the promise of him strained through layers of restraint.

She gasped into his mouth, fingers curling at his collar, clawing him closer like proximity alone could erase months of waiting.

"You still taste like survival," he murmured.

"And you still taste like sin."

The chair groaned when he stood, carrying her with him like momentum had decided for them both.

Mouths locked. Legs tight around his waist.

The safe house blurred; plaster and concrete became cathedral.

He pressed her to the wall, his body pinning hers, his hand sliding up her thigh beneath fabric suddenly obscene in its existence.

Her breath hitched. "Lucien,"

"You belong to me," he said, raw and reverent. "No walls. No silence. No gods in between."

Her eyes burned into his.

"You belong to me as much as I belong to you."

The kiss consumed her answer.

Buttons surrendered. Fabric slid.

His mouth found her throat, biting just enough to mark. His tongue followed, slow, and her knees nearly gave.

He caught her weight, shifted, and carried her back to the chair like ritual. He sat.

She straddled, facing him now, chest to chest, breath to breath.

His hands anchored her hips as she moved against him, a slow grind, wet heat soaking through the last barrier.

His eyes locked on hers, and inevitability settled in her chest.

"Show me," he ordered.

"Show me you didn't wait for nothing."

Her answer was movement.

She undressed him with impatient fingers, knuckles brushing scars like prayers between each tear of fabric.

When she freed him, the weight of him in her palm broke a sound from her she hadn't made in months.

He watched her, unblinking, storm burning.

"Ride me."

She came down to him slowly, breath breaking as the last distance vanished.

Her nails dug into his shoulders. The chair rattled.

For a moment neither moved, just held there, shaking with the unbearable fact of being together again.

Then she moved, hips rolling, finding the rhythm.

He met every movement, his hand sliding up her spine, keeping her eyes locked on his.

Heat broke between them, sharp enough to steal language.

Filthy and sacred, her moans tangled with the creak of wood and the brutal rhythm of him.

His voice scraped out of him, low, wrecked.

"You're the only thing that pulled me back."

"Then take what you came back for."

The kiss that followed was ruin. Tongues colliding. Bodies clawing closer.

Sweat slicked skin, scars and softness binding.

He whispered her name like confession; she whispered his like a dare.

When her body seized, breaking apart around him, he held her tighter and drove into her until his own control shattered.

A raw sound ripped from his chest when he followed.

Buried deep inside her, he marked her the way a storm marks a coastline: irrevocable. Permanent.

They clung there, trembling, gasping, foreheads pressed together.

The safe house walls held their echoes like scripture.

Finally, he whispered, ragged and reverent,

"Never again. I don't come back twice."

Her tears wet his lips as she kissed him.

"Then I'll never let you go."

The silence returned, but it wasn't the silence of Sanctuary.

It was the silence after fire, after thunder, when the world knows it's been changed.

The sun had dropped behind the skyline when the lock on the safe house turned.

Lena rose instinctively, pulse quickening.

Victor stepped through first, city grit clinging to his coat, carrying the sharpness of someone who'd walked streets still learning what fear meant without Lucien's shadow.

Behind him, Logan.

He froze at the threshold, eyes locking on Lucien. His mouth fell open. "Holy shit."

Lucien didn't rise. He leaned back in the chair, letting Logan take him in, alive, leaner, colder, carved beyond myth.

Logan muttered, "You look like someone who didn't come back whole."

Victor dropped his coat. "Whole enough to finish what's left."

They gathered around the stripped-down table, tension pulled tight. Logan dragged a chair forward, still stealing glances at Lucien like he might vanish if he blinked.

"City's changed while you were gone," Logan said. "Lansing's filling the vacuum fast. He's playing crusader, dragging in feds, whispering with governors, promising to purge the rot."

He pointed toward the muted screen where Lansing replayed, flags stacked like threats.

"Crowds still don't know who to believe. Nobody agrees on you. Some whisper ghost. Some swear storm. Nobody says man."

Lucien's expression didn't move.

"Power's fractured," Logan went on. "Not syndicates, crews. Gangs that used to stay in the dark are loud now. Colors on corners again, tagging walls like gospel. Kids calling themselves kings. Half-formed armies with masks instead of names, thinking your absence is their coronation."

He hesitated. "And the worship is everywhere. Murals on brick. Hashtags like hymns. You're not a man to them anymore. You're the ghost that refused to stay dead. Some pray you come back. Others pray you don't. None of them remember the man beneath the myth."

The words filled the safe house until the silence had teeth.

Lucien leaned forward. "Good. Let them think both. Ghost. God. Whatever scares them most. That's what I'll use."

Victor spoke next, voice rough. "And the Corsinis? You heard anything worth a damn, or are they still playing shadows?"

Logan dug a cigarette from his pocket, tapped it twice against his hand, lit it with a shaky flick. Smoke curled as he exhaled a humorless breath.

"Still around," he said. "But they're not calling shots. Rumor says they bent the knee like everybody else. Got absorbed. Folded under one entity, the same faceless outfit swallowing the whole city."

Victor snorted. "Rumors don't keep me warm."

Logan shrugged. "Maybe. But when every corner spits the same story, it isn't gossip. It's pressure building."

Lucien slipped the burner from his jacket and tapped a single key. One ring. Two. Then the line opened, static bending around something that did not sound human.

"I'm here."

"Corsini," Lucien said, iron in his voice. "Word is they're not breathing alone anymore. Trace every whisper. Find their new heart, if they've got one. If they're breathing as one body, tell me where the blood pumps."

"On it. I'll pull the threads. If they're tying knots, I'll know."

Lucien leaned back. "Good. If they're consolidating, I'll cut the head off before it learns to move.

"The Corsinis have written their name in other people's blood for years. I'll write mine in theirs."

Chapter Sixteen

COLLECTION

The city pressed close even here, sirens drifting upward, traffic grinding below.

Inside the safe house, the silence was thick. Brittle. Waiting to be broken.

The phone on the table buzzed once.

Victor slid it toward Lucien without looking.

One key lit. The line opened.

Ghost's voice came low, sanded down by static.

"It's real. The Corsinis aren't freelancing. They've folded under something bigger.

Gangs, traffickers, remnants of the old guard. A hydra. You cut one head, ten watch."

Victor leaned back, arms folded.

"So the whispers weren't smoke."

"No," Ghost said. "They're meeting quiet, pooling muscle, money, reach. Call it consolidation. Call it survival.

But if you strike now, you're not just hitting a family; you're firing on the body they've tied themselves to."

Static thinned, the tone dropping a register.

"We'll all need to go nocturnal for a while.

Daylight's too risky. Too many eyes. Too many phones.

As far as the world knows, Lucien Cole is myth.

Keep it that way.

Nights are your cloak until we decide who gets to see you bleed again."

Lena's gaze snapped to Lucien, catching the faint tilt of his head, the glint in eyes that had forgotten the language of retreat.

His voice landed like steel. "I didn't come back to live in shadows."

There was no hesitation on the line. "Then use the shadows until the strike. It's not surrender. It's camouflage."

Lucien closed his eyes once, opened them cleaner. "Camouflage buys time. Fire wins wars."

Silence bit down.

"I fought through the world between here and hell for a hundred reasons," he said, leaning forward, elbows on steel, voice turned to verdict.

"But killing Giancarlo wasn't one of them.

It was the first consequence."

The words hung, heavy enough to bend the air.

Lena's breath hitched. Logan looked like he'd seen scripture written in blood. Victor only grunted, the sound of a man who'd expected nothing less.

Lucien's tone sharpened, blade to edge. "If we're doing this, we don't limp into it. We strip what's left, cash what we can, and build fast. The feds froze the storefronts. Lansing sent city crews to tape the doors. Fine. We'll turn what's still breathing into teeth."

Victor leaned back, arms folded. "We shut down the noise. We stack payouts and prep safe houses. Everything we need to move and hit without warning."

Lucien's mouth curved, cruel and certain. "They think yellow tape freezes me. They've forgotten I was forged in fire."

His gaze cut to the phone. "Where do I find them tonight?"

"Nothing's changed," Ghost said. "They're dug in at Giancarlo's estate, lights on, phones quiet, cars stacked too neat."

My gut says they're staging. Preparing something big.

The kind of noise their enemies won't hear until it's too late."

Lucien's eyes narrowed, cold. "I hear everything."

"Thermal patterns show extra muscle. Probably pulled in from other boroughs.

Cars lined along the service road, not locals.

I can smell hired guns and cheap ammunition from here.

They're expecting company, but not the kind that cuts their throat before they can raise a glass."

Victor leaned against the doorframe, arms folded. "Guess Giancarlo couldn't resist playing host."

"And tonight," Lucien said. "I'm his guest of honor."

Ghost's tone dropped half an octave, dangerous and amused all at once. "Then I'll keep the eyes blind and the ears deaf while you write his name off the ledger. Consider it a blackout tailored for a funeral."

Lucien stood. No hurry. Every scar a map. "Good. By dawn, Giancarlo Corsini learns what I brought back."

The silence after Lucien's words didn't last. It cracked, stretched, filled itself with motion.

Victor dialed debts that didn't live in contacts.

Logan's hands trembled with hunger he refused to hide.

Ghost's voice slid through the line again.

"I'll blind cameras. Stagger scanners. Drop streetlights. When they know you're there, they'll already be counting bodies."

They weren't discussing a firing squad. They were assembling one.

Lena's chest burned. She stood, crossed to him, gripped his wrist.

"I'm alive. I'm here. There's no need for this, no ledger worth the blood it'll cost you."

Lucien looked down at her hand, then up into her eyes. Storm met flame.

"This isn't just vengeance, Lena. It's law. They betrayed what I swore my life to protect. Men like that don't get to breathe air I paid for. When I end them, it isn't payback. It's balance."

She shook her head, tears cutting sharp against her cheeks. "Balance doesn't bring back what they took."

His mouth curved, half smile, half scar.

"No. But it teaches the world what happens when you take it from me."

The room held its breath.

Lucien crossed the room, each step measured like the prelude to thunder. The others followed, momentum gathering.

Outside, night air hit them like judgment.

Waiting at the curb was the Rezvani, matte black, armored, feral in its lines. The same machine that had carried them through war and bloodshed, now gleaming like a revenant dragged from legend.

Lucien's hand traced the hood, slow and absentminded, the way a soldier might touch an old scar. His fingers left lines in the dust, memory and promise in the same stroke. He whispered low, just for her, though the city could have heard it.

"Hell didn't keep me. Neither will they."

Engines answered. Doors opened. The night stretched wide, ready to witness. Loaded, primed, rolling out.

The truck woke like a predator shaking off sleep, armored teeth humming under its skin. Logan slid behind the wheel, Victor claimed shotgun, and Lucien settled in the back with Lena, his hand heavy on hers, anchoring them both.

The city blurred past, bridges arched like ribs, towers glared with neon eyes, streets dimmed to after-hours silence.

The only voice that mattered came through the dash, stitched with static.

"Traffic eyes blind two blocks ahead. You're ghosts. Take the FDR, I'll bleed it clean."

Victor leaned forward. "Ping the location. Let the others know where to fall in."

"Already ahead of you," Ghost said. "Bread crumbs dropped. Convoy's forming."

They slid onto the FDR. Headlights off. The city's pulse dimmed behind them. One SUV merged from an on-ramp, another fell in, then a third, no introductions, just ghosts finding formation.

Logan cracked a window; river air cut the hum. "Goddamn," he grinned. "I fucking missed this."

Lena didn't look away from Lucien.

The convoy moved like a single animal, but all she saw was him, steady, hunter-still, watching the road like prey.

A mile out from the Corsini estate, all five vehicles killed their lights. Darkness swallowed the street. Engines purred under breath; the night leaned closer.

Lucien turned to her, his hand firm on her thigh.

"For the first time, you stay back."

Her mouth parted, ready to fight, but his eyes stopped her cold.

"I'll call you in when it's just us and Giancarlo. I want him to die looking at your face."

Her pulse spiked. She nodded once.

Ghost's voice cut in. "Perimeter's soft. Two guards at the front gate, four on the walls. Suppressed barrels first. When I say green, move."

Boots hit gravel. A few muffled pops. Bodies dropped without ceremony.

"Courtyard's yours," Ghost said. "Storm the house."

Lucien leaned forward.

"Move."

They didn't run. They advanced, a line of black-clad inevitability crossing the gravel like judgment arriving on foot.

Lena sat back in the vehicle, every instinct clawing her toward him, but Lucien's words echoed: *For the first time, you stay back.* Her fists knotted white against her knees as she watched him go, the storm she loved stepping into the eye of another.

Ghost's voice slid into their earpieces.

"Courtyard's clear. West door's barred. East door open, kitchen line. Too many bodies in one room, loud, comfortable. They don't know what's coming."

Victor checked his weapon, eyes narrowing.

"Let them choke on their last supper."

Lucien adjusted his grip on the pistol and raised two fingers, signaling the split.

"No noise until I speak. Giancarlo breathes last."

They crossed the threshold.

The house fell room by room. Suppressed rifles whispered through the rooms, voices sliced mid-argument, drinks fountained, laughter stopped. Men hit walls, slack and surprised. One toppled over a couch, eyes fixed on the chandelier; another slid across pantry tiles, his last breath drowned by the fridge's small, ordinary hum.

Lucien didn't need to call commands. The squad moved like one organism, every door breached, every corner cleared.

Ghost's voice marked their progress.

"Left wing silent. Second floor cleared. Fourteen down. No alarms tripped."

By the time they reached the dining hall, the estate itself seemed to breathe in blood.

The double doors creaked open, revealing a room meant for ceremony. A long table stretched under chandeliers, now cracked with bullet scars. Plates overturned, wine pooling with blood across linen. Shards of glass littered the floor like salt.

At the far end sat Giancarlo Corsini, his suit sagging where it once fit like armor, jaw grinding as if he could chew rage into something useful. His eyes carried decades of rot and rule, but the room had already stripped him bare.

Beside him, Salvatore, veins straining at his throat, let his hand twitch toward a pistol, but froze as a dozen red dots bloomed across his chest.

The firing squad fanned in, rifles raised, silent as gravestones.

Then Lucien stepped into the room.

The sound shifted. Even the dying seemed to hold their breath. His boots carried him forward, slow and steady, eyes like tempered steel fixed on men who had once dared to call themselves untouchable.

Giancarlo's mouth curled.

"So... the ghost comes home."

Lucien's eyes burned steady.

"Maybe I am a ghost.

Either way, I came back to finish it."

He let the pause sit on Giancarlo's chest.

"And you're first."

He stopped halfway down the length of the table. Every rifle followed his pace, barrels never leaving their marks.

Salvatore's laugh broke, jagged.

"You think killing us fixes anything? You're not cleaning house. You're setting the whole city on fire. You put us down, ten more rise. And not men you know. Beasts you've never met."

Lucien tilted his head, studying him like an insect pinned under glass.

"Then I'll burn the beasts too. Fire doesn't care what it eats."

Victor's voice came from the flank, low and cruel.

"He's not wrong. Ending them lights a bigger fuse. The whole city's going to feel it."

Lucien didn't glance at him.

"Good. Let it burn."

He shifted his gaze to Salvatore, sharp enough to cut flesh.

"You all betrayed me once. You won't get the chance again."

Salvatore sneered, tried for bravado, but his hand trembled against the wood.

"You don't kill me clean, you make me a martyr."

Lucien's reply was a whisper, but it reached every ear.

"You're not dying clean."

Two men from the squad surged forward, pinning Salvatore to the chair.

One snapped a pair of heavy zip ties from his vest and cinched them tight around the wrists, plastic biting deep until the veins bulged.

Another bound his ankles, locking him down like a man laid out for the pyre.

His eyes went wide as a jerrycan slid across the floor, pulled from one of the vehicles outside.

Victor unscrewed the cap without ceremony. The stench of gasoline crawled through the air.

Only Giancarlo remained, forced to watch his brother burn and his house become both grave and monument.

He thrashed, curses spilling out in Italian, in English, in something closer to prayer.

It didn't matter. The liquid soaked through his shirt, slicking his hair flat and darkening the wood beneath him.

Lucien struck the match himself.

Held it steady.

Flame caught in the mirror of his gaze, as if fire had only ever been waiting for him.

"You handed her to Royce," Lucien said. "Now I hand you to hell."

The match dropped.

The scream tore through the dining hall as flame consumed him, flesh blistering, voice breaking. Rifles held steady, no one looked away.

He writhed until he didn't.

Logan looked away first and spat on the floor. The sight of skin bubbling, melting, folding in on itself was more than he could stomach.

Lucien didn't look away. But something behind his eyes flinched, just once, like a man recognizing what damnation costs even when he's the one delivering it.

The flames didn't stop there. They raced down the table, climbing across bodies already cooling, turning the hall into a cremation chamber. Cloth, flesh, and timber caught in quick succession, evidence devoured, history erased in fire. Smoke thickened, black and choking, but no one moved to put it out. There was nothing left to save.

Only Giancarlo remained, forced to watch his house become both grave and monument.

Giancarlo screamed, voice breaking through the roar.

"Put it out! Do you hear me? This house holds a hundred years. This house is our name!"

Lucien's gaze cut to him, calm as a blade unsheathed. He stepped closer, pistol loose in his grip, eyes reflecting the burn. He looked carved from flame and shadow.

"History shines brighter without your family's stench in it."

Giancarlo's breath came ragged, ash streaking his face. The fire surged higher, wood snapping under heat.

Victor hauled him forward by the collar. Giancarlo stumbled, shoes slipping through blood and shattered glass, one leg dragging behind the other as panic finally stripped the last of his pride. He caught the broken edge of the doorway with his shoulder, lost his footing, and went down hard on one knee. Victor yanked him back up and kept him moving.

Through smoke. Through heat. Through the collapsing mouth of the house and out into the night.

Cold air hit him like punishment.

Lucien tilted his chin once at Logan. No words. Logan understood.

"Lena."

A car door clicked open. She stepped out, the blaze painting her in orange and red, her face stark against the ruin. The door slammed shut behind her.

Victor forced Giancarlo to his knees in the gravel. He tried to brace, coughed, nearly pitched forward, then stayed there shaking, smoke still clinging to him. Lucien stood over him, gun leveled at his temple, the fire raging behind like retribution itself.

Giancarlo's breaths came in ragged pulls, eyes wide and red. Gravel bit into his knees. He looked from Victor's grip to the pistol at his head, then up to Lena stepping closer.

The fire behind them threw her shadow long across the ground, joining Lucien's in a shape that looked like a crown in flames. Her chin lifted, steady. No hesitation. She walked until she stood beside him, her presence as sharp as the weapon in his hand.

Giancarlo rasped, voice fraying.

"You don't understand. I had no choice. Royce came for you, for all of us. It was him or us. I only,"

Lena's voice cut clean through the smoke.

"No. I was there. You didn't hesitate. You handed me over like tribute, like my life was just an old debt you could finally pay off."

His mouth worked, but no words came.

Lucien's shadow fell across him, pistol steady.

"And debts paid in blood don't get forgiven. They get collected."

His hand didn't tremble. He pressed the muzzle harder, forcing the man's head a fraction lower. The weight of inevitability hung in the night.

Desperation cracked into rage.

"You think killing me will end it? You think it stops here? There are men above me, bigger, higher. You'll wake them. You'll regret it."

Lucien crouched so he had no choice but to see only him.

"I fought through the world between here and the other side, and it changed me. Not for power. Not for politics. So when I looked men like you in the eyes, I'd know exactly where I was sending them."

Lena's pulse thundered, but her gaze never left Lucien.

Giancarlo's words stuttered into silence. His lips moved without sound, prayer or curse, it didn't matter.

Lucien glanced at Lena, just once. Shadow meeting flame. Her nod was small, but it was everything.

The shot cracked.

Giancarlo collapsed into the gravel, blood spreading dark across the stones.

Behind them, the estate roared higher, windows shattering, roof timbers groaning under the inferno. Then part of the roof gave way with a sound like something old finally breaking.

Victor exhaled through his nose. Logan muttered, almost reverent, "Ledger's clean."

Lucien holstered the weapon, eyes on the blaze consuming the Corsini name.

"No," he said. "This is just the first page."

No one answered.

Behind him, the house kept burning. Ahead of him, the city waited.

Chapter Seventeen

WHAT FIRE LEAVES

They didn't run from the fire. They watched it eat.

Flames climbed the Corsini estate like it had been built for this ending, gutting drapes, chewing through shutters, scaling rafters until the house glowed like a furnace. Smoke curled into the night, black against black, carrying the stink of old money turned to ash.

Victor and Logan dragged Giancarlo's body across the gravel, his suit still intact, blood dark at the temple where Lucien's round had ended him, his face slack in death. They didn't look at him, not really. Just weight. Just payment. With a heave they tossed him back through the shattered threshold, into the blaze that had already claimed his bloodline. For a heartbeat his body flashed in the flame's breath, then vanished, just another log on the pyre.

Rifles lowered. Masks disappeared. The firing team broke off into dark cars that peeled down the service road without headlights, vanishing one by one until only the Rezvani remained.

Lucien stood at the edge of the gravel, the glow of the fire cutting the planes of his face, carving him harder than any knife. He didn't speak. He didn't need to. The first line of the ledger had been answered in fire.

Victor took point. Logan covered the rear. Lucien walked Lena out through the gate, the blaze behind them painting their shadows long over gravel.

"Feeds are blind. Street cams looped," Ghost said in their ears. "To the city it's a house fire with bad timing."

The Rezvani roared to life. Positions held. No one spoke until the estate slipped behind the trees and the blaze died in the mirrors.

Logan broke first, knuckles whitening on the wheel. With his free hand he reached across to Victor.

"Don't know if we can use this. Lifted it from the old man's pocket."

He set a slim black phone in Victor's palm, matte and unmarked. No logos. No ports. Just threat. Then came a steel token, edges cut sharp, heavy for its size, stamped with a sigil older than the metal itself.

Victor whistled low. "Off-grid satphone. Access token."

He turned it once in his hand. "Whoever he answered to, this opens their doors."

"Faraday," Lucien said. "Sleeve it. No signal in, no signal out."

Logan pointed. "Glove box."

"Bag stays shut until I can put eyes on it," Ghost replied. "If it's theirs, it could be wired dirty. But if it's a vein, it could lead straight to the umbrella."

"The what?" Lena asked.

"An umbrella isn't one crew," Ghost said. "It's an entity made of others: gangs, traffickers, fragments of old orders, all welded into a single structure. The Corsinis weren't freelancing. They were plugging in. We cut a branch tonight, not the trunk."

"Then the family was a symptom. We treat the disease," Lucien said.

No one argued.

The city shouldered closer the farther they drove.

Bridges arched overhead; water flashed black between piers.

The night breathed steam from manholes like it had its own lungs.

Sirens stitched themselves into the distance.

Logan kept the wheel steady.

They took the ramp and slipped into the grid like a blade sliding under fabric.

Ghost came through again. "Last note. Lenses are everywhere. Phones, security cams, storefront feeds nobody bothers to secure. I'll keep the grids blind as best I can, but the crowd's always watching. Stay low-profile until I clear lanes. You're not invisible, just harder to see."

Lucien's gaze didn't waver. "Use the dark. Don't live in it."

"Copy," Ghost said, and the line went quiet.

They reached the safehouse on the city's edge. No one spoke as they went up. Fire still clung to their clothes, smoke threading the silence.

Inside, the television was already running headlines.

MANSION BURNS IN OVERNIGHT BLAZE scrolled across the

bottom.

B-roll of sirens and shaken neighbors filled the screen, everyone claiming they saw nothing.

Logan killed the volume with a sharp tap.

Victor double-locked the door and set the Faraday sleeve on the table.

"No," Lucien said. "Don't mute that. Let's listen."

They gathered in front of the screen, the glow washing pale over their faces. The reporter's voice cut crisp, rehearsed urgency laid over chaos.

"Fire crews remain on scene at the Corsini estate, long tied to one of the city's oldest crime dynasties. Flames are still visible behind me, consuming what investigators believe to be one of the last strongholds of the family.

At this time, officials confirm multiple casualties, with bodies pulled from the wreckage, many burned beyond recognition. While no names have been released, sources suggest high-ranking members were inside when the fire began."

Videos slid across the screen, smoke pouring from the mansion, firefighters dragging stretchers over scorched stone.

A neighbor held the microphone.

"We didn't hear anything. The sky just lit up."

The camera cut back to the anchor, lips tightening as though holding back satisfaction.

"Questions are already rising about whether this marks the collapse of one of the city's oldest crime families. Investigators declined to comment on the cause of the fire, but arson is not being ruled out."

Victor pulled out a chair but didn't sit. Logan leaned against the wall, arms crossed tight, his silence mirrored in the crawl of names and rumors.

Lucien didn't move. He let the broadcast play, eyes fixed, face carved from something colder than stone.

Lena's hands finally stopped shaking. It hit her then, not relief, not exactly. Something colder. A ledger line turned from red to black, and left a hollow space in her chest.

Lucien felt it too. He lowered himself into the chair and studied her through a different quiet.

"Say it."

She met his eyes. "I'm alive. I'm safe. Why wasn't that enough?"

"Because what they broke wasn't flesh," Lucien said. "It was the code. They handed over what I love to settle old debts or spit in my face. You don't forgive that. You end it."

She swallowed. "By burning the page."

"By burning the hand that held the pen."

Something clicked near the door.

Logan checked the peephole out of habit. Empty.

Victor tapped the Faraday sleeve once, then unsealed it with a frown.

"Let's see if this thing's carrying anything we don't want."

He broke the seal and slid the satphone out.

The moment it cleared the sleeve, the screen flashed alive.

SEVENTEEN MISSED CALLS

Then it rang again.

All four of them froze.

Victor's mouth twisted into a humorless smile. "Persistent."

Lucien plucked it from his hand, hit accept, and set it flat on the table, speaker live, eyes locked on it.

At first, just breath. Heavy, uneven. Then a voice, recognizable, raw with loss.

Milo Corsini.

"I fucking know someone's there. Answer me. Answer me, you coward."

No one spoke.

"I wasn't even at the damn house tonight," Milo snarled, breath thick with liquor. "Old man didn't want me in the room. Said I turn business into blood feuds."

A bitter laugh hit the mic. "Guess he should have listened to me for once."

The silence worked on him like acid. His voice cracked, stumbled, then sharpened.

"You think you lit a match and walked away? Whoever the fuck you are, you don't have a clue the hell you just unleashed."

He laughed again, broken and ugly.

"You think that house mattered? It was just history. The Coalition owns the streets now."

The name landed colder than the threat.

Lucien muttered under his breath, "Should've known this mouthy little fuck wasn't there."

Milo ranted on, words spilling faster, sloppier.

"Pier Forty-Two. Three a.m. You'll see. You'll fucking see who runs this city now. Not you. Not the old blood. The Coalition writes the future, and you just gave it ink."

Static carried his ragged breathing, then a curse snapped off his tongue. The line cut dead.

Ghost's voice came through the speaker. "He thinks he's scaring shadows. Instead he just gave us a map."

Logan sat back slowly. "He's baiting."

"Good," Lucien said. "Then we bleed the bait before the trap closes."

Victor slid the satphone back into the Faraday sleeve, sealed it, and set it on the table.

"Pier Forty-Two isn't neutral ground. If Milo shows, he won't be alone. Crews, muscle, maybe even someone higher pulling his strings."

Lucien's gaze didn't shift. "Then we make sure there's nothing left to pull."

Ghost came back on. "I'll pull whatever call and node logs I can reach. If Milo used an internal link, we'll get a trail. If he used a throwaway, it'll be noisy. I'll blind the docks and loop visible cams long enough for you to move under blackout. It won't be perfect cover. Treat it like a window."

Lena's hand curled against her thigh. "This doesn't end with Milo."

"No," Lucien said. "It starts with him. Ends with whoever he kneels to."

Logan leaned forward, elbows braced. "And Lansing? He's gonna use the fire like scripture. Your name's already an altar. If you step out of the dark now,"

Victor cut him off. "We don't. Not yet. Ghost is right. Let him be myth until the myth hurts more than truth."

Lucien picked up the sleeve, weighed it once, then set it back down.

"Three a.m. We stay dark until then. We prepare."

Lena crossed to the window, the city's reflection burning against her skin. "And if Milo doesn't bring a meeting," she asked, "but a funeral?"

Lucien rose from his chair, the fire still in his voice.

"Then we bury him. And if the Coalition shows up, we start cutting deeper."

Victor stood and checked his phone. "I'll sweep the truck and safe house. No tags. No tails."

Logan pulled up a dock grid on his phone, the waterfront spread beneath his fingertips in access roads and shadows. "If Milo wants a show, we cut the lights."

Lena turned, studying him. The man who had walked out of Sanctuary wasn't the one who sat here now; this one looked carved for war.

Lucien checked his pistol: a round, a slide, a click. He set it down within reach and looked at the men, at Lena, at the black sleeve between them.

His gaze returned to it once. "Three a.m."

Victor echoed it. "Three a.m."

The television burned on mute now, Corsini flames replayed in endless loop. Lena killed the screen. Darkness filled the room, waiting.

Sleep never came. Only plans.

And across the city, Milo Corsini pressed a gun to his own temple in a

cracked mirror, whispering through clenched teeth:
"Three a.m."

CHAPTER EIGHTEEN

WHEN SYSTEMS EAT THEIR SONS

The hour before three had its own gravity.

It pulled at lids and bones, at nerves thinned by smoke and planning.

No one slept.

Victor worked in quiet layers, checking magazines, aligning optics, sealing the windows against any spill.

Logan mapped routes in pencil, rubbing them out and redrawing until the paper went soft.

Ghost lived in the burner speaker on the table, the room's only voice.

Lena drifted through the room, steady in the small things.

Her hand settled on Lucien's shoulder, saying without words that his body was here, but his mind was somewhere else.

He stood at the window and watched the city pretend to rest. A tugboat turned on the river, its red light smearing across the black.

"Pier Forty-Two," Ghost said. "Thermals are live. Police bands are split. Harbor cams go dark on my mark. Phones near the pier will show signal. They won't have it."

"Confirm our footprint," Lucien said.

"Three signatures," Ghost replied. "Victor. Logan. You."

Static hummed. "You stay out of frame."

Lena's eyes lifted, a question she didn't voice.

He answered without turning.

"I'm not stepping into anyone's light."

Victor slid the compact case shut. "Rooftop across from the pier. Old cannery overlooking their loading doors. We watch. We stay invisible."

Logan tucked the map into his jacket. "We mark what matters and disappear."

Lucien nodded once. "We harvest."

He looked at Lena then, truly looked. She was tired, precise, the kind of steady that had to be chosen minute by minute.

"Stay off the water," she said.

"Until it wants me," he answered. "Not before."

She leaned in and brushed her mouth against his. Brief. Almost silent. It left the taste of promise.

Then they moved.

The city thinned at the river's edge, warehouses ribbed with rust, cranes frozen as if listening. They slid through a belt of fog that smelled of salt and cold iron. Somewhere a chain clinked against a hull, steady as a metronome in this part of the night.

Ghost's voice threaded in. "Two SUVs just parked north side. Six bodies, maybe more. Another pair coming from the ferry lot, staggered. Milo's sedan in five. He's drifting lane to lane."

The cannery wasn't a building anymore, just a hollow shell punched through with holes. The stairs groaned under their weight as they climbed. On the roof, wind pushed grit across the concrete and left the rest to silence.

Victor set the parabolic, a wide-ear dish built to catch voices from far off. Logan lifted the small launcher and checked the tags, thin metal chips that looked like nothing. A pair of high-power binoculars sat beside them, glass steady against the wind. Lucien stayed back from the edge, a darker shape among shadows, letting the city frame the stage below.

Pier Forty-Two held itself like a jaw. Container stacks to the left. A ladder of mooring posts to the right. The long slip of black water between. Sodium bulbs painted everything the color of old paper. Sound carries too far over water; men learn that or they don't live long.

Milo arrived crooked, like his anger had a limp. He got out of the car with his coat open and his mouth already running. He pointed at the night and tried to teach it his name.

Ghost fed them sound, cleaned and sharpened. Milo's voice came through raw with liquor and smoke.

"You hear me?" Milo muttered to no one. "I set the time. You show the respect due. I don't wait."

Two SUVs drifted up and stopped without hurry. Doors opened like the tide, then nothing. The men who got out had the look of docks and corridors. Boots steady. Hands empty.

One of them wasn't like the others. Slim. Quiet. No heavy jacket against the cold, as if it didn't apply to him.

He stepped to the yellow line in the concrete and waited there, hands in his pockets.

"Handler," Logan murmured.

"Name," Lucien said.

"Working on it," Ghost said. "No open social. No ports on the device he carries. That's not a phone. It's purpose-built."

Milo's voice ran out of road. He tried again with volume.

"You don't summon me like a dog. You don't,"

The slim man lifted two fingers, a gesture almost courteous. Milo stopped talking like someone cut his wire.

"You let a house burn that now carried our name too. You let the city watch it fall and talk. And now it's ash in every mouth that matters."

He didn't say the name. The Coalition hung in the air, charged.

Milo snarled, "I didn't light it. I lost what was mine."

The handler didn't raise his voice. "You weren't there to defend it. You let a house tied to us burn while you drank. And now every cop with a badge is wearing out their shoes on our ground."

Ghost's voice cut in. "He's not wrong. He's talking like he wants an audience."

Milo spat to the side, anger flashing. "You think someone's listening? Royce is rot. Cole's a bedtime story. Whoever struck the match tonight, he's smoke. I'm meat and money. I'm what you need."

A gull startled and lifted off the water, white against black. The handler didn't look up.

"You were never a legacy," he said. "We don't keep legacies. We keep systems."

Lucien didn't move. He watched Milo hear the shape of his own end and try to disagree with it.

"You're not killing me at my own pier," Milo said, which is how men talk when they want the air to pick a side.

"No," the handler said. "I'm killing you at mine."

The shot was soft, almost out of time. Subsonic. Precise.

Milo's knee folded.

Another dull pop. His shoulder snapped back.

He hit the concrete and slid, leaving only a darker stain.

No one spoke.

Lucien leaned toward the ledge and let the wind carry the cold.

"Don't be heroic," Ghost said, though no one had moved.

The handler stepped closer and waited until Milo stilled.

"Stories end," he said, to the men, not the body. "Systems don't."

He took something from his pocket, a small steel token cut with the same Coalition sigil they'd seen before. Through the binoculars, it flashed once in the hard dock light. A gloved hand retrieved it, pocketing it like an offering.

"Same mark as the Corsini piece," Logan muttered.

"Get me plate stacks," Victor said.

"Already yours," Ghost replied.

Threads spilled onto their screens. Registrations that didn't exist unless you looked from the right angle. Faces with three names each and no real birthdays.

Lucien watched the handler tilt his head, listening to the voice in his ear. He answered without raising his voice, then lifted his gaze, not to the pier, not to the men, but to the places where the dark might hold witnesses.

For a second, Lena was there in Lucien's mind, fingertips against the glass. *Stay off the water.* He heard it again, as if the wind had carried it back.

"Tag the lead SUV," Lucien said.

Logan raised the launcher. The tag snapped into the wheel well, metal against metal. No one below turned. He placed a second on the sedan that arrived late and parked crooked.

Victor kept count in his head, the way men do when seconds start mattering.

"Audio says they're moving to a 'Blue Room' after this," Ghost reported. "Could be literal. Could be code for a clean space. Could be,"

"A room they don't control alone," Victor finished.

The handler spoke again, lines meant to be remembered.

"Salt the story," he said. "Let it be about old blood and bad insurance. If someone asks for a ghost, sell them a mirror."

He left without looking down.

The SUVs turned in unison, gliding into motion with eerie precision.

Tires slipped once on the gravel, then caught.

Headlights stayed low, never rising higher than the knees of the men walking in front of them.

When they were gone, a smaller crew would come with the practiced care men reserve for money or fear. They would roll the body, carry it like freight, make it disappear. First a man. Then a weight. Then nothing.

"Docks are clean," Ghost said. "Cameras will wake up empty. Nothing from tonight survives the morning."

Logan lowered the launcher and exhaled. Victor broke down the parabolic and packed the pieces into cases that looked like they'd never been opened.

Lucien looked at the water, at the pulse where tide knocked steel, at the dark shape of a dock post across from him. He stood long enough to learn its rhythm.

"Name."

Ghost came back two beats later. "Silas. That's what the handler's inside traffic calls him. Clean. Efficient. No pictures that stick. He's a door that stays closed until someone else opens it."

Victor exhaled once. "He's not calling shots. He's the hand."

Lucien stored the name where unfinished things lived.

They retraced their steps down the groaning stairs, past brine and rust, across a lot that tried to keep footprints and failed.

The car waited, engine low.

By the time they reached the safe house, the fog had thinned and the river behind them looked like it had swallowed what it was given and chosen not to tell.

Lena was waiting upstairs.

For a second she searched Lucien's face for blood she couldn't see. She found none. Her shoulders didn't loosen.

"Well?" she asked.

Victor answered. "We didn't touch the water."

Lucien set the burner on the table and opened the screen. Ghost's feed spilled across it, license plates, faces pulled from the pier, the steel token caught in a gloved hand, a sliver of the handler's profile like a blade laid flat.

"Coalition doesn't keep kings," Logan said. "It keeps men who carry sentences."

"And the one they called Silas," Ghost added. "He writes them. That 'Blue Room'? It's not a place. It's a temperature. A status. It travels with them. I'll follow the tags until they sleep."

Lena's fingers rested on the table's edge. "Milo?"

"Paid," Lucien said.

She closed her eyes for a beat. When she opened them, the color hadn't changed. What sat behind it had.

"What now?" she asked.

"Now we let the city talk to itself," he said. "We give it nothing of me to chew on."

He looked at the token on the screen, the Coalition's mark cut into steel, clean lines repeating like scripture for men who only believe in profit.

"They built a canopy and called it safety," Lucien said. "We'll take their weather."

He shut the feed with a tap. The screen went black, but Ghost stayed in the speaker. The room dimmed, not dark. The city kept moving. Machines hummed. Men stayed awake.

"Stay with him," Lucien said. "Tell me the moment Silas stops."

"You won't close your eyes," Ghost replied, more fact than jest.

Lucien let the silence breathe. "Then keep me company until I do."

He crossed the room. Lena met him halfway without meaning to. Their shoulders touched, an oath without words. He didn't promise her safety. He promised motion.

"Myth is a muzzle," he said. "We keep it on until it's time to bite."

Outside, the river kept moving, indifferent to men and their wars. Somewhere far off, a siren changed its mind and faded.

The city forgets nothing.

Chapter Nineteen

THE WEIGHT OF TRUTH

Mid-morning found them where they fell. Logan slept upright against the wall, chin to his chest, palms open, his guard never fully lowered. Victor was stretched out on the floor with one arm hanging, an empty glass tipped near his fingers, boots still on. On the chair by the window, Lucien sat upright, back straight even in sleep, head tipped forward, shadows carved beneath his eyes. Lena was curled in his lap, her cheek tucked into the hollow of his neck, one hand fisted in his shirt like she forgot to let go. Thin daylight slipped through the blinds and caught in the dust. The TV was dark. The burners were quiet. For a few breaths, the city pretended it didn't know their names.

Lucien's phone buzzed once on the armrest. His eyes opened. He didn't move at first, just looked at the screen, expecting Ghost.

It wasn't.

Dad.

He slipped the phone free without waking Lena. Her hand tightened anyway, a reflex that remembered what waking cost. "One moment," he murmured low against her hair. He gathered her carefully, her warmth still clinging to him, and set her in the chair he had just left. She stirred, breath catching, then evened out.

Only then did he straighten, take the phone in hand, and cross to the window. His voice stayed level. "Father."

Alexander's reply came without warmth. "You're awake."

"I am now."

The line stayed quiet for a moment.

"Your mother has been unwell," he said. "It started while we were away. Episodes. Vertigo. The room tilting when she stood. Headaches she called annoyances, because that is what she does. Victoria flew down last week to keep her company and stayed with her while we were still in Sanctuary."

Lucien closed his eyes once. "You had her seen?"

"Immediately." A pause. "They started with a CT. Then an MRI. They found a mass."

For once, no one in his life had aimed the weapon.

"Where?" Lucien asked. The question came out harder than panic.

"Posterior fossa," Alexander said. "Low in the back of the skull. Pressing where balance lives. The first report calls it meningioma, but one of the specialists does not like what he sees. They will not name anything until the deeper imaging is finished and a surgeon considers approach. It is large enough to explain what she has felt. Not small enough to ignore."

Across the room, Logan shifted and settled again. Victor snored once, a short, human sound that did not fit their world and somehow saved it. Lena stirred in the chair and found the space he left warm and empty.

"When?" Lucien said.

"Today," Alexander answered. "I am bringing her to New York. We will keep it quiet. I intend to have this looked at by people who do not guess. I will be in the city with her while we sort it."

"Keep me in the loop," Lucien said. "All of it."

"I will have Victoria feed you updates," Alexander said. "My lines may be crowded."

A shared awareness settled in the silence, the war breathing under every word.

"Before anything else," Lucien said. "Giancarlo's bloodline is finished. Their house is ash."

Alexander went quiet for a moment, the weight of another chapter closing. "Already making your rounds."

He let the silence sit between them.

"I knew him a long time. But I will not grieve a man who spent blood like coin. I will not mourn that."

Lucien watched a strip of light climb the opposite wall. "Do you need anything you don't already have?"

"Yes," Alexander said, the honesty landing like a new thing between them. "Time. And your discipline. The city cannot see you stand up just because it hurts."

Lucien's throat tightened around something he never gave a name. "Understood."

"She's steady," Alexander added, and this time there was a thread of man beneath the armor. "Annoyed at the fuss. But steady. Victoria is with her now. I will call when we land."

"Tell her..." Lucien stopped. He didn't say I will be there. He would not offer comfort he could not guarantee. He found the truth that cost nothing and carried weight. "Tell her I know."

"I will." A pause softer than anything they had traded in years. "Be smart, son."

The line went quiet.

Lucien stood there a moment longer, phone low at his side. The room's small noises returned one by one, the radiator ticking, the breath of men who survived another night, the city waking past the blinds.

"Everything okay?" Lena's voice, sleep-rough, from the chair.

She drew her knees up, hair mussed, eyes already scanning his face for what he would not let show.

"My father," he said. "He is bringing my mother to New York. They found a mass."

Lena was up and in front of him before the last word faded. No questions to make it worse. Just her hand on his chest, then his cheek, like she could anchor the part of him that wanted to go where he was not allowed.

"Where?" she asked quietly.

"Back of her brain. The part that apparently handles balance. They will look deeper in the city."

"We will get answers."

Her thumb swept the edge of his jaw. "What do you need?"

He thought of orders, lists, a dozen reflexes he could dress this pain in. He thought of Silas moving somewhere under the day, of tags blinking on maps, of myths that kept the wolves at bay.

"Truth," he said. "Not comfort. Not guesses. The truth, and then we decide."

Lena nodded once. "Done."

Logan cleared his throat from the wall. "We good?"

"We're breathing," Victor answered from the floor without opening his eyes.

Lucien pocketed the phone and brought himself back to the room.

"Status," he said, and the word meant two things now.

Lena slid her hand into his and squeezed, a small pressure that said the war was not the only thing moving.

He looked at her, then at the men, then at the blind slats cutting the morning into stripes. "We keep our hours. We keep our myth. And we make space for one more fight."

Lena leaned up, kissed him once, quick and sure, a promise pressed to his mouth, and let go.

The phone on the table stayed dark. Outside, a truck downshifted, the sound dragging gravity back into the world.

Inside, they began to move.

CHAPTER TWENTY

WHO GETS THE STORY

The day dragged them back into it.

The stripe through the blinds had widened.

Victor found the remote and clicked the screen alive.

Banners crawled over footage of smoke curling above the Corsini estate, replayed from half a dozen angles.

CENTURY-OLD CORSINI ESTATE DESTROYED IN OVERNIGHT BLAZE

ARSON NOT RULED OUT

A TURNING POINT IN THE CITY'S WAR ON CRIME

The footage shifted. Not the house now, but the grounds.

Black bags lay in rows across the gravel.

Men in white suits moving slowly between them.

The reporter's voice stayed steady.

"Officials have confirmed multiple fatalities. Many of the remains recovered were severely burned, some beyond immediate identification. Forensic teams say dental records will be required in several cases. Investigators are still searching the structure for additional remains."

The image cut away quickly.

The mayor filled the screen.

He stood behind a lectern flanked by flags, already framed like a campaign photo, his tie chosen to look like authority. Cameras loved him. He knew it. His eyes moved across the room as if it already belonged to him.

"This city does not burn for anyone," he declared.

"It will not belong to ghosts, kings, or families who mistake inheritance for law. We have tolerated too many men who confuse fear with order. That indulgence ends now.

The Corsinis were not a dynasty. They were a symptom. And this city is done mistaking symptoms for sovereignty. Old empires do not get second lives. And if others think to rise in their place, let them understand this clearly: we are watching."

The words cut through static and settled in the room.

Victor's mouth flattened.

"Look at him," he muttered. "Half a night of smoke in the air and he's already building his throne on the ashes."

Logan pushed off the wall. "He's not wrong. Fire like that wakes the city. Forces his hand."

Victor cut him a look. "Forces nothing. He chose this. He's shaping the story before we can breathe."

Lena leaned forward, eyes fixed on the screen. "This isn't about Corsini anymore. It's about who gets to write what comes next."

The volume clicked lower under Lucien's hand, but the mayor's mouth kept moving across the muted glass. Lucien watched without blinking, his reflection faint between frames.

Evelyn's voice was still there. Headaches. Balance. A mass. His father's restraint sat beside it. Now the mayor's voice sat on top of both.

The burner chimed once on the table.

Lucien reached for it.

"Go."

Ghost broke in, low and steady. "Silas is still moving. Not hiding, not rushing. He's drifting through their usual lanes, offices, storage floors, ferry docks. Like he wants me to see him."

"Not panicked?" Lucien said.

"Not even close," Ghost replied. "Coalition's quiet. Too quiet. They're letting the noise work for them."

Victor nodded once.

"Silence is strategy. They wait while the city tears itself up."

Lena's voice cut in. "And the mayor makes himself king of the ruins."

The room held still, the faint hiss of the radiator threading through the muted images on the screen.

Lucien let the silence gather.

When he spoke, everyone listened.

"We don't chase Silas. Not yet. We watch him. And we watch the man who thinks he runs this city."

Later, the feed cut to Lansing again.

Not at a podium this time. He stepped into a black sedan, aides swarming, microphones craning forward. His hand rose to wave, not to answer.

The burner chimed.

"Intercepted chatter," Ghost said. "Lansing's office is moving quiet. Backroom meetings with donors, judges, police brass. Not war. Deals."

Logan watched the screen. "So he picks who burns and who doesn't. Chooses his enemies for the cameras, not the war."

Victor gave a short, humorless laugh. "He's building headlines."

The laugh died.

Lucien stared at the muted footage. The mayor's lips moved in the glow. The room held still.

When he spoke, no one mistook it for a suggestion.

"He's not cleaning the rot," he said. "He's feeding it."

The words lingered.

The burner chimed again.

"I'm sending something over," Ghost said. "Watch your screen."

Lucien tapped the burner open.

Not the mayor.

A raid.

Tactical police in black vests stormed a warehouse. Not SWAT, not uniform, something in between. A nameless strike team in clean armor, cameras already waiting.

Men were dragged out in cuffs, faces pressed into concrete. The crawl beneath read: OPERATION CROWN OF SMOKE

Victor didn't look away. "He's not hunting criminals. He's picking winners."

Logan watched the screen. "He needs the city to see a crown. Doesn't matter what it's built on."

Lena leaned forward, eyes steady. "He doesn't want the war to end. He wants to be the one who ends it."

Lucien watched a moment longer, his reflection faint in the glass.

"He's not after balance," he said. "He's after authorship. If we don't take back the story, he'll write the ending. And us into it."

Lena's hand found his wrist. "Then don't let him make you the villain in his version."

Lucien held the image a moment longer. "I won't."

His gaze returned to the screen.

The myth wasn't enough anymore.

Myth could haunt. It could not answer a podium.

The city had chosen its theater. If he didn't step onto the stage, Lansing would turn his name into a weapon.

When Lucien finally spoke, it wasn't to the room.

"Then I'll give them something to see."

CHAPTER TWENTY-ONE
EIGHTY THREE SECONDS

They didn't plan it like a heist. They planned it like a funeral, tight, fast, every role spoken once, no need to repeat. Nobody in the room believed in second chances.

Ghost's voice leveled to the room's pulse.

"Lansing's raids aren't hunts. They're theater. A private intake bypasses precinct channels, fed by donors, judges, and his pet liaison, Heller, the man who makes warrants appear. They give him empty warehouses and camera angles. He gives them headlines."

Victor didn't sit. He stood over the folding table like it was a map of a war he refused to lose.

"So the city watches him kick down doors that were already open."

"Worse," Ghost said. "While he performs, the real filth moves under Coalition shadow. I traced a string of transfers that never loop back, never land. It just keeps climbing. Every time I follow it, it opens into another shell, another ghost company, another dead city. I can bleed money from it, but I can't see the top. Whatever the Coalition really is, it covers its own tracks."

Logan whistled softly. "So you can touch their money?"

"I can touch enough to remind them money bleeds. I also found the mayor's mouth."

Lena's eyes lifted.

"His mouth?"

"The citywide broadcast stack." Ghost's tone didn't change, but the room did.

"Every station hands video feed to the same choke point before it goes to the towers and boards. It's called CityCast. Their encoder is patched around the edges and rotten in the middle. I can split his speech. I can pour ours down the same pipe."

Lucien's hand closed around the back of the chair.

"How long?"

"I can get you ninety seconds before they wrench the plug. Eighty if Heller panics."

Lucien looked around at the men, at Lena, then at the black glass of the TV that still remembered the mayor's teeth.

"We're done being narrated," he said. "We write now."

The sun dropped straight down the avenues, carving the city into steel and shadow. The mayor had chosen midtown marble for his latest sermon: steps, banners, a hard blue sky pretending to be a ceiling. Cameras flocked. Microphones stretched like hungry throats.

News vans idled at the curb, generators coughing exhaust into the crowd.

In the safe room, there was no lecture. Just mechanics.

Ghost in the wire.

Victor cycled through the handful of cameras Ghost had pulled from nearby buildings.

Logan paced, energy that refused a chair.

Lena moved through the space in a rhythm she chose on purpose, headset check, backup battery.

She glanced at Lucien, a look that said don't die in front of them today.

Ghost came back, stripped to wire.

"We're latched. CityCast handshakes in ten. He'll look down to read the lie. I'll cut him when he breathes in."

Lucien pulled a jacket from the back of the chair. Black. Clean. He looked like a man who could be rich or dead depending on the light.

Lena crossed to him. Pressed two fingers to his throat. His pulse met them without apology.

"Once you step into their light," she said, "no one will ever attempt to make you small again."

"I was never small," he answered.

"But I let them pretend. That ends."

She nodded once. Then she did the only thing she knew that wasn't strategy. She rose on her toes and set her mouth to his. It wasn't soft. It was sure. He took it like a promise and gave it back like one.

"Time," Ghost said.

The mayor opened his mouth to make the city behave.

The screen winked.

Not static.

Absence.

A black that wasn't off, but awake.

Every television in a thousand bars.

Every patient room where the day was measured in beeps and news crawls.

Storefronts. Apartment windows stacked into glass towers.

A deli in Queens. A laundromat in Brooklyn. A precinct break room where three cops stopped talking mid-sentence.

Phones bloomed the same black.

Every screen in Times Square dropped to midnight at noon.

Then it took shape.

A silhouette. Shoulders like a verdict. The suggestion of a face the city once eulogized and then tried to forget.

Somewhere, a bar fell silent.

Commuters froze, phones lighting their faces with the same dark outline.

A train station board, arrivals and departures blinking in rows, wiped clean and gave itself to Lucien's feed.

Ten blocks from the podium, in a hospital waiting room, Evelyn Cole looked up.

She lifted her chin the way she always had when the world tried to take something from her.

"Hello," Lucien said.

There was no amplification in the room, and somehow the city heard it.

"You were told fire ends bloodlines," he said. "You were told ghosts stay dead. You were told crowns grow out of podiums."

He waited.

"Truth doesn't need a stage. It needs a spine."

He didn't raise his voice. He didn't have to. Ghost had poured him through every artery of glass and wire the city owned.

"If you sold safety and called it order, you will answer. If you hid behind office and named it law, you will answer."

He tilted his head.

"If you built your throne out of other people's fear, stand up. While it's still yours."

"I died once. It taught me what you look like without your mask."

Somewhere, someone was trying to take the feed back. Ghost was counting.

"Balance isn't a word," Lucien said. "It's a debt. And I'm the one you owe."

He stepped forward once.

The shadow resolved into a man.

The light cut him leaner. The eyes were the same. The chest carried what the city had never seen, scar tissue under black fabric, a wound that should have ended him.

In the waiting room, Evelyn laughed once, soft and disbelieving. "He always liked an entrance," she said, and then the laugh broke.

Across the hall, Alexander stopped moving, one hand braced against the wall. Victoria lowered into a chair. Her knees had quit.

On the steps behind the mayor, a microphone tipped like it wanted to choose a side.

"If you're looking for reassurance," Lucien said, the smallest cruelty at the corner of his mouth, "don't."

He lifted steel into frame. A token marked with a sigil that had pretended to be older than the men who paid to strike it. The same token pulled from Giancarlo's pocket as his house burned.

He turned it once so the city could see.

Then he closed his fist and snapped it clean.

"Ghosts don't die," he said. "They collect."

The feed cut to black because Ghost let it.

Eighty-three seconds.

The mayor blinked at the black he no longer controlled. His mouth opened. What came out was not a sentence.

Times Square forgot how to breathe for a second.

Then a million voices remembered they were never on the same page.

It started as electricity.

Not metaphor. Real wires. Real signals.

Ghost slipped into accounts never meant to be touched, into systems built on the assumption they were untouchable.

Shells inside shells. Trust layered on assumption and nobody checking.

The city's quiet places opened all at once.

Money began to move.

First small figures, the kind no one noticed.

Then a transfer heavy enough to tilt the room, nine digits moving through a currency no bank would admit existed.

Property deeds tripped like dominoes. Four sites flipped without a single hand signing.

Victor's voice stayed flat, but his eyes were alive.

"Northgate Foundry. Edge of the city. Factory compound with a deep central yard. Two access roads running outside the perimeter. Hard to approach without being seen."

He paused.

"The others are insurance."

Logan let out a low breath, a grin cutting sharp across his face.

"Finally. No more borrowed air."

Lena leaned over the table, blueprints glowing on the phone screen. Her voice was steady. Chosen.

"We build outside their reach. We set our horizon. Then we bend theirs."

Lucien didn't look at the screen.

He looked at her hand on the blueprint, then at the men.

He saw it forming. Numbers becoming ground. Ground becoming rooms. Rooms becoming corridors he could command.

"We build," he said.

This time, not an empire. An answer.

Ghost delivered names like weapons.

Mara Saito. Logistics carved from wars no one admitted.

Imani Kadeh. Intelligence the state shouldn't have let walk away.

Rook. Nobody's real name, but everybody's first call when steel needed a brain.

They didn't swear loyalty. They signed contracts. Money was honest like that.

Their profiles flared across Ghost's screen. Faces. Histories. The scars that explained them.

Lucien saw more than names.

He saw gravity.

When these people met him, they wouldn't see an employer.

They would see weather.

A storm worth orbiting.

The city tried to make sense of what it had just seen. When it couldn't, it made noise.

Newsrooms became hives. Phones found hands that trembled and hit record anyway. The phrase he's alive did not taste the same in every mouth, and that was the point.

The Coalition answered first, because money hated surprise.

Ghost caught the signal, a packet drifting across a dark channel, masked to look like static. To anything else, it was noise.

He rerouted it, scrubbed it clean, and dropped it onto their phones.

The feed showed a table under a single light.

No faces.

Just hands.

A steel token, snapped clean across its old lie, laid flat on wood.

Beside it, a card. Heavy stock. Ink cut deep.

Three words.

BLUE ROOM WAITS

Victor leaned in, eyes narrowing.

"That's not just an invite. That's a rotation key. If that's their token system, it's not decorative. You don't send one unless you've decided someone belongs in the room."

He exhaled once. "And if they didn't know who burned the Corsinis before, they do now."

Ghost had already magnified the card.

Numbers faint in the fiber, almost invisible, riding the grain.

"Coordinates. Time-stamp. They don't print locations. They embed them."

Lucien turned the broken token between his fingers.

"If they're using symbols, a broken one isn't an accident. They're telling us it's under new hands."

Lena studied the dark feed, her voice quiet but certain.

"They want you to answer. That's not fear. It's recognition."

Lucien didn't reach for the screen. He leaned back, eyes steady, as if he had already claimed it. The image lived in pixels, but the meaning belonged to him. He carried it like a knife, invisible but always there.

"We'll keep our appointment," he said.

City Hall smelled like floor wax and ambition rotting under suits.

Tonight it smelled like whiskey poured before a verdict.

Lansing did not sit.

He stood at the head of the long table with a tumbler in hand, the kind of glass heavy enough to break a jaw if the moment required it. Ice clicked once against the rim. It was the only sound anyone dared make.

He took a slow drink and watched the city through the window.

The skyline stared back at him, sharp and black, like it was waiting for him to slip.

"For eighty seconds," Lansing said, "this fucking city forgot who owned it."

He didn't raise his voice.

Power spoke quieter than fear.

Heller stood behind him, pale, sweating through his collar, tablet clutched to his chest.

His chief of staff spoke first. Fear made stupid men brave.

"We can frame it as a foreign breach. A coordinated,"

Lansing turned slightly.

The smile he gave him looked borrowed from a knife.

"You want to tell the city a ghost took its screens?"

The man shut up.

Lansing took a drink.

"No. We tell them what he is. A criminal with timing. A dead man with a camera. That's all."

Heller cleared his throat and instantly regretted it.

Lansing held out his glass without looking. Someone rushed to fill it.

"Build me a personal unit," he said. "I want men who can wear a badge in daylight and bury somebody with it after dark."

He slid the paper across the table.

"Clean records on paper. Filth underneath. If they've kicked in doors for money, good. If they've buried complaints, better."

Someone read the top line. "Civic Shield."

Lansing lit a cigarette, dragged once, then pointed with it.

"Bring me shooters. Bring me raid men. Bring me the kind that hit apartments so hard the neighbors forget what they heard."

Smoke drifted up between him and the window.

"If he wants a stage," Lansing said, "we'll give him one."

He took the cigarette from his mouth.

"Then we'll burn it with him on it."

They drove upriver when the day began to fold.

Northgate waited at the end of a road that had forgotten how to stay paved.

Brick from a century that believed in permanence.

The place smelled like oil and rain that never fully dried.

Windows boarded with wood that outlived belief.

Rust curled along the gate. Logan leaned on the wheel. Victor shouldered it open with a grunt.

Inside, dust. Echo. The bones of industry.

A foundry without fire.

It would do.

Victor set down a case. Metal inside clattered like a promise.

Logan walked the floor, checking angles, marking blind spots like other men count exits.

The burner buzzed.

Ghost filled the room, steady as ever.

"Coordinates sent. If they want the money, they'll walk through that gate. If they don't, you wouldn't want them anyway."

Time passed the way it does in empty buildings, slow and loud.

They didn't wait long.

First came Rook. A duffel slung over one shoulder, steel folded tight inside. He didn't speak. He dropped the bag at his boots and scanned the ceiling, already measuring where the building would break.

Then Mara. Combat boots steady, eyes moving slow, cataloging corners, exits, cover. She turned once in the center of the hall as if committing it to memory.

Imani came next. Laptops under one arm, cables in the other. She plugged into the wall before she spoke, mapping power lines no one else could see.

Lena studied them, then looked at Lucien.

"They don't look like loyalty."

"They're not," he said. "They're skill. Loyalty comes later."

He took the broken token from his jacket and set both halves on the table. No ceremony. This wasn't a trophy room.

It was a worksite.

"Ghost," he said. "Bring me everything that still breathes after Blue Room."

"Already building you a list," Ghost replied. "And for the record, I like your new ceilings."

Lucien looked up. Old beams crossed above, scarred, indifferent.

He liked that.

"Tell the city," he said, voice settling into steel, "the dead man is done being quiet."

"How do you want it told?" Ghost asked.

Lucien's mouth edged toward something that wasn't a smile.

"We already did."

Chapter Twenty-Two

WHERE FEAR LEARNS ITS NAME

The hum of downtown bled through freshly polished glass. It wasn't traffic tonight, it was something colder, a city waiting to be told what to fear next. Lansing ignored it. He stood at the window with a lit cigarette tucked between two fingers, watching the smoke curl back toward his throat. The skyline stared back at him. Sharp. Black. Indifferent.

"I didn't crawl out of a South Bronx walkup to lose this city," he said.

Heller waited three feet behind him with a tablet and a problem. The lights above flickered once, long enough to feel intentional.

"Your approval ticked up," Heller said. "Your credibility…"

"Say it."

"Down. Slightly."

"Because I told the city ghosts don't run it, and then a fucking ghost spoke into every goddamn living room for eighty-three seconds."

He tapped ash onto the floor like the room existed to clean up after him. His voice stayed pleasant, the kind that hid razors until you leaned close.

"Build me the thing I asked for."

"The unit?"

"The story," Lansing said. "The unit is the story."

The door opened without knocking. Cold air slid in behind a woman with shoulders that had known recoil more than rest. Her suit didn't fit like fabric. It fit like a warning.

"Captain Dane," Lansing said. "Your people are the answer to a question no one is supposed to ask. Clean names. Dirty hands. Phones unlock when you touch them. Doors open when you walk in."

He took a slow drag, exhaling through his nose. "I don't care what they did before." He let the pause stretch until the room leaned in. "From now on, they're Civic Shield."

The name sounded clean enough to hide anything.

Dane didn't blink. "Rules of engagement?"

"Win," Lansing said. "Clean."

"Clean is slower."

"Then make it look clean."

Heller's tablet chimed, the sound too loud for the quiet they were in.

"First target package ready."

"Good. What is it?"

"A warehouse in Hell's Kitchen. Old money routes. Nothing left but dust. It's empty."

Lansing watched his reflection swallow the skyline. The city looked hollow in the glass. Hollow meant ready.

"Not empty. Not if we bring a camera."

He didn't say bait or message. The silence already said it for him.

They didn't watch the raid on television. Ghost fed it to them raw. No anchors. No lower thirds. No commentary. Just picture. Cold. Surgical. Staged.

A rollup door on the edge of Hell's Kitchen rattled like it wanted out of its hinges. The task force stacked at the entrance as if they had fought their way in, except the door had already been rolled up. Stillness dressed as chaos.

The camera angle was perfect. Of course it was. Someone had placed it there deliberately, someone who understood how fear moved through a lens.

The men moved like choreography. Black armor. Silent steps. Hands sweeping corners that didn't need sweeping. Weapons raised at shadows already rehearsed.

Then the crates came out. Heavy. Sealed. Carried like poison finally found, except anyone with a pulse could see the crates were light. Nothing inside. Which was the whole point.

The city didn't care.

The city clapped.

Most people had been raised to clap when lights were bright.

Victor's mouth flattened. "He's teaching the city to applaud the noise."

"They're feeding them noise," Logan said. "Real meat's somewhere else."

Imani slowed the footage, eyebrows tightening as each frame sharpened into intent. "They slipped. Digital trace only. Their comms don't touch the police net. Everything they say bounces into a private van off-site. Closed loop. Someone built them a ghost trailer."

Lucien leaned toward the screen, the cold light cutting his face into angles. "So what does that mean?"

"That they can't see us," Imani said. "Not unless we let them."

Ghost's voice threaded through the room. "The mayor wants applause. He's dragging cameras through the city until someone calls him savior."

Victor looked at the screen like it had just spit at him. "And the Blue Room?"

"Twenty-six hours from now," Ghost said. "Still under the river."

No one spoke. Not stunned. Not confused. Just quiet, the kind a city falls into when it forgets the difference between a warning and a show.

The moon climbed above the midtown teeth, sharp and white as a blade the city didn't trust. Lansing watched the raid play out across the tablet on his knee: Hell's Kitchen in full theater, armored silhouettes moving with rehearsed violence, crates lifted like poison someone pretended to find. The applause scrolling under the livestream made him check the numbers, not the bodies.

Good.

The city was already eating from his hand.

The sky went black enough to swallow distance. The streets cooled fast under it, early-spring chill. Soft at first, then sharp once the last of the daylight fled.

Lansing sat in a city car that technically belonged to the taxpayers. It felt like his.

Captain Dane rode opposite him, tablet balanced on her knee, the dark pressing against the windows like it needed a reason.

"We're hearing chatter," Dane said. "People saw the broadcast and remembered how to say his name."

"They'll forget," Lansing answered. "Or they'll remember what I tell them to."

"Not if he keeps making speeches."

"Then we stop the speeches," Lansing said. "We find the stagehands. Then we take their hands."

He watched the glass towers shift from silver to black, reflections sliding over the windshield like confessions.

"Find me old Cole fronts," he said. "Shelters. Charities. Whatever they called themselves. I don't care if they're empty or not."

He adjusted his cuff, the motion feeling ceremonial. "We raid them on camera."

People don't need truth. They need symbols.

Traffic lights bled red across the hood of the car. The whole street looked like it had been baptized in warning.

"And nothing says redemption like burning the ghost of Cole twice."

Dane didn't answer. She didn't disagree.

"People forgive what makes them feel safe," Lansing continued. "So we put eyes on every door that earns sympathy. Churches. Shelters. Hospitals."

He finally looked at her, moonlight cutting across his face. "If he tries to haunt one, we turn it into proof he was never a savior. Just another criminal who learned how to hide."

CHAPTER TWENTY-THREE

TEACH THEM TO BREATHE

Night hadn't quieted the city. It never did. By nightfall it was louder. Sirens traded lanes with news vans. Every lobby TV was shouting.

The mayor's raid in Hell's Kitchen looped in half the bars downtown, applause pretending to be truth.

Northgate heard it through glass and wire.

Ghost let the noise run hot in one ear while the other stayed where it belonged.

"Confirmation. Blue Room drops in twenty-four hours. Riverside Terminal sublevel. Flood-closed since '09."

Victor stood over the table. "We'll be ready."

Logan leaned in. "Blue Room under the terminal. That puts half the city on our shoulders before dessert. The kind who smile for cameras and break teeth offscreen."

Ghost's tone sharpened. "Coalition swept the room an hour ago. New sensors in the walls. If we don't map it tonight, we walk in blind."

The warning settled, sharp and cold.

Lucien absorbed it. Not the image, the weight.

"We do not bow," he said. "We measure. If they want to breathe under the same sky, they learn how to breathe beside us."

The words set behind his eyes the way warnings do.

BLUE ROOM WAITS

It lived in the space between them, heavier than anything they could lay on the table.

"We do not walk in blind. Tonight we map it, all of us. We leave eyes where they will never think to look."

Northgate shifted around them in small, sharp movements, the kind a room makes right before it stands up.

Rook climbed a ladder, bolting steel into old beams, turning echoes into angles that could be defended.

Mara paced the hall, dropping tape in clean lines. Kill zone. Cover. Fallback.

Imani's laptop glowed faint on a crate as she teased new nerves through old walls, power and cameras and hidden antennas.

Little by little, the place shed its past.

Rooms that once held dust became stations.

Halls narrowed into sightlines.

Corners turned into decisions.

Northgate was no longer a foundry.

It was learning to be a fortress.

An hour later the noise had lowered, not gone, just tucked into corners where work kept breathing. The overheads were dimmer now, the maps cleaned up, the room no longer bracing for impact but holding its breath for whatever came next.

Across the table, Lena watched him.

Not his posture. The strain beneath it.

The way he stared through the blueprint like it was a future he wasn't sure he had permission to touch.

The faint tremor he thought he hid, the one that came from carrying too many wars at once.

She knew he wasn't seeing the blueprint anymore.

And that was the moment she moved.

She broke the one thing she never wanted to break.

Her silence.

"My mother hated the city," she said. Her voice lowered, like she was opening a door she'd kept locked for years. "She called it a mouth. Said if you stood too close too long, it would learn your name and swallow you whole."

Her eyes didn't blink. They just fixed on something only she could see.

"My father loved maps. He used to trace roads with his finger like if he smoothed them enough, nothing bad would happen on them. He said places had personalities, not destinies. That nothing was written unless you were too afraid to change the ending."

She laughed once, the kind of sound that came from remembering how wrong you were.

"We fought. Not once. All the time. About everything that didn't matter until it did. I said I needed to leave. They said leaving wasn't a plan. I thought staying gone meant I'd proved something."

Her throat moved, the swallow of someone bracing for impact.

"I didn't call," she said. "Not out of hate. Out of pride dressed up like distance. I thought time was something I could come back to."

The room stilled around her. Even the screens seemed to listen.

"Then a truck ran a light on a county road that wasn't built for speed." Her voice thinned.

"Metal folded. Glass did what glass does best. And the next time the phone rang, I thought it was them calling to make me admit I'd been stubborn. I almost didn't answer, because I wasn't ready to lose the argument yet."

She drew a breath she didn't want.

"But they weren't calling."

A beat.

"They weren't calling ever again."

Her next breath shook. Just slightly. Enough.

"I stayed in New York because there wasn't a home left to go back to. You don't forget the sound of an empty house. The clocks still tick. The refrigerator still hums. But it's not a house anymore. It's a place where voices used to live.

And hallways get longer when all the things you didn't say are the only things walking beside you."

She finally looked at him.

"Go see Evelyn," she said. "Don't be brave. Don't be stubborn. Don't think there's more time. Just go."

Lucien studied her like she'd finally opened a door he didn't think he deserved to walk through. He almost stepped through. Almost.

"That night at the hospital," he said quietly, "you told me you had no family."

He had believed her then. Now he heard the grave inside it.

Lena met his eyes and didn't flinch. "Yes, Lucien. In that moment, I realized family was a word that didn't belong to me anymore."

The war maps and screens faded under something quieter.

Lucien almost asked more, but he didn't. Some doors didn't need kicking down when she was already bleeding just to open them.

The silence after wasn't empty. It was full of everything she had never said until now.

Victor frowned. "Wait, what the fuck is going on?"

"Nothing," Lucien said.

Lena's voice softened. "Tell them. They're your family too."

Lucien rolled his eyes like the words cost him extra.

"My mother has a brain mass. We don't know what it is yet. Alexander's here with her now. He wanted her checked into the best place."

The word mass hung in the room, worse because it had no final shape yet.

Lucien didn't blink when he said it. That was the worst part.

Logan stiffened. "Boss, you don't tell us that?"

Victor shook his head, disbelief curdling into something steadier. "Evelyn? Christ, Lucien, you drop this in the middle of a war council?"

Lena shot him a look. "Really, Victor? Right now?"

The edge left his mouth.

"I didn't feel the need to say anything to anyone," Lucien said.

Victor held his gaze. "We're not just partners. I walked beside you in the dark when the world said you were gone. Every second you spent beyond the line, I carried it here. Don't shut us out now."

"Yeah, boss," Logan said. "We're family. I mean... I killed my sister for you."

Lucien smirked, a dry edge in it.

"Half-sister."

The room held its breath. No one was sure if they were allowed to smile.

"Yeah," Logan said, his mouth twitching. "Half-sister for you."

Victor lifted a hand like he was keeping score.

"And I shot his dad's hand off for you."

A low chuckle moved through the room, dark and human.

Not because anything was funny.

Because they were alive.

For a moment it wasn't strategy or vengeance holding them together.

It was the fact they had survived each other.

Victor cleared his throat, stepping into a different version of himself.

"We can build a tunnel that isn't a tunnel. Laundry bay, service lift, oxygen line running the length of the ward. Hospitals are full of back doors. They just call them health codes."

Imani didn't look up. "Give me a wing map and two custodial IDs. I'll convince the badge reader it's last Tuesday."

"Blue Room is twenty-four," Ghost added quietly. "You have time to be a son and still walk into a meeting as a king."

Lucien breathed once through his nose, a small sound that knew it had lost the argument and was grateful for it.

"Build it."

Rook finally spoke. "And the Blue Room. Mara and I will run recon alone. Imani stays here and watches the feed. Quiet. Fast. No signature on their side."

Mara nodded, certain. "Say when."

Lucien hesitated, the kind of pause that came from wanting to carry everything at once.

"You win," he told Lena, softer.

"I wasn't trying to," she said.

It landed heavier than any victory.

He turned away before gratitude looked like weakness.

"Ghost."

He steadied his breath, the room narrowing to purpose.

"The path."

Twenty minutes later, the room had changed shape.

Not louder, not softer.

Just sharper.

The quiet where decisions got made.

Ghost came back on the line. "Mercy West, east wing. Service lift drops into a laundry bay with a broken sensor I can keep down. Night nurse loves Sudoku and won't look up between midnight and twelve-fifteen. Oxygen corridor camera's capped, but the cap has a cap. We're in and out in under an hour."

Victor leaned over the table. "We'll dress you like a problem no one wants to make paperwork about."

"Tonight," Lucien said.

Lena's shoulders dropped a fraction, like she had just let go of a weight she had been pretending belonged to someone else.

"Tonight," Ghost repeated. "And two nights after, Blue Room."

"Say the time," Victor said.

"Twenty-one hundred for the hospital," Ghost replied. "Twenty-two hundred we're ghosts again."

Logan grinned without humor. "Careful. That word's getting crowded."

"Let them have the echo," Lucien said. "We're the source."

Lucien thumbed a magazine, felt the weight settle, and locked it in with a clean click.

No flourish. No hesitation.

He adjusted his jacket, fabric chosen so it wouldn't snag on a draw.

Lena stopped him at the door, two fingers against his wrist.

"Don't armor yourself so much you forget why you're going," she said. "She doesn't need a king. She just needs her son."

He kissed her, nothing theatrical, just truth. A promise he meant to keep even with the whole room watching.

"Victor."

"Car's ready."

"Logan."

"Say when."

"Ghost."

"I'll keep the city looking at the wrong street."

Lucien nodded once, the kind that settled a room.

They didn't rush the door. They moved with him, steady and sure, past every bolt Rook had driven into the beams, past Mara's tape lines that cut the floor into choices, past Imani's cables humming through the walls like a nervous system coming online.

The weight wasn't lighter. It simply wasn't his alone anymore.

By the time they reached the stairs, something unspoken had built itself between them, something steadier than orders and louder than fear.

Family.

Not the kind you were born into.

The kind that stayed when the world didn't.

They pushed into the night, the city breathing hot and restless around them, and for the first time in hours Lucien let himself inhale without bracing.

This was what a family looked like when it moved.

CHAPTER TWENTY-FOUR

A MOTHER AND HER BOY

Night held its breath outside Mercy West.

A service bay yawned open because it was told to.

Three men no one would remember stepped into the freight lift. Broad shoulders, lean angles, one in scrubs between them.

It smelled like bleach and rubber gloves.

A fourth voice lived in their ears.

"Left at the linen cage," Ghost said. "Camera two is thinking about last Tuesday. You have three floors before anyone's luck gets tested."

Victor hit the button with a knuckle. Logan adjusted a cap low over his eyes. Lucien stood between them in borrowed hospital greens, the kind of ordinary that didn't belong to him. He touched his pocket once. Not for a weapon. To steady his hand.

"Breathe on the fours," Ghost murmured, steady as a heartbeat. "Keeps you quiet. Keeps you sharp. Four in, four hold, four out. I'll tell you if you need to stop breathing."

The lift shuddered upward.

At twelve-oh-nine, a badge reader forgot its job.

At twelve-ten, a door opened because someone who wasn't there was holding it from the far side.

At twelve-eleven, the oxygen corridor blinked and decided to look the other way.

A nurse looked up once, saw only routine in their shapes, and went back to her crossword beneath a lamp that turned everything gold.

Fifth floor, east wing.

He could feel it before the number stenciled on the wall confirmed it.

509.

510.

"Room 512," Ghost whispered. "Two right turns. Custodial closet on your way. If someone asks why you're here, you're not. Oxygen closet beside the door. Staff passes every few minutes. Time your turn."

Lucien moved.

Not like a myth. Like a son.

He turned the second corner and the world did that trick it saved for very few people, narrowed to a single person and widened around them at the same time.

She was coming toward him with a flimsy hospital sweater draped over her shoulders and a magazine folded at the spine because the crossword was insulting. Paper bracelet on one wrist. A faint tape mark from an IV on the other. Eyes that forgave first.

For an instant he saw those same eyes looking down at him through playground bruises and cheap apartment light. The decades collapsed into a single reach.

She looked up at something that wasn't a sound.

For a heartbeat they just stood there, ten feet of tile and months of silence pressed into it. Then the magazine slipped from her fingers. She moved, and so did he, and the hug landed like the end of a long fall.

She smelled like the same soap she'd used his entire childhood, a scent no city had been able to erase.

"Hi, Mom," he said into her hair.

"Don't 'Mom' me like you were just upstairs getting ice," Evelyn said, voice steady but leaking. She leaned back to stare at him like he was a painting some fool tried to throw away. "Let me see."

He let her.

She checked the line of his cheek, the old cut near his brow, the new hardness under his shirt where the bullet did not take him. She found what she was looking for, and what she was afraid of.

Her thumb hesitated at the scar. For a heartbeat he thought she might scold him for it, the way she used to when he scraped his knees.

"You're thinner," she decided.

"You're bossy," he answered.

"And you're here." She breathed once like permission. "Come on, before I start crying in the hall and make the nurses feel useful."

They went into her room. It was a small, expensive kind of quiet. A wide window gave the city its distance back, all glass and softened light. Fresh flowers sat in a real vase, not hospital plastic, and the chair beside the bed looked built for long waits people pretended were temporary. The monitor still beeped, polite as ever, as if good manners could make a room like this hurt less.

He closed the door. The click was a sacrament.

"Three minutes clear," Ghost said. "Then footsteps."

Lucien took the small earpiece from his ear and set it on the counter, cutting the channel to Ghost.

She sat on the edge of the bed like a woman who didn't want help but would allow the idea of it. She patted the spot beside her like he was eight again and too tall for it. He sat anyway.

"I watched you," she said, like it was a show she didn't recommend but still caught every episode. "Everybody watched you."

"I didn't do it for them."

"You looked like your grandfather the day he told the priest he paid for the roof and that was the only donation he was making."

He laughed once, because he had to. "I broke something," he said, thinking of the token, the city, the silence.

"I heard it." She glanced at his hand, then back at his face. "You always did like a simple truth. Cracks travel. They tell you where the weak is."

Her words landed heavier than he expected, and he felt them settling under his ribs. He didn't want her seeing the weight he was carrying. "Headaches?" he asked, as gentle as he could make it.

"Boredom," she said. "Which feels like blasphemy when people are scared for you. Vertigo when I stand up too fast. I refuse to stand up slowly."

He stared at her bracelet. At her. "They'll fix it."

"They confirmed what they were afraid of this afternoon," she said. "Cancer."

The word didn't land like a sentence. It landed like a room losing air.

Lucien went still in a way even violence had never made him still.

For once, there was no enemy to name. No throat to close his hand around. No door to kick open.

Just his mother sitting beside him, warm and alive, saying the one word he couldn't turn into war.

His hand closed against the edge of the bed.

Evelyn covered it with hers. "Everything is going to be okay. Not because it's easy. Because we will do the next thing, then the next, until there is nothing left to fear today."

She squeezed his hand once. "So yes, they'll try. And I'll let them. That's the deal we make with doctors and hope." She looked at him. "I'm not scared of what is, Lucien. I'm only scared of what I leave you with if I don't say it now."

He looked at her, and for the first time tonight, maybe the first time in years, he let himself look like a son who wanted to be told.

"Say it."

She didn't look away. "Don't make war your address. Visit it if you must. Win when you have to. But don't get your mail there. It eats men who think they're immune."

He swallowed. The monitor ticked on.

"Don't punish yourself by refusing joy," she went on. "Punishment is easy. Joy is work. Do the work."

He set his palms on his knees. "I'm trying."

"Try better." She studied him for a moment. "You found someone who makes you walk like you're walking toward light. Don't make her wait in the doorway. She'll convince herself she was wrong to open it."

He looked down like a man who didn't want to show his face to a truth that knew his face too well.

"How did you,"

"Please," she said, smiling. "You say Lena's name like you're thirsty and someone set down water. I didn't raise an idiot."

He let a laugh out, and it hurt in a good way.

Silence. Not empty. Just big.

Then she reached for the drawer, past the comb and lotion, to the thing the nurses wouldn't understand.

She took out a small velvet box that looked like it had been kept near a heartbeat for years. No flourish. No speech. Just a mother placing an object between them that turned the air different.

He noticed the faint worn crease where her thumb had traced it over and over, a prayer she refused to say aloud.

"Before you ask," she said, "yes, I knew."

He did what she expected him to. "How?"

"Every mother knows when her child is standing on a threshold," she said. "The way you look at that girl carries for miles. The way she looks back at you, it's rude to physics."

He exhaled, and it almost became something else.

She opened the box.

The ring was simple and not simple at all, thin gold that held light instead of reflecting it, a setting so clean it didn't need to announce itself to be seen.

"It's old," Evelyn said. "Worn by women who knew what they wanted. Men think diamonds are about shine. They're not. They're about pressure and time behaving."

He stared. He didn't reach. He couldn't.

She took his hand, not gently. Softer things had never convinced her of love.

"Don't wait forever," Evelyn said. "You asked between worlds. Ask again in this one. Give that girl a place to put her yes." Her thumb moved once over his knuckle. "And don't you tell me you don't deserve it. You don't get to be humble at the cost of someone else's future."

Her voice shook on the last word, but her hand didn't. She had decided long ago she'd give him this moment if she ever got another chance.

"How did you know my plans?" he asked, and it wasn't a deflection. It was a boy asking permission to be the man he'd already decided to be.

"Because you came back different," she said. "And the difference wasn't rage. It was direction." She closed her hand over his. "Because God doesn't get to take everything. If He decides He wants me early, I can forgive Him if the price of it is that you live long and loved, my Lucien."

He closed his eyes. The room swayed once, not from vertigo. He nodded because anything else would undo him.

She set the ring in his palm and pressed his fingers around it. It was warm from her. Heavy in a way that had nothing to do with metal.

"You'll make a beautiful husband," she said, like a prophecy spoken in a kitchen. "Not because you're good at the theater of it. Because you remember what you move for."

"I don't know how to be small enough for this," he admitted, and it was the truest thing he'd said in the building.

"Then don't be small," she said. "Be kind. Be precise. Power that isn't kind and precise is loud and stupid. I didn't raise you to be loud and stupid."

The monitor ticked. A cart rattled somewhere far. The room held its breath with them.

"Your father is pretending not to be terrified," she added, soft. "Let him pretend. Call him anyway. He needs you to ask him about nothing."

"I will," he said.

"And your sister." She shook her head, amused and fierce. "She's sharper than both of you and has been since she was six. Listen when she cuts to the truth; she's usually right."

He nodded.

"Come here," she finished.

He did. He leaned in and she framed his face in her hands like she was memorizing it all over again. She kissed his forehead the way she did when his knees were scuffed and the sky was something you could conquer with a bike and a dare.

"I'm proud of you," she said into his skin. "Not for the noise. For the choices you're trying to make in the quiet."

He breathed once, then reached for the small earpiece on the counter and set it back in his ear. The world widened again.

"Thirty seconds," Ghost said, a thread, apologetic but unbending.

Evelyn heard nothing and somehow heard everything. "Go," she told him. "Before going turns into staying and staying turns into trouble."

He stood. It felt like standing on a ship.

He couldn't think of a line that could carry the room, so he didn't try. He held up the ring. "I'll do this right."

"You'll do it honest," she corrected. "Right is a story. Honest is a spine."

He nodded again because there wasn't language for what was moving through him and out into the hall.

"There's an oncology fundraiser at The Atria later this week. I promised them I'd be there, depending on how the day treats me. Lately every morning has its own idea."

He almost said, I'll make sure it's safe, but she was already moving on.

He touched her hair once. She swatted his hand and fixed it herself. Some rituals don't break.

He almost said "I love you," but the words felt too small for what she had just given him, so he let the door close on the ache instead.

"And Lucien," she said. His name from her stopped him the way it always had. He looked back.

"If it gets dark again, if it ever does, remember where the light lives." She tipped her head toward his chest. "It's not out there. It's in you. It always was."

He swallowed a ghost and opened the door.

The hallway breathed again, low light pooling on polished tile, the muted rhythm of monitors, a soft laugh from the nurses' station that almost sounded like mercy.

Logan appeared first, then Victor. Neither spoke.

Victor's hand brushed the doorframe once, a quiet signal only Lucien would hear.

Logan shifted his stance so Lucien stayed half-hidden when the nurse looked up and saw only two ordinary men leaving an unremarkable room, carrying something no chart would record.

They walked.

"Move steady," Ghost said. "Elevator in ten. Alley in twenty."

Lucien closed his fingers around the ring. It printed a small bright circle into his palm, a pain so clean it felt like instruction.

They moved past the vending machine with the dead bulb. The badge forgot its job again. The elevator whispered them down and the service bay opened without protest.

Outside, the night took them back. Logan opened the rear door. Victor watched the street the way he watched threats.

Lucien paused before getting in. Mercy West stood quiet behind him, every window anonymous except one.

Fifth-floor, east-facing. Her light dimmed as she settled, unaware he was still watching.

He memorized that square of glow the way some men memorize prayers.

Lucien slid into the seat and didn't let go of the ring until they were moving.

He didn't leave as a king.

He didn't leave as a myth.

He left as a boy who let his mother touch his face and tell him the truth.

CHAPTER TWENTY-FIVE

TWENTY-TWO HOURS

Northgate's concrete was gridded in tape and low blue lights, like a rehearsal for a storm.

Lucien, Victor, and Logan stepped in from the cold. Imani was already at the main table with Lena, her laptop open among cables, camera feeds, and mapped entry points.

The overhead lights dimmed.

"Blue Room clock: twenty-two hours," Ghost said. "Riverside Terminal sublevel. Same coordinates."

Rook and Mara pushed through the side door a moment later, river chill still on their jackets.

Rook dropped a coiled rope on the table like he wanted it to confess.

Mara wiped rust off her palms. "Utility gate opened clean. No live cameras. Motion sensors were asleep."

Imani turned the screen toward them. Grainy images sharpened into a steel chamber drowned in shadow.

"Temperature dropped the second we stepped inside," Rook said. "Flood scars on the walls. Felt like the river tried to bury the place and missed."

Ghost highlighted sections of the digital blueprint. "The system is in low-power mode. Structural sensors stay blind for twelve minutes. After that, the room wakes up."

Victor leaned in. "Show me the room."

Imani zoomed tighter.

A round platform. Black composite. Wires running out from it like veins.

Mara studied the screen. "It's a stage, not a room. It's wired for confession, not conversation."

Rook tapped one point on the map. "Infrared beam at knee height. Coalition sensors, not city. I killed them for sixty seconds. Long enough to map the space."

Imani nodded. "Hidden microphones in the steel. Every breath gets recorded. Lansing's private loop rides the same feed. He wants eyes and sound in that room."

Logan frowned. "They didn't build a meeting place. They built a ritual."

Ghost circled the platform on the screen. "Exactly."

Mara leaned back. "Silas probably isn't hiding. He wants an audience."

Imani folded her arms. "We marked everything. Cameras. Exits. Walls. If they mean to trap someone, that platform is where it happens."

Ghost's tone tightened. "Blue Room rules: three attendees max. Ten-second rotation key at twenty-three hundred. Door locks at twenty-three ten. Once it seals, no one gets in without making noise."

The screen dimmed back to the map overview.

"New development," Ghost said. "Lansing's new task force, Civic Shield, goes fully active at dawn. Closed loop. Off-grid. He hired an ex-military operator who calls herself Captain Dane. She's running the unit. Their first target is a Cole Foundation property, an old shelter they kept alive as a tax writeoff."

Lucien didn't look up. "Which one?"

"West 48th Outreach," Ghost answered. "Clean building. Cameras everywhere. He's staging a victory."

Victor frowned. "I thought those assets were frozen."

"On paper," Ghost said. "They were restructured years ago under shell nonprofits. Different boards on the paperwork. Same ownership underneath."

Lucien watched the feed without blinking.

"If I show up," Lucien said, "he gets his spectacle. Me on camera. Me in his frame. After that, he owns the story."

Silence settled, honest and heavy.

"If we pull people out of a place that looks safe, he calls it destabilizing the city," Lucien said. "If we leave them there, he gets his footage anyway. Either way, he gets his show."

"Then we empty it without giving him a frame," Lena said. "No panic. No cameras. No bodies for his speech."

Victor's mouth edged toward something like approval.

"So we don't play," Logan said.

Lucien finally turned from the screens. "I'm not walking onto a stage he built."

His eyes stayed on the map.

Ghost's voice dropped lower. "Private message on the Coalition loop. Meant for us."

"Play it," Lucien said.

A voice came through, calm and unhurried. "No theatrics. No speeches. We'll know in the first minute if he's real."

Logan shifted. "A test."

Victor looked at Lucien. "What do we give them?"

Lucien studied the waveform until it vanished. "Presence. Proof I'm back. Then names."

"And if it's a trap?" Victor asked.

"Then we walk out under our own power," Lucien said. "They asked for me. They'll meet me on ground I choose."

Victor held his stare. "And if Silas refuses?"

"Then we end it on our terms."

His eyes returned to the map.

"The Blue Room is the objective. Everything else is just noise around it."

Lena stayed where she was. "Anything else?"

He looked at the crew, at the skill that made them useful and the loyalty that made them family.

"Tomorrow night," he said. "We don't walk in as guests. We walk in as the cost of their decisions."

Chapter Twenty-Six
THE CORONATION

The day didn't end. It thinned. Hours stretched, frayed, and folded into each other until time felt like it was holding its breath. By dusk the city had worked itself into a noise it couldn't swallow. Anchors rehearsed fear. Councilmen practiced outrage. Lansing chased cameras like absolution lived in a lens. Every screen wanted a ghost. Every mouth wanted a name. Northgate didn't answer.

While the city repeated itself, Northgate moved in silence. Concrete kept its own counsel. Steel remembered how to wait. The work filled the hours without applause, and no one asked it to.

They traced wires, blinded cameras, and watched patrol routes until they could predict them. The Riverside sublevel was rebuilt in schematics until every corner had a purpose. Angles were tested. Exits were timed.

No one said Blue Room. They didn't have to. It lived in the rhythm of hands, in the pacing, in the quiet that settled like weather choosing a direction. By nightfall the war room smelled of oil, solder, and the metallic ghost of cordite that lingers once a place chooses a side. Across the river, Silas surfaced long enough to be seen, then disappeared again. The digital clock over the worktable kept counting: 22:00. And Northgate finally stopped pretending it wasn't about to step into someone else's light.

22:15, Gear.

The table was cleared of anything that wasn't survival. Steel waited in quiet rows, matte grips catching the low light, small instruments designed to end arguments without raising a voice.

Victor checked each piece like a man signing something permanent.

Logan loaded magazines without looking away from the clock, rounds sliding into place with patient force.

Rook wrapped a slim coil in cloth, hands steady, expression unreadable.

Imani stepped in and taped a strip to Lucien's wrist.

The ink was simple.

22:58: Move

23:00: Door

23:02: Commit

No poetry. No interpretation.

"Reminder," Ghost said. "Three attendees max. Sidearms scanned at entry. Extra bodies trigger gas. Coalition controls the floor. Lansing's van will stage on West End. I'll make his eyes blink."

Lucien dragged his thumb across the tape. Not to smudge it. Just to feel it.

He tilted his head toward the stairwell.

"Walk."

Concrete held the building's chill. They stopped on a landing that had never been meant for tenderness.

"You're shadow. If I call you in, you move. Before that, you don't exist."

"Copy."

She touched his wrist, her fingers settling over the thin line where plan becomes consequence.

"Three inside. You, Victor, Logan."

"Yes."

"You'll be on camera?"

"Yes."

"What do you want it to look like?"

"Presence. Proof. Then questions that cut."

"Keep it simple."

"I'm trying."

Her hand moved to the front of his jacket, right where the ring rested.

"Don't let them take this. Not the fight. The reason."

"I won't."

"We come back."

He nodded once.

"We come back."

"Come back with your name still yours."

It wasn't superstition.

It was instruction.

Below them, Victor snapped the last latch shut. The sound landed like a period on a sentence no one wanted to reread.

"Thirty-five minutes."

No one spoke after that.

Air shifted. Metal cooled.

Above them the city kept pretending it was normal.

On the wall, the clock continued its small, indifferent violence.

And for the first time that night, the room understood it was about to be judged.

22:40, Transit.

The city thinned into sodium and glass. Neon dragged across the windshield and broke into color. Traffic lights changed for no one. A bus sighed at the curb. A siren rose somewhere, thought better of it, and went quiet again.

Victor kept the wheel steady, posture taut, every movement measured.

Logan sat angled toward the window, scanner on his knee, tuned to the subtle betrayals that lived in open air.

Lena sat beside Lucien, silent because he'd told her to be, eyes fixed on the dark ahead.

Lucien said nothing. His thumb rested on the tape at his wrist. Time pressed back like a pulse.

Ghost's voice drifted through the cabin. "West End van is parked. Captain Dane posted a perimeter ten blocks north. They're pretending to watch traffic. I'm stepping on their eyes."

"Coalition?" Victor asked.

"Already below," Ghost said. "Silas is in the room."

The words settled hard.

"Once it starts," Ghost continued, "I can blind the outer feeds for twelve minutes. After that, the system wakes up and starts remembering."

The engine settled into a controlled rhythm as they turned toward Riverside. The terminal rose out of the dark like something the river had tried to bury, brick scarred by old flood lines, steel ribs exposed, one of those places the city stops claiming after it finishes profiting from its ruin.

They parked without ceremony.

Stairs spiraled down into the sublevel, the temperature dropping step by step. Power pressed closer with each descent, steady and patient, like the place was preparing to meet them.

At the base waited a steel plate with a slit the width of a breath, its edges glowing faint green.

"Window," Ghost said.

Imani's counterfeit rotation key slid into the slit clean. Rook's coil kissed the seam. A green light blinked once. The lock exhaled open.

They stepped through.

A narrow corridor waited beyond, all concrete and wire. At the far end, a scanner arch stood poised like a question with one answer.

Victor passed first. Clean.

Logan next. Clean.

Lucien last.

The arch chimed once.

They crossed the threshold, and the Blue Room didn't greet them.

It watched.

23:00, The Room.

Same bones as recon. Different skin.

The Blue Room burned white. The platform waited at its center, and the silence was thinner.

Four men sat along the far wall, winter-hard faces behind expensive suits. Two shifted when Lucien entered, hands tightening on armrests. Another leaned to whisper, disbelief flashing across his eyes.

Silas stood on the floor before them, hands in his pockets, carved out of someone else's quiet. He didn't posture. He didn't reach. He looked at Lucien once, the way you look at a storm you've prayed for and feared at the same time.

Three months of candle vigils outside shuttered clubs, murals painted on loading-dock walls, whispered prayers in basements had turned Lucien into a ghost-king. Now the ghost walked in.

"Thank you for coming," Silas said, voice steady, eyes flicking like a man tasting voltage. "The city has worshipped your memory for months. We needed flesh to know the myth was real after all."

His smile didn't quite reach his eyes. "And next time you plant pins in my rafters, tell Rook to clean his solder off the conduit. It leaves a fingerprint."

Victor's weight shifted, just enough to mean noted.

Lucien stayed still. "You knew."

"We always know. You left reflections in the seams and ghosts in the junction box. We left them there." Silas gestured around the chamber. "Consider this our first agreement. I don't swat your hand for touching the walls, and you don't insult us by pretending we didn't feel it."

Lucien stepped onto the edge of the platform. "Now you have it."

Silas motioned toward the four behind him. "Council delegates. No speeches tonight. We don't trade myths. We trade terms."

Victor and Logan flanked the platform, a step off the light. Their hands were where everyone could see them. Their eyes weren't.

Silas tipped his head. "Two understandings before we begin. First: if the mayor tries to make this his show, we cut our feed. Second: if you're just a ghost, we end it here. This room isn't built to humiliate you. It's built to be sure."

"Be sure."

A Coalition tech approached with a small tablet and held it up.

"Thermal and biometrics," Silas said. "One sentence to camera."

Lucien faced the lens and gave his name like a verdict. "Lucien Cole."

The tablet chimed. Live heat. Live pulse. No deepfake. No mask.

Silas studied him, something sharp behind his calm.

"That token you broke, every man in this room understood what it meant. The Corsinis didn't fall. They were erased. Only one hand in this city writes endings like that."

Two of the seated men froze. Another swallowed hard. The last looked anywhere but at Lucien.

The temperature in the room dropped as if the lights had dimmed.

Lucien didn't look away. "I don't deal in warnings. Only finales. I gave the Corsinis the ending they earned. Anyone who stands in that debt joins them."

Silas flicked his eyes to the tiny red LED overhead. "The mayor's siphoning the room. Cut his access."

Above ground on West End, Lansing's van lost the feed, not cleanly, not quietly. Ghost had turned the signal to static before Silas ever called it.

Imani murmured in their ears, "Their screen just started stuttering."

The red LED in the rafters winked out.

Silas's shoulders eased. "Now we talk. You think we're just another crew. We're not. We're the brokers, the wires under the street, the hands behind the donations. Lansing's rise? We built it. We fed him money, optics, theater. We gave him empty fronts to burn so he'd leave our corridors alone."

One of the men in the chairs shifted, as if wishing Silas would shut up. Another stared at Lucien like he was trying to decide if the man was bulletproof or just lucky.

"We know every message, every donor, every backchannel he's touched. We set up his private comms, routed his money off-books, held the leash he thought he'd hidden." Silas reached into his jacket and set a phone on the platform. "Start here. Three months of him talking to ghosts. He thinks he deletes. He doesn't."

Lucien let the silence stretch until the weight of it changed. "So you're done feeding him."

"We're done pretending he's bigger than you," Silas said. "We invited you to the Blue Room to see if the myth was real. You walked in."

He lifted a slim metal case and set it on the platform.

Inside were three cold-wallet tokens. Direct access to their off-book vaults.

He pushed them forward an inch.

"Collateral. Take them if you're real. Return them if you're not. Either way, we know where we stand."

One of the four barked a short laugh. "You're just going to hand him our money?"

Silas didn't look at him. "I'm going to see who he is."

Lucien didn't touch the tokens yet. "My rules are simple. No trade in children. No blood on shelters or churches. No street wars for headlines. You move quiet or you don't move. The docks stop being your playground; they're corridors again. And if you ever put your hand on what's mine, your line ends."

One of the four leaned forward. "Define 'yours.'"

Lucien didn't raise his voice. "You'll know it when you see it."

Silas watched that land. He nodded once, almost to himself. "And the mayor?"

"We cut him out. You hand me everything you have on Lansing and Heller. Evidence. Accounts. Back-channel donors. I won't share the stage with a man who sells fear."

Silas looked at the men in the chairs. The skeptic opened his mouth, then closed it. Another rubbed his face like he was recalculating.

"You understand what you're asking," Silas said. "Lansing's not just a mayor. He's tied to federal grants, Homeland task forces, the people who signed off on Civic Shield. If we cut him out, he'll know exactly where it came from. By morning he won't be crushing anyone, he'll be screaming. And when men like him scream, they drag in every badge, every byline, every oversight committee that wants a headline. He won't beat us. He'll light up the dark."

He stepped closer. "We build balance by keeping faces out of the frame. Be the hand that moves the board, not the king that stands on it."

Lucien didn't flicker. "Kings move the board."

"Then you'd better pray the board doesn't decide to move you," Silas said.

Lucien didn't blink. "Then let it try."

From the rafters came a muted vibration. Not intrusion. A door sensor cycling upstairs. The mayor's perimeter testing its leash.

Ghost's voice stayed level. "Civic Shield is probing the outer sensors. Jamming remains clean."

Silas didn't look away from Lucien. "Civic Shield's already sniffing at the door. This isn't a trap, it's a choice. We can run your city with you or against you. Running against you is stupid. We're not stupid."

Lucien reached for the cold wallets. He didn't pocket them. He weighed them in his palm. "Then stand up with me. On record. Now."

Silas moved first. No drama. He stepped onto the platform and went to one knee. His voice stayed steady, charged. "Ghosts don't kneel. Kings do. Welcome to the throne."

One delegate hesitated, then bent.

Another followed, not looking at anyone.

The last held a second too long, until Lucien looked at him. Then he dropped.

Cameras caught it from three angles.

Lansing's feed was blind. History's wasn't.

Victor didn't shift.

Logan didn't breathe.

Ghost stayed silent.

Lucien didn't make them hold the floor long. "Up."

They rose.

The room had changed. The ghost they'd summoned had become weather.

"Under one canopy. No little kings. One ledger."

Silas held still. No smile. No resistance. "We can live with that."

Imani's whisper threaded through his earpiece. "Outer count is blind. Ten seconds."

Lucien turned his head. "Lena."

She stepped out of the side corridor, clean and composed. The platform light found her, and the room reorganized around her.

The last skeptical delegate's face shifted. Shock gave way to calculation.

Lucien placed his hand at the small of her back and brought her to the center. "This is Lena. She carries my protection and my authority. Any hand raised against her ends without discussion."

Silas stepped off the platform and lowered his eyes. "Understood."

Another man stepped forward holding a thin band of black steel, stamped with the mark they had retired minutes ago, now re-coded to Lucien's ledger.

"For her," Silas said. "Access to our corridors when she chooses. Highest level."

Lena looked to Lucien. He nodded once.

She slid the band onto her wrist. No hesitation. No ceremony.

She stepped back from the platform and moved into position for their exit.

Imani's whisper threaded through their earpieces. "Mayor's van just lost power. They think it's a transformer. They've stopped probing."

Lucien faced the room. "We're done tonight."

Silas didn't argue. "Then the city shifts."

He lingered a fraction longer than necessary. "There's one thing you should understand. The House survives because it remembers what it builds. It builds weather, not names. If you try to make the storm about you, if you put your face on it, the House will do what weather always does."

Lucien tilted his head. "And what's that?"

"It erases anything that tries to crown itself the sun."

"Good."

Lucien looked across the platform, across the cameras, across the men who had once whispered prayers to a ghost. "Then let the weather learn a new name."

Silas didn't move. "Names fade. Just remember, storms outlive kings."

23:19, Egress.

They left the way they came. No hurry. No backward glance. Scanner arch. Corridor. The steel slit that knew their names for ten seconds and forgot them on purpose.

Up the stairs, Lena fell into step without a sound.

Air returned with taste in it. Chill. River-metal. City breath. West End pulsed red and blue three blocks north, Civic Shield busy guarding nothing. Traffic cones lit like trophies. Officers paced inside their own theater. They never looked toward the terminal.

Logan opened the rear door without speaking.

Victor took the driver's seat and turned the engine over, low and patient.

Lucien guided Lena in and followed.

The SUV merged into traffic as if it had never left. To their right, the river ran black and indifferent, carrying reflections it would not keep.

Lena turned her wrist under the cabin light, feeling the weight of what she'd been given. The Coalition band sat there, dark steel, re-coded to a ledger that had changed hands. She pressed it into her palm, testing whether it would bruise.

"Queen?" she asked.

"Protected."

Then softer, not for the city.

"Untouchable."

She studied him, not the word.

"Then act like it."

"Soon."

"When?"

He took her hand and set it over his chest, over the steady drum that had survived fire, the mountain, and a room built to measure him.

"When it's just us. When the city can't listen."

She held his gaze and nodded once.

Outside, bridge lights strobed across the windshield, slicing them into pieces and putting them back together.

His eyes stayed forward, already calculating.

"Tomorrow. We start pulling Lansing apart."

Victor drove.

Logan watched the mirror like he expected the past to follow.

No one asked how.

Ghost's voice slid back into the cabin.

"You just took the board."

Lucien watched the river flash between pilings, dark water swallowing light and returning nothing.

"No. We took the pen."

Lena looked out at the water, then back at him.

"Then write."

The SUV disappeared into traffic, and for the first time that night, the city didn't know the story had already changed hands.

Chapter Twenty-Seven

FOREVER

They rolled back into Northgate just before midnight. Headlights carved white arcs across the courtyard.

Victor eased to a crawl, eyes scanning the perimeter.

Logan flicked a glance at Ghost's encrypted feed, fingers already moving.

Rook and Mara stepped from the loading bay, took the cases, and sealed the door behind them, steel on steel.

Upstairs, Imani unplugged the last feed and sank into her chair like she'd been holding the city up by herself.

Lucien leaned forward, palm on Lena's knee.

"Slide up front with me."

She blinked. "Why?"

"Because there's one more thing I'm fixing tonight."

Victor eased the truck under the overhang.

"What's going on?" His eyes flicked from the rearview to Lucien. "We've got hours of intel to scrub."

"Then scrub it," Lucien said. "You and Logan run it. Ghost keeps the feeds blind. I'll be back."

Logan frowned, one hand still on his scanner. "This a good idea?"

"It's the only play. Out."

Victor started to argue, then caught the look in Lucien's eyes and decided against it.

He put the truck in park.

"Understood," he muttered.

Lucien opened his door. "Keys."

Victor handed them over without another word and climbed out with Logan, both already talking about access logs and shell accounts.

Lena slid into the front as Lucien took the driver's seat.

"Call if anything shifts," Victor said. "And keep Ghost on."

"Looped and logging," Ghost cut in.

Lucien looked back at them through the glass. "You've got the board. Tonight it's yours."

Then, softer, to Lena: "Buckle up."

The engine purred back to life. Northgate's floodlights fell away in the mirrors. Ahead, Manhattan opened, steel and glass breathing in the dark.

The streets ran quieter than they had any right to. No sirens at their back. No coded knock. Just night. Lucien drove without music, one hand on the wheel, the other on Lena's knee like touch alone could keep her here.

"Where are we going, baby?" she asked.

"A place I owe you."

He turned off the main artery and slid into the city's underbelly, concrete swallowing the tires as he descended into a private underground garage, no signage, no parked cars, just polished floors and cameras watching from the corners.

Lena's pulse kicked. She knew exactly where they were. She just didn't know why he was bringing her back tonight.

The gate read the vehicle tag and rolled open without a sound.

Lucien parked in the far bay, tucked away like a secret. Brushed steel doors waited at the elevator.

He swiped a key.

The elevator rose in a smooth, private glide, floor numbers blinking toward the night clouds.

The doors opened to the penthouse, stone-dark and waiting. No lights. No sound but the hush of their footsteps.

Lucien reached for the main switch. Soft light slid across glass and steel, easing the dark back.

"With everything going on, I had Ghost loop the elevator log and burn the entry feed for the ten seconds we crossed in."

Lena's mouth curved, small and knowing, and she still didn't look at him.

"Always one step ahead, Lucien Cole."

The penthouse revealed itself in layers, each one hitting her like a memory she had no right to survive.

The air held the stillness of a place left alone too long, leather and wood sealed in quiet, the faint metallic chill of untouched space.

Lena stopped.

"Lucien,"

"I know."

He set a flat black folder on the kitchen island and let his hand fall away.

She walked deeper into the space, like someone stepping back into a room that still remembered her.

Her fingers trailed through the air, reaching for shapes she remembered. She drifted to the windows and pressed her palms to the glass, as if she could pull the city closer, as if she could pull time back.

Everything looked sealed. Preserved. Like the night he died had folded itself into the walls and waited for her return.

She turned, eyes burning.

"How?"

"I didn't bring you back here by accident. I brought you back when I could say it clean."

He opened the folder.

Two keys. A slim silver fob. Documents stacked with the kind of care that meant he had touched every page twice.

He slid the first document across the stone.

"Cole–Hart Residential Trust," he said, plain. "Established fourteen weeks ago. Delaware trustee. You're the managing member."

Lena stared at the line that mattered, the one her heart latched onto like a lifeline.

TITLE HOLDER, LENA HART

Her throat tightened. She read it again, slower, like the words might change if she blinked.

Lucien slid the second packet across.

"Heaven on Fifth," he said softly. "Hart Atelier LLC. Filed months ago."

Lena's breath caught, sharp and small.

He didn't crowd her. He let it sit between them, heavy and real.

"After everything, when I knew you weren't a moment but forever, I started moving pieces. Shells, trusts, quiet protections. I can't stop every shadow that comes looking. That's not a promise any honest man can make. But I can keep what matters from being taken."

He tapped the folder once, the sound small inside the expensive silence.

"Your name's on it because I put it there. No tricks. No courier games. It's clean."

A faint smile pulled at his mouth, not cocky, almost shy, like he was admitting something he had never known how to say.

"I don't lose things I intend to keep."

Lena laughed once, disbelieving, and it broke close to a sob.

"You stole my signature."

"I protected it," he said. "I did what I could before anyone had the chance to touch you through paper."

She looked down at the documents again, then back at him, the heat in her eyes sharpening through the tears.

"The Feds can tape my doors, but they can't unwrite your name."

He slid the third document forward.

"Operating account. Clean. Money I can explain in daylight. Runway to breathe."

Lena went still, like moving too fast might make the whole thing vanish.

"You already gave me everything I asked for," she whispered, "without asking."

"No. I gave you what I should've given you before anyone ever had the chance to threaten it."

"You never had the chance. Everything ended the moment we tried to start clean."

The silence settled right.

Not comfortable.

Not easy.

Right.

Lucien reached into his pocket and pulled out a small velvet box.

He walked to the windows with her, close enough that their heat touched, close enough that the glass caught them both in reflection with a city behind them.

"I never forgot what I asked you. Between worlds."

Lena's breath hitched. The hospital. The beeping. The question that bent time and made it ask permission.

"I came back different. Not softer. Not cleaner. Just certain. I can't promise peace. It isn't mine to hand out. But I can promise direction. I can promise that everything I build from here will have your name somewhere inside it."

He dropped to one knee and opened the box.

The ring caught the low light and held it like a secret. It looked less like jewelry than something time had finally learned to keep.

"Lena Hart," he said, and the room made room for the words.

"You made me real when I was a rumor, even to myself."

His voice stayed steady, but his eyes didn't.

"Will you marry me?

Not at the end of a war.

Now.

While the world is still loud.

While we're still breathing."

Lena didn't speak at first. She just stared at him, the man who had been a myth, then a wound, then a home, and her eyes filled like her body finally understood it was safe to feel.

Then she nodded once.

Tears slid. She didn't hide them. She smiled through them anyway.

"Lucien Cole," she said, voice breaking around his name. "Yes.

In every lifetime."

Lucien's exhale broke like a dam finally giving up.

He slid the ring onto her finger. It found its place like it had been waiting there the whole time.

She pulled him up and into her.

The kiss was not a performance. Not a claim.

Just them, trying to breathe in a world that kept demanding blood.

When they separated, she looked past his shoulder toward the folder on the island, like she needed to confirm reality was still sitting on stone.

"So the penthouse?"

Lucien's hand stayed on her back, steady.

"Yours. We move in when the time is right. Until then, Northgate holds us."

"Heaven on Fifth?"

"Yours to open when you say. The rest is logistics."

"We build it clean," he added. "If the world tries to make it dirty, it comes through me."

Lena smiled into his chest.

"They always do."

He closed his eyes for a beat, as if the answer had settled into his bones.

"Tonight we memorize this view, so if it gets dark again, we remember where the light lives."

Lena laughed softly. She pressed her hand to his chest, right over his heart.

"Inside," she murmured.

"Inside," he echoed.

They walked the rooms together, slow, like mapping a country they were taking back.

In the bedroom, Lena paused at the edge of the bed and looked over her shoulder, playful and reverent at the same time.

"Mr. Cole," she said, voice sweet with trouble, "show me our home properly."

Lucien's smile came slow, dangerous, and full of memory.

"Come here. Let's make the past behave."

She didn't climb onto the bed. She leaned back against it, hands behind her, legs crossed at the ankles, and let her eyes drag over him like a secret she intended to say out loud.

The ring burned against her finger, equal parts vow and weapon.

Lucien stood in the doorway, shirt half-unbuttoned, watching her like a man watching a fire decide whether it would devour or spare.

"Old sins?" she asked, head tilting.

He stepped closer.

"Let's start with the ones we'll never finish."

She uncrossed her legs. Let the hem of her dress slip higher as her thighs parted.

"Then stop looking at me like a prayer and come prove it."

Lucien caught her jaw with the same hands that had held guns to gods and monsters, the same hands that had clawed through death and memory to reach her again. Thumbs tilted her face up like it was something fragile, but the kiss that followed said otherwise.

The kiss wasn't soft.

It was possession melting into homecoming.

His mouth drank hers like a man who came back to taste one last thing, only to find it wasn't the last at all, it was the start.

The first kiss remembered the vow.

The second remembered the war.

By the third, there was no world left outside them.

He undressed her with a reverence usually reserved for altars. Silk slid off her shoulders like a secret revealed, the dress falling away in one slow surrender.

"Mine forever," he breathed.

Her hand tightened in his hair.

"I was yours before you knew what to call it."

For a heartbeat she saw the boy under the king, the one who had survived too much too young, hands shaking, eyes too young for everything they'd done. It flickered there, raw and human, before the fire returned.

He dropped to his knees, like gravity had claimed him.

"You want an answer?" she whispered, voice trembling.

He wiped his mouth on her thigh and looked up, eyes black with hunger, waiting for her signal.

"Give it to me."

She pushed her panties aside. "Then listen."

He buried his face between her thighs and worshipped her without mercy. Not gentle. Not polite. Devoted in the way only a ruined man could be, like every sound he pulled from her proved he had made it back. Her moans were low at first, then louder, then something near-shattering. When she came, her thighs locked around him like iron gates. Her whole body broke around the sound, and he held her through every violent second of it.

He didn't stop. Not until her legs shook like aftershocks.

"Inside," she gasped, yanking at his belt. In one word she told him everything: enough teasing, enough distance, come back to her, all the way.

He stood. Let her undress him, piece by piece. The ring caught the moonlight like a circle that had finally closed. He was alive under her hand, hot and trembling and real in a way death had tried to steal.

"You were dead," she whispered.

"I was," he said, guiding her hand. "Now I want to come back to life inside you before I come back to the world."

Every step back to the bed was an echo. Every breath, a build.

He entered her slowly, not as conquest, but as a vow finding its body.

It wasn't fast.

It was grinding. Possession. History.

Her mouth fell open in a stunned, breathless oh, back arching as she took him all in, inch after inch, slow and agonizing and divine.

"Fuck," she choked, nails digging into his shoulders.

He held still, fully buried, trembling against her.

"You feel like,"

"Say it."

"Like home with teeth."

Then he moved.

A slow pull. A deep return. Not frantic. Not casual. A rhythm built for her only, each movement dragging another yes from somewhere deeper than breath.

Her moans turned ragged, near-feral.

"Harder," she begged.

"No," he said, biting her shoulder just hard enough to brand. "Not yet. I need you to remember this. Every fucking second."

Her hands tangled in his hair, her legs around his back, her breath catching with every deep, unrelenting push.

"You burn better than the world deserves," he groaned, mouth at her neck.

She gasped, rocking up into him. "Then burn it with me. Start with me."

He did.

When she came, her body clenched so violently it punched the breath from both of them. He held her wrists to the mattress, kissed her through it, whispered filth and reverence into her mouth as her body seized around him.

"I missed the way you fall apart," he murmured. "Missed ruining you."

She brushed her thumb across his lips, catching the shine there, a shiver passing between them like an unspoken dare.

Then he turned her beneath him and brought her to the edge of the bed, the edge of breath, the edge of every promise they had made in that room.

He grabbed her hair, pulled her head back, whispered into her ear:

"You're gonna come again. And again. Until this house remembers every fucking sound you make, my queen."

He reached around and found the place that made her breath break. Kept the rhythm merciless, exact, until her body forgot how to hold itself together.

"Lucien, fuck, I'm gonna,"

"Then come. Give me what the world can't touch."

She did. Shattered. Shuddered. Legs collapsed.

He unraveled with her, hips locking, a tremor running through every muscle, a sound rising from somewhere deep and ungoverned as he gave her everything death had failed to keep.

They lay there afterward, panting, tangled, wrecked, and something steadier than hunger took hold of him.

He made love to her like he meant to write her into whatever survived him.

"Tell me something true."

He breathed her in.

"I died somewhere you couldn't follow. You still found me. You named me. You brought me back."

"Then what am I to you?"

"The only place I ever stopped bleeding."

She kissed him, and whispered the two words that ruined him more than death ever had.

"Build me."

So he did.

With his hands at her hips.

With his mouth at her throat.

With a rhythm slow enough to be remembered and deep enough to make fear change its name.

He gave her every shattered thing in him and felt her make room for it.

She took the worst parts of him without flinching and turned them toward light.

They moved until breath became language.

Until her yes was everywhere.

Until the room could no longer remember the shape of grief.

Outside, a train moved beneath the streets. A cab cut through neon and vanished. Traffic lights kept changing for people who still belonged to time.

But above it all, in a room the dark had failed to keep, they made something the city could not touch.

Not peace.

Not safety.

Something stronger.

A future with both their names on it.

And below them, Manhattan kept breathing, unaware it had already been rewritten.

Later, skin warm from the shower and hair still damp, the city shone outside like it couldn't help itself. They ate delivery on the living room floor with their backs to the couch and their feet tucked under the coffee table, tequila in whiskey tumblers because that's what they had. Steam ghosted from the cartons while a black and white movie flickered on mute, some couple at a train station promising each other impossible things.

She lifted her glass. "To the world trying to keep up."

He touched his tumbler to hers. "To us not slowing down."

The clink was small and perfect. He watched the spot where her glass had touched his, like he could memorize the sound and wear it.

They ate in easy silence, the city doing its indifference outside, the movie doing its ghosts. Every now and then he stole a bite from her carton and replaced it with something better; she let him fuss, because that was a kind of vow too.

"What does it look like," she asked, eyes on the window, "when we say it for real?"

"The wedding?"

"The beginning," she said softly. Then, "Yeah. The wedding."

He breathed out like a weight changed shoulders. "Away from microphones. Away from men who think a camera is a crown. Somewhere the world can't hear."

"Coast or mountains?"

He pictured both, the iron Atlantic and the cold patience of pines. "Water. The kind that never stops moving."

She nodded. "Off season. Wind a little mean. A chapel with no roof or a dock with splinters. My hair up, then ruined. Your tie on, then gone."

"No aisle."

"Just you walking toward me."

His smile came slow, quiet, the kind that makes promises without witnesses. "No speeches either. Ten words each. Maybe twelve if I can't shut up."

"You never could."

He let his cheek rest in her hair. On the wall, the movie threw a train across the frame. He unmuted long enough to hear the woman say, "I'm not afraid anymore," then silenced them again and let the line hang like a candle.

"Who's there?" she asked.

"Two witnesses. Three if you want to pretend we're respectable."

"Victor signs like a disapproving uncle. Mara pretends to hate it, cries anyway. Imani runs the music from a phone in her pocket. And nobody tells the wind what to do."

"And Ghost keeps the horizon empty."

"Of course he does."

She looked at him full, already chosen. "No press. No permits. Just paper. And a name."

"Two names. Yours and mine."

She studied the ring like a blueprint, checking its stress points and secret strengths. "Engrave something inside?"

He poured a finger of tequila for both. "One word. The only one that ever mattered to us."

"Inside."

"Inside," he echoed, and both of them breathed easier.

She nudged his knee. "Colors?"

"Whatever you want. But you in white is a weapon."

"I was thinking winter white. Thick fabric, clean lines, no lace. Armor that looks like grace."

"Bare shoulders."

"Gloves," she countered, enjoying the way he lost composure and found it again. "To the wrist. A little defiance in silk."

He took her left hand gently, thumb at the base of the ring. "Shoes you can run in."

"Or kick in."

"Same thing."

She watched him while Manhattan's glow stroked their ankles. "Where do we go after? When it's done."

"Not back here. Not yet. A road no one's watching. A room with wood that smells like sap. A place with a lock that answers only to us."

"A cheap motel with bad curtains?"

"Something better. Something honest. Windows that open. A chair that knows the weight of our jackets. Coffee that tastes like a morning you can keep."

"You planning to seduce me with a chair and coffee."

"I'm planning to spend the rest of my life making your name the safest room in every house we own."

She went quiet in the way people do when they've been correctly seen. Snow flickered on the wall. Outside, a helicopter prowled the sky, searching for someone the city had already swallowed.

"Ten words," she said. "I should practice."

"Say the first draft."

"I loved you at rumor. I choose you in daylight."

He closed his eyes. "Then my ten. I was built for storms. You are my weather and home."

"That's eleven."

"I'll pay the fine."

She slid closer until her thigh pressed to his. "Do we tell anyone before we do it?"

"We tell the people who would forgive us if we didn't. And the ones who'd kill me if they found out later."

"Alexander."

"He can bless it or not. Either way, it happens."

She considered that, eyes on the ring. "People will expect spectacle. Dresses. Flowers. A thousand pictures proving it happened."

"Let them expect. We'll give them a legend later. For now we keep the gold quiet."

She kissed his temple. "A secret marriage, and then a city that figures it out in pieces. They won't know whether to be jealous or terrified."

"Both. That's balance."

They ate until the cartons were light and the tequila had started telling the truth. Her feet settled in his lap; his hands found their way under the blanket without agenda, just warmth. On the screen, the couple at the station boarded their futures without waving or looking back. It felt right.

"Tomorrow?" she asked.

"Tomorrow."

Not a date, a direction.

She turned off the TV. The room remembered how quiet could feel like wealth.

Below them, the streets whispered their secrets.

Above them, the sky kept its indifferent watch.

Between them, two people chose a life and wrote it in their own names.

Some promises don't need witnesses. They just need a pulse.

And when they finally went to bed, with no audience or ceremony, New York rolled onto its side and pretended not to notice, the way all great cities do when something sacred happens without asking permission.

By morning, nothing in the skyline would look different.

But everything would be.

Chapter Twenty-Eight

THE FIRST TO KNOW

Gray light pooled against the glass, laying a thin gloss over abandoned cartons and two spent tumblers. The penthouse held their shadows like it wanted to keep them. Somewhere a radiator ticked as if remembering how to breathe.

Lucien woke to the phone shuddering on the nightstand, a low buzz building like it meant to shame him.

Lena shifted, hair across his shoulder. The ring glimmered against his chest, a small star where her hand had slept. He watched it for a beat, then reached for the phone vibrating beside the bed.

Missed calls stacked like dominoes. VOICEMAIL (3). VICTORIA, VICTORIA, VICTORIA.

A recent thread from Ghost parked at the top.

He opened it.

Lansing files syncing. 2TB scraped
They're triaging and building the map. Eat first

He stared at his sister's name for a long second, then hit FaceTime and waited.

The screen filled with fluorescent ceiling tile, then a face too much like his own, gone blotchy with tears before he said a word.

"Are you," her breath caught, "you're actually on my phone. You're alive on my phone."

"Hi, Vic." His voice sounded like it had slept in gravel.

Her laugh cracked, breaking into a sob before she could stop it. "Do not 'Hi, Vic' me like you ducked out for a cigarette. You've been back in this world how many days and you didn't call your sister?"

"I had to feel like myself again before I could be your brother. I didn't want the first time you saw me to feel like a ghost."

That bought him two seconds of mercy. Then she swiped at her eyes with the heel of her hand and set the camera so he could see more than a ceiling.

Family lounge, low chairs that never got comfortable, a bulletin board with cheerful flyers that lied about food, a window that gave nothing back. He heard a coffee machine somewhere die and start again.

"Are you with Mom and Dad?"

"I've been here all night." She shifted the phone again. "Mom's getting ready for morning labs and neuro checks. Dad's on the phone with billing. He thinks if he says 'MRI' and 'urgent' in the same sentence enough times, they'll move faster."

"Of course he is."

"And he's right."

She dared him to argue.

He looked down at Lena tucked into him, at their hands tangled.

"Show it."

He lifted their joined fingers into frame.

The ring caught the gray light and held it.

Victoria made the sound people make when something hits them in the chest. She bit her fist, the camera jittered. "You, you," she broke into laughter that hurt. "Oh my God. Oh my God. I hate you. I love you. Give me two seconds, MOM!"

A voice off-screen, Evelyn's, steady and threaded with the hospital's morning, "What are you shouting about, Victoria Marie?"

Victoria dragged the phone like a kid hauling treasure. The picture lurched past a hall, a floral arrangement earning its keep, a whiteboard that said TODAY'S GOAL: WALK THREE TIMES.

"Hold on," she hissed, then, to someone else, "Dad, can you chill with the hospital codes for five seconds?"

Alexander's voice, precise and impatient, bled in. "If they think I'm authorizing,"

"Dad," she said, and whatever was in her tone made even a Cole stop.

The camera found Evelyn. Paper bracelet. Lipstick applied with a warrior's precision. She was pulling her cardigan straight like an execution of dignity, and then she saw the screen.

Her face changed without moving. Something in it opened.

"Of course he did." It wasn't surprise, it was recognition. "Of course he asked her."

"Hi, Mom." For a second, he sounded twelve.

Evelyn's eyes softened. He had been back almost a week, and still, every time Evelyn heard him say it, something in her rewired.

"You have no idea what it does to me to hear you call me that. Let me see her."

He turned the phone. Lena managed to look both fierce and suddenly shy. "Hi, Mrs. Cole."

"Evelyn," she corrected gently. "I always wondered who could stand where you are standing. Now I know."

Lena's eyes went bright. "I only got here because he kept reaching back."

"Good," Evelyn said. "Then you will spend your lives arguing over who saved who, and nobody will win, which is how you know you are doing it right."

"Let me see," Alexander demanded from off-camera, because love and control had always sounded the same in his mouth.

Alexander appeared over Evelyn's shoulder, tie already knotted like a threat, jaw tight enough to remember what ruling used to cost. His mouth went soft when he saw Lucien. He hid it immediately, which only made it louder.

"You look like hell."

"And you look like you have been carrying this family on your back," Lucien replied.

For a flicker Alexander's face broke, surprise, maybe gratitude, a tiny smirk he had not planned escaping before he could kill it. His gaze slid to the ring glinting on Lena's hand, then back up to his son. "About time."

"About time," Evelyn echoed, her thumb brushed the pale groove where her own ring had rested for decades.

There was a beat where nobody spoke and everybody did, one breath, sealing a new circle.

Lucien chose his fight before it arrived.

"We are going to keep it small. No press. No pageantry. We will do it somewhere the world cannot hear."

"Nonsense," Alexander said at once, reflex and strategy. "We will make every call we have to. No one will come within a mile of you unless you invite them, and the ones who try will remember their manners. We are not hiding your marriage like contraband."

"Dad."

"Listen to me." He leaned closer, voice lowering, not for secrecy but weight. "You have been on the front page on and off for almost four months. Right now every headline writes you. A wedding, your wedding, is the one time you write yourself. Public relations matter when the truth is thin on the ground. Optics are not the truth but they are a weapon, and I taught you not to leave your weapons unused."

"You taught me not to point them at people I love."

"Then point them at the world," Alexander returned. He softened, barely. "And let your mother wear a dress."

Evelyn swatted him without looking. "I was going to say that part."

Victoria had stopped crying and started plotting. It was the same posture.

"We're not talking circus." She rolled her eyes, already building it in her head. "We're talking, I dunno, guest list so tight even Secret Service would pout, some kind of jammer towers, or whatever your friends do, a couple of fake vans to throw off the creeps, and an aisle I dare anyone to step into without losing a foot. Mom gets actual flowers, Dad gets to pretend he likes them, and the world can mind its own business for one day."

Lena squeezed Lucien's hand where Victoria could not see. He felt the decision in it before she spoke.

"We wanted to elope. We wanted one thing the world did not get to claim."

"You can have two. Have the secret one you keep under your ribs, and have the one you let us stand in."

Lucien looked at the three faces on the small screen that contained every version of him from skinned knees to now. Evelyn's lipstick. Alexander's unlearned tenderness. Victoria's sharpened kindness, weaponized on his behalf.

He looked past the phone to the woman beside him who had said yes like a door opening, who would love him in a basement or a cathedral because the address was not the point.

"We do not do spectacles."

"No," Evelyn said. "We do sacraments."

That word lodged.

A text banner slid across the top of the screen:

Lansing's shell companies are tripping over each other

A second banner followed:

Victor's pulling the threads

Then a third, slightly later:

Also, congratulations, or whatever humans say

"Mom." He had learned to choose the thing that mattered most first. "How do you feel?"

She lifted her chin. "Like myself, plus an IV pole." Then, softer, "Like I want to see my son put a ring on a woman worth the good china."

Alexander made a sound that might have been a laugh if it weren't wearing armor. "Your mother's subtle way of saying we're doing this properly."

Victoria was already typing with one hand, wiping her cheeks with the other.

"We'll talk details later. When you're off whatever op you're not telling me about."

"Victoria," Alexander warned.

"Oh, please. He's breathing like he's measuring a hallway and the lighting in his room screams 'classified files someone's not supposed to have.'"

Lena couldn't help it; she laughed. It cracked something in all of them.

"We'll find a way to see you today."

The promise and the caution lived in the same breath.

"You'll try," Evelyn corrected. "You'll succeed tomorrow if you don't today. I'm not going anywhere in the next twelve hours except down for scans and back up for a terrible sandwich. Give me your faces again before the day is done."

"Yes, ma'am."

He meant the yes the way you mean a word that has rooms inside it.

"Remember what I said before," she added, a last stitch. "Call your father about nothing, like I told you. Let him pretend."

Alexander grunted as if affection were a debt he was paying with interest. "Bring me coffee that tastes like coffee."

"Black," Victoria said. "From the place on the corner. He'll tell you it's wrong no matter what."

"Family tradition," Alexander said dryly.

"Go. Before I keep you and call it fate."

He didn't hang up. He let Victoria end the call. She needed to be the one sometimes. The screen went black and held his reflection up like a stranger he recognized.

For a long breath nobody spoke. Outside, the city sat in half-light, half-shadow. The color of decisions.

Lena looked toward the black phone screen. "They're not wrong." Not because she liked spectacle, but because she understood love when it asked for witnesses.

He nodded, the motion barely there and absolute. "We give them a day. And we make sure we survive the telling."

His phone buzzed again. Then again.

Ghost didn't bundle bad news.

One more thing
Lansing's calendar shifted
Noon just opened up, and it shouldn't have
Victor says it smells like a meet
Your call

Lucien looked at the room they had reclaimed, at the future they had named, at the woman who had put her hand in his and made the air turn different. He lowered his head to her temple and spoke into the place his voice was already allowed to live.

"Breakfast first. Then we choose how the world sees us. Then we choose how it falls."

Lena smiled into his shoulder. "Order of operations," she murmured.

"Always." For the first time in months, it sounded like a future.

She swallowed hard and buried the thought before it could speak: the last time he'd promised breakfast, they never made it to the table.

A gunshot had stolen the morning and the man with it.

The penthouse watched them rise.

Manhattan's pale light pressed its face to the glass.

Far below, sirens chased someone else's emergency.

In a different building, a nurse tightened a tourniquet and said, "Little pinch."

In the family lounge, a man in a suit argued about codes again, because numbers were easier than feelings.

In this room, a brother finally called his sister.

A son took instruction.

Two people chose the kind of day they would make.

And then they went to meet it.

CHAPTER TWENTY-NINE

BEFORE THE NOISE

Morning slid under the door with coffee on its breath. They took a booth in a place that had seen more confessions than churches, grease paper gone translucent under egg and cheese, coffee black enough to ink out sins. No one spared them a glance. The few tired souls stayed buried in their own small worlds, in the kind of stop no one remembered.

Lena sat across from him, collarbone lit by gray daylight. Lucien watched her like he was storing the last still frame of quiet. The menu was taped and curling. The mugs were chipped. The griddle worked through bacon and something sweet. She'd tied her hair up, strands escaping, softening her in the light.

They didn't talk about the Lansing files syncing back at Northgate, each thread pulling the city tighter. They talked about burnt toast still worth eating and the man in the corner with a crossword he never completed. Lucien's phone buzzed face-down. He ignored it.

When the plates were nearly empty, Lena pushed her mug aside. "How loud is it going to be when we get back?"

"Messy." He turned the pen between his fingers. "Nothing we can't walk into."

"And you're sitting here with me."

"And I'm sitting here with you." His voice changed the silence between them.

She brushed the ring. "Victoria is already building a wedding plan."

"Of course she is. Alexander will hate it."

"He'll survive. Will you?"

"If she lets me survive it."

Silence settled full, not tense. They finished the last bites, the last swallows. Outside, a delivery truck braked hard, and a kid cut across two lanes. The city opened its eyes without recognizing them.

Lena watched sunlight tremble against her mug and felt the quiet for what it was, brief.

Lucien tucked bills beneath it and stood. "Back to Northgate."

She slipped her hand into his. "Back to Northgate," she echoed. "And then?"

"We put the day back together."

They stepped into the morning, hand in hand, carrying the quiet with them like something stolen.

Northgate came awake like a machine that preferred the dark.

The gate swallowed the car. Cameras watched from the corners. The engine's last growl vanished into concrete.

Inside, the war room was already breathing. Maps pulsed across glass like veins. Code streamed in a language only Ghost spoke. The hum didn't sound mechanical. It sounded hungry.

Victor looked up first. "About time."

Then he saw Lena's hand, and the room went still.

He studied the ring, then looked at Lucien. "Good."

High praise.

Logan's grin went feral. "Damn, Lena. You actually pulled it off."

"Finally," Mara said. "Something in this building is legal. Congratulations."

Imani didn't turn. "I'll handle the security. Preliminary plan's already running."

Rook passed with a mug and set it in front of Lena. "Well, that settles it. We all answer to you now."

Lucien's look could have cut steel. Rook vanished.

"Focus," Victor said. "Let me see it."

Lena offered her hand. He studied the stone like evidence. "Good choice."

Lucien's gaze stayed on the stone. "It was my mother's."

Victor's expression softened by a fraction. "Then it's more than a ring."

Screens around the room were already chewing through Lansing's files, names and shell companies branching across the glass.

Ghost's voice rolled through the room, stripped of everything but war.

"Fairy tale is over. Listen."

The main screen flickered. A single red dot pulsed on the city grid.

Ghost put the city grid on the screen. "Civic Shield expanded surveillance. Four corridors. Rotating cameras. Routing approved by one person."

"Lansing," Lucien said.

The move had come too fast to be policy. It was fear dressed as infrastructure.

"They bought analytic coverage at two in the morning," Ghost said. "Targeted to pick up movement patterns, faces, anything that smells like you. Or her."

Lena's pulse ticked once.

Victor's jaw tightened. "Fishing."

"Panic fishing," Ghost corrected. "He doesn't know what happened. So he is throwing cameras into the dark hoping the dark blinks."

"Reaction," Lucien said.

"Which means he overcorrects," Ghost said. "My guess, twelve to twenty-four hours."

Lucien looked at Lena. Lena met him without flinching. Their silence felt like a shield.

"We stay ready."

Ghost lowered his tone. "Stay normal. Stay boring. Stay close. I'll call it when it moves."

Behind them, on the screen, the red dot pulsed again. Closer.

Lucien tapped the table once. "We keep the day quiet."

Lena slid her hand into his. "Until it's not."

"Let's get back to work," Victor said.

The room did what it always did, built a life inside a war.

Lucien looked at the people who had chosen him on purpose. He thought of a hospital lounge, burnt coffee, and a woman fighting for every breath, reminding him not to build his life in conflict. That moment stayed with him.

Outside, the city drew a long breath, waiting to see who exhaled first.

CHAPTER THIRTY
THE FIRST MARK

A few hours later, the call hit while the city pretended to be ordinary.

"Pick a cake flavor," Victoria said. No hello. Just orders. "If you say vanilla, I'm filing an injunction."

Lena stood in her room at Northgate, the ring no longer feeling like jewelry, but evidence.

"We're not choosing a cake on the phone."

"We're not choosing it through encrypted paranoia either. Lunch. SoHo. We'll look at dresses. I'll bully you into joy."

"I need to clear it."

"You're marrying a Cole. Clear it fast. I need one afternoon that doesn't smell like antiseptic."

Lena breathed once, steadying the ache behind her ribs, then stepped into the hall.

She passed one camera, then another, each blinking like it was pretending not to watch her, and pushed through the double doors.

The war room waited in a wash of quiet pressure. Lucien was already at the table, jacket off, head bent over the files.

He looked up the moment she filled the doorway.

Ghost's voice rippled across the screens. "You're leaving?"

"An hour or two. Maybe three. We're not a convoy."

Victor took a thumb-sized matte-black fob from a drawer and set it in her palm.

"Pulse key. Silent panic. Press and keep walking. Logan is the driver. Eyes on both of you."

Lena pocketed it with a small, tired smile.

"We're looking at dresses and eating lunch, not robbing a bank."

"With everything going on," Victor said, "caution is cheap."

Ghost again, colder. "Keep it close. I'll have your route the second you step outside."

She nodded once, not unkind, just finished being managed.

Lucien looked at her.

Not a warning.

Not permission.

Just the wire between them, pulled tight and real.

"Let Logan do his job. Keep me bored. Come back to me."

"I will." She adjusted her coat. "Back this afternoon."

Logan rose, keys already in hand.

"Ready when you are."

Lena gave Lucien a soft look.

"No action without me."

"Never without you."

She followed Logan down the service corridor.

Steel doors opened into the courtyard, late-morning sun and hard air hitting her all at once.

The Rezvani waited low, all angles and armor.

She slid in. Leather. Cold metal. The city holding its breath outside.

Normal was the best armor.

Normal was bait.

Logan slipped them off Canal and slid the car into a dead space at the curb, the kind of spot most drivers missed. Spring light hit the windshield and found the faint scar along his jaw, a pale reminder of a conversation that had ended badly for someone else.

Lena was already reaching for the door.

"I'll be an hour."

"One pretzel, one coffee, always visible," Logan answered, scanning the foot traffic. "You'll see me before you need me."

She stepped into the street's breath and let the city's pulse settle under her ribs.

SoHo carried its own weather. Paint-scent drifted from an open studio. Brass door handles held the warmth of the last hands. A street vendor snapped a plastic spoon in half and laughed like it was ritual. Victoria waited under a web of fire escapes, umbrella perched on her shoulder like a flag she refused to wave.

Victoria hugged Lena with her whole body. "You're late. Come on. We're using this city like a fitting room."

"You look like you borrowed that jacket from someone who scares their tailor."

"I stole it." Victoria linked arms. "Today we commit boldness. Emerald napkins. Scarlet shoes. Real music. Real flowers. No boring people."

"Lucien lasts forty seconds."

"Then we'll aim for thirty-nine."

She was already walking, scanning windows like the city had dressed itself for her.

Lena let the chatter glide past. A neon sign blinked DON'T BLINK. Deckled paper lay in soft, feathered stacks. A mannequin in a silk gown posed like sin dressed for applause.

"You'd break necks in that," Victoria said. "And a few laws."

"I prefer my crimes off the rack."

Victoria smirked. "You prefer them in a tux."

The ring felt heavier in the sun, less like a promise than proof the future had found her.

For a heartbeat the future was real, ink and vows, applause from the living. It was so clean it almost hurt.

And happiness made a bigger target.

Lena breathed slow and let her eyes drift. Reflection. Chrome. Shadow. The black pane of a dormant window.

Across the street, a man stood too still. Mid-thirties. Gray beanie. Coffee cup gone cold in his grip. The kind of height that vanished in a crowd, but his stillness betrayed him.

People moved. He didn't.

He watched the bus-shelter ad like he expected it to answer.

Victoria nudged her. "That's your thinking face. What's up?"

"Deciding between scarlet and emerald."

"Scarlet. Emerald for napkins. Scarlet for the world."

A bicycle chain snapped against a curb. A busker hit a wrong note that clung to the air a moment too long. The hair on Lena's neck lifted. She touched the pulse key in her pocket, not pressing, just acknowledging the choice waiting under her thumb.

They slipped into a café choked with green, the kind of place that grew its own atmosphere. The counter girl clocked Victoria, and just like that, they got the good table, the one everyone pretended not to watch.

"Mom wants a swatch," Victoria said. "She'll pretend to hate whatever you choose, then cry when you walk down the aisle. Dad will deny he cried too, which is how you'll know he did."

"We'll send her options tonight."

"After we feed you. You look like you slept on adrenaline."

"We're pushing a lot of intel. It makes its own coffee."

"All this. Whatever Lucien's running." Victoria leaned in. "You know he's proud of you, right? He won't say it. He thinks praise dulls people. It doesn't dull you."

The waitress set down the water. A spoon slipped and hit the table. No one reacted. The quiet settled in like it had been waiting for its cue.

Out the window, the beanie man again. Closer now. No cup. One hand in his pocket, maybe a gun, maybe nothing. He wasn't facing them, only angled, listening to exits instead of conversations.

"Try the grilled bread," Victoria said. "The olive oil's violent."

Lena chewed, watching his shape through a chrome pitcher. He scratched the bridge of his nose, casual, but the finger tapped twice on the way down. A private code meant for no one visible.

She smiled like someone amused by a harmless joke. Camouflage.

"So, scarlet."

She kept her tone weightless.

"Scarlet, huh?" Victoria teased. "Emerald is jealous. The world will choke on envy."

"Maybe."

She lifted her phone as if checking a message. First frame, nothing. Second, nothing. Third: a flicker. Him. She sent it. Ghost would have it before the second hand reached the next number.

They ate like civilians and left cash under the plates because civilians tipped well.

Outside, the light sharpened.

Victoria pointed toward West Broadway. They moved through a block of facades, a gallery, a bodega, a shuttered space marked only by a serial number sprayed on glass.

A sedan idled thirty yards behind. Matte black. Windows dark as wells. The driver's eyes lifted once, met theirs in the reflection, then disappeared.

Lena pulled her phone like she was checking veils.

One message:

West Broadway. Black sedan. Thirty yards. Low profile

She sent it.

Her hand brushed Victoria's wrist, subtle as a breath. Victoria adjusted their pace without speaking. They slid past a mural of a crowned wolf gnawing a clock. Time with teeth.

At the corner, Lena gestured toward a line of boutiques. "Two minutes. You'll hate every dress. Then we leave."

Victoria laughed. "You're finally catching on."

A bell chimed when they stepped inside. Cedar and starch filled the air. The mannequins faced the wall like they were waiting on a verdict.

Victoria swept the space.

"Okay. We start with silhouettes."

She touched a column dress, then a ballgown shaped like it was catching breath. "This one says timeless. That one says I dare you to blink."

Lena's attention lived in the mirrors. Movement made more sense in reflection. Intent exposed itself.

Victoria paused at a display.

"That veil. It suits you."

"Me?"

Victoria smiled. "You. I'll take the crown."

The clerk vanished. Lena studied a bolt of silk and the mirror that admitted no lies.

The beanie man stopped a foot inside the doorway, right where customers stalled before choosing a direction. He raised his phone. His lips moved without sound. Dictation. Or a relay.

The mirror caught his wrist as he fixed his cuff. A single bar flanked by five slashes, repeated like a tally of lives. A kill ledger carved into skin.

Lena's stomach tightened. Not prison ink. Not gang ink. Something older. Earned.

Her hand slipped into her pocket and pressed the pulse key once. No light. No buzz. Just Ghost waking on the other end.

She lifted her phone like she was admiring lace and snapped a photo. Proof.

Behind her, Victoria stepped out with the veil perched in her hair like a dare.

"Try me."

"You're dangerous," Lena said. And it wasn't about the veil.

Outside, the man smiled at no one, his expression practiced in mirrors. He pocketed his phone and scanned corners before moving. Not spooked. Repositioning.

"Too much?" Victoria asked.

"Perfect." Her voice didn't waver.

The mirror answered. The sedan driver now stood at the alley mouth.

Arms loose. Waiting. Not a guard. A net.

The clerk returned with pins in her mouth. "Alterations can,"

"Not yet. We're still in the part where everything's possible."

They stepped into the street.

The war room seemed to shift when Ghost's console pinged, the sound sharp enough to change the air.

"Pulse key," Ghost said. "Signal from her channel. Marking it now."

Imani rolled her chair across the floor, fingers already moving.

"Overlaying city permits."

Her movement stopped.

"That's not good."

Victor looked across the table.

"What's not good?"

"The Civic Shield shell we flagged earlier just activated a temporary analytics license on that block. Vendor feed. Public safety mask. The city only sees crowd data. Their shell gets faces. Lena's entire stretch just lit up inside the zone."

Victor stood.

"That's not city business. That's stalking with a badge."

Lucien spoke from the far side of the table, hands still, voice colder than the screens.

"Not a blind spot. A curtain. City sees safety. Their shell sees people."

Mara lifted her head from her drafts.

"They can do that?"

"They can pretend," Imani said. "The invoice cleared."

Ghost cut back in. "They didn't know she'd be there. The corridor was already flagged. Whoever's tailing her is using coverage Lansing bought before sunrise."

Lucien lifted his head. Coincidence didn't survive in this room. His attention narrowed.

The city map shifted. Heat bloomed across SoHo like breath on glass.

"Sedan parked too clean," Ghost went on. "Driver trying to disappear. Walker gliding like he's allergic to attention. Tapped his nose twice when he adjusted pace. Training, not a tic."

A beat.

"One more thing. One of the permits was rubber-stamped by a lawyer who used to move Coalition favors. Lansing isn't just buying eyes anymore. He's pulling old strings."

Victor was already moving.

Rook tossed him a set of keys without looking up.

"Take my van. Plates are mine. Registration's Imani's problem."

Imani didn't look up.

"Spoofed and layered. Contractor shell. Utility subcontractor. Boring enough to disappear in."

Victor caught them. Lucien took them from his hand.

"Good. I'm not in the mood to be loud."

They headed for the garage.

The white contractor van waited under the lights, dented along the side, ladder rack bolted to the roof. Nothing about it asked to be remembered.

Victor slid behind the wheel. Lucien took the passenger seat, routing his phone to the van's dash.

"Give me the update."

The engine turned over and settled into a low idle. Headlights washed the concrete in pale light.

Ghost's voice came through the speakers.

"Lena just sent a photo. Wrist tattoo. One vertical bar, five tally marks. Looks like a kill ledger. Ex-military or contract. Not street ink."

The van stayed quiet around that.

Lucien checked his pistol, the chamber silent and waiting.

"We'll walk it down."

"No sudden moves," Ghost said. "Stay boring until you're fire."

Lucien checked the mirror.

"Drive."

Victor shifted into gear.

"Boring's a costume."

The van rolled into daylight.

They trailed Lena from a block out, close enough to see the pressure forming, far enough to look uninvolved.

Victor drove like a man allergic to urgency, letting every yellow light stretch thin before surrendering. The van moved with the patience of something built to be ignored.

Lucien sat beside him, silent, eyes scanning angles, blind spots, escape lines, and the invisible hands trying to herd Lena where they wanted her.

"He's not overeager," Victor said. "He's patient. Steering them toward a choke point."

Lucien didn't look away from the mirrors.

"He's building a funnel. If we move too soon, he builds another one around us."

Lucien's thumb moved over his phone.

Logan. You got eyes on Lena? She hit the fob. Something's moving

He waited, screen open.

No reply.

Ahead, the black sedan kept perfect distance, half a block, never more, never less.

Around it, the city played normal. Crowds crossing. Doors swinging. Steam rising from the gutter.

Victor's grip stayed loose on the wheel.

"Feels like déjà vu."

Lucien didn't smile.

"I don't do déjà vu. I finish what tries to repeat."

Victoria stepped into the city like she owned the day, and Lena moved beside her, quiet, listening to more than footsteps. Window glare flashed. People crossed without looking. The city did what it always did. Pretended nothing was wrong.

A white contractor van sat double-parked two storefronts down, forgettable on purpose. A man checked his sleeve for a watch he didn't need.

Victoria ticked them off with a pen like the afternoon belonged to her.

"Emerald napkins. Scarlet shoes. The veil if you refuse the crown. Simple ceremony. Complex consequences."

"Simple is a luxury."

Victoria angled her a look. "You make it look expensive."

They passed a shop with vintage typewriters stacked in the window like broken teeth. The space between sounds narrowed. Cars drifted with too much intent. People walked with too much rhythm. The street was starting to feel arranged.

Lena kept them moving.

"We'll send Mom three options."

Victoria stepped off the curb.

"She'll pick the one Dad hates. Which is my favorite part."

The alley ahead opened like a slit in the city's throat. Brick. Dumpsters. Rust. A space made for cutting someone out of the day.

"Not that way," Lena murmured. "Let's check across the street."

They crossed into a narrow row of art-supply shops, long counters, short aisles, windows smudged with the fingerprints of impatient lives. Behind the register, a clerk wrestled with a glue bottle and lost.

Victoria drifted toward a display of wax seals, colors bright as spilled secrets. Lena stayed by the window, phone in hand, pretending at errands while using the glass like a second pair of eyes.

The alley reflected behind them.

A shoe.

A knee.

The beanie.

Lower now.

Posture bent, ready to move or reach or vanish.

A man who could tie his shoe if he needed a reason to get close.

Victoria lifted a packet of red and black seals.

"We'll use these for the invitations. Real wax. No stickers. If people break them, it means they wanted it."

"Old-world validation."

Victoria wandered deeper with a length of ribbon held to the light.

"So, are you excited to marry my brother?"

Lena touched a row of paper swatches, her reflection sharper than the colors.

"Excited?" Lena touched the paper swatches. "I don't pick safe."

Victoria laughed. "No. You pick what could burn you."

Lena didn't smile. The reflection froze the block in place. The beanie man lingered behind them, a weight with a pulse.

Victoria paid.

They stepped outside.

The street breathed differently now. The sedan had glided a half length down. The driver's eyes were empty windows. The beanie man had moved closer.

He passed behind them, close enough to brush Victoria's sleeve by a fraction of a hair. A touch so controlled it could have passed for accident.

He kept walking, straight toward the cross-street, his gait slow, confident, calibrated. The kind of walk men used when they already counted exits and lives.

Lena memorized him. The angle of shoulder. The weight in his step. The timing between breaths. Lucien had taught her how to read a body the way other people read a room.

This wasn't a snatch.

This was a survey.

Someone wanted room to work.

Victoria turned the seals in her hand.

"We're buying napkins, right?"

"We're buying napkins."

Her voice was steadier than the moment deserved.

The store windows rolled by. The street shifted around the man. The sedan shadowed him, adjusting in half-length increments.

Two storefronts away, Victor stepped out of the van in a jacket that made him look like a lawyer who'd missed a meeting. His hands empty. His presence precise. He did not hurry.

Lucien stayed inside, eyes on mirrors, listening to the comms with a focus that didn't drift.

Logan circled the block, phone lifted, murmuring to silence. His gait loose. His focus locked.

"Wind's shifting," Victor said. "He's got prey and witness. He wants isolation." He didn't look at Lena. He looked past her like distance belonged to him. "We take him soft or softer?"

"Soft," Ghost said. "I want to know who paid the invoices."

Logan tracked the sedan driver's rhythm. Blink. Mirror. Corner. Blink. Men like that always gave themselves away.

The beanie man dipped his chin in a yes to no one and moved along the curb. A decision taking form.

"Copy," Victor said. "On your count."

"Not yet," Ghost said. "Let him choose a street."

Lena and Victoria walked onto a block of candles and bowls. The city played normal. Paint-splattered wrists. Laughter about dogs. Flyers stapled to poles. Lives rolling forward without knowing a different life was moving between them.

At the next window, Lena paused to adjust an earring. It didn't need adjusting.

In the reflected glass, the man crossed behind them. He measured stride, arm swing, hair movement. Studying them from a distance.

It felt like theft.

He turned the hydrant corner with the same gait he'd used earlier. Routine. The kind men fell into right before they died.

Lena's phone buzzed once.

We have him. One more block. Turn left. Talk about cake

They walked.

At the corner, Lena turned left.

"We still haven't decided on cake."

Victoria groaned. "You're impossible."

Inside a bakery that smelled like warm sugar and escape, they ordered sample slices under names they didn't own. The clerk boxed them like treasures.

"Chocolate. With salt. Layers like a secret you meant to keep."

"Sold."

Outside, the city tightened again.

The man entered his funnel.

He didn't know the funnel bent.

He cut down a delivery-choked street. The sedan rolled forward and owned the mouth. Logan gave ground ahead like a civilian. Victor approached from the side like a passing thought.

From the van, Lucien let the circle close around all three.

"Now."

Victor stepped in just enough to force a polite swerve.

"Hey. Is this Prince Street?"

The man's eyes flicked to Victor's mouth, then his hands. Work first. Threat second. He shifted a quarter inch off his line.

Logan drifted behind him, closing the tail.

The sedan idled, blocked by a delivery truck.

To everyone watching, it looked like nothing.

Lena watched everything in a reflection.

"Do not burn him," Ghost said. "Trail him. He was casing. Not hitting."

Victor fell into step. Logan watched the sedan without turning his head.

Victoria let the wax seals clack in her hand like tiny dice.

"How many of these do we need?"

"Enough to buy time," Lena said.

"Time for what?"

"To get through today."

They turned a corner and let the street look easy again.

Behind them, the city adjusted. A predator in daylight realizing something had looked back.

Back at Northgate, the war room hummed, monitors washing the room in moving light. Code crawled across glass.

Ghost came through the speakers.

"Coalition felt the CityCast takeover. When I bled a few of their accounts after, they panicked. Two city contracts froze. A PAC donation got yanked mid-transfer. Three shell accounts scattered into new banks. No press. No retaliation. Not yet."

The map shifted.

"Lansing's people felt it before he did. The Coalition was his donor machine. When their money froze, his whole operation choked before he knew whose hand was around its throat. That was panic, not strategy."

Mara, drowning in half-written headlines, let out a humorless snort.

"Convenient, isn't it? Lose the money, and suddenly Civic Shield's shell buys temporary AI surveillance on multiple corridors under the label of 'public safety.'"

Ghost's tone thinned, clean as steel.

"Not coincidence. He smelled the shift and started buying eyes. This wasn't about Lena. He was fishing for Lucien through Lena and the properties. Panic paid for cameras."

Imani slid between feeds, fingers skating the map like she was reading a pulse.

"Two of the four corridors sit right on top of the properties Lucien put in Lena's name."

Mara looked up, mouth tightening like a stitch pulled too hard.

"Someone did a little digging on their own."

Ghost tilted the heat map until the four corridors flared across the wall like wound markers.

"Exactly. He wasn't just watching the street. He was tracing the paperwork."

Ghost pulled up the wrist mark from Lena's photo, isolated the ink, and ran it through his private library of contract markings. The system tagged it with today's date and hour. A mark entering the archive.

"Welcome to the vault," Ghost muttered. "Probable match on a 2019 Brighton fight-camp shot. Same ear nick. Same ink pattern. Alias, Trask. Confidence, seventy-two percent."

The SoHo grid glowed across the big screen. The idling sedan. The drifting walker. The invisible lines of a trap slowly revealing their shape.

Ghost went quiet for a second.

"Got you."

Not to any of them, but to the man who had just stepped into the story.

They gave the day one last minute to pretend.

They wandered a bookstore that smelled like old paper and glue, a sanctuary built from other people's unfinished thoughts. Victoria bought a blank notebook and wrote LENA on the first page in block letters big enough to signal satellites.

"For your vows."

"For my crimes."

"Same folder."

Victoria capped the pen with a sharp click.

Lena's phone buzzed again. Northgate, not emergency. She ignored it. Some battles were won by looking away.

Outside, the mid-afternoon light turned unforgiving, nowhere for shadows to hide.

The man slipped around the corner Victor already owned.

The sedan drifted forward again, trying to pass for ordinary and failing.

Logan vanished into a knot of tourists, tracking without leaving a ripple.

Lena stopped at the curb and looked at the city straight on. She let it look back.

"We're done."

It was not a retreat.

They started across the street.

A construction vest brushed Lena's shoulder. The man apologized in a language he didn't speak. The apology came too quickly, the smile held one second too long. His vest was too clean. His badge read CITY EVNTS, one letter missing.

He kept walking. The typo stayed with her like a shard of glass.

Up the block, Victor tailed the beanie man as he drifted toward a florist wrapped in a tired green awning and buckets of half-wilted carnations. A crooked security camera hung above the service door, blinking over the alley.

Ghost slipped into the feed and froze the frame. "Got his keypad code. Three-seven-one-nine. Rehearsed, not improvised."

Logan shadowed the sedan's driver for a block, silent as a hinge. He memorized the plate, the bumper stickers, the rental barcode ghosting the windshield. He snapped a photo of the registration through the glass and sent it to Ghost without breaking stride.

He peeled off at the next corner, circled wide, and flowed back toward the Rezvani like a man retracing a thought he didn't want to forget.

Back at Northgate, Imani was already pulling apart the ownership tree, stripping the rental down to its bones.

Ghost pinged Lena's phone with a weather alert that had nothing to do with rain.

We're in your pocket. Go home slow

No sirens on the screen. The words didn't need any.

"Go home slow" meant the watchers had become the watched.

Lena kept walking, thumb drifting over her screen like she was checking a shopping list.

She typed:

Did you get photo? Wrist mark, vertical bar, five tallies. Calm but trained

Ghost replied:

We got it. Beautiful

Not praise. Classification. Beautiful meant useful enough to hunt with.

She pictured Lucien that morning at the table, a man who had survived by never being the softest thing in the room.

He had told her to keep him bored.

She would fail, gloriously.

And he would forgive her for it.

Victoria nudged her.

"Now that's a poster line."

Across the street, a mural stretched along a shuttered storefront: a heart painted like a target, rings bleeding outward, the words LOVE IS THE EASIEST THING TO AIM AT stenciled in chipped white.

Lena let her eyes rest on it.

"So we build better armor."

Victoria nodded once, knighting her.

"Then we don't decorate it. We defend it."

Lena's mouth curved.

"We do."

Logan pulled to the curb. Victoria slid in first, Lena after her, both sinking into the dark interior like stepping back into a fortified room. The doors shut with a dense, sealed thud.

They didn't travel in a single line. Logan held the truck half a block back. Victor and Lucien matched their pace from the next street over. The formation staggered itself, precise as pieces on a board. They never looked back. People who needed the illusion of leading were happiest when you let them keep it.

Four blocks from Mercy West, Logan peeled away.

At the curb, Victoria kissed Lena's cheek, already talking about cake, already dialing upstairs.

Lena waited until the hospital doors closed behind her before signaling Logan to move.

She almost spoke. Almost told Victoria what had hunted them beneath the city's heartbeat. But Victoria had spent the day wreathed in veils and wax seals, and dragging her into the crosshairs would have been cruelty dressed as honesty.

And Lucien's mother, fighting for her life in the oncology wing above them, didn't need another shard of fear lodged in her chest.

Lena swallowed it and let the silence harden.

Some things were safer kept.

Under the city that thought it still owned its stories, Trask sat at a stainless steel table in a basement that smelled of metal and detergent. He slid his phone into a signal pouch. A list of venues lay in front of him. He circled one with a pen that cost more than his boots.

He wasn't thinking about brides.

He was thinking about air flow. Entry points. Exits that narrowed.

He touched the ink on his wrist. Felt nothing. The marks weren't for memory. They were for accounting.

He checked the date.

He still had a route to finish.

Above him, the city moved like cities do. Loud. Blind. Predictable.

He believed that.

He was wrong.

The main wall showed the city again, grids of light moving across the glass like nerves under skin.

Lucien stepped into the war room. Victor followed, rolling his shoulders like he was shaking off rain that never came.

"Lena's inbound with Logan. Victoria's clear."

"Tell me you've got something worth my time," Victor murmured.

The central screen shifted. Lena's photo filled it. The tattoo, one vertical bar and five fine tally slashes, stood out in stark contrast, a private kill ledger carved into skin.

"There's your anchor," Ghost said.

Lucien's eyes stayed on the screen.

"He was careful."

"He was careful," Ghost echoed. "But he's ours now."

Victor's eyes swept the map, then the door, then back.

"We cut him tomorrow."

"Tonight we let him dream," Ghost said.

"Dreams leave footprints," Imani murmured, not looking up.

Rook appeared, or had always been there. His voice rose from the corner like a shape forming.

"He used the alley keypad. We have the code."

Lucien studied the screen.

"We'll need a quiet door."

Rook smiled like he already had the door.

"We'll get it."

Lucien's phone lit in his hand. Lena.

He answered before the first ring finished.

"Bored yet?"

"Not even close."

"I told you to keep me bored."

"I tried. The city had other ideas."

"What did it give you?"

"A wrist mark. A face I won't forget. A pattern I didn't like."

"Bring it upstairs. Show me."

"I brought chocolate cake instead."

A pause.

"Salted?"

"Always."

"Come home."

Lena ended the call as the Rezvani turned into Northgate. The gate ahead rose like a curtain lifting on the next act.

Logan eased the Rezvani through the courtyard.

The garage door descended behind them, metal grinding along its track. Through the narrowing slit, Lena caught the suggestion of a black sedan sliding past the far end of the block, measured and patient.

Then the door sealed, and the image stayed carved behind her eyes.

She told herself it was nothing. She didn't believe it.

She stepped into the hush inside and walked straight to the war room.

On the main screen, a message waited from Ghost:

CONTRACT TAIL CONFIRMED. NET IN MOTION

Lena set the cake box on the table and ran her finger along the seam, opening it in one clean line. When she lifted the lid, chocolate and salt rose through the room, cutting the tension in a single breath.

"Eat. Might as well train for the wedding menu, if we survive long enough to need one."

Victor took one slice for himself, then cut a second and set it beside the nearest speaker.

"For Ghost," he said.

Ghost came through flat. "Sentimental idiot."

Victor picked up his fork. "You're welcome."

Logan wiped frosting from his thumb, grinning like a man who knew tomorrow wasn't promised but was willing to bet on it anyway.

Lucien swiped a finger through the frosting.

Lena caught his hand, took the frosting from his skin, then wiped a bit from his mouth and kissed him.

A pressure valve disguised as affection.

The war room kept breathing around them, pretending it hadn't felt the shift.

Ghost's voice cracked through the speakers.

"Your tail moved."

"Good."

Ghost came back on the line.

"So did the cameras."

Her eyes locked on the map blooming across the wall. Cross streets. Choke points. The tail's last vector. The camera grid. Her heartbeat leveled into focus. The city's undercurrent matched it.

Their phones buzzed.

A single image appeared, pulled from a maintenance feed Ghost was never meant to touch. Trask stepped through a florist's service door, entering a code with the same calm precision he'd used on the street.

The photo settled under Lena's ribs, heavy and exact.

She lowered the phone, the moment tight in her chest.

Ghost's voice slid back in, softer now. "We'll pick him up tomorrow."

"Then we end it."

Her eyes stayed on the frozen frame of the man disappearing through the door.

Outside, an engine turned over once and cut out.

Like a throat clearing.

Tomorrow, the city would learn his name.

CHAPTER THIRTY-ONE

BLACKSITE ON WHEELS

The clock on the van's dash flipped to 3:00 a.m.

Three in the morning was the hour when bad decisions stopped pretending to be temporary.

Waiting until daylight had not been an option. Nobody in the van had the patience. Moving under the sun was a risk; moving now was a promise.

Northgate carried its command center in whatever shell the night required. Tonight it wasn't the Rezvani's black growl but the plain white contractor van with Rook's plates and Imani's spoofed registration, anonymity dressed as utility.

Earlier, Ghost had pulled the keypad code off the florist's exterior feed, freeze-framing the beanie man as he slipped through the service door with the confidence of someone who had used that route before. That same feed had caught a pallet delivered hours later, a crate stamped in rough block letters: THE ATRIA, routed for tomorrow's oncology fundraiser where Evelyn Cole's name sat on the host list.

The basement itself was a blind spot their cameras couldn't see.

A box tied to her event sitting in that kind of darkness was enough to send them out now.

Cold vinyl pressed faint lines into Lena's fingertips. Hard benches and stripped-down walls, built for hauling gear, not comfort.

The city's witching hour slid past their windows: streets that had carried its worst on their sidewalks, dumpsters stacked in silent rows, traffic lights holding red for no one. Victor drove with the radio dead and the headlights on until the last turn.

Ghost's voice came low through the dash speaker.

"Florist basement confirmed. Civic Shield shell still owns four corridors under 'public safety.' You've got one blind window in their feed. Ninety seconds."

Lucien scrolled once on the image Ghost had pushed to his phone, the florist's exterior feed frozen on the pallet being rolled through the service door, the crate stamped THE ATRIA clear in the frame.

One panel showed a stylized flame climbing upward. Another, a skull stripped of humor. A third, a black gas cylinder thin as a coffin.

Beneath each icon sat a class number, the kind you only notice when it's too late: 2 for gases, 3 for flammable liquids, 6 for toxins.

Under the cheap sodium light, the hazard diamond stopped looking like paperwork and snapped into focus as what it really was: a countdown written in symbols.

Lucien's thumb paused. For a heartbeat the diamond stopped being a symbol and became a room, place cards and water glasses, Evelyn's lipstick ghosted on a rim.

The skull wasn't a warning. It was a promise someone had already decided to keep.

The room wasn't just a room anymore. It was a camera waiting to turn her and everyone else inside into footage.

"Hazard diamonds on the crate," Ghost added. "Training aerosol if it's honest. Something nastier if it's not."

"Air," Lena said quietly, and the word felt heavier than metal.

Rook checked the tool roll at his feet. "Quiet door off Broome Street. Keypad. Camera I can kill without leaving fingerprints."

Logan touched his comm bead. "Soft or quiet?"

"Quiet," Lucien said. "Not soft."

Victor slowed. The van's suspension groaned against the curb.

Lena slid her hand deeper into her coat and met Lucien's eyes. "With you."

He didn't smile; his eyes did, once, just for her, and then he went to war.

Rook worked the lock, and the door sighed open.

Cold concrete. Fluorescents flickered like the room didn't want them there. A fridge hummed somewhere, the kind of sound that made silence feel sick.

Logan moved first, a shadow with manners.

Victor took rear, boredom worn like armor, dangerous by nature.

Lucien moved in without sound, already measuring the room.

Lena kept her hands loose and her mind on air.

At the bend: the florist's side door, a four-digit keypad with four clean keys. Above it, a camera with a strip of electrical tape that hadn't been there this morning.

"Don't touch their eye," Ghost murmured. "It's not ours."

Rook's fingers stopped. "Understood. Going dark."

"Adjusting approach," Ghost said, his voice low. "Also, Civic Shield's system pings each camera every five minutes to prove the grant works. I can slip you a two-minute blind. That's it."

Lucien set two fingers against the wall, his only tell. The hazard diamond burned behind his eyes. It wasn't just a kill op. It was a broadcast. He put the thought away. Later. "We're in and out."

Rook typed the code Ghost had freeze-framed from earlier. The latch clicked.

They slid through.

The room was bigger than a basement should be and emptier than a place where people planned to hurt strangers.

Stainless table. Wire racks. A steel locker stood there, its stickers scraped off, only the adhesive ghosts left behind.

On the table: a portable air sampler.

On the floor: a crate stamped THE ATRIA, RECEIVING, marked with warnings no one was supposed to read in time.

"Right place, wrong time," Ghost murmured.

Lena pressed two gloved fingers to the crate, the way you quiet something that shouldn't wake. Cold. Seals unbroken. Cold meant patience. Patience meant planning.

She pictured vents high as balconies and donors wearing fear like perfume. Cancer patients seated beneath banners meant to honor them. Evelyn sitting at a table beside her name. Breath that had fought to stay in the world, stolen and weaponized for spectacle. She made her own breath obey.

Rook popped the locker with a pry bar and the calm of a man who considered locks temporary opinions. Inside: a pocket drone with a blade cage, clear tubing, nitrile gloves, a cheap notebook with its corners chewed by work.

Lena flipped it open. Bones of dates. Addresses. Arrows that assumed fluency. And four words carved hard enough to scar the next page: AIR FIRST. ROOM SECOND

"Eyes up," Lucien said, head cocked to a door only he heard.

Rook flicked a glance to the taped camera above the interior door. "He watched us arrive."

"He piggybacked our blackout," Ghost said. "I dropped their feed; he dropped his too. Something in his system pinged, a trip sensor or a seal alarm. He thinks he's coming to check a glitch, not a team."

Logan faded left, setting his back to a pillar. Rook slid behind the locker. Victor took the hinge side.

Lucien stepped three paces in, bait that didn't look like bait. Lena stayed a yard off his shoulder, close enough to cut.

The lock turned.

The man in the gray beanie came in like he belonged there. He closed the door with his heel. His hand brushed the pocket where the black pouch sat.

Logan's forearm was already across his throat.

They moved at the same time, like violence had a conductor.

No space. No sound. No chance.

Metal slammed his spine into the concrete. Breath burst white against the floor. He reached for a blade, Rook took it before steel showed. He tried to rise, Victor dumped him flat again.

The pouch in his back pocket shifted; Lena crushed his median nerve with her heel until his hand let go like a dropped tool.

Two seconds. One sound. A thud a room doesn't forget.

"Sleep," Victor said, almost polite.

He sagged under their weight and stayed down. Victor flipped him onto his side while Logan pinned his wrists. Tape tore loud in the quiet. Zip cuffs cinched his hands and ankles. A bead of spit clung to his lip, and he tongued the split there, once, twice, like a tic he couldn't stop.

Rook ran a cloth over the patch of floor where his head had hit, wiping away the last mark of the struggle.

Lucien didn't look at the man. He looked at the crate.

"Van."

They carried the quiet out the same door.

They hauled him into the van and slammed the doors. The ignition turned, the engine catching with a low growl. Dash lights flared. Lucien's phone synced to the system on instinct.

The van smelled like chemical cleaner losing a fight. A moving blanket went up fast, turning the back into a square of nowhere.

Ghost came through as Victor dropped it into gear. "Civic Shield's shell feeds just pinged. They noticed the florist feed blink. You've got a narrow window before someone checks nearby cameras. Keep transit clean. Don't give me a headline."

Victor was already rolling before Ghost finished speaking.

The man snapped back to himself, sharp and sudden. Logan kept a knee on his shoulder, almost polite.

At the wheel, Victor kept one hand loose, eyes on the street.

Lucien didn't sit. He stood over the man and let him look up. "What do I call you?"

The man said nothing. His eyes stayed on Lucien, not the doors. Recognition moved behind them.

Ghost put a name into the van. "Trask. Scrubbed deeper. Overseas tours, off-book work. Men like that keep tricks. Treat him as dangerous."

Trask's mouth split into a thin, crooked smile. "Well... you're not cops."

"Correct," Victor said from the wheel. "Cops wouldn't be this polite."

"I know who you are," Trask said.

Lucien tilted his head. "Then you know what happens next. You followed her. You mapped exits she already owned. You weren't just tailing a woman, you were tracing a line to me. Who sent you?"

A flicker crossed Trask's face. Calculation, not guilt.

Then came the curl of a dry, needling smile. "Big day coming up, Cole? Dresses, cake tastings. SoHo looked busy."

Lucien didn't blink. "Careful. You're close to saying something I'll make you regret."

Lena kept her voice reasonable on purpose. "Who hired you?"

"I don't talk."

Victor watched the road like he wasn't listening. "Everyone talks. Some of us like the price better than money."

Trask looked at Lena, the way men like him always searched for softness, and found nothing he could use.

Lucien held up the notebook. "Air first. Room second. Is Atria the rehearsal or the show?"

No answer.

"Release or scare?" Lena asked.

The answer came out like a calculation. "Enough to make them run."

Victor took the next turn clean. "And when they run, they choke."

"Who do you answer to?" Lucien asked.

"A net," Trask said. "Not a tree."

"Names," Logan said, patience gone thin. "Or I start at the wrist and work to the elbow."

Lena didn't look away. "There are people in that room fighting for their lives. If you aim air at them, you don't leave this van."

His gaze flicked to Lucien, recalculating.

"Vance," he said. "You won't find him written down. Buys corridors. Never attends."

Victor's eyes flicked once to the mirror. "Vance what?"

"Just Vance." Trask tongued the split in his lip. "He's the hand. The head's clean."

The name changed the van. Lucien went still. Logan's eyes narrowed, like he'd seen that name once in a margin the city pretended didn't exist.

Mara's voice cut into their ears. "So who's the head?"

Lucien said it aloud for Trask. "Civic Shield?"

Trask's smile went thin and wolfish. "Higher than them. Lower than God." He leaned forward until the tape on his wrists creaked. "You know the name. You've just been afraid to say it out loud."

At the wheel, Victor shook his head once. "Lansing built this."

Trask's laugh scraped the air. "Built it? He laid the pipes. Drew the diagrams. Thought he was the genius in the room."

His eyes glinted.

"But he answers up. They all do."

He lowered his voice. "Every corridor. Every camera. Every panic plan. Lansing thinks he's proving he can keep order. But the Atria isn't his idea. It's the headline someone else wrote for him."

Rook pointed at the small black pouch Trask had been eyeing since they pulled him into the van.

"Don't."

"It's not for me," Trask said, breath catching on something close to a laugh.

A warning chirped through the dash. Ghost's tone dipped. "Heads up. Civic Shield's system just did a forced check-in. Someone noticed the florist feed blink. Not long enough to send help if you keep moving. Long enough to send a hello."

Lena studied the tallies on his wrist, old ink, brag retired. "How many of you will be at Atria during the gala?"

He almost lied. Chose math instead. "Two on the roof. One in the kitchen talking vents. One at the service corridor."

"Plus you," Victor said.

Trask didn't confirm. He didn't need to.

Lucien's grip tightened on Trask's jacket. "Time?"

"Load-in at eighteen hundred. Dry run at nineteen-thirty. Portable unit standing by in a Civic Shield van. If it goes live, twenty hundred."

Logan's knee settled harder against Trask's shoulder. "Dry run of what?"

"Fear," Trask said. "Cameras catch the right faces running. That's the product."

"Not killers," Lena said, contempt thin as glass. "Editors."

He sneered. "Editors get paid more."

Lucien tilted his head. "Then explain it. What's the play?"

"You still think it's about the air."

Lena's eyes sharpened. "It's not."

Blood shone at the corner of Trask's mouth. "It's about the picture."

Lucien's gaze sharpened. "Footage."

"Fundraisers. Donors. Officials. Sick people gasping under banners with their names on them." Trask's smile thinned. "That's the product. The aerosol's just the switch."

The words hung too long. Lucien's hand closed on the front of Trask's jacket and hauled him up, a single, precise motion that put their faces inches apart.

Lucien's voice dropped until calm became the threat.

"With my mother gasping at one of those tables? You think you're selling panic. You're selling a headline built on her breath, and on the breath of every sick soul sitting there to receive help instead of harm."

Ghost's voice came again, colder now.

"Their camera's waking up. So will the city if we miss."

Lucien studied Trask like something that had stopped working. The hazard diamond flared again in his mind, now with Evelyn at that table and a journalist's camera blinking red.

"You don't get the upstairs anymore."

"You think that's mercy?" Trask said.

"Mercy's a bedtime story. I don't sleep anymore."

Lucien glanced at Logan.

Logan understood.

Logan hit him once, low and clean, catching the weight before it hit the floor.

No scream. Just the van settling around them.

They taped his wrists to his belt, ankles together, beanie back on to shade his eyes. Logan rolled him into a recovery position with the bored care of a man who had triaged enemies before.

"Drop spot?" Lucien asked.

Rook checked the route on his phone.

"Cold room on Canal. Cleaner than my first apartment."

"Stash this piece of shit," Lucien said. "We collect if the net tightens."

They ghosted the van off Canal, shoved Trask into the cold room, and left him breathing but locked out of his own part in a much bigger play.

Tonight, poison got nothing.

Panic got nothing.

Back at Northgate, the screens lit the room in quick pulses. Ghost painted The Atria across the wall, rooflines, kitchen runs, the thin veins of intake vents that fed air to people who thought ceilings were safe.

"Host committee's unchanged," Mara said, eyes on her notes. "Donor list still reads like a favor you can't pay back."

Imani dragged icons into place. "Roof access here and here. Service corridor off Twenty-Sixth. Kitchen vents are narrow, someone could crawl them, but they'd scrape metal the whole way."

"The crate?" Lena asked.

"Diverted," Ghost said. "We pulled their crate tonight and parked it where it can't hurt anyone."

Lucien's eyes stayed locked on the map. "Then we act like it's already in motion."

Ghost hesitated. "Atria's calendar just went private. That's not canceling. That's closing the blinds."

"Lansing," Mara said.

"Or Vance paying his tab," Ghost replied. "Either way, eight o'clock is still air, unless we own the room."

Lucien's hand flattened on the table. The image of the crate and his mother's lipstick ghosting a glass rim welded together in his head and refused to come apart. Evelyn's breath wasn't a variable. It was the line.

"Give me a roof map. A kitchen map. Every intake vent a human with a ladder and a bad idea can reach."

"On your screen before the elevator doors open," Ghost said.

The room's hum thinned.

"And Lucien, table three has your mother's name. If Lansing wants panic footage, he picked the wrong family."

Lucien's voice came quiet but final. "Then we give him a different film."

"What do we shoot?" Victor asked.

"Nothing," Lucien said. "A room that doesn't move at all."

He looked at Lena, and the look itself was a plan.

"We go break the air."

The night bent around that promise.

By sunrise, the florist's camera saw nothing but clean concrete and a strip of tape that had never been there.

The crate had a new address, and the map glowed with a new grid: vents, ladders, exits, every path the building offered.

"Air first," Lena murmured, the dented words still living on the page she'd found.

"Not tonight," Lucien answered, eyes on the map. "Tonight, the air belongs to us."

And in this city, whoever owned the air decided who got to breathe.

Chapter Thirty-Two

THE AIR WE BREATHE

At 19:41 the air inside The Atria stopped belonging to the city and started belonging to fate. The waxed oak floor gleamed like wet gold beneath a hundred soft soles. The walls smelled like old money and decisions no one apologized for. Light climbed the velvet drapes and refused to touch the room.

Waiters carved silver arcs through the glow, priests moving through a ceremony. Every gesture whispered the same fragile lie: tonight was safe. The banner over the stage promised HOPE FOR ONCOLOGY in tall, clean letters, as if language could bless what time refused.

Evelyn Cole sat at Table Three in ivory silk that made color feel like a rumor. A cannula traced her cheek, hissing with the patience of a tide. Not a constant need, the doctors had said, but a guardrail for when breath forgot itself. The mass sat too close to the place that taught the lungs their rhythm.

Each breath was an act of defiance.

She knew the threat. The plot. The danger. The fact that the air itself might turn against her. And still she had chosen to come. To sit. To breathe.

Earlier, Evelyn had taken Lena's hand and made the choice sound simple.

"They don't get to steal the night from us. They don't get to teach my breath fear."

So Lena stood beside her, not as a guest but as a daughter. Emerald silk, chosen because it read as family and moved like warning. Her hand corrected a fold that didn't need correcting. She kept time with Evelyn's inhale and exhale the way soldiers count seconds before a breach.

"Where's Alexander?" Lena murmured. "He should've been here by now."

Evelyn's smile curved, soft but tired. "Alexander has never been built for these kinds of nights. Galas. Manufactured hope. Pageants for people pretending the world isn't on fire."

She adjusted the cannula, breath steadying. "He's been carrying too much lately. You. Me. Lucien's storms. I saw it in his eyes this morning. Even men like him need one night to put the weight down."

Lena nodded. The truth settled between them.

Evelyn's gaze stayed soft on the room.

"He'll be here to retrieve me after. He always comes for me."

A certainty. A promise the world hadn't broken.

Lena's hand stilled against Evelyn's sleeve. "You didn't tell me if they confirmed anything."

Evelyn didn't look away from the room. "I told them not to waste my breath dressing it prettier than it is."

Lena swallowed. "Brain cancer."

Evelyn's chin lifted a fraction. "Yes. And still I'm here."

The specialists in New York had confirmed what Florida first saw in shadow and caution. Malignant meningioma. No softer language left. No more maybe.

Lena's eyes glassed before she could stop them. "You should be resting, not down here where everyone can look at you and pretend that's the same thing as saving you."

"Don't make me cry in front of donors," Evelyn murmured.

Lena leaned closer, lowering her voice. "Then breathe with me."

Evelyn's smile softened. "Terrible liar."

Their soft laughter disappeared beneath the clinking of glasses. Something shifted in the room, too thin to name but impossible to ignore.

Lansing drifted through the fundraiser like a rumor in a city that no longer trusted its own saints. A host with no podium. An architect with no fingerprints. He left nothing behind but the smiles he manufactured on other people's mouths.

His gaze brushed Lena and clung a second too long. Not threat. Not warmth. Something colder than both. Then he moved on, and the room pretended it hadn't felt the chill.

The chandelier light glowed hot, stage light dressed as charity. The room believed it was a mirror.

Tonight, it would be a screen.

High above the chandeliers and champagne, two rifles waited on the roof, shadows stretching long across the cold concrete bones of the building. A signal was meant to come, one that would never reach them.

A traffic chopper ripped past, rotors hammering the sky, blades chewing the air. The men on the roof shifted, hands jerking to their brims, eyes narrowing against the dark, faces carved from grit and sweat.

Then Logan hit the roof like gravity.

The door didn't open. It surrendered, metal shrieking off the jamb as he came through sideways, low, a black shape cut out of the night itself. The first man had half a second to register the wind shifting wrong.

That was generous.

Logan's hand speared up into the soft notch at the base of his throat, fingers locking the nerve pocket, and drove upward. Not a strike. A shutdown.

The man went limp.

Before he even began to fall, Logan pivoted inside his collapse and swung him into the second guard. Dead weight hit the man square in the chest. Ribs cracked.

The rifle came up.

Logan let it.

He caught the barrel with one hand and twisted. The sling tore skin off the man's neck as the weapon spun free and clattered across the gravel. He stepped in close enough to smell the fear-sweat and slammed his forehead into the bridge of the man's nose.

The third hit wasn't a headbutt anymore, just a man driving another man's face into the roof with the patience of someone hammering a nail.

Blood sheeted warm across Logan's cheek.

The guard fumbled for a knife under his jacket. Logan caught the wrist, rotated, and folded the arm the wrong way until the joint gave. The scream started somewhere in the diaphragm and never made it out. Logan's other hand was already clamped over the mouth, thumb digging into the hinge beneath the jaw.

He leaned in, foreheads almost touching.

"Shh," he whispered, almost tender. "Listen."

Far below, a siren dopplered and died. The city kept breathing, indifferent.

Logan lowered the man until the back of his skull kissed the rooftop. Then he dropped his full weight through a single knee. Something deep inside gave way. The body spasmed once and went still.

Zip ties bit into wrists that would never feel them again. Duct tape sealed silence.

The burner phone in the second man's pocket buzzed like a trapped insect. Logan thumbed the screen.

TARGET STILL IN PLAY

He smiled the way winter smiles and crushed the phone in his fist, plastic and glass raining across the gravel.

Logan dragged both bodies by their ankles, heels carving twin furrows through the blood-wet gravel, and parked them behind the HVAC unit.

He looked out over the city lights. "Tell him it failed."

Then he stood and walked back toward the stairwell without looking down.

Behind him, the rooftop was quiet except for the slow drip of something thick hitting gravel and the wind dragging itself over the roof.

Downstairs, the poison waited.

It hadn't moved yet. It crouched inside the canister, colorless, odorless, heavier than air, ready to pour across the floor the instant the valve cracked and ghost along tile hunting lungs.

The kitchen sat in its pre-gala lull. Prep stations abandoned. Burners left on low. No one watching the intake duct. No one close enough to hear anything until it was too late.

A man in a gray catering jacket knelt beside the main return, canister cradled like a newborn. His thumb settled on the valve. One twist and the building would breathe wrong in under four minutes.

Rook came in low and fast, shoulder driving into the man's spine before sound registered. The impact lifted him off his knees and folded him over a prep table.

The canister spun free. The valve clicked loose on impact.

A thin hiss started.

Rook caught the canister, slammed a heavy stainless bowl over the nozzle, then whipped it into the bus tub he'd pre-filled with brine. Water surged. The hiss became a death rattle and died.

"Not HVAC," Rook muttered, eyes flicking to the stamped hazard diamond. "Portable unit. Clever bastards."

He was already moving.

The side door banged open. Second hitter. Knife out.

Logan filled the doorway like judgment.

The knife came up. Logan crashed into him shoulder-first, driving him sideways into the wall. The blade skittered across the floor. He caught the stagger and drove the man's skull into the corner of the butcher block.

Wood split.

Bone followed.

Blood striped the grain.

The hitter clawed for balance. Logan hauled him up and slammed him face-first into the boiling stockpot. Steam burst. The scream went high, then broke as Logan held him there. His legs kicked once, twice, then stopped.

He let the body drop.

Rook locked the last filter into place. "Health inspection."

Logan stepped over the body. "Failed."

Rook glanced at the stockpot, where red clouded through broth. "This was the distraction."

Logan rolled his neck once. "Distraction's over. Where's the real push?"

They left without looking back.

Behind them, the poison met new filters and went nowhere.

The building kept breathing.

The service corridor stank of bleach and something metallic someone had tried to hide. Fluorescents stuttered overhead, throwing hard light across the concrete.

Victor waited in the dark between two strobes, motionless, breathing through his mouth so the smell wouldn't burn his sinuses.

The hitter came in quick, shoulders high, thumb locked over the trigger fob in his fist. One press and the building would die through its own vents. His pulse jumped in his throat.

They met at the corner.

He stepped in, not out. His left hand drifted up, almost polite, and hooked behind the hitter's elbow. A small turn of his wrist levered the arm straight, then over the line.

The joint let go with a small surrender, more insult than injury.

The fob ripped free and skittered across the floor.

The scream never happened. Victor ended it with one short strike to the throat.

Momentum carried them forward. He used it, steering the collapsing body head-first into the fire-hose cabinet. Metal boomed. The glass panel shattered. A shard lodged in the man's cheek and trembled.

He grabbed a fistful of hair and drove his head into the cabinet one last time.

The metal buckled inward.

The body slid down, slumped against the wall. Blood pooled under the lights.

He crouched, retrieved the fob, wiped it once on the man's sleeve.

Still warm.

He pocketed it.

He dragged the body behind the linen cart. One boot stuck out. He nudged the cart forward until the foot disappeared.

Clean enough.

He rose and breathed out slow.

"Wrong god. Wrong day."

The fluorescents flickered once, twice, then steadied, like the building had decided it was safer to keep the lights on.

Victor walked away without looking back.

The bleach smell was already losing its fight against copper, and somewhere above, the party continued.

Deep in the building, the city's lungs changed direction.

Ghost's voice slid across comms. "Their cameras are waking. The city will too if we miss. Mara's on mezzanine feeds. Imani's got corridor analytics."

Rook's filters were already seated behind three grilles, waiting to choke whatever poison they tried to push. In the control panel, the fan reversed, pulling instead of pushing, starving the ducts before they could feed the room.

A red override Lansing had paid for clicked uselessly beneath a technician's thumb. It wasn't a weapon anymore. Just expensive plastic pretending to matter.

Three blocks out, in the dark hush of the Rezvani's cabin, Lucien watched Table Three on a private feed. He didn't need the angle. He needed his mother's breath, the slow, stubborn rhythm of the woman he was doing this for.

The vents did the one thing the enemy never planned for.

They refused.

For six minutes, nothing happened.

The roof stayed quiet. The kitchen held its breath. The corridor hitter lay crumpled behind a linen cart, unconscious. Ghost's feed stayed calm and green.

Then the world shifted.

Lucien's eyes stayed on the feed. "Talk to me."

Ghost's voice tightened, stripped of its usual calm. "HVAC's clean. Pressure steady. Filters holding. But service just rolled in a maintenance cart. Something's live. Thermal only."

Imani cut in. "Cart's not on the staff log. It's a ghost entry."

Mara followed. "Tracing its path now."

Lucien looked at Ghost's feed. "Meaning?"

Ghost's feed split again.

"Meaning Trask gave us their first play. They pivoted. Not the vents. Portable. Hidden. Already on your floor."

Mara's cursor snapped to the upper level. "Tagging heat signatures on the mezzanine."

"Pressure shifts confirmed," Imani added. "Something's moving across the mezzanine."

"Kitchen feed," Lucien ordered.

The split-screen told the story: a Civic Shield van that hadn't been there at 19:30 now parked in service. Two techs pushed a covered floral cart through the doors. Ordinary enough to ignore. On thermal, the underside glowed hot. No tie-in to ductwork. No path but the room.

"Backup," Lena breathed.

Victor's jaw tightened. "Or decoy."

Lucien's pulse didn't change. "Or both. We adapt."

Lucien stopped watching.

The myth started hunting.

Someone tried to make panic worth more than poison.

It started as etiquette, a single cough at Table Eight, the kind people apologize for. Then the lights dipped, soft enough to pass for ambience but deeper than mood should fall. Waiters paused in doorways. And through the hush crept a whisper, thin and contagious:

Is the air wrong?

Evelyn's eyes stayed on Lena.

Lena knew the taste of wrong. Bitter chalk under the tongue. Not death. Performance.

Ghost's voice cracked across the comms. "Localized pressure anomaly, mezzanine three, directly above your position. Not HVAC. Handheld dispersal unit."

"They're already in the room. Above Table Three."

Rook cut in. "Copy. We stopped one in the kitchen. He never got the chance."

"Meaning there's more," Victor said.

"Meaning it's coordinated," Ghost replied. "And it's happening now."

Lena's pulse slowed. "They knew we took Trask."

Evelyn's hand found hers under the table, cold but steady. "If my son is coming, it will be now."

Lena met her eyes. "Then we let the city watch."

The chandeliers flickered.

A hiss came from the mezzanine. Not the deep breath of HVAC. Something smaller. Closer.

Evelyn's hand tightened around Lena's. "He's here."

The doors opened.

Lucien walked in.

Ghost's voice slipped into his ear. "It's live. The uplink is hot. Whatever happens next, we can put it in front of the whole city if you say go."

The room didn't gasp. It came apart in pieces.

A ripple tore through silk and sequins as heads turned. Phones lifted. Whispers collided with shouts. Chairs scraped. Someone screamed a name that wasn't answered.

Cameras found him and wouldn't look away.

No badge. No cover. Midnight suit threaded with steel. He moved down the center aisle, and nobody stepped in his way.

He didn't look at Lansing.

He walked to his mother.

Evelyn looked up at him, sovereign even with oxygen at her cheeks. "You'll burn everything."

"Then light the match," he answered.

The coughs multiplied.

A florist's cart squeaked along the mezzanine rail, white roses piled high like a disguise praying to be believed. Beneath them sat a compact dispersal unit, valved, rigged, built to turn a fundraiser into footage without ever needing a coroner.

A man's thumb hovered over the trigger.

Lena's hand found the steak knife beside her untouched plate, not with hesitation but with certainty. She felt the weight of every night she had survived, every enemy who learned too late what she was capable of. Love had forged her long before this moment.

She moved before thought could finish.

Not a throw. A thrust, vicious and exact. One stride and her arm snapped forward, driving the steak knife through the back of his hand and into the wooden lip of the flower cart. His scream tore loose, high, human, involuntary, as he twisted, desperate to escape his own pinned flesh.

"Stay," she said, leaning her weight into the hilt until nerves begged for mercy they would not get. Blood pooled fast, hot and dark, dripping over the rail.

His free hand clawed toward the unit.

Lucien was already there. He seized the man by the collar, slammed him backward into the iron rail hard enough to make bolts jump, and tore the device from his grip. A thin hiss sang against his wrist, a venomous little song that promised headlines and hysteria.

Lucien twisted the valve until metal screamed.

The hiss died.

He turned with the dead unit in his hand. "Phones down."

He didn't raise his voice. He didn't need to.

Some people lowered their phones at once. Others kept recording, hands shaking, bravery cracking under the weight of being seen.

Lansing stepped into the aisle with a host's concern and a tyrant's posture. "Ladies and gentlemen, security has the situ,"

Lucien cut in cleanly:

"Security works for whoever buys their leash." Lucien's eyes stayed on Evelyn. "Tonight, that isn't you."

Lucien's shadow fell over Lansing before the mayor realized he had stopped backing away.

Lansing's voice lowered into the shape of calm. "You ruined nothing. They'll still think this was you. Panic sells, and fear needs a face."

Lucien stepped close enough for Lansing to smell the metal on him. "You were going to spray the room. Turn their panic into proof. Make the city fear the face you chose."

Lansing straightened, clinging to authority. "This city believes what it sees."

"And tonight it sees you choking on your own story."

Lansing's eyes flicked to the cameras that were no longer his. Ghost's blackout swallowed every angle he had paid for. The narrative he'd built crumbled between breaths.

Lena kept the knife buried. "Who sent you?"

The man smiled through his teeth. "Public safety."

"Cute." She turned his face to the floor with the flat of her hand. "Try a name."

Victor took position beside the flower cart and snapped the battery from the pinhole camera none of the donors knew was watching them. The feed died without a sound.

Lucien set the cylinder on a linen-draped side table. He took a table knife, cut his palm without flinching, and smeared the fresh blood across the hazard diamond on the canister, skull, flame, gas. Then he lifted his hand and pressed it to the O in HOPE above the stage, leaving a faint print the whole room would see.

He stepped onto the ballroom floor.

"This is simple. Nobody moves. You breathe. Slow. Anyone who runs turns themselves into someone else's product."

Lansing found his public smile. "Mr. Cole, this is a charity gala."

"It still will be," Lucien said. "When you're gone."

A man stepped out of the wings, comm in his ear, hand heavy behind a lapel. He angled his body between Lucien and the room.

"So you're the one they've been whispering about."

Lucien's eyes flicked over him once, taking in the stance, the weight on his heels, the kind of bravado that broke easy.

His smirk barely moved. "And you must be Vance. Trask made you sound dangerous."

Vance's smile thinned. "You can't walk into another man's narrative."

"I brought my own."

Vance's hand twitched toward his jacket.

Lucien caught his palm mid-reach and slammed it onto the podium's edge.

Bone crunched under the weight he drove through it.

The room flinched.

Vance didn't scream. Something older than pride strangled the sound before it could exist.

Lucien plucked a folded napkin from the table, wiped the blood from his palm without breaking eye contact, and let the cloth drop onto Lansing's empty plate.

Lansing's face shifted by a single millimeter. The mask slipped.

He raised a hand toward the microphones, a reflex, a grasp for control. Lucien reached past him and killed the sound at its source, flattening the switch beneath his palm.

The room settled into a heavier quiet.

His voice cut cleaner than any weapon.

"You used my mother's breath as a prop for your story."

A ripple. Not outrage. Understanding.

"You hired men who think a city is a stage and fear is a funding model."

The donors looked at one another and didn't like what they saw.

"Tonight, your button was plastic."

Ghost in their ears: "Curtain's blind. Lansing's feed is teeth without a throat. We own the eyes in the room."

Lucien looked from Lansing to Vance.

"Your corridors belong to me now. Your footage is blank."

He took a breath. The room took his with him.

"If you want panic, look at me. If you want order, sit down."

For the first time all night, Lansing sat.

Lucien turned back to the room. "This is how it works. You stay seated. You breathe slow. You walk out in order when I tell you. The cameras outside will hear one story: a malfunction was corrected before it became a tragedy. Don't say my name if you don't want to. You'll be saying it soon enough."

He looked back at Evelyn. "Tell me to go."

"Go," she whispered. "And come back to me."

He nodded once. It landed like a vow.

He checked Evelyn's oxygen flow with the care of a man touching something holy.

The line held steady.

Only then did his hand fall away.

He looked at Lena.

Heat and promise and the cruel luck of being seen in front of everyone.

His voice dropped low enough to belong only to her. "Queen."

Lena didn't blink. Didn't bow. "King."

He turned to the room. "Nobody moves. Breathe."

They obeyed.

Chapter Thirty-Three

THE COLDEST ROOM

Outside The Atria, the city was pretending nothing had happened.

Sirens didn't scream. Headlines hadn't broken.

But in the alleys between streetlights, something had already shifted.

Most of the guests had made their way to waiting town cars. Alexander reached Evelyn quickly, Victoria with him, and they took her back to Mercy West the moment the room settled.

Rook, Logan, Victor, and Lena came up the block at different cadences, the way shadows check the light before stepping in.

Rook cut along the curb pretending to text.

Logan drifted a pace behind a couple arguing about parking.

Victor moved steady as a man with nothing to hide.

Lena let the space widen and narrow until the pattern vanished into the city noise.

Groups drew eyes.

Singles slipped past.

They met at the corner where the streetlight buzzed.

The Rezvani nosed to the curb, black glass, engine a rumble under armor. The passenger door cracked, and Lucien's voice came from the dark inside.

"In."

Rook slid into the back first, Logan after, Victor last. Lena took the front seat and closed the door, and the city slipped away.

The truck smelled like ozone, sweat, and a job that wasn't done yet. The dash was alive with Ghost's grid.

"Tonight was clean," Victor said. "No donors panicked. No headlines. Vance lost five hitters and a kitchen toy."

Logan watched the city slide across the black glass. "Clean means unfinished."

Rook stretched one arm along the back of the seat, too comfortable for a man who had just helped save a room full of people. "Let's go see how our friend Trask survived all day tied up with no food. Maybe he left us a thank-you note."

Victor's mouth twitched. "All day in a cold room will make anyone re-think life."

"Or write a recipe for vengeance," Lena said.

Lucien shifted gears, eyes on the road. "Cold room on Canal?"

Victor tapped two fingers against his knee, confirming the route before Ghost could. "Cold room on Canal."

Logan cracked a grin. "Boys' night."

Lena turned her head just enough for the front-seat silence to sharpen.

Logan lifted both hands. "Figure of speech."

Lena's lips curved. "Good. Because I brought heels, not cigars."

Ghost slipped through the dash. "Keep it boring."

Nobody believed him.

The truck rolled south. Streetlights broke across the hood like police lights with nowhere to land. On the screen the city opened for them in real time, corridors sliding past, cameras muted, dots blinking where they shouldn't.

No one spoke once the truck picked up speed. The tires worked the pavement as Ghost's signal breathed low through the dash. Beneath it, Lena heard her own pulse and the faint scrape of Victor's thumb over the safety on his sidearm. Everyone in the cabin already knew what waited at the end of the ride.

The cold room on Canal smelled abandoned, old drywall, stale ductwork, dead air rotting in the corners. Frost feathered the hinges where Victor turned the key. The lock gave too easily, as if the door had been waiting to be opened.

Inside, their prisoner was still there, rearranged into a message.

Trask's body had been folded forward at the waist and pinned to the chair, a steel rod punched through wood, spine, and concrete like a butcher's skewer. Tape still bit his wrists blue. His head hung at an angle against the wall, beneath a black-red arc sprayed up the concrete. Two black florist pins crossed where his eyes had been, neat as a signature. A white lily bloomed between his teeth, petals rimed with blood.

Victor pulled his phone from his coat as they stepped inside, camera already streaming to Ghost, a live window on everything the room wanted to hide.

The floor was a map of methodical violence. Lines of spray marked angles, not chaos. In the congealed slick, a single bootprint faced the door, heel cut to a pattern Ghost couldn't immediately place from the live feed.

"Florist pins," Ghost said. "Two black. Crossed over the eyes. They're telling us he saw something he shouldn't. Or that we did."

The cold room swallowed their breath; each step pressed against air gone stale and wet.

On the table: a square of florist's paper folded into perfect quarters, crease aligned with the grain. Five words in steady black marker:

NICE TRICK. NEXT MOVE'S OURS

Rook lifted the note with gloved fingers. Reading it was better than letting the silence do it. "They didn't give him a chance to scream."

Logan's gun came up, low, sweeping corners. "No cameras. No door alarm. Ghost,"

"Already on it," Ghost said. "They didn't move fast. They waited for the one window we couldn't see, walked in during it, and wiped themselves off the map. He's been dead for hours."

Victor crouched, eyes flat. "They knew the gap."

Ghost's voice returned. "They weren't fast. They were patient. That's worse."

Lena's stomach went cold. In their world, speed killed. Patience inherited. Her throat worked once. Lily. Flowers not as a gag, but as a mark, funeral and gala folded into one. She thought of emerald silk and a woman in ivory under a chandelier. She thought of vows and air and how the world always learned your taste before it tried to kill you with it.

Lucien didn't move. Shadows clung to his coat collar like wet ink drying. He looked at the lily, the pins, the neat bootprint. "Not cleanup," he said softly. "Instruction."

Victor held his phone out, camera angled toward the doorway, the screen flickering with Ghost's live feed.

"Hold up," Ghost said. "Back up a step. Right there."

Victor shifted his hand. The frame steadied on the doorframe.

"Yep, just what I expected. Someone taped a magnetic reed switch to the frame. Cheap. One-shot transmitter. It burst the moment you opened the door. They didn't care how long you left him; they just wanted the alert when you found him."

"Watching us watch," Rook murmured. "Classic."

Logan nudged the steel support bracket jutting from the floor where the chair had been bolted down. "You bring tools like that to stage a body, you've been in slaughterhouses or training rooms too long."

"Or politics," Victor said.

Lena took a breath that felt like a decision. "We steal air, they steal time. We can't keep letting them choose either."

In the quiet that followed, the cold room felt like a church that had learned the wrong god.

The truck's cabin held the team like a fist. No one liked the silence; no one disturbed it. Canal slid by outside, shuttered bodegas lining the block, a lone smoker under a streetlight, a dog moving like it understood the city better than its owners ever had.

"Florist paper isn't generic," Rook said, studying the note on his knee. "Watermark's a crown with a tiny serif on the right. That brand probably runs through three wholesalers in the Flower District, give or take."

"And those pins," Logan added. "Black enamel, long corsage pins. Not standard. Most venues use shorter silver ones."

Ghost grunted. "Already slicing invoices. Cross-referencing night deliveries, Civic Shield shells, city-stipend trucks."

"Boot sole?" Victor asked.

"Pattern's Vibram commando with a missing outside lug," Ghost said. "It's either custom wear or a blade cut. I'll build you a shoe out of data before breakfast."

Lucien rested three fingers on the dash as if feeling the city's pulse under it. "They found our cold room, timed our window, walked in and left a sermon. This wasn't a hit. It was rehearsal."

Lena stared at the lily on the note. "Then let's write their third act."

Lucien's lips moved half a millimeter. That counted for a smile in this weather. "We stop being reactive. We hunt."

"Where?" Victor asked. "Civic Shield hub? Flower District? Vance's handler?"

"Yes," Lucien said.

What came off the team then was simple. Permission.

Outside, the city slept like it didn't know it had been marked.

Night didn't end.

It just changed temperature.

The war floor inside Northgate sat under a low, watchful glow. Every screen looked hungry. No headlines yet. No sirens. Only the quiet before systems catch up to violence.

Ghost ran every feed they owned on a loop, back-of-house cameras from The Atria, service corridors, the mezzanine angle they had stolen before the blackout.

Grainy cellphone clips were already surfacing in group chats across the city. People coughing. Lucien tearing a device from the vents. Lena driving a knife through a man's wrist. Nothing viral yet, but the spark was there, moving through the boroughs like rumor-fire.

Victor watched a still of Trask's body on another monitor, and the smirk he'd worn earlier faded out.

"Tell me I'm not the only one asking this," he said quietly. "Are we even sure that was Civic Shield that hit Canal?"

Rook shook his head. "Shield couldn't choreograph something that clean if you stapled the plan to their foreheads."

"No," Mara said. "They didn't track the room. They tracked us."

Lucien stood with one hand braced on the table, watching a silent clip loop: Evelyn under the lights, oxygen trembling at her cheek, his blood bright against the banner behind her.

The city hadn't crowned him publicly yet, but someone was already deciding how to tear the crown off before it even settled.

A new alert slid across Ghost's interface. Not a text. A system-level push, deep encrypted and never meant for civilians.

Victor's mouth bent into something that wasn't a smile. "Spoke too soon."

Rook leaned in. "That's not Shield."

Ghost's voice cut in. "No. That's the hand behind the hand."

The message opened by itself.

Black text. White field. No timestamp.

They paint murals. They chant your name. They crown you king.

Good. That's how we draw the blade from its sheath.

Silas spoke for a room. We speak for the house.

You were never king. You were always a weapon, and weapons don't get to choose where they strike.

The Coalition.

A second file arrived. Just a thumbnail.

Ghost hesitated the width of a breath, then opened it.

The photo wasn't performance. It was ritual.

A table. Polished oak.

A single head placed dead-center like an offering.

Silas.

His body was gone, but his head had been arranged with surgical care. Two black florist pins crossed over his eyes. A white lily sat between his teeth, petals stiff with dried blood. A strip of florist's paper was wrapped tight around his jaw like a gag turned elegy.

Across the wood, written in something darker than ink:

ROOMS CLOSE. HOUSES STAND

Lena's breath caught. "Same as Trask. Same pins. Same staging. Their signature."

Imani exhaled, eyes narrowing. "So it wasn't Shield at all."

Silence pulled tight, heavy and exact.

Victor finally said what all of them knew. "We never had partners. We had handlers."

A third message followed. A single sentence:

You built walls; we built the weather, and stone always thinks it rules the storm until it drowns.

"They're not in the shadows anymore," Lena whispered.

Lucien didn't move. His eyes stayed fixed on Silas's head, the lily blooming pale between dead teeth.

"No," he murmured. "This is them stepping into the light to declare war."

The room went still in the way rooms do when everyone realizes death has learned the address.

Ghost's monitors flickered, one by one.

Not dead.

Just blinking out for a half-second each, coming back weaker.

"Signal interference," Ghost hissed. "Short burst. Intentional. They just touched every camera we own. Not enough to cripple. Enough to say hello."

Lena felt her pulse kick once, sharp. "A warning?"

Static breathed once through the speakers.

"A promise."

Lucien sat back while the war floor flickered around him. He saw Evelyn under the lights, breath thin, HOPE hanging behind her like a joke. Something cold locked into place.

"They crowned me king. And tonight, they announced the war meant to unmake me."

Chapter Thirty-Four

WAKE THE WOLF

Lucien opened his eyes to absence.

Not darkness, something emptier. A sky drained of color. A horizon without shape. The ground beneath his spine was the wrong temperature, grit biting his shoulders like glass. The silence wasn't quiet here; it had weight.

He knew this place. Or rather, his bones did. It hummed with the familiarity of a nightmare half-remembered, a world he might have lived in another life but couldn't name.

Only this time, it was different.

The air wasn't dead. It moved, thin and hollow, sliding through skeletal trees, carrying far-off screams that sounded too human to be wind. Not loud. Distant. Like a memory echoing from the end of the world.

The road beneath him was broken, buckled asphalt ghosting into dust. Trees rose on both sides in dead ranks, their bark stripped in pale, hanging ribbons. Shadows jittered in the periphery where no wind stirred them.

A sound broke the stillness.

A growl.

Ahead, a wolf stood in the road. Its coat was the color of smoke and ash, its eyes a feral yellow that pinned him in place. It didn't snarl. It simply stared, the sound rumbling in its throat like a warning the earth itself might give.

Lucien clenched his fist. If it lunged, he would meet it.

But the wolf turned, slipping soundlessly into the black line of trees. It paused once at the edge, glancing back at him as if to ask whether he would follow.

Something older than thought answered for him.

Forward.

The forest swallowed him whole.

Branches knotted above his head like ribs, blotting out what little sky there was. The trunks shifted under his gaze, faces flickering in the grain, watching, whispering, gone when he blinked. Roots curled across the path like fingers trying to trip him.

The wind carried words now, tangled and sharp:

"Wrong son... empty crown... killer king..."

He kept walking.

The forest opened into a clearing where nature had built a cathedral from ruin. Vines gripped a stone altar choked in moss, and atop it rested a single book, its leather cover split and swollen with age, its pages mottled and stained.

A Bible.

It should have rotted to pulp long ago, yet one page was impossibly untouched, the ink still black, the words still clear. At the top, the heading read:

BEHOLD, HE COMETH WITH CLOUDS; AND EVERY EYE SHALL SEE HIM, AND THEY ALSO WHICH PIERCED HIM: AND ALL KINDREDS OF THE EARTH SHALL WAIL BECAUSE OF HIM. EVEN SO, AMEN. REV. 1:7

The wind died. The forest held its breath.

Beside the altar, half-buried in black earth, rested a severed head.

Silas.

His eyes snapped open and locked onto Lucien's. His lips cracked into a rictus smile.

"You were never king," he rasped. "Only a weapon."

The trees shivered. The sky seemed to lean closer.

Then came the voice.

Faint at first, low and frayed, threading through the dead leaves.

"Lucien..."

He turned, searching the gray.

Again, louder now: "Lucien!"

His chest tightened. He knew that voice.

"Lucien!" A third time, urgent, breaking. "You have to wake up!"

The trees parted. Through the fog and skeletal branches, he saw her. Lena. Half-formed, haloed in mist, her hand outstretched, her mouth shaping his name again and again.

"Lucien, wake up!"

He ran. The forest clawed at him, branches slashing his arms, roots catching his boots. Whispers howled in his ears. The wolf growled somewhere behind him. Silas's dead eyes followed as the verse burned against the back of his mind. But none of it mattered.

Only her voice mattered.

"Lucien!"

The ground vanished beneath him.

The world shattered.

He slammed back into his body, breath ragged, heart jackhammering against his ribs. The ceiling above was no longer a colorless sky but dark rafters stretching overhead. Machines hummed low. Real air filled his lungs.

The dream was gone. The war wasn't.

"Lucien."

The voice was still there, real now, right beside him.

Lena's silhouette stood by the window, the faintest glow cutting across her cheekbone. Her voice was a whisper, but it carried more weight than any scream.

"Get over here."

He pushed himself upright, disoriented and sweating. She didn't look away from the glass.

"Look."

He was beside her in three steps. She lifted the shade a fraction. Outside, in the courtyard's dead air, three matte-black drones circled silently above the compound at different altitudes, lights dark, flight pattern controlled, their red eyes blinking like omens against the night sky. Not scouting. Marking.

Lucien's breath fogged the glass.

No sirens. No insignia. No hurry.

Lena's breath brushed his jaw. "They're not city."

He didn't answer. He was already moving.

Lucien crossed to the wall and dragged the blackout panels shut by hand, metal tracks groaning as he hauled them into place, sealing the windows in seconds.

Before he could reach the stairwell, the internal alarm pulsed once through the floor, silent to the world but loud in the bones.

Rook's fail-safe. A seismic whisper: we're being watched.

Lucien grabbed the comm set off the emergency cradle by the door, clipped it into his ear, and keyed the line manually.

"Ghost."

Rustling answered first. Then his voice came through, sharp and awake, dragged clean out of sleep by Northgate's call.

"Already on," Ghost said. "Your perimeter tripped my quiet feed. Three drones on a passive loop, low EM chatter. They pinged us at eighty-seven seconds, then tightened the loop and pinged again at sixty. They're mapping your bastion."

"Our bastion," Lena said, and the word gave the room a spine.

Lucien pulled on a shirt one-handed, holstered the pistol, jammed his feet into boots, and left them untied. His voice carried down the stairwell like a verdict.

"Up," he roared. "Now. All of you. We're under attack."

Doors snapped open. Sleep fell off the building like a skin.

Victor was first into the corridor, bare-chested, boots unlaced, a loaded mag clicking into place with muscle memory. Logan vaulted the third-floor rail instead of trusting the stairs. Mara came out already on a call. Rook moved like a man who had been waiting for this moment all his life. Imani slipped out silent and lethal.

Lena stayed at Lucien's hip, jacket over silk, ring catching the emergency glow, defiant even in the dark.

They pounded down the stairs.

Lucien re-keyed the line. "Ghost. Status."

"Not blind yet," Ghost said. "They are probing the walls first."

The lights flickered once.

Ghost's voice tightened. "There it is. Someone's jamming us. Low power, wide band. They're checking which cameras die first."

Victor's eyes moved across the feeds. "Closer than they should be."

"They always are," Mara murmured.

Screens flared blue-white. The building snapped awake.

Imani dropped her rig on the table, cables already hunting ports.

The war floor was the core, a hardened interior level set behind layers of steel and glass, built to hold when everything else gave.

Mara pulled up the city map and locked it with both hands.

Rook cracked his kit open, metal hitting steel in clean lines.

Logan took the perimeter, pacing once, memorizing angles.

Victor planted himself center mass and steadied the whole room.

Ghost's waveform rippled across the main screen. "Three drones. Tri-ro-tor, matte hull, no FAA transponder. Two are running a lazy figure-eight. The third is scanning the north wall like it's hunting for a breach point."

Logan cracked his knuckles. "We shooting them down?"

Lucien didn't look up. "No. We let them watch what we want them to watch."

"Copy," Ghost said.

Ghost hijacked the feed they were trying to steal and gave them quiet. Empty hallways. No movement.

Let the other side think the house was asleep.

On their screens, a secondary window bloomed: the falsified loop Ghost was feeding the drones. A hollow echo, repeating foyer, empty halls, false angles.

The men watching from out there would think they were reading a house.

They were reading a story.

Ghost's voice cut through the line. "This isn't a grab. It's a pressure test. They want to see how fast you move and how clean your grid is."

Victor exhaled once, slow. "We don't even know whose eyes those are."

A tremor went through the floor.

Not an explosion. A touch, like a shiver up steel.

Rook's head turned. "Sublevel. East corridor."

Imani didn't look up from her screen. "Seismic pickup says east service hatch just flexed. Not brute force. Something precise. Better bite than a crowbar."

She slid a window open with her thumb. "Bringing the basement feed online now."

Black and white. Concrete corridor. A thin ring of dust disturbed around the hatch at the far end. Then the floorline shifted, just a ripple, and heat lifted off the steel like something rising to breathe.

Ghost cut in. "They're inside your fence."

Logan's grin went feral. "Finally."

Lucien planted three fingers on the map and felt the building under them. He traced the path in his head: service hatch, east corridor, the dead angle under camera three, electrical closet, sublevel stairs, war floor door.

"Positions."

They moved without speaking.

Mara took the south windows.

Imani dropped her laptop into the grid and Ghost rode the lines the second she touched them.

Rook vanished, reappeared at the west door, and marked the lock seam with a thin run of black epoxy only he would recognize.

Logan and Victor hit the east stair, one high, one low.

Lena slipped left toward the corridor that would meet the sublevel stairs.

Lucien stayed where a king belonged, hand on the table, eyes on the feeds, voice in the wires.

"Ghost. Mute the house. Keep our ears. Feed them noise."

"On it," Ghost said. "House is deaf and polite. We're not."

A second tremor. Stronger.

The service hatch buckled a centimeter and came easy, too easy, like it had been opened before.

The camera saw nothing.

The thermal saw everything.

A heat mass slid through the crack, stretched thin, and resolved into a man.

Then a second.

The third stayed in the dark, patient enough to wait his turn.

Victor breathed once into his mic. "Door."

"Copy," Lucien said. "Let them commit to the stairs."

On the roof feed, a drone slid low and vanished behind the parapet. The camera lost it. The microphone didn't; it caught the faintest insect hum and a whisper of displaced air.

"Topside," Mara said. "I don't want a shooter coming through the skylight while we're quoting scripture."

"I'm already on your skylight," Rook said in her earpiece.

"Good," she said.

The house made breathing noises, pipes, compressors, vents. The human sound slotted in among them, a weight on a stair, a boot on concrete, cloth against stone. Enemies who believed in quiet like it was religion.

"Left," Logan whispered.

"I see him," Victor said.

The first man took the last step and died halfway through Lucien's name.

Not messy. Not loud. The kind of kill you only learn by walking through too many doors first.

Victor's hand closed, something soft cracked, and the body slid without announcing itself to gravity.

Logan caught the next one by the belt and jaw and folded him to the floor so quietly nothing in the room thought to object.

The third stopped on the third stair from the bottom and smiled.

He had found them, and he wanted them to know it.

Lucien didn't move. He watched the abandoned body-cam on the man's shoulder, the tiny lens winking like an eye that hadn't decided if it was dead yet.

"Could be building a private loop," Ghost said. "Footage they might reshape into whatever story they want told."

Lucien stepped off the map and into the corridor. He didn't take the gun. He took the knife. A small, ugly length of metal meant for proximity and answers.

"Bring him," Lucien said.

The man came anyway, slow and confident.

Logan stepped aside just enough to trap him.

Victor anchored the corridor like a weight.

The hitter took the last two stairs slow, muzzle down, shoulders loose, the posture of a man who thought losing surprise didn't mean losing control. Gloves tight. Boots with heavy tactical lugs, the outer edge sheared clean.

Lena's voice drifted in from his flank, low and cold. "Look at him."

He obeyed, and Lucien slid the tip of his knife across the camera clipped to the man's shoulder, slow enough that the lens caught its own reflection before the metal severed it.

"Let whoever sent you guess," Lena said.

The feed went dead. The only red light left in the stairwell lived in Lucien's stare.

Lucien stepped close enough for the man to feel the heat of his breath. "You think this is still your story?"

The hitter swallowed once. No answer.

Lucien tilted his head. "Who writes it, then?"

A flicker, fear or faith, hard to tell. "You don't want that name."

Lucien's mouth barely moved. "I already have it. I just want to see if you break before I say it."

Ghost's voice filled the corridor.

"Two more teams peeling off north and west. Small arms, bolt-cutters, tight spacing. Not local muscle. They move like ex military who never stopped being military. Whoever sent them is running a professional play."

"The Coalition," Mara said. It wasn't a question.

Ghost didn't argue. "Fits their spine," he said.

The hitter's smile died as if someone took it away.

Lucien tilted his head. "You brought drones to circle our roof and knives to kiss our doors and cameras to steal our faces. You came to perform."

He pressed the knife a breath deeper until the man's ribs remembered pain.

"Wrong theater."

Rook slipped past without a word.

He headed back to the war floor's west side and checked the line of epoxy he had laid along the door's lock seam, a thin, dark sheen no one outside would ever notice.

Without waiting for orders, Rook vanished up the service ladder.

"East corridor neutral," Victor said. "For now."

"Roof," Ghost said. "Talk to me."

Rook's voice came over the line, steady. "One drone clipped the roof and dropped something under the edge. I'm cutting its signal, not the device it left."

"What did it leave?" Mara asked.

"A tracker," Rook said, and crushed the transmitter between his fingers.

The screens flashed once. The house hummed twice.

Outside, the drones' lazy orbit broke, jerked, corrected, tried to find their gods again and failed.

"They'll push harder now," Imani said without looking up. "Pride is a breach tool."

"Let them," Lucien said.

Imani tapped a key and the floorplan bled to gray, corridors shifting from light to dark at her command. "If they cut the main grid, I can give you nine minutes on our own power." Her eyes flicked to the room. "After that, we're holding candles."

"Nine's a lifetime," Victor said.

"Then spend it like one," Lena murmured.

"West wall," Ghost said, timbre shifting to speed without panic. "Movement in the shadow line. Heat signatures low and staggered. Two, four, six, eight. They're hitting the lock seam with cryo spray. Flash-freezing the metal, making it brittle, cracking it clean. This isn't brute force. This is craft. This is an execution team."

Lucien didn't look up. "Then they chose the wrong house to learn in."

"Affirmative."

The first real blow landed.

A dull pop at the west wall and the sound of a steel tendon letting go.

Cold air sniffed under the door like an animal and then withdrew, satisfied.

The second pop hit the hinge.

The third woke the bars.

The fourth was silence held like breath.

"Now," Ghost said.

The building killed its own lights.

Inside, the interior circuits and the front-facing windows went dark. The yard still held its own dim spill of city power.

Dark fell like an executioner's hood.

For a heartbeat, the war floor was nothing but breath.

Then the house learned to see in its own night.

Imani's emergency rig birthed a thin red that made edges into weapons.

In that light the room looked like the inside of a beast's mouth.

The west door shifted. It moved slightly out of alignment.

Two men pressed tight against it from the outside, a two-man stack working the breach.

A gloved hand slid through the gap with a slender saw and reached for the lock.

Lucien spoke to the house. "Bite."

Rook's epoxy line along the lock seam hissed once, then hardened into a thin, invisible sheet. The saw teeth hit it and stopped cold. The man jerked, confused. Men who lived on rehearsals didn't like surprises.

The saw kept moving. It never reached the lock.

Logan moved first, fast and quiet. One arm locked around the first man's throat through the narrow breach, one twist, and the hitter went limp before he understood the fight was already over.

Victor dragged the body clear of the doorway.

The second man in the stack lunged to grab the saw, trying to finish the breach.

Mara kicked it out of his reach, metal skittering under a shelving rack.

He hesitated just long enough.

Lena fired once. The round blew the weakened hinge into shards.

The second man jerked back too slow, a raw sound tearing out of him, not strategy, just fear.

Silence fell in a circle and then got cut to ribbons.

"North wall," Ghost said. "They just went loud."

Suppressed fire stitched across the brick, controlled and disciplined. Not meant to kill. Meant to pin and probe.

"They're forcing us to react," Lena said.

Lucien watched the yard flare with muzzle flashes. "Then we take away their angle."

Imani didn't look up from the console. "On it."

The floodlights along the yard snapped dead.

The rusted work lamps over the loading bays blinked out.

The old crane above the scrap pit stood frozen in its last rusted position.

Even the motion sensors scattered throughout the courtyard went blind.

The entire compound fell into darkness except for the low red emergency wash inside the war floor.

Outside, the intruders lost their visibility in a heartbeat.

No ambient light.

No silhouettes to track.

No fallback illumination.

Just the courtyard, black and unforgiving.

For the first time tonight, the advantage shifted.

Ghost's voice dropped to a near-whisper. "They just realized what kind of room they're in."

"What kind is that?" Logan asked.

Ghost's voice dropped colder. "One that was built for this."

A dead man lay at the stairwell, folded where Logan had put him.

Lucien didn't spare him more than a look. He spoke to the room, not the body.

"This is simple. We hold. No one runs. We make them come inside. We don't give them a headline. We give them a lesson."

He didn't think of anything but the room, the walls, and the men coming to die in it. Focus sharpened him like a blade.

"Hold the house," Lena said, not loud, not soft. A benediction.

"Hold the house," came the answer, from every corner.

The west door hit for real.

Steel screamed. Hinges learned humility. Cold air slammed into warm.

"Full breach," Ghost said. "All stacks committed."

Lucien smiled without humor and stepped into the red light.

"Then let's teach them how to die politely."

The first man through the door learned the difference between a target and a stronghold.

Behind him, more shadows pressed forward, certain of their script.

The building rewrote it.

And the night decided whose doctrine would stand.

CHAPTER THIRTY-FIVE

THE HOUSE THAT HEARS

The corridors carried the smell of war.

Gunpowder clung to the air, metallic as blood drying on steel. Scorched wiring still buzzed faintly where Ghost's countermeasures had fought the last wave of the breach and nearly cooked the grid. Blood slicked the old iron seams of the floor, pooled in the gouges between century-old bricks.

Bodies slumped where they fell, some twisted, some neatly folded, all silent now.

Mara crouched over a half-ruined console, one hand trembling just enough to betray the cost. Logan wiped a smear of blood from his jaw where a graze had kissed too close. Lena dragged a sleeve across her cheek, leaving a streak of someone else's life behind. Even Ghost's voice sounded thinner in the speakers, like the night had reached him too.

Lucien walked the length of the corridor without speaking. Slow steps. Claiming every inch back from the chaos.

Northgate still stood. It had teeth in it now, but it still stood.

"This wasn't the strike," he said quietly. "This was the signature."

Near the west stairwell, Rook and Victor knelt over a man who should've been dead but wasn't. His breathing came shallow.

Half his gear had melted and rehardened where one of Rook's epoxy traps had triggered during the breach. The chemical burn had eaten through nylon and plate edges before turning glass-hard, freezing him mid-motion.

A jagged shard had sliced a bright line across his thigh. Enough to bleed him out slowly. Not enough to finish him. He had crawled maybe ten feet before Logan caught him and drove him to the concrete.

He lay on his side, pinned where they had put him, vest half-charred, one arm trapped beneath the cooled sheath.

A red failsafe clamp sat untouched on his chest plate.

Logan had ripped his hand away before he could reach it.

Victor pressed two fingers to the man's neck and felt the pulse. "Alive."

The man stirred and groaned through clenched teeth.

Logan stepped into his shadow. "Good. We need him awake."

Rook crouched closer, studying the ruined gear. "He hit the second line. Didn't expect anyone to make it past the first."

They dragged him upright. His teeth were filed flat, every edge taken down to something blunt and uniform. A sigil was carved into the skin of his wrist, not ink, not branding, but scar. He didn't blink much. Didn't look scared, either.

"Wrist," Mara murmured. "Same mark Trask had."

Logan exhaled once. "Not Shield, then."

"No," Mara said. "Something worse."

Lucien stared at the man's face and saw what was left after soldier and mercenary were stripped away. Belief. Cold, absolute, weaponized.

"Take him below."

He took Victor, Logan, Rook, Mara, and Lena with him.

Imani stayed on the war floor, fingers buried in the console's gutted wiring, eyes on the exterior feeds. She rode their audio from the sublevel through a protected copper hardline, analog and sealed, a line no signal could crawl into.

They dragged him through the wreckage and down into the cold.

Rook palmed the sublevel lock, and the system remembered him. The door slid on its seals with the soft sigh of a vault. Concrete swallowed them.

The room wasn't big. Poured walls. Floor drain. A stainless table bolted to chemical anchors.

The Faraday mesh in the paint gave the concrete a faint graphite sheen, Rook's handwriting in metal. A single camera ran on a short, closed loop.

No microphones that talked to the world.

No windows. No angles.

Victor set him into the chair and cinched the cuffs until metal bit down. Logan pressed gauze into the crease where a graze had soaked his sleeve.

He swallowed and stared at nothing, teeth pressed together so hard his neck twitched. Too young for the dead man's calm, but trained into the posture. Eyes counting exits and prayers. Breath rationed. Gloves neat.

His boots were Vibram, outside lug missing, the same wound that had smudged the cold-room floor on Canal.

Lena studied his wrist in the better light. Tally marks crossed the skin in that same obsessive hand. A single spine, then fives built off it, old muscle memory rewritten. Trask's had been older ink, more sets, edges worn to a prisoner's blue. His were darker. Newer. Fewer.

Her voice cut cool. "You knew Trask."

The kid's eye twitched. Not no. Not yes. Recognition that the name had weight in this room.

He didn't take the head of the table. He stood opposite Decker. The red wash made his shirt look darker than black, his face carved down to angle and intent.

"We don't have long," he said. "I'm going to be fair and you're going to be honest. You'll find out the difference."

Imani's fingers stayed on the patched copper line.

"Grid is clean. No RF. No bleed. If anyone is listening, they're doing it with angels and math."

"Good," Lucien said. His eyes didn't leave the prisoner. "Name."

A second passed. His mouth stayed closed like it belonged to someone else.

"Masks are for upstairs," Victor murmured. He reached across and pressed his thumb hard into a nerve below the ear. His eyes shot bright with pain. Breath hissed. He swallowed fight. He didn't break.

"Name."

Not louder. New gravity.

The kid took the breath he'd been saving and spent it. "Decker."

"Decker," Lena repeated, like deciding if it fit.

"Wrist," Lucien said. "Tell me what I'm seeing."

Silence stretched thin. Decker studied the marks like his obituary had been carved there.

The words came slowly, his voice like gravel learning to be a sentence. "It's how we start over. You come back from over there, you bring tallies with you. Numbers you think mean something."

He glanced up to measure the word in their faces. "You join the House, and you cut the old off at the bone."

He drew a slow breath, eyes hollow. "You start counting again."

Mara spoke from the corner, half a question. "The House."

"Coalition," Decker said. A tiny smile cracked like dry paint. "You call it that cause it sounds like donors and speeches. We don't. We call it home."

"The Coalition is what the city calls the room. House is what owns the rooms."

Rook leaned on the wall, arms crossed. "Home doesn't put a lily in a man's mouth."

Decker's smile twisted. "Rooms close. Houses stand."

The sentence didn't land; it settled. Lena felt it sit next to *ROOMS*

CLOSE. HOUSES STAND written across the photo Ghost had dumped on their wall. Same creed. Same hand.

Decker's voice went flat. Not pride. Inventory.

"Most of us wore uniforms first. Came back with skills the world pretended it didn't need. The House didn't pretend."

His eyes drifted toward the blood drying on his sleeve.

"They don't use gangs for work like this. Gangs are noise. Crowds. Flash. We're what comes after the room gets quiet."

Lucien watched Decker's eyes when he said it. There was no pride in them. Only devotion.

"SoHo. The sedan on Greene Street," Lucien said. "That was you."

Decker's gaze flicked to Lena, then away so fast it read as apology or fear.

"First assignment I ever got. They told me to measure you. Not your guards. Not your reach. You."

His tongue found the split in his lip again.

"Every turn she took was a page in the script they'd already written."

Lena felt her stomach knot. They hadn't been improvising. They'd been studying.

"And Trask?" Victor asked.

"Ours." Decker's tongue found the split in his lip and worried it. "We called it crosstraining. City work. He was good, less noise than most. He knew how to be a maybe."

His eyes flickered to Lucien with something close to faith. "You weren't meant to be crowned. That was never the script."

Victor folded his arms. "You think Lansing was the storm?"

A shadow of something like pity crossed the man's face. "He's weather," Decker said. "The House is climate."

"Vance?" Logan asked.

Decker almost smiled. "That's a seat, not a person. Burn one, they slide another in and tell you he was the same all along."

Victor leaned forward. "So where is he now?"

Decker's eyes flickered. Fear. Resignation. Something cracked at the edges.

"Gone," he said. "The seat emptied the second he failed you at The Atria."

A small shake of his head.

"The House doesn't wait for reports. It reads outcomes."

Lena's brow tightened. "Meaning?"

Decker drew a slow breath. "They pulled him before you even hit the street."

Imani's voice drifted through the hardline, steady but edged. "Can that be confirmed?"

Decker let out a humorless breath. "You don't need your ghost-tech for this. The House doesn't hide its lessons."

He lifted his bound hands as far as the cuffs allowed. Victor hesitated, then released one wrist just enough for Decker to reach into his pocket. His fingers shook, whether from blood loss or belief, none of them could tell.

He pulled out a phone. Not civilian. Matte black. Edges worn smooth from use. No logo. No shine. Built to disappear.

He tapped once, and the screen came alive with a vertical list of names, stacked in clean rows. No ranks. No titles. Just positions in something structured and intentional.

One name blinked red.

VANCE

Then it didn't blink. It dissolved.

Quietly. Completely.

As if erased by a god that never explained itself.

The lattice closed around the empty space like a throat closing.

Decker stared at the blank gap where the name had lived, the ghost of red still burning in his eyes.

"They show us this so we don't mistake our place."

The phone dimmed. The absence didn't.

"The House doesn't demote," Decker said, voice thinning. "It retracts."

Cold threaded down Lena's spine.

"He's gone," she said. "Just gone."

Decker nodded to himself. "He failed the room. The House closed it on him."

Victor exhaled through his teeth. "That's how they handle their own."

Decker's smile was small and ruined. "That's the mercy version."

He looked up then. Really looked.

And for the first time since they'd dragged him into the chair, the fear in him wasn't for them.

It was for himself.

"They want us to see it," he whispered. "So we remember what happens next."

No one spoke.

The phone's screen faded to black, taking Vance's existence with it, leaving only the empty space where a man had been.

"Who sits at the head of the table?" Mara asked, calm as a chalk line.

Decker shook his head. "You don't meet the head. You don't say the head. House isn't a staircase."

His gaze found Lucien, and something moved behind it. Curiosity. Fatalism.

"It's load-bearing."

He winced when Victor tightened the wrap. Fresh gauze bloomed red. The cuff bit into skin. The tally lines flared bright beneath it.

Lena stepped closer and set her palm on the table, her ring clicking softly against steel. "Why the lily for Trask? What message were you writing?"

Decker's eyes drifted toward the blank wall, as if the concrete might answer.

"We don't write messages." His eyes stayed on the blank wall. "We write warnings."

"Rooms close. Houses stand. You put your hand on a door you weren't given, the House makes sure it closes on you. Pins in the eyes so he can't see. Flower in the mouth so he can't speak. That's a sacrament."

"Who knew we stashed him on Canal," Imani said over the copper. "No network. No chatter. Someone still found him."

Decker let out a thin laugh. "You think we exploit pings," he said. "You still don't get it."

"Enlighten me," Lucien said.

Decker leaned forward, lowering his voice like the concrete might overhear.

"You think you're safe because metal keeps signal out. It doesn't matter. House doesn't listen for signal."

He looked up, something hollow behind the stare. "It listens for decisions."

He said it like scripture.

It landed like one.

Lucien didn't move, but the sentence found a place beside every wound the city had taught him.

"How?" he said.

Decker shrugged. For a second, he looked young.

"You want a wire in the wall," he said. "You want a device. We're not tech, Mr. Cole. We're doctrine. You make a choice in a room, where to stash, who to trust, and somewhere, someone isn't sleeping. The House adjusts."

He shook his head, like he remembered being taught and never being given the option to refuse.

"It isn't mystic. It's reach. It's hands."

"Hands," Victor echoed. "Like yours."

"I'm a finger," Decker said. "They don't let us be hands."

Lena's question slid gentle and exact.

"Did you come tonight for snatch," she said, "or spectacle?"

"Neither," Decker said, almost offended. "We came for proof."

"Of what?" Logan asked.

"That your kingdom is a room," Decker said, smiling like a disciple at prayer. "And rooms close."

Lucien let the quiet be long enough to change shape.

"You don't have long," Decker said.

The temperature in the room lowered in a way metal couldn't explain.

His eyes weren't on the door anymore. He was staring at the ceiling, like something lived beyond it and the idea hurt.

"They saw I walked into this. They always see. They always come."

"This room is scrubbed," Imani said, steady as a heartbeat. "Faraday mesh. Analog lines. Closed loops. Nothing leaks."

Decker laughed. Bigger this time. It frayed at the edges. "You still don't get it. You think copper saves you. You think they need my voice. They needed the moment I chose to be here."

His teeth showed. "You can duct-tape the world. They'll still find the shape of the decision."

Lena saw the tremor start. Left thumb. Then eyelid.

Something steady was burning itself down to wire.

He wasn't looking for an exit anymore. He was looking for a way not to be present for what he believed was already walking down the hall.

Lucien eased his voice. "Decker."

Weight in the name.

"You still have a choice. You can keep being a finger pointing where they tell you. Or you can put that hand on the scale."

Decker didn't hear mercy. He heard math.

"You broke the city for eighty-three seconds. You woke the House. You think that makes you king."

The smile returned. Same shape as fear.

"You're just noise they can aim."

Lena's eyes dropped to his hand. "You're shaking."

Not pity. Fact.

"I know what happens to people who talk in closed rooms. It's not a bullet. It's like the air stops recognizing you."

His eyes flicked to the corners. "I'd rather pick my door."

Victor's voice tightened. "Search him again."

Logan was already moving.

Too late.

Decker's free hand snapped to the seam inside his burned vest, fingers vanishing beneath melted nylon and plate.

Rook's face changed. "Holdout."

Lucien saw the shape come free. Small. Flat. Ugly. A last-door gun, built for one decision.

"Decker."

He held it low against his own ribs, turned inward.

"Tell me the name above Vance," Lucien said. "Who writes 'Rooms close. Houses stand.'"

Decker swallowed. "You want a head. We don't say heads."

His gaze ticked to Lena. Not for forgiveness. Just acknowledgment.

"We call him House."

"You already said that," Mara said.

Decker's eyes stayed on Lucien.

"I said it like a place. I mean it like a person."

He never aimed at them.

He aimed at the only thing left that was his.

His eyes found Lucien. Then Lena. Then nothing.

"They already know. They always know."

Lena stepped forward. "Decker."

He smiled. Not brave. Not bitter. Just tired.

"Better the devil I choose."

The muzzle rose to the hollow beneath his jaw.

Lucien moved, palm open. "You're not theirs anymore."

Decker's eyes shone. "I never stopped being theirs. I just stopped pretending."

His finger tightened.

The shot was small in the room. And enormous in the skull. A single, vicious cough of thunder that punched the air out of every lung that heard it.

The bullet took the shortest path it could find between regret and silence.

Blood left him in a brief, upward sigh, warm mist catching the overhead light for one heartbeat before gravity remembered its job.

It rained down across the tally marks carved into his wrist; black ink washed suddenly, violently red; then drained to nothing.

The chair legs scraped once as the body sagged, cuffs singing their last metallic note against the ring.

Then even that stopped.

He lay on his side like a soldier whose war had finally run out, one hand still cuffed to the chair, the other finally, mercifully free.

No one spoke. The room simply adjusted its breathing to make space for the new quiet.

From the hardline panel, Imani's voice came thin and careful. "North-gate's clean. No signals out."

Mara stared at the small lake spreading across the concrete, at the way the overhead bulb painted it the color of dark wine.

"No one chooses an exit like that for nothing."

Lena reached across and pressed Decker's hand flat on the steel.

Not mercy. A test.

His fingers twitched once. Then they didn't.

Her gaze climbed the tally marks. Old war turned to new doctrine. The same chill she'd felt in the florist's basement crept back. Different delivery. Same sermon.

Saying it out loud shifted the air.

"Trask wasn't Shield. He was House. Decker was House. So were the men at Atria. Lansing's not building the room. He's renting it."

Victor scrubbed a palm down his face. "We keep thinking agencies. They're congregations."

Logan stood very still. For him, that was a warning.

"He said the House listens for decisions. What did we just decide?"

Blood found the drain.

Not straight. Never straight.

It split around bone, hesitated at the cuff still locked to the chair, then slid on.

Lucien set his palm on the steel table and felt the cold bite through skin.

Sixty seconds.

That was all it took for a man to choose his exit and for the room to remember it was mortal.

He saw the ruined Bible again. The untouched page. The verse.

Prophecy never arrived gentle, he thought.

He looked up.

His voice came low and precise.

"Bag the hands. Print the soles. Photograph every tally."

He turned his head toward Rook.

"Burn the footage into something that survives fire. Nowhere else."

Rook moved without a word.

Lucien stepped to Lena's side.

The overhead bulb struck her ring and flung gold back into red.

He didn't touch her. The air between them held enough.

"He didn't think we could keep him," Lena said.

"He didn't think it mattered," Lucien answered, eyes still on the table.

The hardline crackled. Imani came through.

"Multiple city feeds just blinked. That wasn't a breach. It was alignment."

Mara frowned. "Alignment with who?"

"Not with us," Imani said.

Ghost slid into the channel.

"The 'Special Council' Lansing floated? They just got a private switchboard. The press will call it coordination. The House will call it a choir."

Logan exhaled. "They're tuning the city."

"Rooms close," Victor said.

"Houses stand," Lena finished. She was still looking at the tally marks. "Not tonight."

Lucien set his hand over hers. Not tenderness. Structure.

"We flip the doctrine."

Mara's voice came quiet but steady. "Into what?"

"Nothing gets out. Nothing gets through. Not a slogan. A law."

Imani's fingers moved across copper lines. "I'll need fresh diagrams."

Rook zipped the body bag. Logan and Victor lifted the weight like it belonged to them.

Lena turned the spent bullet casing once against the steel.

"The House listens for decisions," she said.

"Then let's make one they can't live with," Lucien answered.

Above them, a tremor ran through the steel. Small. Intentional.

The building felt it and didn't flinch.

They stood one breath longer with doctrine cooling at their feet.

Then the war resumed.

Chapter Thirty-Six

THE BLOOD CROWN

Northgate's bones weren't screaming anymore. They were remembering.

Gunshot haze hung thin in the vents. Blood sketched dark constellations along the seams of old steel. Someone had righted a chair and left a handprint on its back, five red fingers drying toward rust.

The building breathed like a cathedral after vespers. Hushed. Haunted. The air thick with everything no one had said.

Lena stood over the steel table where Decker had chosen his door.

His body was gone now, taken upstairs to be dealt with alongside the rest of the dead. Still, the air here felt carved by him.

When she closed her eyes, she saw the tally marks on his wrist. Scar tissue raised and angry. A history rewritten into skin.

She knew she would always see them.

"It wasn't a message." Her voice didn't sound like it belonged to this room.

Victor glanced up, a strip of gauze ghosting his knuckles. "What was it?"

Her gaze swept the blood on the floor, the empty cuffs, the space where Decker's body had been. "It was a census. A record. Proof the House is counting. Not just the dead. Us. Every step we take. Every breath we think is ours."

Logan paced the dark. His boot tracked a smear and kept going.

"We didn't just take a swing at a crew. We declared war on a religion."

One of the interior screens flickered and steadied.

Ghost's voice arrived.

"External feeds are aligning again. Not pushing. Listening. Streetcams tilt a few degrees every time we move. City maintenance reroutes crews when we reach for a door. They aren't trying to get in. They're waiting for us to choose."

Imani's voice came thin over the copper line.

"Call it decision telemetry. We choose, they breathe. We hesitate, they blink. The House doesn't respond. It pre-responds."

Lena kept her eyes on the steel.

"They don't need microphones. Not if they already know what we'll say."

Lucien hadn't spoken since the shot.

At the west door, where the steel wore a fresh dent, he stopped.

"This wasn't their strike. This was scripture to them."

He looked at them. "So we burn it."

No one mistook the sentence for heat. It was a command. His voice cleared the hall and left only direction.

On the wall, Ghost threw up a map. Veins of light ran through the city. Heat clustered where the House was building pressure. Cold spread where it had quieted the streets on purpose.

"If they're listening for choices," Imani said, "let's make one."

Lena looked at Lucien. He had nothing left of sleep on him. Only resolve, and the shape of a crown you don't wear on the skull, but carry in the spine.

"If you want a king, be one."

He turned to the table and pressed his palm into the steel. The red emergency light stamped his handprint against it like a seal.

"Open the wire," he told Ghost.

"To who?"

"To everyone."

A choice this time. Not a leak.

Ghost didn't argue.

Lucien lifted his head and gave the city his eyes through the building's cameras. No preamble. No brand. Just a man who had stepped out of a rumor and refused to return.

"This has two pages. You're on one. The House is on the other. They think their page is scripture, untouchable, ordained. They think ours is graffiti, angry, meant to be scrubbed away."

He leaned closer, letting the camera take him in full.

"Kings move the board."

He didn't sign it. He didn't need to.

Ghost opened the line.

The city twitched.

Not murals. Metrics.

CDN logs spiked. Dead group chats woke. Three encrypted channels that had never named each other pushed the same six-second clip: a crown emoji, nothing else.

Scanner chatter shifted codes. Units rerouted for crowd control that did not exist yet. Streetcams outside Northgate ticked two degrees and held.

On the Council's private press line, a draft appeared.

CONDEMN ANONYMOUS INCITEMENT

It vanished.

"We're in the bloodstream," Ghost said, voice low. "No art yet. Just pulse."

By the hours before dawn, the city had started to answer in paint and paper.

Chalk crowns bloomed at curb height where tires had washed this past winter's grief away. Underpasses wore a new square stencil, four dark blocks on white, three words beneath:

MOVE THE BOARD

Civic Shield decals peeled from light poles and reappeared on trash lids. Open palms stamped over them in cheap ink.

WE DECIDE

None of it was neat. All of it was fast.

Victor didn't smile. He did something rarer. He let his shoulders drop a fraction, like the weight had finally found somewhere to land.

"Reckless."

"Necessary," Logan answered.

The word closed the room.

Imani's fingers chased the copper paths. "I can build you a decoy decision," she said. "A false plan with tells meant to be found. If the House is listening for choices, let's hand them one they can't ignore."

"Do it," Lucien said. "Make their weather system chase a storm that isn't real."

From the mezzanine, Mara's voice drifted down, steady.

"They escalate when they're embarrassed. You want them angry, not cautious."

Lucien's mouth twitched.

"Good. Maybe then they stop thinking they're the sky."

He turned to Lena.

Not for approval. For alignment.

"Decoy is live," Imani reported. "I seeded breadcrumbs into six of the

House's listening posts. The fake plan says we're shifting north to intercept one of their courier lines near the waterfront. If their whole doctrine is prediction, let's see which prophet flinches first."

The external map pulsed once.

Then the city answered.

Streetlights along Pier 19 flipped from amber to white. Three surveillance drones changed altitude in perfect sync. Two Civic Shield vans rerouted toward the docks without a single call being placed.

As if an invisible hand had traced new lines through the air, and the city obeyed.

"They took the bait," Lena whispered.

Lucien's gaze didn't leave the screen.

"Good. Now trace it. Every adjustment. Every reroute. If they just showed us their teeth, we break the jaw."

The east wall screens bled into morning footage. Grainy. Unfiltered.

Altars lined stoops and curbs, candles still burning in the blue dark before sunrise.

A chalk crown marked a doorway, the one yesterday's rain hadn't washed away.

A boy in a hood brushed a fingertip over the crown, like he wanted to know why it lasted.

Murals climbed brick and underpass. And where the paint dried rough and fast, the same message rose again:

MOVE THE BOARD

Victor exhaled once.

"You really want to ride this?" he asked. "You really want to put your face on a weather report?"

Lucien didn't blink.

"The House told us to be the hand and not the king. They forgot who moves pieces."

Ghost cut in, voice level but tightened at the edges.

"Heads up. Decoy drew them, as predicted. We just got another tremor."

"Where?" Victor asked.

"Everywhere that matters. House signals lighting up across the grid. They're repositioning shooters around a municipal maintenance yard five blocks from an old Union distribution hub. They think it's our play. It isn't. But it tells us where they count."

Logan shrugged into his jacket.

"How do you want it?"

Lucien studied the map. The intersection where the House had just, unknowingly, planted its foot.

"Louder than their cameras."

Mara already had the phone to her ear.

"One vehicle. No plates. No convoy. We go in as a rumor and leave as smoke."

Victor racked the slide on his pistol. Metal snapped into place.

"The hour's chosen."

They moved.

Sunday morning wore a quieter skin, the kind that looked like night pretending to end. The city moved slower, as if even its ghosts slept in. Storefront gates stayed down an hour longer. Delivery vans idled at corners without honking. A priest on Delancey walked alone with his homily in one hand and a cigarette in the other. The sun hadn't risen yet, just a pale seam on the horizon, thin as breath, promising light it hadn't delivered.

Lucien drove through that stillness, the hour when the city pretended it could be forgiven, and planned how to spill blood after sunrise.

They parked wrong. No one stopped them.

The municipal yard looked like every place a city hid its sins, dull razors on the fence, floodlights straining, signs that promised nothing but liability.

Ghost's voice cut in.

"Two cameras on swivel. One dead blind under the east pole. Heat signatures in the main shed, four moving, two seated like they believe chairs keep bullets out."

"Failsafes?" Lucien asked.

"Someone wired the breaker to a panic strobe," Imani said. "You trip it, the cameras go full white and your retinas get rewritten."

"Then we don't trip it," Lena said.

Logan slid along the fence and became a hinge.

Rook cut the wire clean, a breath disguised as motion.

Victor went first because doors were made for his shoulders.

Lucien didn't crouch. He didn't shrink for men. He descended, unhurried, like a shadow that chose its own height.

The shed's breath came hot and oily. Pallets rose like tombs. Crates marked as city property wore their lies badly. House symbols lived inside the letters if you knew how to squint.

The men at the table wore the same quiet arrogance Decker had carried into the world.

Lena tilted her chin toward the far wall.

"Fold the light."

Two suppressed pops answered her. The floodlights died without drama, and the dark folded in on itself like a broken stage.

The first guard reached for a radio that wasn't there anymore; Logan had stepped through the light and lifted it on his way past. Victor met the second at the corner and introduced his face to steel.

The third tried to bring a rifle into a conversation Lucien's pistol was already controlling. Lucien tapped the muzzle with his palm, redirected it, and let the round find the ceiling. Then he put the man on his knees and made the floor remember weight.

Two more came out of a side room dressed in city orange, guns under municipal virtue. Lena shot the first in the hinge of his shoulder and the gun spun away. The second raised his weapon and a blade punched through his wrist before he understood why. He screamed, not loud. Human.

"Lights," Ghost said. "You have ninety seconds before they wonder why this block stopped pretending to exist."

Lucien walked to the nearest crate, read the label WATER METER COUPLINGS, and laughed once without humor. He jammed his fingers under the lip and pried it open.

Inside the first crate: rifles, four to a bed in foam cut with care. Beneath them, stacks of cash bound with bands stamped by a bank that hadn't touched cash in ten years. Beneath that, paperwork, permits, sign-offs, the city signing its name to silence.

He moved to the next. Drones, sleek little killers with enamel-black bellies and glassy eyes. Then cases of filters. Then a roll of pendant cameras like pretty jewelry with ugly intent.

"Proof," Victor said, low.

"Spectacle," Lucien corrected.

He found a five-gallon can tucked behind a stack of pallets. Accelerant.

He dragged it free. The metal edge of a splintered pallet scraped his forearm, shallow and hot. He didn't look.

Logan met his eyes. "We torch the cash or the fuel?"

"Both," Lucien said, and dropped a match.

The flame took the room like it had been waiting.

Heat climbed fast. The firelight stretched their shadows into giants. It pulled the guards' faces open, every regret laid bare in the glare.

On the back wall, Lena grabbed a spray can from a shelf, the kind used to mark cable paths, and pressed the nozzle down. Red paint hissed across gray.

She left six words for them:

THE HOUSE BLEEDS WHEN IT LISTENS

She paused. Looked at Lucien. He finished the sermon.

LAW DOESN'T KNEEL

Sirens woke three blocks over.

The remaining floodlights blinked out when Ghost cut the yard's grid. The perimeter dropped into deeper dark, brushed at the edges by the first light of morning.

Heat shimmered along the ceiling, bending the air into ghosts. The sprinklers considered it. Then changed their minds.

Victor dragged a corpse to the door and tossed it into the cold like garbage returned to the curb.

Logan kicked a case across the floor. It burst open. Money lifted into the fire, paper flurrying like sacrament.

"Time," Ghost said.

The word carried a grin he wasn't wearing. "You just put a knife in the city's pocket."

They left the way they came. Wrong and quiet.

In the rearview, the yard became a furnace. Inside it, the House's careful symmetry melted into anonymous ash.

Back in the car, Ghost rode the wiring, translating in real time.

"Redeployments across four boroughs. Civic Shield standing down where it matters and flooding where it doesn't. Coalition chatter just escalated. You've been moved from nuisance to priority."

Lena leaned back, firelight fading from her skin as the city took its place.

"They'll call this terrorism," she said.

"They'll call it treason," Logan said.

"They'll call it prophecy," Victor said.

Lucien watched the mirrors. He watched the dark. He watched the small parts of himself that still wanted a ledger to confirm what the street already had.

"They'll call it what they want. We'll answer."

The phone on the dash lit without ringing. Not a call. A picture. Someone had snapped his wall in the burn, letters scorched into concrete, the hiss of the paint still alive in the shot.

Below it, a caption in a stranger's hand:

KINGS MOVE THE BOARD

Lena's hand found his, fingers lacing with the casual inevitability of people who had learned they were each other's horizon. Her ring pressed bone. He liked that it hurt.

"Without the money?" she said softly. "Without the networks?"

"A king doesn't need a vault. He needs the city willing to move."

Behind them, the yard collapsed inward, a star burning out.

Ahead, in eight places he could name and ten he couldn't, the city began to kneel without kneeling. Shrines rose where murals once mourned. Doors opened. Men who owed men who owed men took markers out and crossed off debts, because fear had found a new address.

Ghost cut in over the engine's hum. "Coalition just moved their next session off-grid. Closed site. No shell. They think underground means invisible."

"Nothing is invisible," Lucien said. "Not today."

Northgate's silhouette lifted out of the dark ahead, battered and standing, a house that had decided it would be a kingdom.

Chapter Thirty-Seven
THE QUIET BETWEEN WARS

Morning light cut across the war floor in thin, cold stripes. Nobody had slept. Coffee sat untouched beside keyboards. Ghost had muted every alarm but left the screens alive. CityCast ran the same overnight segment on a loop.

Not chaos.

Not the truth.

Just the version the city had been allowed to keep.

A still frame of The Atria entrance under emergency lights. Overnight replay. Paramedics escorting coughing donors toward ambulances. Security guiding guests down velvet runner carpets now stained with spilled champagne and fear. A reporter pressing a mic too close to a trembling donor in an evening gown. A councilman shielding his face from the camera with a program he'd signed minutes earlier.

It wasn't footage that showed violence.

It was footage that showed failure.

Mara muted the segment the moment Lansing's face appeared.

"Let it play," Lucien said.

She unmuted.

Lansing stood on the City Hall steps in a navy suit that fit like a lie. The podium bore the city seal; two public safety commissioners flanked him like furniture. No questions allowed.

"Last night's brief equipment malfunction at The Atria," he began, "was contained within minutes. An over-responsive air-quality sensor triggered a false alert. At no time were donors or patients in danger. We thank the oncology community for their continued generosity and calm."

Imani snorted. "He didn't even blink when he said it."

"His eyelids are unionized," Rook said.

Lansing kept going, smooth as laminated paper.

"The contractor responsible for the ventilation irregularity has been placed under review. Civic Shield's rapid presence ensured order, and we remain committed to transparency as we evaluate the system's performance."

Logan leaned back in his chair. "Translation: blame the AC guy."

Ghost's voice slid through the speakers. "I intercepted the internal memo. They're banning the word 'incident.' Official term is now 'HVAC irregularity.' Anyone who says otherwise gets pulled off comms rotation."

Lansing pressed a hand to his chest. Rehearsed sympathy.

"I want to assure the public there was no threat, no intentional harm, and no ongoing danger to anyone in this city. Civic Shield acted swiftly, professionally, and I personally commend their response."

Victor leaned forward. "He's doing it. He's burying the whole thing alive."

Lena watched without blinking. "He's not apologizing. He's performing."

On-screen, donors stood behind barricades, eyes wide, breaths shaky. Lansing pretended he didn't see them.

"I understand the fear many of our honored guests experienced," he continued. "Especially those with medical vulnerabilities. For them, I offer my deepest apology for the distress caused."

Lucien didn't react. He'd gone still.

"We're launching a full internal review," Lansing said. "If a malfunction occurred, we will find it. If protocols failed, we will fix them. This city must remain a place where its sick, its vulnerable, and its strongest citizens can gather without fear."

He offered a practiced smile that never reached the edges.

Lucien's gaze stayed locked on the screen.

"He thinks if he names it small, it becomes small."

"No," Lena murmured. "He thinks if he names it small, we'll play small."

Then Lansing shifted his stance, that tell he didn't know he had, the one he used right before sliding a knife between numbers and calling it policy.

"On a related note, we're accelerating our Civic Shield expansion initiative. More officers, updated training protocols, and an integrated rapid-response division to ensure these rare irregularities are handled quickly and calmly."

Logan's eyebrow climbed. "Translation: more boots. Bigger boots."

Lansing kept going, smooth as wet marble.

"Civic Shield will also be entering its next operational phase. We'll continue adding additional tactical support teams in the weeks ahead, expanding our presence citywide to help safeguard residents and assist law enforcement in stabilizing high-risk areas."

Mara's mouth tightened. "There it is."

Victor leaned forward, grim. "Building a private army in broad daylight."

Lansing continued. "To address unrelated reports of overnight disturbances across several boroughs, our administration has confirmed there is no coordinated threat. These incidents are being handled individually, and there is no risk to the wider public."

Lansing ended with a line meant to reassure, but it landed closer to threat: "The city remains safe. We urge residents to continue their day without concern."

Ghost killed the feed.

Silence tugged at the room.

Victor cracked his knuckles once. "He's burying the body before the autopsy."

Lucien exhaled, slow. "Let him. He just taught the city to look the other way."

Lena met his eyes. "Then we teach them how to look again."

The morning held its breath around them, waiting to see which truth would win.

Northgate settled into the hush of an old church after the last hymn.

The bodies were gone by first light, but the building still stank like a slaughterhouse left in the sun.

Rook and Victor had hauled them out in the dark and sealed what was left into six drums behind the scrap pile, all of it tucked beneath Ghost's blind loop. Fifteen men reduced to anonymous weight and a smell that would thicken by noon.

Weld-light stuttered against the brick as Rook crouched at the breached service plate. Sparks skittered across the floor and died.

Along the south wall, Imani and Mara rebuilt the nervous system. Doors rerouted to manual. Cameras forced local. A half-dead row of monitors buzzed over coffee gone cold.

Logan sat on the mezzanine rail, gauze taped to his neck, smirking at the ache in his shoulder.

Victor retaped his knuckles, pulling each wrap tight, smoothing it down with his thumb.

The war floor was awake, but the people in it moved on whatever lived between instinct and exhaustion, the strange hour where fatigue sharpened everything instead of dulling it.

Lena came down the steps with a field kit and a look that said this world could bleed and still be made clean.

Lucien waited at the base of the stairs, jacket peeled to the elbows, quiet in the way men were quiet when they'd already made dangerous choices and lived past them.

"You're cut."

In her mouth, it meant I see you.

He looked down as if only now remembering the line on his forearm, a shallow kiss of metal, not worth a report.

She swabbed it with antiseptic. He didn't flinch, but he watched her hands the whole time.

She taped a small square of gauze into place and smoothed it twice, the second pass more tenderness than bandage.

"Consider yourself patched."

"Do I get a sticker?"

"You get a pulse. For now."

He caught her wrist, light but certain, before she could pull away. The ring caught the first light of morning and threw it back at both of them. A small, private smile touched his mouth and vanished.

Above them, Rook lifted his mask and inspected the seam he'd welded shut.

"She'll hold," he said, voice warm with metal and certainty. "Loud or quiet, they'll have to work for it next time."

"Clever's the only way they know," Imani added from the console. "So I rewrote our door protocols. They won't slip through the same cracks twice."

Mara tore a strip of tape with her teeth and pinned another corridor onto the map.

"We're on independent power now. If the House so much as exhales in our direction, we'll hear the breath."

Logan checked the time and let his foot tap the air. "Anybody else want to pretend sleep is a thing?"

"Sleep's a rumor," Victor said. "Like mercy."

The phone in Lucien's pocket buzzed, low and insistent. Not an alarm, not a code.

He glanced at the screen.

Alexander.

He stepped into the shadow of a pillar, turned just enough for privacy, and thumbed the call open.

"Dad."

"Lucien." Alexander sounded like a man who had survived many kinds of storms and learned which ones answered and which ones didn't. "We're at Mercy West. Your mother's updated scans are back."

Lena's eyes flicked to Lucien's and held. He tilted the phone slightly, a gesture that said listen without saying the word. She came closer, shoulder to his.

"How is she?" Lucien asked.

"She's herself," Alexander said, which meant the truth. There was news and it wasn't kind, and still Evelyn had woken with her chin up. "The numbers aren't what a man prays for, but they're not a verdict either. Her doctor wants us to pick a window, sooner rather than later. We can talk about that when I see you."

Lucien's mouth went still.

"There's something else." The words dipped into that rare softness that made Lucien feel, for a fleeting second, like a boy again.

"There's a place up north. The Vale of Saint Arden. Forty-five minutes, maybe less. Stone and cedar over a river, tucked into a quiet fold of the hills. Your mother and I stood there once, years ago, and promised each other a life. We said till death do us part, and right now I'm fighting that part with everything in me."

He paused, the silence beneath him heavy with years.

"I thought, what better place for my son and the woman he loves to promise eternity? The air up there is clean, the kind that makes lungs remember what they were built for. It will be good for everyone."

Then, quieter still:

"Tomorrow isn't promised, Lucien. Not in the world you walk in, and not in the one I once did. And it may not be promised for your mother, either. So let's start making moves now, while now is still ours."

The line held for a beat, then softened into something warmer, something close to hope.

"And if we're choosing windows, your mother would like to look at one that faces a wedding."

Lucien's throat tightened before he spoke.

"You think she's ready for that?"

"She's the one who asked if you and Lena could meet us there," Alexander said. "This morning. No speeches. Just walk the ground and see if the future can stand there."

Lucien let the silence stretch long enough to mean respect and not fear.

"Text me the address. We'll be there."

"She'll like that," Alexander murmured. His voice had a gentleness Lucien still wasn't used to, the kind a man grew into after years of not knowing how to speak to his own son. "And tell Logan the road up there isn't a racetrack. If he puts a wheel wrong, he'll answer to me."

A ghost of a smile touched Lucien's mouth.

"He'll take that, as a dare."

"I know," Alexander said, and hung up before sentiment could be mistaken for weakness.

Lucien slid the phone into his pocket and looked at Lena.

"My father wants us up north. Where he and my mother were married. Today. Just to walk the ground."

Lena's nod was small and fierce. "Then we bring them with us. We stop at Mercy West. I walk her to the car myself."

"I like that."

"And Logan stays here," she added. "Let him keep the grid breathing while we go be people."

Lucien's mouth tipped. "He can mind the city."

She found his hand. "No convoy. Just family. The armor stays with the car."

"Family," he echoed.

Lucien pulled his phone, thumb already moving. He typed a short message and showed her the screen before sending it.

Change of plans. We're on our way. We'll ride up together

The message blinked sent.

Lena exhaled once. "Good."

Logan strode in, palms slapping together once.

"You two go play fairy tale in the woods. Try not to get married ahead of schedule. We'll keep the monsters fed."

Victor's mouth ticked. "If anything catches fire, I'll let it burn politely."

"Leave the east cameras on a local loop," Imani added, already moving to a new panel. "I don't want the House learning our faces in better light than we deserve."

Rook flipped his mask up and wiped a streak from his cheek. "I'll keep the doors remembering who owns them."

Mara packed a coil of cable into a tight circle.

"I'll keep the lights honest."

Then, to Lucien, softer:

"Bring her back smiling."

Lucien met her eyes. "That's the plan."

On the way to the stairs, with Northgate moving again around them, Lena paused and pulled Lucien into the narrow slice of shadow between two columns. There, with the day not yet fully born and the night not yet fully dead, she put her forehead to his chest and let herself hold still.

"You sure we should be thinking about vows," she asked without lifting her head, "when they're sharpening knives?"

He put a hand in her hair, gentle where he was never soft.

"Because they're sharpening knives. We write our oaths louder than their threats. We promise the thing they're trying to steal."

She breathed him in, steel, smoke, that faint clean cut that meant adrenaline fading. When she looked up, the doubt had been filed down to purpose. "Then we go."

They climbed. The building watched them go with the quiet patience of an old warhorse, steel bones and tired eyes following a son stepping out to chase the next chapter.

At the top of the stairs, Lucien stopped and looked back along the length of the war floor. The weld-sparks were dying down to cooling orange. The map. The red wash along steel. The men and women who had decided his life was a good place to put theirs.

"Inside lives," he said quietly.

Lena answered first.

"Inside lives."

Then the room found it, low and uneven, a creed being born in real time.

"Inside lives."

They stepped into the morning.

The city in the distance hadn't woken to its own headlines yet.

There was only the bright sweep of light over the river, and the low murmur of a world pretending it didn't know the war humming beneath its skin.

The truck waited where they had left it, its tinted windows catching the waking sky and hardening it into something sharper.

They crossed into the courtyard.

The iron gate wore fresh scars. The city wore old ones.

Lucien opened the passenger door for her with a courtesy he never forgot, even when the ground moved. Then he rounded the hood and slid behind the wheel.

The engine woke like a predator deciding to stretch.

Logan leaned over the rail above and called down, all dry sarcasm.

"Bring back pictures. Hell, set the date while you're there."

Victor lifted two fingers in a soldier's blessing that wasn't a prayer so much as permission.

"See you later."

They pulled out into a world trying on forgiveness for a day.

Lena reached over the console and laced her fingers through Lucien's, their hands a small architecture of promise under a sky that had not yet chosen its weather.

"Ready?"

He glanced at her. At the ring. At the road.

"Always."

He took the turn that would carry them down the river toward Mercy West. Toward his mother's eyes. Toward a quiet place forty-five minutes north where a future might learn to stand.

Behind them, Northgate's lights steadied.

Ahead, the sun climbed the edge of the skyline and put a crown on the city it didn't deserve, and on the man who had decided to wear one anyway.

For the first time in hours, he felt something different from war.

Something heavier.

And somehow softer.

Something like a life beginning anyway.

Chapter Thirty-Eight

A ROAD BACK NORTH

Mercy West wore its Sunday quiet like gauze.

The automatic doors breathed and closed. A volunteer wheeled a cart of paperbacks past a row of sleeping televisions. Somewhere, a machine kept time for someone who couldn't.

The Rezvani idled at the curb, a black animal made polite for the day.

Spring had come, but the morning still carried a thin chill that lived in the shade and under trees.

Lucien stepped from the Rezvani as the hospital doors parted and let the hospital air spill into the street.

Evelyn came first, not out of ease, but insistence.

Alexander moved at her side without touching. When she faltered, his hand was simply there, the way a banister existed for one exact step and no other.

She was radiant in a way that had nothing to do with health. Ivory scarf. Fine bones. That wry light that made nurses obey and doctors explain themselves.

Lena was already moving, wordless care, a soft blanket from the back seat, her palm at Evelyn's elbow. The kind of steadiness that didn't announce itself because it never had to.

Evelyn's fingers found Lena's and squeezed once, gratitude folded inside mischief.

"Don't look at me like I'm made of spun glass," Evelyn murmured. "I'm not glass, Lena. I'm decisions."

"You're trouble," Alexander said, and the love in it hurt.

"Trouble needs air," she replied. "And views."

They settled her gently into the back seat. Lena tucked the blanket and lifted the oxygen line so it wouldn't catch. Lucien adjusted the vent without being told, the reflex of a son still learning to measure rooms by his mother's breath.

"Where's Victoria?" he asked, glancing toward the doors. "Thought I'd see my sister before we took off."

"She's been here every minute they allow," Evelyn said, a soft smile touching her mouth. "Today she let herself step outside."

Alexander glanced at Lucien. "Some friends wanted to see her. She needed a day to remember she's more than worry."

Evelyn tilted her chin, that old sovereign angle returning like a crown she hadn't misplaced. "Then let's go," she said. "The day won't wait for us to be brave."

Alexander claimed the front seat. The door closed on the hospital's noise, and the city's slower heartbeat took over.

They rolled away, four people and a future that felt both fragile and inevitable, heading north into air that promised to hold them a little longer.

The city shifted gears around them.

It wasn't the hush of dawn anymore. It was Sunday mid-morning. Manhattan stretched awake with noise and intent.

Vendors rolled carts to corners that had names before maps. Brunch crowds gathered under awnings, voices rising in waves to meet the street. Joggers traced the edges of the park, earbuds sealing them off from the world. Somewhere, church bells rehearsed for noon.

The river moved beside them, gold waking on its skin. The skyline stepped back and let the horizon speak.

They slipped through it like a thought not yet spoken.

Glass thinned to brick. Brick surrendered to bridge. The bridge emptied into air that felt older, cleaner. The kind the city could never afford to waste.

Inside the car, the world slowed just enough for them to feel the weight of what they were carrying, and the strange, borrowed peace of a city still waking.

For a while, nobody talked. It wasn't silence. It was respect.

Love measured in heartbeats. Comfort born of presence.

Alexander broke it first, eyes on the road, voice pitched for his son and the quiet hills.

"Tell me. Tell me what you're really at war with?"

Lucien didn't posture. He didn't reach for a speech.

"While I was gone, the city rewrote its skeleton. Every crew that wanted to survive, every syndicate that wanted tomorrow, folded themselves into a single structure. Not an alliance. A merger written in blood. The ones who refused vanished. The ones who stayed became part of something colder, older, and more disciplined than any flag they ever flew."

He watched the skyline fall away in the mirror. Just road and sky ahead.

"They call themselves the Coalition. But inside it, to the ones who matter, it goes by another name."

Alexander waited.

"They call it the House."

He didn't raise his voice. He didn't need to.

"The House isn't men sitting around a table. It's an organism. Each part does one job. One seat runs ports. One runs enforcement. One writes press cycles. One controls grant money and charity boards. Courts. Contractors. Civic Shield for theater. Financiers in the dark. Gangs sewn together until you can't tell where one ends and the next begins."

Evelyn's smile ghosted the window.

"You always hated politics."

"This isn't politics. Politics ends at term limits. The House does not. It scripts the story before the city wakes up. It decides who gets oxygen, who gets indicted, who gets erased. It rewards obedience and makes disobedience look like coincidence. Lansing is a mouthpiece. Weather, not climate."

He let that sit.

Alexander's hands tightened in his lap.

Lucien went on, quieter, sharper.

"They don't govern. They curate. They don't respond to events. They predict the decisions people will make and adjust the board so their result looks inevitable. They built a doctrine around it. Rooms close. Houses stand."

Lena's voice cut soft from the back seat.

"They don't call themselves leaders. They call themselves load-bearing."

Lucien nodded.

"Every node, every lieutenant, every disposable soldier. Fingers. Hands. A body big enough to survive losing parts of itself. A climate system, not a crime family."

He looked back at his father, at the man who had weathered older storms.

"And right now, that climate is shifting toward war."

Alexander listened without interrupting, the way men did when they were assembling an old fear with new information.

"I heard whispers of consolidation years ago. Nothing with a name. Just crews bending knee where they never had before. I thought it was rumor. Politics. A temporary truce."

"It wasn't a truce. It was scaffolding."

Alexander nodded once, slowly.

Lucien looked out at the highway, at the horizon getting wider instead of closer.

"And I don't think it ends at the city limits. No structure this coordinated builds itself for one skyline. I think the city is just the room we can see."

He let the silence run long enough to sharpen.

"Royce kept saying the world was rearranging itself. I thought it was arrogance." His voice dropped, quieter, colder. "Now I think he was echoing a prophecy he didn't understand. Something fed to him by people who move in darker rooms."

Alexander exhaled like he'd already known that but hadn't wanted it spoken aloud.

"Storms blow in from somewhere. They don't start on your doorstep."

He watched the highway unspool. Late morning stripped the color from the clouds until they were nothing but truth.

"And your plan. What's the end state?"

"Balance." The word landed like a weight placed where it belonged. "We flip their doctrine. We make fear too expensive to trade. We cut off the ledgers and the lungs, their money and their myth. We take the cameras out of their hands so the city stops auditioning for pain. Shelters and churches stay off the board. Kids never touch the ledger. And the corridors go quiet again."

"Quiet is a fragile god. But in every war I've lived through, the quiet started with a name. Yours is already echoing. Storms kneel to men who teach the world how to listen."

"Let them kneel if they want. I'm not building a kingdom. I'm rewriting the rules they've been breathing for years. The House runs on fear. I'm going to make fear cost them more than it buys. When the math breaks, the doctrine breaks. And that's when the city learns who it really belongs to."

Lena reached forward and set her fingers on his shoulder, light, steady. He didn't look back. He didn't need to. She was there. The world confirmed it.

Alexander nodded once, satisfied with the shape of the answer if not the odds it implied.

"You don't win by outshouting storms. You become the sky."

He paused, long enough for Lucien to feel the lesson sharpen.

"And never forget. A man feared for his wrath is a tyrant. A man feared for his silence is a king."

Evelyn chuckled.

"I married a poet by accident."

"You married a man who learned to keep his volume for the last sentence."

"Maybe I raised one." She looked at Lucien through the mirror, and the joy there was laced with pride. "Poets see the shape of things before they're built. Maybe that's what you've been doing all along."

The silence that followed carried weight, worry, and all the questions they weren't asking. Lucien broke it with the only one that mattered.

"Scans?" Not because he didn't know. Because he needed her to say it.

Evelyn made a face at the word.

"Shadows and maybe. We do another pass this week. Your father has fifteen research papers printed and folded like paper cranes, God help the man who tries to explain risk curves to me. I know what the curves mean. I also know what doors mean."

Alexander's mouth twitched.

"Better to meet the storm on your feet than wait for it on your knees."

"Don't talk like I'm gone." Not a scold, a boundary. "I'm still choosing doors."

Lena squeezed her hand, wordless agreement.

"And today's door opens to fresh air."

"To fresh air."

They passed a weather-beaten farm stand, its chalkboard still blank for the day's harvest. A pair of vultures traced patient circles above a distant field, their shadows looping over the road like omens too old to mean just one thing. A faded county shopping center blinked past, hardware store, feed supply, a diner with six cars out front and a neon sign that hadn't been off in decades.

Traffic was a memory now. The last billboards had surrendered miles back, leaving the trees to do the advertising. The city had shrugged off its armor. Light slid through the branches like grace, and the air carried the first hint of pine.

After a mile of thinking, Alexander turned that measured gaze inward.

"What do you need from me?"

Lucien shook his head. "Nothing you haven't already given. You stood guard while I clawed my way back into this world. You're standing guard now while she fights to stay in it. That's more than enough."

He looked back to the road, the words lowering until they carried weight without needing volume.

"The rest of this, Lansing, the House, the city trying to name its god, that's on me. I was born for storms. I know how to walk into them."

Then he glanced at Alexander, and something like softness edged the steel. "And if I know how, it's because you taught me. You built a man who doesn't flinch when the sky breaks. You gave me the spine to stand inside the wind."

Alexander's mouth twitched. "And when you make them bleed, you'll do it politely."

Lucien allowed the smallest ghost of a smile. "Polite is a weapon."

"Good boy," Evelyn murmured, pride warming her voice. "Make them thank you for it."

They crossed a ridge and the air cooled as if someone had cracked a door into a different season. Pines stood like old soldiers who liked this uniform best. The road narrowed into a promise and then kept it.

"Tell me the truth," Evelyn said, softer now, the window framing a slice of morning. "Are you afraid?"

Lena answered before Lucien could. "He doesn't get afraid. He gets precise."

Evelyn smiled at the glass. "That's fear with a better tailor." She turned her head slightly toward Lena. "And you?"

Lena didn't look away from the road ahead. "Always. It keeps me honest."

"Honest, not right," Lucien said, and the car held the weight of it, four souls stitched by blood and choice, all knowing it was true.

They crested a final curve, and the world opened.

A weathered wooden sign stood beside the road, the paint worn to ghosts but the name still legible: THE VALE OF SAINT ARDEN.

Stone and cedar rose from the hillside as if the earth had decided to build a chapel for its own prayers. The main nave pushed forward in a long, swept roofline, its high windows staring downriver like eyes that had chosen not to close. Beside it, a quieter annex, part hall and part haven, waited for laughter, for wine, for promises spoken under softer light. A hand-laid wall of old stone circled the grounds, patient and permanent. Below it all, the river ran silver and slow, not a mirror, but a memory in motion.

Lena said it before she could stop the words.

"It looks like a place you'd build a future."

Alexander looked at the grounds, and the years softened his face.

"We did. Once."

He pointed with two fingers, a gesture that remembered who he'd been.

"There. Under that stand of oak. Your mother wore a dress she argued with. Too simple, she said, and it made every other thing there look gaudy. We promised each other the usual lies and meant them like the truth."

Evelyn's eyes stayed on the oak.

"They weren't lies. They were terms. And we kept them."

Lucien cut the engine. The quiet that followed didn't feel empty. It felt earned. Birds negotiated in the canopy with the confidence of things that never read headlines. The grounds regarded them without hurry.

No visible cameras. No sirens. No eyes close enough to matter.

"Come on," Alexander said, suddenly younger by twenty years. He stepped out like his body remembered how to do it without thinking.

He drew the rear door open for Evelyn, and Lena was there before he asked, a hand, a brace, a soft word.

Evelyn turned and set one foot carefully on the gravel. She paused, not to pose, but to gather. The smallest labor. The largest meaning.

Lucien moved to her other side. This close, he could see the shadow under her eyes that good makeup couldn't erase, the subtle tremor when she lifted her chin against gravity. He could also see the thing that hadn't diminished at all, the look that said she lived by choosing, not by being carried.

"Give me the view."

They did.

The valley stretched out below them, wide and indifferent. Wind combed the hillside until the leaves confessed they were lighter than they pretended. Far off, birds circled above the ridge, too distant to trouble the peace.

Alexander pointed again, ritual in his voice now.

"We stood there. Vows there. Reception there, if you can call champagne and stolen pastries a reception."

Evelyn laughed, small, clear.

"We were poor and uninterested in pretending otherwise. It made the promises easier to keep."

Lena looked from the sky to the river to Lucien. It wasn't calculation. It was building. The ring on her hand caught morning and wrote a tiny flare on the stone.

"What would you want?" Lucien asked her, quiet, as if speaking too loud might disrespect the place.

"Nothing that doesn't belong. Chairs that accept being wood. A song we don't have to justify. Your mother sitting where she can see me walk toward you."

Evelyn drew a slow breath, steadier than the last, and her smile reached further than her strength did.

"If I can see my boy standing at the end of that aisle, then my time here will have meant something."

The line cut him deep and clean. Lena's hand found Evelyn's, squeezed back with the promise of a daughter who refused to be merely hopeful.

Alexander looked away a moment, the way men did when water surprised them in their eyes and they'd rather it didn't. When he looked back, he was all purpose again.

"We'll need permits. We'll need a date. We'll need,"

"We'll need now," Evelyn said. "We'll need to choose it and not wait for it to choose us."

Lucien stood there with three kinds of love inside a single rib cage and felt something settle. Not surrender. Not even peace. A decision.

He stepped forward onto the gravel toward the trees and measured the distance. He turned back toward them and saw her steady herself against the weight of her own bones, smile catching the light like a promise she meant to keep.

Time had joined the enemy's ranks. It wasn't neutral. It was tactical now. It would take what it could unless he made it behave.

He looked across the clearing, then at Lena, then at Alexander, and finally at Evelyn, who was both the past and the vow.

"We set the date. We make a window face a wedding."

The breeze answered in its own language.

Evelyn stepped forward from the shelter of them and paused, her strength gathering itself before resolve smoothed it out. She moved on, and the world made room.

She lifted her chin again, queen without a crown, and let the morning write itself across her face.

Lucien watched her and understood the math completely. In this war, bullets weren't the only things that missed, and time wasn't the only thing that killed. He would have to fight both.

He offered his arm. Evelyn took it.

"Show me where you'll stand," she said.

He did.

Chapter Thirty-Nine

THE AISLE AND THE ASH

The chapel wasn't something they stood before anymore. It was something they had already stepped into, a vow that had been waiting for them.

They walked the garden first, flagstone winding through lavender and thyme. The air held their scent, sharp and clean. Wind moved through the clearing, leaves whispering overhead. At the edge of the hill, a stone bench waited, facing a sweep of green.

"This is where the picture was taken," Alexander said, pointing. "The one we never framed."

"We didn't frame it because we didn't own a frame," Evelyn said, and the laugh that followed carried twenty small rebellions. "We had one suit, one dress, and more will than furniture."

Lena smiled, bright, then quiet. "I like that."

Alexander's gaze swept the grounds. "We can afford chairs now. But we don't have to pretend with them."

Somewhere beyond the hills, helicopter rotors turned the air. Not close enough to matter. Not far enough to ignore. A faint thrum that said the world kept circling.

Lucien's burner buzzed once in his pocket. A message from Ghost:

Council chatter's shifting. They're not changing plans. Just pulling the timeline closer

He shifted his weight where stone met grass and typed back. His eyes traced the valley beyond the birches, where the horizon held its own silence.

How close?

Ghost replied a moment later, sharp and economical:

Close enough to test the edge. Not close enough to draw blood

Lucien's thumb paused over the glass. Behind him, the chapel doors stood open.

Let them circle. We're walking holy ground

Ghost answered.

Copy

They crossed to the office side, stone cool underfoot, the scent of paper and lemon oil meeting them at the door.

A woman near sixty stepped into the foyer, spine like a metronome. She glanced from face to face and, without asking, understood this wasn't a tour for strangers.

"May I help you?" she asked.

Her name tag said DUARTE. Her eyes said she had kept more secrets than most people.

Alexander offered his hand. "Alexander Cole. My wife and I were married here. In another life."

Recognition softened Mrs. Duarte's posture. "Then welcome back." Warmth threaded through her professionalism. "Saint Arden remembers its own."

Evelyn didn't let him answer. "We'd like to see about dates. For our son." She tilted her head to Lucien. "He's stubborn enough to be worth the trouble."

Mrs. Duarte's mouth worked toward a smile and arrived. "We're blessed to be busy. Usually eight months to a year."

"Of course," Alexander said, already nodding, ready to accept the wait.

"But," Mrs. Duarte continued, her eyes narrowing, not in suspicion but in calculation. She studied Evelyn's face the way people studied weather, gauging what it would demand. "There was a cancellation yesterday. Six weeks from Saturday. Afternoon. The couple eloped to Sicily. Good for them. Bad for my calendar. If you can be ready, the room can be too."

Silence settled over them.

"That's fast," Lena said, and something in her tone made it sound like a thrill, not a warning.

"You'd be surprised what people can do when the day requires it," Mrs. Duarte said. "Six weeks is long if you use all of it."

Evelyn met the woman's gaze and saw a kind of mercy there she hadn't asked for and didn't resent. "Can the chapel accept our kind of light?"

"I don't know your kind," Mrs. Duarte said, unflustered. "But the building likes honesty."

Evelyn turned to Lucien. "Take it." Not an order. Not a plea. Permission.

Lucien looked at Lena. Her nod wasn't small. It was exact.

"We'll make the day keep up."

"Then it's yours."

Mrs. Duarte set a ledger on the desk.

Paperwork appeared, not much. Names. A refundable deposit. A florist who didn't punish people for simplicity. A note about sound levels, which Evelyn crossed out, then uncrossed when Mrs. Duarte raised one eyebrow in dry amusement.

"Anything else?" Mrs. Duarte asked.

"Windows," Evelyn said. "I'd like to sit where I can see him walk."

"Here." Mrs. Duarte circled a pew on the floor plan with a soft pencil. "It isn't an aisle until a mother sees it."

Lena pressed her lips together. That was the line that found her.

They stepped back into the green and drifted down the gravel to the chapel again. The river below kept moving, patient and unhurried.

On the far side of the lawn, three gardeners lifted a trellis into place. The metal frame caught the sun and threw it in lines across the grass. One of them straightened, shaded his eyes, and gave the polite nod of a man who worked the grounds and knew how to leave visitors alone.

Not threat. Community.

"Walk with me," Evelyn said.

She took two careful steps and only needed help on the third. When Alexander's hand was there, it wasn't show. It was marriage doing its work.

At the chapel doors she stopped and turned to Lucien. "Promise me."

He didn't ask to what.

"Promise you'll walk that aisle. No matter what storm you're walking through when the day arrives. Arrive anyway."

"I'll walk through fire. If it's the only way in, I'll walk through fire."

She studied him for the flicker where bravado lived and didn't find it. "Good. Then all that's left is the part where you stand."

Lena let her fingers skim the pew ends again, memorizing texture as if memory were a weapon. "I never planned a wedding." The confession was so quiet it didn't need privacy to be intimate. "I thought that was for other women. Softer lives."

"You're not other women," Evelyn said. "And this isn't softness. It's selection. Killers don't stop being killers when they pick their church." She smiled, faint and knowing. "Besides, you know Victoria. She's been planning this day since she saw the way you two burn for each other. She'll treat it like a military campaign and love every second."

Alexander looked toward the edge of the woods where they gathered like men in dark coats. "We'll handle what's outside. You handle what's inside."

Lucien returned his gaze. "I am."

They drifted to the overlook one more time. The horizon ran like a slow blade. The air up here belonged to itself.

Lucien's burner buzzed again, a thread from Ghost lighting the screen:

Council planted a meet. Four hours from now. Midtown. They think the address is quiet because their donor bought the floor above it

He exhaled once through his nose, the kind of sound that wasn't quite a laugh.

Let them think it.

Evelyn took his hand and turned it palm-up. She placed her fingers in the center the way mothers did when they checked a fever without a thermometer. "You're warm," she said, relieved. "Stay that way."

"I intend to."

A breeze crossed the hill and folded the chapel's open doors back a degree. Not a sign. Not a story. Just air doing what it did. Still, Lena watched the movement and felt the hinge turn in her chest.

They returned to the office to finish what the paperwork required. Mrs. Duarte had set four thin paper cups of water out the way sacristans set small chalices, to be used, not admired. Evelyn sipped without ceremony. Lena signed where the line asked. Alexander tucked a receipt in his chest pocket, near his heart. He would call it paperwork, not faith.

"Six weeks," Mrs. Duarte said, handing over a folded page with dates and times printed in neat rows. "Bring what matters. Leave what doesn't."

"That was always the plan," Lucien said.

They stepped back into the light and took the long way toward the car, as if the short way would spend the morning too quickly. At the chapel doors, Evelyn paused, not to gather breath this time, but to gather the scene for later, the chapel, the bench, the stone, the sky with its earned blue.

"If this is where we promise forever," Lena said, half to the view, half to the man whose hand she took and didn't let go, "then forever starts now."

Lucien looked once through the open doorway, at the aisle that would soon divide their lives into before and after. Then back at her. Then at his mother, whose eyes had taken on that bright, glassy depth where pain and joy met.

He kissed Lena's knuckles once, not as show but as oath.

"Now," he said, and the word carried as far as the trees.

When they reached the truck, they helped Evelyn settle into the back seat, her head tipped just so against the leather. Alexander slid into the passenger side and let his palm rest a second on the dash, the way men did before they drove into what was coming.

They rolled under birch shade and out into the day.

From across the grounds, the chapel kept being a chapel. From the road, the land kept being the land. Far beyond their sight, the city they were heading back to stayed unaware of what had just been chosen.

A mile down the road, Lucien's burner buzzed again.

One more thing

House channels went quiet for ninety seconds. Not static. Reverence. Like they heard a bell you didn't ring

He watched the road unspool ahead and typed back.

Then maybe they're listening

A moment later:

Always

The car took the curve, and the river far below showed its dull silver again. The four of them carried the day with them the way you carried a flame cupped in both hands, not precious, but essential.

They drove toward a city that had already started to build shrines, toward hours that would refuse to make room for them, toward a war that had changed costumes but not intent. The vow had a date now. The storm had a calendar.

Between the aisle and the ash, they chose both.

Chapter Forty

DAYLIGHT COUNCIL

Mercy West took them back without questions.

Lucien eased the truck to the curb, every movement steady.

The day had hardened into afternoon. The sun hung high, pale and unmoving against the glass.

Inside, the lobby smelled of sterility trying to make room for care. A volunteer at the desk glanced up, saw nothing she recognized, and nodded with practiced comfort.

Alexander offered his arm. Evelyn accepted it without apology. Lena moved to her other side, her palm finding the exact place where help looked like respect.

Evelyn paused in front of the reception desk, straightened the flower arrangement that leaned too far left, and adjusted the edge of the sign-in clipboard until it aligned with the counter.

"Now it looks like someone cares."

Alexander watched Evelyn fix the clipboard. "She set a wedding date this morning. Now she's adjusting furniture. I've learned not to interfere."

Evelyn lifted her chin a fraction. "We made an agreement. Keep it simple. Let the day do the lighting."

"Kings listen. Carpenters build. Women decide how it stands," Lena said, smiling.

They reached the elevator. The metal doors held their reflections for a second, then parted. Alexander pressed the button for the floor that knew their names without loving them.

Before the doors closed, Lucien looked at the two of them framed there. Evelyn leaned the smallest bit toward Alexander, and he shifted to meet her without thinking. A quiet geometry built over a lifetime.

He felt the tug that came before grief and called it by another name. Fuel.

Lena's fingers found his. "She's fighting for more than time. She's fighting for moments."

Lucien's gaze stayed on the doors until they closed. "Then we give her one worth watching. She's not asking for forever. Just a front-row seat to the part where we begin."

The doors sealed. Somewhere above, the machinery carried his parents away like a promise being held for the right hour.

They didn't linger. They had a city to meet.

It was a little after one-thirty when they reached Northgate.

Northgate held a different temperature. It didn't care about vows. It cared about outcomes.

The elevator took them up into a long, echoing corridor.

The glass didn't brighten the hall. It sharpened it.

The war room was already in motion, sharp and unsparing.

Logan reclined in Lucien's chair like he owned it, coffee balanced on the armrest, eyes bright in a way that meant he'd slept none at all. Mara sat cross-legged on the table's edge, boots resting on a file she had already dismissed as unworthy. Imani moved without looking up, three channels running in her periphery like she'd been born with another set of senses. Rook dragged a strip of steel along the glass in slow, steady passes. The sound was almost meditative. Or threatening. Depending on your conscience.

Victor stood at the window, hands folded behind his back, Manhattan cut into silhouette across his shoulders.

They all looked up at once.

Not curious.

Counting.

Logan broke the tension the way only Logan could.

"So." Logan stretched the word. "Did we secure eternity or are we still shopping?"

Lena didn't blink.

"Six weeks from Saturday. Afternoon."

Mara grinned first. "Armed."

Imani, still scrolling. "Coordinated."

Rook, without missing a stroke of steel. "Properly catered."

Victor exhaled through his nose. "Unholy."

Logan raised his cup. "Photogenic."

The room laughed. Not loud. Not long. But real.

It was the sound of people who had chosen each other and never asked the price again.

Lucien let it move through them. Let the building feel less like a fortress and more like something worth defending.

Then the speakers clicked.

Ghost.

"Focused."

The room adjusted. Not dramatically. Just enough.

"Six weeks is long enough for them to move three pawns, reinforce two bishops, and try to shoot a king."

The warmth didn't disappear. It condensed.

Victor straightened first. "Status."

Imani flicked her wrist. Midtown bloomed on the screen, an address steeped in donor money and bad intention. "Council meet confirmed. Two hours. Donor-owned floor above it. Elevators scrubbed. Cameras compliant enough to pass inspection and not a pixel more."

Logan leaned forward now. "Staggered arrivals. No one wants to be seen together, but they're wearing the same perfume. Three ghost vans. One convoy too expensive to stop."

Ghost cut in. "Language unchanged. Cult phrases intact. They're not calling him a man anymore. They're calling him weather."

Lena's eyes slid to Lucien.

He didn't react.

Before anyone could answer that, his phone buzzed.

The room went quiet without being told to.

He checked it once.

Then set the phone face-up on the table.

The image stared back.

Grainy. Intentional. Fresh.

Alexander's hand on Evelyn's back. Mercy West entrance. Timestamp still warm.

No caption.

The temperature didn't drop in the air.

It dropped in bone.

Mara froze.

Imani's scroll halted.

Rook's steel stopped mid-pass.

Logan forgot his coffee existed.

Victor stepped closer, eyes narrowing on the image. "They weren't across the street. Too clean. Too low. This was taken from inside the drop lane."

Logan leaned closer to the screen. "They're checking response time."

Lucien picked the phone back up.

He didn't let anger be first.

He set it down with the precision of a blade going back to its sheath.

"They know what matters," Logan said.

"They're measuring how much," Lena replied.

Ghost's voice dropped colder. "This isn't threat posture. It's calibration. They're testing the edge before they press."

Lucien felt something inside him settle into its proper place.

He looked at his people.

Not soldiers.

Family.

"We watch. We listen."

Orders moved without volume.

"South stairwell feeds," Mara said, fingers already moving.

"Elevators," Logan said.

"Street sightlines," Rook said.

"Every channel they think is quiet," Imani added.

Victor adjusted his sleeve once. Ready.

Ghost layered over them.

"Roof mics. Street corners. Lobby dead drops. They're listening for footsteps before they see faces."

Lucien slid his jacket on. The fabric remembered him.

"Let them listen," he said.

Ghost didn't hesitate.

"Then they'll hear you."

Lucien glanced once more at the photo.

His father's hand.

His mother's spine.

A threshold crossed, and the war stepped over it with him.

"They will never walk unguarded again."

No one asked what perimeter he meant.

The oath covered all of them.

The room needed air before the weight broke something.

Logan stood, rolled his shoulders, reclaimed his grin, and lifted his cup.

"Six weeks from Saturday. Afternoon wedding. You two shall remain..."

Lena answered without missing rhythm. "Uninterrupted."

Rook: "Documented."

Mara: "Defended."

Imani: "Delivered."

Victor, smallest nod. "Witnessed."

Ghost, perfectly timed. "On schedule."

Lucien looked at each of them until the room believed itself.

Then, "Let's go."

Chairs shifted. Screens woke. Doors opened.

Outside the glass, Manhattan pretended not to listen.

And did.

Ghost fed live data into the air. "Two stairwells. Four exits. Eight lenses. No alarms worth respecting. Council begins in one hour, forty-three minutes."

Lucien walked toward the door without ceremony. "We stage first. Not in their shadow. On our terms."

He paused long enough for the room to align with him.

"We'll teach them what they orbit."

They moved as one body.

On the screen, Midtown drew itself like a target that hadn't realized the arrow was already loose.

The wedding had a date.

The war had a schedule.

And Northgate was done pretending they were separate.

Chapter Forty-One

THE TABLE WITH NO WINDOWS

The elevator didn't rise. It climbed. Like a confession with no mercy waiting at the top.

No music. No voice. No floor numbers. Just pressure in their ears, the soft pull in their stomachs, and the quiet that came before revelation.

They weren't invited. Men like Lucien didn't get invitations. They made their own.

Not after dawn.

Not after the municipal yard burned.

Guns, cash, drones, permits. All of it went up while someone painted a message across the wreckage:

THE HOUSE BLEEDS WHEN IT LISTENS

By sunrise, every feed carried the smoke. Before the light settled, the Council moved. They pulled their session off-grid, behind money and glass.

Lucien went anyway.

If they wanted shadows, he would bring judgment into them.

He didn't come to talk. He came to be seen.

The doors opened.

Glass on every side. Floor-to-ceiling panels that erased the room's edges. The city fell away beneath them, distant and indifferent, traffic reduced to suggestion and soundless motion. The carpet was white, too white, the kind that punished footprints and forgave nothing.

No receptionist. No assistant pretending to type. No movement at all.

One door stood open at the far end of the corridor, the light behind it bright enough to be deliberate.

They walked toward it.

Inside, the table dominated the room.

It wasn't built for conversation. It was built for spectacle.

Oval. Seamless. Polished to the point of distortion. The kind of surface that reflected faces back at men who preferred not to see themselves clearly.

A murmur rolled around the perimeter as Lucien stepped in.

Recognition first, then doubt, then the careful stillness of men who understood storms did not knock.

One voice, dry as old paper and twice as brittle.

"Look who decided to join us."

Lucien didn't sit.

Lena stopped one step behind him, close enough that her presence altered the air without touching it. Victor and Logan remained near the threshold, relaxed enough to look harmless and lethal enough to make that a lie. Rook drifted along the wall, counting exits, measuring angles, reading the glass.

Ghost was already inside their system, invisible and listening, and the room knew it. He'd piggybacked the Council's own display feed. Whatever they saw, he saw.

Imani stayed back with Mara, running the backend grid Ghost wasn't touching.

In his pocket, Lucien felt the small weight of a recorder, already live, already listening.

The donor smiled with his teeth first.

"Daylight makes everything clean."

Lena stepped forward. Her shadow split the table.

"Clean is what men call it before they kneel in the dark."

The donor's cuff link twitched.

A monitor behind him lit up.

Mercy West. Room 512.

Evelyn Cole was resting against her pillows, oxygen cannula tracing her cheek. Alexander sat beside her, his hand moving in small circles between her shoulders.

Timestamp: 15:37.

No caption. No warning. Just the feed.

No one looked at Lucien. That was their first mistake.

They thought a man broke when you showed him what he loved. They had never met one who turned love into a reason.

"Your myth is forcing our hand," the donor said. "Choose your words carefully."

Lena shifted her weight, a quiet refusal taking shape in her stance.

"That's a mother."

"Also a detonator," a woman at the table's edge said.

Her voice held no tremor. No softness. She offered no name. She didn't need one.

Lucien didn't look at her. He looked at the screen.

The image didn't blink.

He let the anger settle into weight.

"Say it plainly."

The donor's smile slipped, then settled back into place.

"Declare a truce. Redirect your war. Blame whoever you need to blame. We set the terms."

Logan tapped the glass once with his knuckle.

A small, hollow note. Like a bell rung for something already dead.

The donor continued. "Your mother keeps her breath. Your father keeps his pulse. The candles go out. The crowns get scrubbed off the pavement."

The room didn't react.

That unsettled him more than outrage would have.

A soft click entered their earpieces. Shared. Controlled.

Ghost.

"Unknown presence. One floor up. Not staff. Moving toward you."

Lucien didn't turn.

He kept his eyes on the donor.

"Finish your sentence."

The donor swallowed.

The door opened.

A woman stepped inside with the kind of composure that didn't need to announce itself.

Gray suit. Clean, unforgiving lines. Hair pulled back tight enough to suggest she hated anything loose. Sixty, maybe older, with nothing softened by time. Her eyes didn't scan the room for approval. They assessed it.

The Council didn't rise. They froze, then recalibrated.

Lucien registered it instantly. This was someone they feared.

She took a seat no one offered.

The silence introduced her.

She set a slim device in the center of the table and tapped once.

The Mercy West feed shifted, then divided.

On one side, hospital logs. Nurse access records. Medication timestamps.

On the other, this room, this table, this moment, filmed from behind the donor's head.

Lucien knew instantly it wasn't Ghost's angle.

Ghost did not borrow eyes he could not control.

The donor's color drained. Calculation rushed in.

He had realized something crucial.

This was not his room. It had never been.

"Your city's running hot," the woman said.

"We prefer cold."

Her voice carried control without apology.

Even the Council lowered their eyes when she spoke.

Whatever she represented, they served it.

Lena didn't move. "Define we."

The woman regarded Lena for a single, precise second.

Not dismissive.

Not impressed.

Just measuring.

"People who own the buildings. The cameras. The signatures. The doors."

The donor tried to smile. It died halfway up his face.

"Friends of stability."

She didn't correct him. He wasn't qualified to define anything.

He was furniture that had spoken out of turn.

Logan's smile stayed flat. "Stability doesn't knock."

Her attention returned to Lucien.

Not hostility.

Inventory.

"I heard the earlier proposal. Candles extinguished. Crowns removed. Parents preserved."

She let the silence stretch.

"That was his offer. Small terms from a small man."

She paused long enough for the room to understand the hierarchy.

"Now here is the doctrine."

The air tightened. Not from fear. From focus.

Her voice was as smooth as a vault sealing. "If you push, the candles die out. The crowns disappear."

She gave the room the weight of that.

"If you stop, your mother keeps her suite. Your father keeps his breath."

Her final line landed light as a signature on a death warrant.

"We don't negotiate. We decide."

"Kings used to say that," Lucien replied. "Right before the fire found their curtains."

The woman in gray adjusted the slim device on the table, aligning it perfectly with the grain of the wood.

"We decide what matters."

Victor's voice cut the air, level and sharp.

"Then stop using mothers as leverage."

No one corrected the word.

Lucien met Lena's gaze.

Not a question. A decision.

Lena spoke like steel finding its lock.

"We don't answer to doctrine. We write it."

The woman in gray tapped the device again.

The feed flipped to a drone angle outside the glass, showing the room from above the skyline.

Access no one at the table had purchased.

The donor went pale. "Pennington," he muttered.

She killed the screens with her thumb.

"The one these men serve is watching. Daylight's crowded."

Logan's grin sharpened. "Honesty. So rare it should come with a safe-word."

Lucien set both hands on the back of the empty chair.

"You dragged my mother into your glass tower and called it mercy."

He didn't raise his voice. "You think daylight makes you brave. It doesn't. It just makes it easier to find you."

Now Pennington didn't blink.

"Then we negotiate in pain."

Lena's reply stayed steady. "Pain doesn't negotiate. It remembers."

Lucien stepped back. The chair remained untouched.

"Remember this room. Remember the angle you chose."

He looked at the dark monitor.

"The next time you look at us, know we are already looking back."

Victor opened the door.

They left.

Pennington's voice followed them, smooth as a contract.

"You'll miss the light."

Lucien didn't turn. "I don't need it."

The elevator swallowed them. The doors sealed. The descent began.

Ghost came through the comm.

"Clear."

Lucien adjusted his cuff.

"They priced mercy like a product. Let's see what they charge for war."

Outside, the late light glazed the towers. Traffic thickened. Engines caught.

Victor watched the tower glass erase their reflection. "They'll scatter."

Lucien shook his head. "They'll climb."

Lena's thumb traced her ring once. "Then we raise the price."

Logan checked the mirror, grin thin as a scar.

"Let them climb. Ladders break."

The city swallowed them.

Above, the towers kept their secrets.

Below, the candles kept burning.

And somewhere between the glass and the street, the House learned something new.

They were no longer watching alone.

Chapter Forty-Two

REVOLUTION SIGNAL

The war room felt like a tomb wired to the city. Northgate's concrete held the blue glow from twelve screens, each one showing men who had confessed without knowing anyone was listening.

Lucien stood dead center, jacket off, sleeves rolled, ready to open the city and let the truth bleed. The air smelled like ozone and old blood from the breach they never really scrubbed out.

Ghost's voice came first, cold and clipped.

"Feed goes live in ninety seconds. Your move, king."

Imani didn't look up, her typing settling into a surgical rhythm. Mara perched on the table's edge, eyes tracking the monitors. Rook leaned on the far wall, arms folded, watching angles and exits. Victor stood by the door, back to the steel, ready to shut down anything that ran too hot. Lena was the only one still, just outside the circle of light, her silence heavier than the servers.

Eighty.

Ghost came again, lower now, like he had already seen the ending.

"Routes are set. Hijacked bands. Backrooms only. Chop shops, trap houses, precinct basements, old men's clubs. No billboards. No CityCast. They'll feel it where they live."

Lucien's voice stayed level, past anger now, past mercy.

"Let them see what survives when we stop asking."

Seventy.

The main screen bloomed. The Council room, caught mid-breath.

The donor froze with his mouth open.

Pennington's thumb hovered over a little black box, bored and waiting.

Then came the moment they realized the lens wasn't theirs.

Imani's voice cut through, clean as wire. "Backroom TVs are waking. Pawn shops. Card rooms. Boiler rooms. Crews on burner phones passing the link hand to hand."

Mara didn't look up. "South Dock just went dark."

She waited a breath. "Three more followed."

Rook's grin cut the gloom. "They're choosing sides."

Sixty.

Lena stepped forward. Her shadow cut across the table.

"This isn't daylight. It's a bonfire. What if it burns us first?"

Lucien looked at her. A flicker in the eyes, there and gone.

"Then we burn the world with us. And we make it look like sunrise."

Fifty.

Another window blinked open, donors in velvet suits toasting the devils they had bankrolled.

No data dump. No code. Just names, wire transfers, and smiles that had cost lives.

The receipts hit like bullets.

No one in those rooms called the police. They called their accountants.

Ghost's voice cut in, calm as static settling.

"Bronx hears it. Brooklyn's awake. Floorboards across the boroughs are starting to talk."

Forty.

The donor's voice crawled through dying speakers, cutting in and out like it hated to be heard.

"Call a truce... your mother keeps her breath..."

It rolled through basements and back offices, through smoke shops and cheap liquor stores.

Men stopped talking. Women leaned in. Cards paused mid-hand.

Thirty.

On a battered feed, Captain Dane handed an envelope to a judge's aide tied to Civic Shield's launch.

A priest of law took his tithe.

Another screen showed a list of shelters marked for raids.

Another showed a wire room counting blood as profit.

Twenty.

A few monitors flickered. One died.

Silence pressed its thumb on the room.

For one heartbeat, the picture went black.

Then the image came back, harder than before.

Ghost didn't celebrate. "We're still in."

Ten.

The city didn't roar. It held its breath.

In a backroom on East Third, a bodega TV hummed behind bars. An old man watching didn't move.

In a precinct basement, two uniformed officers stared at a muted screen and said nothing.

On a Brooklyn rooftop, a kid lifted his burner toward the river like a flare no one sane would answer.

Candles appeared in windows where curtains never opened.

Not many. But enough.

Lena's hand found Lucien's.

Not comfort. Anchor.

Zero.

The footage looped once. Then the final frame stuttered.

Something tore through the static.

A wolf.

Yellow eyes. Smoke-dark fur.

One frame only.

Gone.

Lucien had seen those eyes once before.

Not on a screen.

In the dark behind his own eyes.

Black paws on dead leaves.

A Bible open to Revelation.

He had never said a word about it.

The thought came cold and strange: prophecy did not arrive as a voice.

It arrived as an image.

Ghost's voice scraped through the speaker.

"Static hit every feed. Just noise."

Lucien didn't move. Didn't answer.

They saw static.

He saw the wolf.

He watched the blank corner of the screen as if it might breathe.

Mara broke the stillness. "Riverfront's blind. Backrooms too. Something killed the feed."

Imani froze. "That wasn't us."

Rook pushed off the wall. "Civic Shield?"

Victor's hand found the door. "Or the Coalition."

Lena's whisper cut the room in half.

"They're done watching. They're moving."

Lucien's reply came calm as a trigger under pressure.

"Then we move first."

Northgate didn't exhale. It armed itself.

War didn't start with gunfire. It started with decisions.

His eyes stayed on the place where that single frame had lived, the seam where nightmare and reality touched.

Outside, a few candles burned harder. Inside, everything held. The underworld had heard. Something else had come with it.

The air had changed. Static ate the last frame, and encrypted telemetry blinked across the lower monitors in red.

Imani frowned. "Telemetry spike. Doesn't match any of ours."

Ghost sharpened as code spilled across the screens.

"Coalition drone net just woke up. Flight path over Midtown. Pattern's wrong for recon."

Lena stayed low. "What's there?"

Imani didn't answer. She was already looking at it.

Ghost pulled the location. "Mercy West."

The war had found a room number.

Silence didn't fall. It locked.

Lucien's pulse didn't change. His voice dropped. "Kill the broadcast. Put Mercy West in a cage. Lock elevators, stall stairs, blind every camera we don't own. I want eyes on that floor now."

Imani's hands moved. "Pushing alerts. Hospital security's live."

Ghost didn't hesitate. "Routing cameras. Exterior and roof."

Lucien was already moving, jacket on, keys in hand.

Rook called after him. "Where the hell are you going?"

Lucien didn't answer.

A minute later, the truck's engine answered for him.

His mother's room number burned behind his eyes.

Midtown didn't know it yet, but Lucien was already on his way.

CHAPTER FORTY-THREE

MERCY BURNS

He left Northgate without explaining. It felt half-truth, half-ritual. Lena had already seen it in his eyes.

The Rezvani tore through the city, black armor swallowing light, engine coughing thunder.

Every red light became a suggestion. Every turn screamed against pavement.

Victor's name flashed across the dash. Incoming.

He ignored it.

Lena's name lit the screen next.

He killed the call on reflex.

Her text followed:

Don't make me chase you

He thumbed back, eyes on the road:

You already are

He called his mother twice. No answer.

Fired a text anyway:

Get away from your room. Now

No dots. No read receipt.

Only the city sliding past in streaks of light and static.

He gunned the accelerator, the armored frame howling through Midtown, plates rattling.

The sky above was dark and restless, clouds slick with moonlight that didn't belong to the earth.

The HUD flickered, brief interference, faint but wrong. Something moved inside those clouds, too fast, too steady.

He felt the air tighten, like the city itself was waiting for impact.

Mercy West rose ahead like a cathedral built on tired hope. Fifth floor, east-facing window, that was hers. He'd memorized it the way some men memorize prayers.

He slid to the curb by the service entrance, engine idling rough. The sodium lamps made everything gold and sick.

Then, a hum deepened.

He looked up.

Three black shapes cut against the night sky, too low, too steady.

He exhaled.

"No..."

The air drew tight. Light bent inward.

The first drone dropped through the roof vent above Oncology, fifth floor, east wing.

A shaped charge found the oxygen closet beside Room 512, white tanks waiting like saints for martyrdom.

The explosion didn't roar. It exhaled the world.

Windows turned to glass rain. The façade folded. The east wing lit slow and holy, then hungry.

The Rezvani rocked back on its axles.

The street bucked beneath him, a brief earthquake that shook the entire block.

Parked cars jolted and screamed, alarms wailed in a discordant choir.

Streetlights flickered. Then died.

A bed rail skidded across the asphalt like driftwood in a flood.

Lucien's cigarette hit the ground, a red ember dying in the wind.

He was already moving.

The Rezvani's doors gaped behind him as he sprinted into the smoke.

Paramedics shouted.

A nurse dragged an IV pole like a broken mast.

Fire sprinklers turned to steam the second they touched the heat.

Above it all, a freelance news drone hung motionless, already feeding the city its tragedy.

He remembered the hallway by heart: fifth floor, rooms 509–516, oxygen closet beside 512.

Whoever planned this knew the anatomy or guessed cruelly right.

Smoke filled the stairwell like a tide.

He should've grabbed a mask.

He didn't.

He clawed through insulation and ash, coughing specks of blood into his sleeve. Habit and devotion moved him more than breath.

Somewhere in the collapse, a shape kept pace, four beats in the dust, gone when he turned.

He found her not in 512, but in the corridor's wreckage. She'd been walking her late-night loop when the roof gave way.

She was still on her feet, coughing like the air had fangs.

"Lucien?"

Her face was streaked with ash, her hair threaded with gray light.

He dropped to his knees, caught her before she fell.

"Hey, hey..."

The words meant nothing.

He pressed his forehead to hers, one of the only warm things left in the world.

"You were supposed to be in 512. You were supposed to be safe..."

He couldn't finish.

He just held her.

Paramedics pried them apart.

Quick hands. Blanket, mask, vitals climbing.

Smoke inhalation, burns, shock, but alive.

Barely.

Outside, Lansing's people were already sculpting lies for the cameras.

"An isolated act of terror," one recited.

"Gang-related. The city will not bow."

Paramedics were everywhere now, pulling the wounded into order, voices sharp against the smoke.

One of them shouted for vitals; another cleared the path to the stairwell.

They started to roll her out.

She lifted a trembling hand.

"Wait."

The medic tried to hush her. "Ma'am, we have to move."

She pointed past him to a half-collapsed prayer table near the nurses' station.

A wooden basket lay on its side, rosary beads scattered like spilled stars.

"Please," she whispered.

Lucien reached it, sifted through ash and glass until he found one still whole, sealed in a little plastic sleeve.

She took it from him, closed her fist around it, then pressed it into his palm.

"For you," she said.

Her voice was barely breath.

"Keep it safe."

He nodded because his throat would not work.

The medics pushed her stretcher on, wheels squealing through the debris, and the noise swallowed the rest.

Lucien's phone buzzed in his pocket, Ghost, clipped, furious.

They lit the whole oncology wing. Either they didn't know about the oxygen tanks, or they wanted it biblical

Lucien stared at the fire chewing through Mercy West and typed back with steady thumbs.

I know. It's real war now

The phone buzzed again.

He didn't need to read it to know the shape of the words.

Beeps. Curses. Tiny order inside chaos.

He'd chased the fire and found the ashes waiting.

Something inside him settled, iron cooling into a blade.

Not grief.

Not rage.

A contract written in fire.

"I'm here," he said.

"I'm here."

He followed the paramedics out through the lobby doors.

The avenue was chaos, sirens stacking over one another, red and blue washing the smoke to purple.

Fire crews shouted coordinates.

Stretchers lined the curb.

White sheets turned gray as ash settled.

Nurses were counting survivors, clipboards shaking.

A priest knelt beside one of the bays, whispering last rites no one had time to finish.

The whole block had become a triage ground, engines idling, doors slamming, the air thick with metal and prayer.

Lucien walked beside her stretcher until they reached the ambulance row.

They rolled her in.

The city glared like a church on fire. No one in power would call this war. Reporters would build myths. Politicians would build shields. The Coalition would call it necessary.

But Lucien saw the truth in the drone's black scar across the sky.

It wasn't strategy.

It was personal.

That was their second mistake.

He watched the doors close, smoke wrapping the night like breath.

From the ruin, something unfastened behind his eyes. Two yellow slits shimmered in the heat, watching.

He thumbed the rosary band she'd given him, the plastic still warm from her hand.

His phone buzzed again in his pocket, Ghost, clipped, relentless.

The same message.

Or maybe the one he had missed while the world burned.

Then we answer

Lucien looked at the screen, at the word answer, and felt it settle inside him like ignition.

The city would hear it soon.

The truck's engine still idled where he'd left it, headlights cutting through drifting smoke.

A second buzz, Lena.

We know where you are

Then another:

We're all on our way

He slipped the phone into his pocket and turned toward the ambulances.

Sirens stacked over one another. Fire crews shouted numbers into radios.

Then a new noise cut through the rest, human, angry.

"Sir, you can't step into this area."

"Fuck you! That's my wife in that ambulance!"

Alexander pushed through the chaos with the force of a man who would not be stopped.

The perimeter tape snapped against his coat; paramedics yelled, flashlights strobing through debris.

He stopped when he saw Lucien.

Two men. Same jaw. Same eyes. One built the city. The other set it on fire.

Lucien's throat tightened.

"They wanted her to burn for me."

Alexander stepped closer until their shadows merged in the flame-glow.

"Then they've already lost," he said.

"They made you remember what you are."

He looked toward the ambulance where his wife lay beneath the pulse of red and blue.

The color washed the lines of his face, war etched over age.

For a long beat, the old general said nothing.

Then his voice came low, carved from command and grief.

"You were never built for peace, son. Neither was this city."

Lucien met his eyes.

The fire painted them both in the same ruin.

Alexander's hand came up, rough and shaking, and landed on the back of

Lucien's neck.

"You finish this. You take back every inch they stole. But when you bury them,"

His voice caught, then hardened.

"Make sure the world watches."

Lucien's fingers tightened around the rosary.

"And you?"

"I'll hold the line. Once again."

Something ancient passed between them. Blood. Oath. Smoke.

Lucien nodded once.

"Then we move."

Alexander's grip tightened, then fell away.

"Go make them remember why they should fear the name Cole."

Lucien turned back to the fire.

The sky over Mercy West burned the color of judgment.

The rosary bit into his palm; the city's sirens sounded like mourning turned to march.

He whispered to the smoke:

Not the ward.

Not the broken.

Not the lie.

Not the city.

Not the machine.

The rest could burn.

Chapter Forty-Four

SUBWAY GOSPEL

Sirens ripped the night to shreds. Mercy West still burned in sheets of orange and shattered glass. Fire crews carved corridors through heat; ladders clanged in metal.

An ambulance door slammed. Then another.

Alexander climbed in with Evelyn, his palm against her cheek like a vow. His thumb traced the soot along her temple.

The rig shouldered the smoke and tore east for a hospital across town.

Lucien stood in the glow, the taste of iron in his throat, rosary in his fist.

A van knifed in from the dark and braked hard.

Doors flew open. Victor. Logan. Rook. And Lena, already running, already reaching him.

He smelled of smoke. She held back tears she refused to let fall.

She pressed her forehead to his. "Tell me."

"She is alive. Barely."

"She's stubborn. She'll make the doctors earn their names."

He let out a rough breath. "You sound like her."

Lena's thumb touched the singed edge of his cuff.

"I'm learning life again from a woman who refuses bad endings. And from her son."

Victor's hand found Lucien's shoulder, solid, anchoring.

"We move when you say."

Logan looked at the broken windows and did not bother with swagger.

"They brought church to a hospital. I hate this fucking war."

Rook stared at the aftermath like a man measuring what needed breaking.

Ghost came through the static. "I'm hearing chatter."

"What kind?"

"Coalition command. Tonight was not supposed to go biblical. They didn't account for the oxygen closet beside five-twelve. They're spooked.

Council is evacuating underground."

"Where underground?"

"Old lines. Abandoned junctions under Civic Hall. I can trace them."

Lena's screen lit her face with feeds, rumors, and shaky footage of Lucien walking beside paramedics. Headlines were already multiplying.

KINGPIN COMFORTS VICTIMS

COLE SEEN AT MERCY WEST MASSACRE

She showed him the glow. "You cannot hide anymore."

He closed his fist on the rosary. "Then we walk in daylight."

"Copy. Sending coordinates."

They loaded.

Logan slid behind the wheel of the truck, the engine still ticking with the heat it had carried from the fire.

Lucien took the passenger seat, earpiece in place, eyes forward.

Lena climbed into the back, one hand still on his shoulder like an anchor.

Victor and Rook took the van behind them, eyes on their six. The convoy formed without a word.

Lucien keyed his comm. "Keep us linked. Mara, Imani, Ghost, stay in our ears until this city sleeps."

"Copy. You'll have me the whole way down."

"Mara here. I'll blind their eyes on approach."

"Imani on the spoof. Feeding maintenance IDs, kicking their timers out of sync. Give me thirty seconds."

The city parted for sirens and refused everyone else. Midtown's towers stole light from the flames and the moon and made it cruel.

Ghost spoke in their ears. "Two blocks south of Civic Hall. Service gate for a sealed spur. City capped it in seventy-six when the curves couldn't take the new trains. Left it to rot."

"Eyes dark in three blocks," Mara said. "Thermals and feeds go trash on my mark."

"I've fed them false routes," Imani added. "Their GPS will lead them in circles if they trust it."

Logan took the turn without slowing.

The convoy slid into the service street behind Civic Hall, tires whispering against wet asphalt. The alley rose up ahead, narrow, gated, forgotten.

They stepped out.

"That gate should be open," Ghost said in their ears. "They pulled security to the west access. You're coming in clean."

"Keys don't matter."

Rook popped a latch and shouldered the chain open.

The alley smelled of damp brick and rot.

Headlights cut through the mist and caught movement, figures watching from the trash line, jittery and young.

Footsteps came toward them, quick and stacking, too many to stay quiet.

Victor pivoted, hand settling where violence lived.

Rook lifted his chin, eyes mapping the dark.

Logan smiled. Trouble waking behind his teeth.

A pack of young men slid out of the dark, early twenties, skinny and loud, trying to look fearless. Hoodies. Cheap knives. Eyes too young for this.

The first one skidded to a stop, voice cracking before it steadied. "Holy shit. It's him. You're Lucien Cole."

Another kid nodded like he was trying to convince his own heartbeat. "We saw the feed. We saw you put 'em on blast."

The smallest one looked at Lena, then dropped his eyes to his shoes. Respect shaped like shyness.

Lucien faced them. "Names."

They started talking over each other.

He cut it with a hand. "Not all at once."

A few had pistols tucked wrong. Grip too high. Waistbands snagging on the metal. Fingers fumbling cheap safeties.

Lucien counted them anyway. Amateurs or not, numbers were numbers. Tonight, numbers mattered.

He looked at each face until it had weight.

"You came to help. Help means rules."

They went still.

"If you want in tonight, you choose the way. Not out of loyalty to me, out of loyalty to the kid next to you. No crowns. No trophies. You don't outrun your radio. You don't shoot what you can step around. If you fall, you get carried. If your brother falls, you carry him."

One of them, tattooed knuckles, a half-healed split in his lip, nodded so hard his neck hurt.

"Say when."

"Now. Heads down. Shoulder to shoulder. Twenty bodies, one line."

Rook looked at the busted lock.

"Then let's go see what the city forgot."

He swung the chain loose.

They moved in.

The dark wasn't hunting him anymore. Tonight, it moved when he moved.

The mouth of the old line yawned, brick and rust, cold air spilling out.

Condensation dripped.

Graffiti layered graffiti until it read like scripture, names over years, prayers over curses.

Rats watched from the cracks, the quiet landlords of places the city forgot.

The city had buried its dead under churches and rails. Tonight, they walked on both.

Someone's light swept a wall and froze.

Red letters. Years of paint under them, years of paint over them, but the words sat on top like a fresh wound:

THESE SHALL MAKE WAR WITH THE LAMB, AND THE LAMB SHALL OVERCOME THEM: FOR HE IS LORD OF LORDS, AND KING OF KINGS: AND THEY THAT ARE WITH HIM ARE CALLED, AND CHOSEN, AND FAITHFUL, REV. 17:14

No one spoke.

Lucien's beam drifted past the verse and slid down the throat of a side tunnel.

The dark there sat wrong.

Two yellow eyes opened inside the dark, not catching light, swallowing it.

Around them, the shadows tightened and took the rough shape of a wolf, as if the night itself were remembering what it once feared.

No fur. No breath. Just a shape held together by intent.

Stillness so perfect it felt chosen.

Watching him like prophecy waiting to be confirmed.

Not memory.

Not dream.

Here.

Lucien didn't breathe.

He blinked.

The tunnel was empty again.

The dark rushed back into the space the Wolf had taken, settling too quickly, too neatly, as if covering its own tracks.

Brick. Damp. Silence.

Nothing there, but the feeling stayed.

No one else reacted.

No one else had seen anything.

Water trembled in a pothole at his feet. No drip. No footstep. Just a ripple.

"Movement," Ghost whispered. "Council guards pulling out through the east maintenance ramp, old service grade, connects to the street behind City Hall. Three cars, two vans. Staggered. If you're going to block them, it's now."

"Got it," Mara breathed. "I've nuked their cams on the east ramp. No eyes but ours."

"I'm desyncing their real-time," Imani said. "They'll hear echoes, not orders. If they move, they won't move together."

Victor was already moving.

"Logan, east catwalk."

"I've got the lower grate," Rook said.

Lena thumbed the safety off and pointed to the kids.

"You guys with me. Tight line. Don't drift."

"Ghost. Kill their map. I want them guessing."

"Lights are flickering."

Somewhere above, a panel snapped dark.

"You're welcome."

"Feeds gone," Mara confirmed. "Thermals spiking, anything with eyes is blind."

"Their GPS is chasing ghosts," Imani added. "They'll be two streets off for the next five minutes."

Boots on metal.

Voices that didn't belong down here.

Flashlight cones jittered across the ribs of the station and died against the dark.

"Block the exits," Lucien said.

Logan stepped into the beam and became a problem the guards had to solve.

Rook vanished and reappeared where steel met weak weld.

Victor took the center and walked straight into the gunline.

The first muzzle flash tore the dark.

Their answer came back from four corners at once.

Sound became physics.

Sparks made brief stars on old tile.

"Down," Lena said.

She pulled two kids behind a pillar and blew out the portable floodlight the guards had dropped on a tripod.

The world went dark again.

Better.

The boy with the split lip stumbled, caught himself, and kept moving.

Another kid with a bracelet made from wire and faith dragged a friend down and took the bullet instead.

The kid froze mid-breath, bullet already inside him, shocked that heat could feel so cold.

"Left flank!" Rook barked.

His knife dropped a man before he could turn.

Victor read the shift in their shoulders and cut the angle.

He moved to block the ramp.

Gunfire found a rhythm and then broke.

Dust lifted.

Steel rang.

When the last guard broke, he threw a flashbang and ran.

The blast rolled through the junction and hit like a punch to the chest.

Silence returned.

The living came back injured, limping, present.

Five kids didn't get up. Lena knelt by each one, touching their foreheads like a mother who expected no thanks. Logan swallowed hard and didn't pretend he wasn't doing it. Rook stood guard with his back to grief. Victor counted the living and said nothing.

Lucien stood over the bodies and let himself be a son, a brother, a king with no throne beneath him.

"No nameless dead."

"Not in my city."

It wasn't loud.

It didn't need to be.

"You're not smoke. You're not footage. You moved with us and you don't stop moving here."

He looked at the kids who were still breathing.

"I will carry their names to their mothers. If you want out, you walk out now. If you stay, you make their lives worth the breath you keep. We waste nothing, least of all you."

Lucien crouched beside the bodies.

Wallets scorched. IDs warped. Faces still visible if you could bear to look.

He took each card gently, five in all, sliding them into his pocket.

Lena watched but didn't ask.

She knew what it meant to remember by hand.

Ghost came through softer. "Cars are peeling out up top, Pennington's convoy. They're running east for the river."

"Pennington's blind. I clipped her patrol feed. She's trusting a dead camera."

"I've painted the east route two blocks north," Imani added. "If they follow what they see, they'll miss the bridge."

Lucien closed his eyes for one beat.

One prayer that didn't ask.

"Then we're not done."

They gathered the fallen.

Their jackets became shrouds.

Rook found a piece of cardboard, clean on one side, and wrote the names the kids gave him, letters uneven, holy.

They set the bodies in a row where the tunnel's draft was kindest.

Lena brushed dust from a face.

Logan tucked a bracelet into a palm.

Victor stood at the head of the line and looked like the kind of man who would murder a city for five sons he never met.

Lucien turned toward the ramp.

Firelight from Mercy West still lived on his jacket.

Black rain tapped the rails.

In a puddle at his feet, a ripple caught two yellow eyes, then turned them into nothing a human could prove.

He didn't look down again.

He looked forward.

Breath steady.

"We follow them into the dark."

The tunnel agreed.

The city listened.

And somewhere above, the night went still, unwilling to admit what it had seen.

CHAPTER FORTY-FIVE

COME AND SEE

Dawn split the night with sunlight.

They climbed out of the tunnel like men surfacing from a grave.

The city above was quiet, streets washed, windows blind, nothing left of the chaos but echoes.

Victor had the van rolling, metal settling as it moved. Rook took the passenger side without a word. Logan slid into the truck and let the engine remember rage. Lucien climbed into the back with Lena, silent, eyes on the road ahead. The air between them felt wired, not empty. No one talked. They were breathing.

The city had changed colors while they were underground. Sirens were memories now. The smoke at Mercy West thinned to a stain on the skyline.

They pointed north.

Northgate's elevator hauled them up in a silence that felt nailed shut.

The corridor reeked of damp concrete and solder flux.

The war room thrummed, twelve screens flickering inside its steel skull.

Ghost's voice slid through the comm, cold and precise.

"Feeds live."

Mara spun, eyes bloodshot over the keyboard.

Imani's station pulsed with code, maps sliding alive on the screen.

Headlines crawled:

COLE AT MERCY WEST RUIN

TUNNELS SEALED
UNDERGROUND WAR, RUMOR OR RECKONING?
CITY HALL GONE QUIET
One clip slowed him into a monster.
Another slowed him into sainthood.
The city swallowed both.
Lena stepped beside him, eyes moving over him the way soldiers read terrain. Fast. Accurate. Nothing tender about it.
"Anything broken?" she asked.
"Not enough to matter," Lucien said.
She studied the scorch on his jacket, the dried blood on his knuckles, the smoke that lived in the folds.
"You look like you walked out of fire."
"I did."
She nodded once, the closest she'd come to softness in a room like this.
"Then stay upright," she said. "The city's already trying to fall."
Lucien didn't answer. He didn't have to.
Their silence wasn't distance. It was recognition.
Logan stood at the corner of the table like a man who finally understood what the word cost meant.
"Those boys in the tunnel," he said. "Five. That's on us."
Rook didn't look up from the blade he wiped clean.
"It's on the city that made them cheap."
Victor watched the screens change like weather.
"They'll fill the quiet with worse men if we leave it."
Imani flicked a window to the front.
"Underworld's fracturing. Half the crews are waiting to pledge to the loudest story."
Ghost's voice bled through the speakers. "So we make the story."
"Status on Pennington?" Victor asked.
"Eastbound convoy hit the river, split across the bridges," Ghost said. "She thinks the cameras are her friends again. She's wrong. Odds are she won't surface until night."
"Mayor?" Logan asked.
"Lansing's statement in thirty," Mara said. "Draft already leaked: isolated terror act, city unbowed. He'll try to bury the oxygen explosion under the word gang."
Imani pinched and dragged across the map, downtown blacked out, Midtown crawling with cameras, South Dock a warzone, the East End locked down by Civic Shield.

"We need one move they can't edit," she said. "No CityCast. No donor floors. A dead zone big enough to hold a sermon."

Ghost's voice tightened. "Not a truce. Not peace."

"A reckoning," Lucien said.

Lena's eyes never left his.

"They'll all bring guns."

"Good," he said. "It means they'll remember."

Logan scratched his jaw. "South Dock?"

Ghost slid through the audio.

"South Dock is a grave yelling over itself. No one hears a sermon there."

Rook leaned back. "The old courthouse basement? Certain crews used it for off book drops back when it still passed for forgotten."

Victor didn't blink. "One way in, one way out. They'd bottle us."

Imani zoomed wider. "Then look here."

Three grids overlapped, power dead, cameras blind, patrols thin.

A single patch stayed dim, like the city had forgotten it existed.

"Bronx stadium," she said. "Roof half gone. No feeds. No patrols. Enough open concrete to hold an army and every ghost that ever sat in the stands alone."

Mara pulled up an old photo, sunburned concrete ribs, vines swallowing the old seats, the sky showing through broken beams.

Lucien leaned closer. The ruin filled his eyes like something that had been waiting to be spoken.

Something in him understood it at once: they could build a kingdom out of ghosts.

No one argued with the ruin.

"Lines?" Victor asked.

"Four ingress," Ghost said. "Three clean exits if we don't light the whole place. Rooftop perches. I can put eyes on the rim."

"Snipers?" Logan said, half-hope, half-habit.

"Witnesses. I don't want a crosshair for a conscience."

Lena's voice was quiet enough to make them listen closer.

"If you speak there, you stop hiding. You become the thing they've been naming. Prophet. Warlord. King."

He held her look.

"I won't be their word. I'll be the space where they meet."

Imani's fingers were already moving.

"Message packet going to dark boards, burner trees, backroom chains. One meet. No kings. No crowns. Bring truth, not banners."

Mara killed the wall, revived a blank slate, and drew a single line in white:

COME AND SEE

Logan watched the words like a man about to jump into cold water.

"That's it? No time, no sermon, no schedule?"

Ghost came back on.

"Everyone reads come and see. Only the right ones read the clock inside it."

Victor looked at Lucien. "We'll need roofs."

"Done. Cash buys saints with long lenses for a day."

Rook opened an ammo tin and set it aside.

"I'll bring scaffolds. I'll keep it clean."

A phone buzzed across the table, sharp in the quiet.

Lena caught it, read it, and handed it to Lucien.

Victoria:

Mom's stable. They moved her to Saint Dymphna's on 70th
Oxygen, burns, observation, but she's awake
Dad hasn't left her window

Lucien set the phone down as if the truth inside it was still burning.

He looked at each of them as if taking account.

"We say the names of the five," he said. "We say Mercy West. We say Lansing's lie. We don't promise heaven. We tell them how to breathe."

"Route the call," Ghost said.

Imani's code turned the room into a relay of whispers.

Mara stacked the message under a hundred other messages and let it rise on the right screens, the right phones, the right mouths.

The city listened.

It would deny it later.

The sun cut through the dirty windows and turned the dust holy.

Lena stepped in close, just enough to ground him.

"Say it out loud," she told him, not asking, not soft.

He did.

"Bronx stadium. Late light. No crowns. No banners. You come to speak for someone who can't."

Ghost pushed it through.

Something left the room and didn't come back.

No one cheered.

No one spoke.

Lena leaned her forehead to Lucien's chest for one second.

He let her.

They watched the packet hop boroughs, multiplying. The screen pulsed with confirmations.

Ghost dimmed them until only one remained: a live shot of the skyline, smoke lifting, the day being brave.

By the time the sun fell behind the Bronx, the city already knew where to gather.

CHAPTER FORTY-SIX

THE NEW ORDER

Dusk bled copper across the Bronx. The convoy knifed through a jagged fence mouth. Victor rolled the van slow, tires spitting glass and old banner shreds. The Rezvani followed, engine low, like a blade sliding home.

Wind scraped the stadium's steel ribs, rattling ghosts in the rebar. Half the roof gaped open to a violet sky fading toward night. Floodlight poles bowed under their own weight. Weeds clawed through the concrete aisles as they passed.

Tires crushed bottles and bulbs and splintered bleacher slats.

The convoy came to a stop at the edge of the infield.

Engines went quiet.

Logan jumped down first. He yanked the tarp off a portable generator they'd hauled in the van. He kicked the choke twice, and the generator coughed, spat, then threw one cone of jaundiced light across the dirt.

Shadows stretched, jail bars forged from rusted steel.

The air tasted of diesel, wet stone, stale beer, and the ash of old fires.

Lucien stepped out.

He shouldered fatigue like a loaded vest. No crack in his stance.

He clocked angles: player tunnel, maintenance gate, two breaches in the outfield wall, a stairwell to the concourse, half-buried and still open to the dark.

Exits and entries.

That was breath in a city like this.

Victor and Rook climbed the upper stands, never turning their backs to the field. Counting heads before any heads appeared. Sightlines, corners, nests.

Lena moved with him until the silence asked something of them.

She stopped, eyes tracing the torn sky, the leaning lights, the relic ache of a place built for noise, now held together by silence.

"They built a church for games. And left a kingdom for ghosts."

The centerfield wall was raw concrete, streaked black where rain had tried to wash old graffiti away.

Lucien stared too long.

For a second, a shadow shaped itself into something that watched back.

Then the wind took it.

He didn't blink.

"Eyes on you from the roof and the rafters," Ghost said in his ear. "No lasers. Just witnesses."

"Good."

He felt the exhaustion in his bones and buried it behind his ribs. Never his face.

The crowd arrived without invitation, exactly on time.

Not just the Bronx.

Brooklyn. Queens. Uptown. Downtown.

Crews that usually only saw each other through gun smoke stood in the same field without reaching for steel.

Every crew that mattered sent bodies.

If this went bad, the city would burn before morning.

School buses armored in scrap metal growled through the gate, windows barred like teeth.

Low-riders hissed and dropped low, chrome catching the last light like exposed bone.

Dirt bikes screamed through the gaps and carved circles in the dust, engines snapping like hornets.

Motorcycles rolled in behind them, long and low, headlights burning like single eyes.

A stolen ambulance lurched through the gate, lights torn out, siren box ripped open so its guts showed. Its back doors were chained shut, and something heavy slammed inside with every rut, a slow coffin knock that carried across the field.

Barrel fires rose inside oil drums stamped with old team logos, the paint blistering and running in black lines down the metal.

Then came the horse.

A black police mount stepped onto the warning track, iron in its mouth, breath smoking in the cooling air.

Its rider wore a riot vest with KING slashed in white across the chest, the paint still drying.

Not costume.

A procession.

High above, three figures stretched prone along the upper deck, long lenses steady, bodies wrapped in pale cloth and scavenged armor.

One wore a priest's collar under Kevlar.

They weren't hunting.

They were documenting.

Ghost's witnesses.

Saints with cameras.

Vendors bled out of shadow because cities sell you something at the end of the world.

A boy, thirteen at most, dragged a cooler like it carried relics. Inside, bullet casings polished bright and strung on wire. Necklaces for the dead.

Lena stepped to him.

"Two please."

He looped one into her palm and one around his own wrist, a ritual learned by watching.

She slipped a folded bill into his sleeve, more than the necklace was worth.

Then she tucked the necklace into her pocket, where gauze and ammunition shared space.

"Whole city came to see if legends bleed," Rook muttered, pacing the stands.

Lucien walked down the player tunnel alone.

The generator coughed. Pigeons burst from the rafters, wings scraping dust into the light.

The field received him with a hush that remembered crowds and expected sound.

He crossed to the mound and stood where games once began.

He didn't rush.

He took the field with certainty.

Lena followed halfway, then stopped, her hand falling from his sleeve like a quiet ceremony no one spoke over. He felt it leave and did not look back.

A plastic traffic cone lay by the dugout, sun-faded and cracked along one side.

He lifted it like an old instrument and held it low.

He didn't have to call for quiet. The place did it for him.

Conversations fell apart.

The generator steadied.

The first word would carry.

He reached into his jacket and pulled out five laminated cards, edges burned, photos half-gone.

The IDs of the boys from the tunnel.

He laid them on the dirt one by one, careful, like prayers given weight.

"Luis. Malik. Javi. Romy. Isaiah."

No last names. No details.

The city knew the rest already.

If it didn't, it would learn.

"They died underground. They died because men above the ground sold numbers as truth. They worshiped quiet like it forgave them. They died because the strong forgot to stand between breath and the knife."

He looked up through the torn roof.

The sky offered nothing back, but he measured it like a man taking inventory of what was left.

"They burned the room where my mother breathes. They called that order. They put scripture on a budget and called fire clean."

He let the quiet thicken until it had weight.

"You want a doctrine? Here it is."

He drew breath like a man drinking water in a desert.

"Protect what breathes.

Everything else is just territory."

The cone didn't make him louder.

It made him unavoidable.

"You want money?" His gaze swept crews and colors, men and women who slept with knives for friends. "I'll fill your pockets."

"You want power?" He let the word sit. "Bleed with me.

You want this city back?" His hand opened. The traffic cone lifted a fraction, a bright plastic chalice. "Fight for someone else's lungs."

On the field, mothers held photographs in both hands.

Men who had come to posture lowered their guns without noticing.

The kid with the cooler stood still, open-mouthed, as if church had a sound he'd just found.

Wind slipped through the open roof.

A pigeon called once and went quiet.

Somewhere, a fence rattled in a decades-old breeze.

A man stepped out from the home-side tunnel, swagger blind to the hour.

Gold tooth. Machete in a sheath too clean. A coat that wanted to be a cape.

He wore fear like cologne. He thought no one could smell it.

"You ain't God," he said. "You talk like you got the book."

Lucien walked to meet him.

He didn't hurry.

He didn't slow.

He looked the man in his one honest eye and gave him no higher ground.

"No. I'm what happens when you stop listening."

Someone whispered his name.

Vega.

He snatched for his blade, thinking speed was a prayer.

Lucien's hand found a splintered bat half-buried near the dugout, its handle rotted, nameplate long gone.

Old wood came away with a reluctant creak.

He swung once.

The crack reminded the stadium what bats were for.

Vega's wrist dropped the machete.

Lucien moved without flourish.

He pinned Vega's hand to the pitcher's mound with the man's own blade.

The sound was not pain.

It was metal finding earth.

A stake in the ground.

He leaned close. A city only hears what it is ready to echo.

"These shall make war with the Lamb, and the Lamb shall overcome them," he said, voice low at the man's ear.

He let the silence carry it.

The crowd didn't see the end.

It felt it move through the field.

Not spectacle. Just quiet taking hold.

On the upper deck, one of the ash-white men traced his long lens across the horizon as if praying lines into the city.

He wasn't hunting. He was recording.

Somewhere in a dark packet, the footage began to travel.

"You just rewrote jurisdiction," Ghost said, almost amused.

The generator chose that moment to die.

The field exhaled into darkness.

Engines along the loop coughed, turned, and headlights blinked on one by one in a circle, a rough halo around the mound.

Light washed over faces and found what it needed: men with new thoughts, women with old ones, kids who would carry both by morning.

A lone rival up in the seats fired into the rafters, an idiot's flare.

Feathers burst loose and drifted down through the lights.

No blood.

No drama.

Just hush made visible.

A boy pushed forward from the lip of the dugout with something in both hands: wire twisted from fence scrap into a small crown.

It looked like a dare.

Lucien accepted it.

He pressed it down into his hair until it bit.

A line of red rose and stayed where it was.

He didn't wince.

He didn't bow.

He breathed.

Lena watched from the warning track, hand on her pistol, silhouette cutting through beams.

She could see the half-second the tired ran across his mouth before he closed the door on it.

He wasn't invincible.

Just a man teaching his body what faith costs.

Her fingers brushed the bullet necklace in her pocket. She didn't pray, exactly.

She asked for enough breath.

Logan's whisper ticked the channel.

"If they shoot, the roof catches their names first."

Victor's answer was iron.

"No one's that stupid."

Stupidity was a sacrament in cities like this.

But not tonight.

One boss broke first.

He walked to the mound and knelt.

He set two fingers to the clay like he was checking a pulse, then kissed his fingertips.

Not worship.

Claim.

Another came.

A third.

Knees found earth, leather and metal surrendering.

No chant.

Only breath.

And that was enough.

Lucien let it happen and never claimed it.

He lifted the cone one last time because closing was a kind of mercy.

"The city forgot how to breathe. Tonight, we remember for it."

"Congratulations," Ghost said. If wire could carry a smile, this one did.

"You just crowned yourself in a graveyard."

Lena's voice came next, soft and firm.

"And buried the old gods."

The wind shifted, cold and sudden, like breath too close to the back of his neck.

Ghost again.

"Coalition chatter spiking. Pennington on with Lansing. Civic Shield moving north. They're naming it already."

Across the city, the sermon reached screens it was never meant to.

Ghost's feed bled through Coalition servers before he could lock it.

In Pennington's command room, the screens stilled. Analysts froze the frame. Lucien caught in the headlights, blood at his temple, wire crown bright as confession.

"This isn't a riot," Pennington said. "It's doctrine."

In City Hall, Lansing watched from an office built for speeches, not confessions. Civic Shield alerts crawled along the edge of the feed like static.

"Then call it what it is," he said. "A cult."

Ghost fed the word into Lucien's ear.

The weather had changed. The men who owned its silence had heard the thunder first.

Lucien looked out over the field.

"Then they finally learned the word."

Victor and Rook swept the upper deck where the sniper-priests held their posts, eyes set in dark angles no camera could reach.

Logan put heat back into the Rezvani's engine.

Lena drew mothers inward, hands on elbows, photos tucked away, a human lane forming where chaos thought it owned rights.

"Move before the light lies to them," Lucien said.

Engines turned.

The dead generator smoked in the corner like a spent lung.

Headlights swung toward the exits.

The horse stamped once and tossed its head.

The kid with the cooler counted the necklaces left and found the number wasn't what he'd brought.

Somewhere up top, the ash-white witnesses crossed themselves and went back to filming a sacrament they didn't need a bishop for.

Engines rolled.

The convoy found the gap it had made and pushed through.

On the field, the wind leveled the mound as best it could.

Pigeons settled into the rafters. The old stadium remembered what to do after the shouting stopped.

As the last taillight slid through the broken gate, the old stadium took its breath back.

Headlights died to memory.

The night cooled.

The place went back to what it had been built to be: a house for noise that now remembered prayer.

And the city, cruel and faithful and hungry, had a new sermon.

Chapter Forty-Seven

BEFORE THE TRUMPETS

Northgate, 8:22 P.M.

They coasted through the courtyard and into the garage, tires coughing dust through the headlight haze.

Victor rolled in close behind, lights off.

The metal door sealed behind them with a final clang, no echo, no mercy.

Inside, Northgate felt alive in a way places like this shouldn't.

Imani and Mara stood at the monitors, eyes locked on feeds.

Ghost's voice came through. "Coalition pulled the lever. They're rolling Mercy West and the stadium into one story. Coordinated attack, organized network, armed political movement. They're calling Mercy West a terror strike on medical infrastructure. That lets them escalate fast without saying the big words yet. Governor signed the emergency order. Mayor pushed a citywide curfew for 2200. You've got about ninety minutes before the streets start getting teeth. Drones already mapping curfew zones."

Imani tapped the screen, bridge cameras freezing one by one. "They're not locking down districts. They're cutting arteries. By midnight, the city won't even bleed right."

Ghost cut back in. "Civic Shield went to crisis posture. Every reserve unit is spinning up. They're moving bridges and tunnels to controlled access. Transit will start folding in the next hour. They're setting checkpoints at the bridge mouths and major avenues. Air units overhead all night. And the language is shifting. Feeds aren't saying gang anymore. I'm hearing network, doctrine, recruitment. By morning they'll be using the word insurgent without saying who yet."

Lucien stared at the static, eyes reflecting broken pixels.

"They're not reacting to what you did tonight," Ghost said. "They're reacting to what they think happens tomorrow when the city wakes up and picks a side."

"Let them put on their show," Lucien said. "We'll see who the city listens to."

Lena moved to his side, close enough that he could feel the warmth of her arm without either of them looking at the other.

Before he could lean into it, his phone buzzed once.

Victoria.

He put her on speaker.

"Vic."

Hospital noise moved behind her.

"Yeah. Listen. Saint Dymphna's. I ran into someone in the hall. Celia Armand. Private atelier on Forty-Seventh. Old-school. No website, no front window, no staff. The kind of women who can't be seen in a bridal shop go to her. No records, no photos, no questions. Nights are the only time she can open right now, her husband's in ICU and she spends her days here. She gave us one hour. Cash. No names spoken twice."

Lucien's face hardened.

"Vic, the city locks down in less than two hours. By dawn they could have my face under every word they need. Cult. Terrorist. Insurgent. Whatever sells best. I'm not sending Lena into Midtown for silk."

The line went quiet for half a beat.

"Then stop talking like we have six peaceful weeks left, Lucien. Lena can't do this in daylight now, and you know it. By morning every lens in this city will know her face next to yours. This woman is quiet. You go in, the door locks, and the world doesn't know you were there. Nights are the only time she can open right now. And this curfew isn't going anywhere. If Lena waits for a safer night, there might not be one before the wedding. If she wants to lay hands on that future, this is the window."

Lena looked at the wall of monitors. Police lights were stacking at the bridges. Barricades were going up. Traffic was thinning block by block. The city wasn't locked yet, but it was getting ready to be.

Ghost came through, thinner now, less certain.

"It's not clean. The city just hasn't closed its hand yet. Midtown's still pretending to be normal. Cameras are sparse, not blind. Most of the eyes are leaning north and the bridge approaches are taking most of the attention. Getting there isn't the problem. Getting back is when the streets start asking questions. I can give them a hole, not safety."

Lucien's jaw set. "Not tonight."

"It's the window we have," Ghost said.

Mara pushed off the wall.

"Oh, good. For a second I thought we were pretending this gets safer next week."

Imani looked at Lena, then at Lucien, like she was measuring the distance between them.

"Waiting doesn't improve the math," she said quietly.

"In six weeks, we could be married. In six weeks, we could be ash. The way this is going, that day isn't getting closer. It's moving away from us."

Lucien looked at Lena.

She held his gaze without softening for him.

"If they name you something worse by morning," she said, "then let them. I'm not waiting for a safer city to pick the dress I plan to survive in."

That hit him where armor didn't reach.

He looked away first.

For one second he hated the truth of it, not her, not any of them, just the world that made this reasonable.

Victoria's voice came back, quieter now.

"She's not asking for a fairytale, Lucien. She's asking to lay a hand on the future before they try to outlaw that too."

The room stayed still.

No one tried to help him out of it.

Then Lucien exhaled once, and some of the fight went with it.

"All right.

I'm taking her."

Lena arched a brow, finding a spark of humor because that's how you survive nights like this.

"You're not supposed to see the dress before the day. That's the rule."

He looked at her a second too long.

The wire crown still ghosted his scalp, the dried blood tight where the wire had been.

Every vow he'd made tonight had been carved from someone else's lungs.

Hers was the only breath he refused to gamble.

And still, she was asking him to.

That was the wound.

Lucien looked at Rook. "Those plates still say we fix things?"

"Utility contractors," Rook said. "Emergency work order. Boring and official."

"Good. Logan, pull the van around. If you're caught in the open, hazards on. You're not hiding. You're supposed to be there."

"Copy," Logan said. "Utility, not ghosts."

Mara grabbed her coat.

"You think we're letting her do this without witnesses? Absolutely not."

Imani was already reaching for her sidearm.

"We're the only ones who understand silk under siege."

Lucien looked at the ceiling speaker.

"You stay in her ear the whole way."

"I'll watch the streets," Ghost said. "If something shifts, I'll see it first."

"Good. I want them home before the city remembers what time it is."

An engine came alive downstairs.

The women were already moving. Coats. Sidearms. A last check in black glass.

Lena turned back once, eyes catching his in the cold light of the screens.

"Don't do anything unholy without me."

Lucien held the look until she was gone.

"No promises."

Their laughter, faint and nervous and human, trailed out into the blackout night.

Victor watched Lucien watch them go.

"You hate this," Victor said.

Lucien kept his eyes on the door.

"Yeah."

"But you let her go."

Lucien looked at the dead monitors, the frozen bridges, the city learning how to close.

"I let her be right."

Northgate, 8:49 P.M.

The garage doors sealed behind the taillights.

Quiet pressed in, thick, wrong, like the building had swallowed sound.

Ghost bled in. "Lockdown clock's ticking. They're walling the bridges and scanning plates. Anyone caught past ten gets picked up."

Victor set the truck keys on the table and left them there.

"We staying open until they check in, or do we button this place up now?"

"Hold," Lucien said. "Until they're locked in."

Rook killed the overheads. Only the lamps stayed on, small circles of light in a dark room.

The next half hour went to doors, guns, and maps while the city disappeared from the screens.

Ghost again, softer. "Atelier confirms arrival. Cameras dead on that block. Logan's parked nose-out. I'll run noise if anyone hunts."

"Keep them dark."

He walked the corridor alone. The building smelled like wet concrete and old paper. Pipes hissed somewhere above.

A maintenance door stuck halfway, then gave. Inside was a sink, a cracked mirror, and a bare bulb that couldn't warm the room.

The glass had a fingertip smear across it. He didn't see the letters until he looked straight at them.

AND IT WAS GIVEN UNTO HIM TO MAKE WAR WITH THE SAINTS, AND TO OVERCOME THEM.

REV. 13:7

He didn't breathe for a second.

The bulb hummed.

The mirror found his face, then something over his shoulder the glass had no right to hold.

Yellow eyes, fixed in the glass. Close. Patient. Smoke-dark fur around a mouth too calm for hunger.

No sound. No drama. Just presence.

The room seemed to lean with it.

Lucien didn't turn.

He watched the wolf watch him, two forces that understood the cost of standing still.

He hadn't slept right since the coma. Not real sleep. Just hours where his body went still and his mind didn't. The back of his head still throbbed where the crown had cut him, and when his pulse climbed too fast the room tilted, then settled. He stood there a second longer than a steady man would, waiting for the floor to stop moving.

The bulb flickered. The eyes were gone.

He stepped closer. The glass caught his reflection wrong. Too many shadows, not enough man.

His fist moved.

The mirror shattered, a hundred Luciens breaking at once.

He opened his hand and closed it. Blood from the glass threaded into his palm. He pressed it into the shards and felt the cut answer.

Behind him, boots on concrete.

Victor in the doorway. "You picking fights with mirrors now?"

Lucien didn't look up. "It wasn't a mirror."

Blood slipped from his knuckles, ticking into the sink.

Victor swore and grabbed a towel. "You're bleeding and talking to glass. That's a problem."

Lucien didn't flinch. "There was writing on it."

Victor paused. "What kind of writing?"

Lucien met his eyes in the broken reflection. "The kind that already had my name on it."

Victor wrapped the hand, pulling the gauze tight. "Under pressure?"

"Under vow."

Victor tied it off. "Talk."

Lucien watched the broken frame hold a smaller, meaner reflection.

"When I flatlined, there was nothing waiting. Just a sky that forgot what color meant. Roads to nowhere. I walked for what felt like forever through a world that didn't know it was dead."

Victor didn't interrupt.

"But there's this thing," Lucien said, eyes flicking to the mirror shards. "This Wolf. It didn't come from there. That world was empty. The Wolf found me later. I saw it in a dream the night of the raid."

He flexed his bandaged hand, the gauze already pink at the seams.

"I dreamed I was back in that place, but wrong, like someone had redrawn it from bad memory. There was a forest. A Bible on an altar. Silas's head beside it, still talking. The page was Revelation 1:7. Behold, he comes with the clouds. And I heard Lena calling me back."

Victor exhaled through his nose. "And you woke up."

"Yeah. Heart kicking like it had something left to prove."

Lucien tapped one of the broken shards with his knuckle, dust shifting where the letters had been. REV 13:7. Gone now. He'd seen it before the glass broke.

"The verse back in the subway was just graffiti. Anyone could've painted it. But this one wasn't written by a hand. It showed up while I was standing here. Same book. Different warning. I've seen the Wolf in the tunnel, and now in the glass. It's not just dreams anymore. It's like it's crossing over."

"I don't know if that's God, a wolf, or a head injury," Victor said. "What I know is you're here, and you're bleeding."

Victor looked at the bandage like a man checking a weld. "So what is it asking you to do?"

Lucien thought about Evelyn under glass and heat. About five boys laid out in a row where the draft had been kindest. About Lena in a dead city choosing a dress like a dare.

"It isn't asking. It's reminding me."

Victor leaned into the jamb, the posture of a man who had stood at too many edges.

"Listen. Anyone can make a vow when the room is on fire. The real ones, you keep them in the smoke after. Right now you have two vows. Lena, and breath. Whatever that wolf is, beside you, behind you, or nowhere at all, it doesn't change the work. We still carry the same stretchers."

Lucien nodded once. The small kind of yes that fixes bigger ones.

They walked back into the war room. Screens showed bridges going to sleep and avenues folding in on themselves. Men in armored vans made noise for the cameras and moved quiet for the work. Somewhere choppers hovered in overwatch, covering the curfew routes.

Ghost's voice came in. "Update. Curfew line's moving north. Lansing's sending Civic Shield into the Bronx with it. They're going to salt it with curfew arrests and call it mercy. That's where they'll make the example. He goes live from City Hall in five."

Rook called from the hallway. "You want me on the roof with the long eyes?"

Victor answered without looking up. "The rifle. Two positions. Stay low. Don't light a cigarette."

"Copy. Throwing the drone up instead."

"Keep it low and launch from shadow," Victor said. "If they see it go up, they'll start looking for where it came from."

Ghost came back. "They're locking Downtown and pushing into Midtown. Once they seal the Harlem River crossings and the tunnels, we're boxed in. Lena needs to head back before the line reaches her. Once it does, every road north turns into a checkpoint."

Lucien stepped past Victor, voice low. "Put Lena on."

"You're live," Ghost said, and the line opened in his ear.

Logan came first, voice muffled under static. "We're here. Storefront's dark. Back room only. Work lights. Women are marking and pinning. Feels like a bank job."

Mara came over the line. "More like surgery. The woman works like she's stitching someone back together."

Imani followed. "Sutures. We're on the clock."

In the background, Victoria's voice, calm and warm. "He doesn't get to see the dress."

Lucien let himself breathe that line in. "I'll pretend I didn't want to."

Lena came last. "We're safe, my love. It's quiet. Sirens. No footsteps."

"Hold that quiet," Lucien said. "You have a half-hour window left. Don't miss it."

Victoria again. "She found it. It's the one. The woman says she'll work through the night."

"I'll see you when the sirens stop," Lena said.

"Count on it."

The channel clicked dead.

For a second the room held her voice like heat after a door closes.

Then the world pushed back in.

CHAPTER FORTY-EIGHT

WERE THE POLICE NOW

The main screen no longer showed traffic. It showed the mayor.

His face filled the screen, softly lit, flag behind his shoulder, eyes reading from a teleprompter built to forgive tone.

"An isolated terror act," Lansing said. "Gang violence. Necessary measures. Curfew saves lives."

Lucien closed his eyes while the words rolled past.

He had never learned how to hate cleanly.

He put the feeling into verbs instead.

He opened them. "Mute him."

Victor cut the sound.

"Read me the streets," Lucien said.

Ghost's voice came through. "Curfew line's still pushing north. NYPD and Shield mixed units. Slow and wide. Barricades, floodlights, checkpoints. Lansing's main Shield units are still staging to hit the Bronx once the curfew line reaches it."

Lucien glanced at the clock.

9:50

His jaw tightened once. "If they enter the Bronx, I want our doors ready and everyone on their feet."

Rook's voice cracked through the comm. "Drone's up. They're setting portable light towers at the intersections. Big ones. Lighting the streets like day. Barricades are staggered, not straight. They're funneling traffic where they want it."

"Good," Victor said. "Let them think the wall is the point."

Rook went quiet. "Hold on. Change in the pattern. Large convoy just peeled off the closure line. Heavy vehicles. Not heading north. Heading for the river."

Victor frowned. "Staging supplies before they seal the crossings."

Lucien's head lifted. "Cargo?"

"Armored transports," Rook said. "Fuel trucks behind them. Not patrol cars. Logistics."

Ghost cut in. "ID matches Pennington's requisition. Civic Shield supply convoy. Armor, radios, riot packs, diesel. Enough to hold a lockdown in place once they bed it down."

Lucien's voice went quiet. "Where?"

"Harlem River industrial yards. Manhattan side. They want the gear inside Manhattan before they seal the bridges."

Victor looked at Lucien. They both understood it at the same time.

Lucien nodded once. "Then we hit it before they close the door."

Ghost stayed calm. "If that's where they're staging, they won't be settled yet. Yard cams run on an old industrial loop. Bad angles. Dead zones. I can give you a window, not a war."

Lucien looked at the screens a second longer, then turned away from them like the decision was already finished.

"Rook, bring the drone home. Pack it up and get downstairs."

"On it."

Lucien stepped back into the maintenance room and picked up a broken shard from the sink. The letters were gone. Only his blood proved they'd been there.

"What are you doing?" Victor asked.

"Remembering."

He slipped the shard into his pocket and went back to the war room.

Rook came in a few seconds later, rifle off his shoulder, drone controller in hand. He set both on the table and stepped up to the monitor wall, city cameras flickering across his face. Victor cupped a hand to light a cigarette.

Ghost came back. "Two minutes to ten."

"Bring the truck around," Lucien said.

Victor moved first.

Engines turned over below. Doors opened. They moved with the quiet speed of people who had already decided.

The night slipped into Northgate, thin and cool, the air rationed.

By the time Lucien stepped outside, the city felt different, like something large had just leaned its weight onto the grid.

Phones screamed first.

Then the city alert bled through the dead feeds.

Somewhere beyond the walls, cruisers rolled orders out through bullhorns.

The city didn't have one voice. It had a thousand cheap speakers saying the same thing.

"ATTENTION. BY ORDER OF THE CITY OF NEW YORK, A CITYWIDE CURFEW IS NOW IN EFFECT. ALL CIVILIANS RETURN HOME IMMEDIATELY. BRIDGES AND TUNNELS ARE SUBJECT TO CLOSURE. FAILURE TO COMPLY WILL RESULT IN DETENTION."

Lucien looked at Victor.

"We move before they get comfortable."

10:04 P.M.

Curfew sirens smeared through light rain.

The streets were a wet lung breathing through loudspeakers.

The Rezvani rolled dark through the district, headlights off, and nothing on the street questioned it.

From every pole, the same recorded voice, tired already:

"Curfew in effect. Remain indoors. Enforcement in progress."

Helicopters stitched slow circles overhead.

Floodlights washed intersections in hard white.

Somewhere, a drone dragged a red eye across empty asphalt.

The city repeated itself until even fear sounded bored.

Inside the truck, light leaked from a single instrument dial. Lucien rode in the passenger seat, gloved hand on the dash. The other was wrapped in gauze, darkening to the color of old sins. He flexed once, knuckles pale, and steadied.

Ghost's voice filtered through the comm speaker, compressed, clean. "Yard lights holding. Two fuel carriers. Three Civic Shield transports. One command jeep. Patrol in pairs."

Behind the wheel, Rook drove like the city was glass and he knew where it cracked. His eyes lived on angles no stoplight ever saw.

"Rain's helping," Rook said. "Keeps the streets empty and the dark thick."

Lucien kept his eyes on the dark ahead. "Keep the headlights off. Use thermal. If anything's alive out there, I want to see it before it sees us."

Victor sat behind them, checking his rifle with the patience of a man who had survived his own temper. Each click landed like a quiet prayer in another language.

Lucien watched rain stripe the windshield.

"They call it curfew."

Victor's mouth curved, short of a smile.

"What do we call it?"

"Clarity."

The loudspeaker continued talking.

The city continued not listening.

Ghost laid the route over the night.

"Pier C gate. Two exits east. Yard cam grid loops every seventy seconds. Industrial maintenance cycle. Strike inside that silence. You'll have thirty seconds of perfect dark when I step on the flood array."

Lucien watched the world by reflection, storefront glass. He mapped their entry onto every surface.

Victor glanced up. "You ever get tired of scripture?"

Lucien's grin was tired but real. "Only when it stops coming true."

"One mile to the Yard," Ghost said.

Rook sniffed once, eyes narrowing. "Fuel's already in the air."

They rolled under a warehouse awning that had sagged long before any of them were born. Tin roof, holes punched by weather, rain coming through in slow, steady taps.

They cut the engine. Doors didn't slam. Black wraps. Suppressed rifles. Pry bar. Zip kit. Two crow's feet for tires that needed sleep.

Rook checked the gate tablet, fingers a quiet blur. Victor shouldered the rifle and measured the street.

Lucien adjusted the rearview. The mirror caught a thin wash of dashboard light, splitting his reflection in half, one eye lit, the other lost to shadow. He let the two versions of himself settle.

He slid the shard into his pocket.

"Time to finish the sermon."

Ghost came in. "Grid loop starting now."

Lucien nodded, the kind of nod that starts wars.

"Move."

They moved.

The first gate met Rook's grip. The lock cracked. The hinge screamed.

They slipped into the yard's throat.

Containers stacked like mute tenements. Cranes loomed like skeletons taught to kneel. Floodlights spilled cold white on everything. Rain made it shine, like the city trying to spit them out.

Footsteps went quiet when men moved with intent. They ghosted along the hulls of fuel carriers, wet metal against wet sleeves.

Civic Shield stood thirty yards off. Riot armor. Helmets canted. Laughing like night-shift men when the city stopped being a city and started being a paycheck.

"They think they own the fucking city," Victor murmured.

Lucien watched a raindrop walk the length of his barrel.

"Then we evict them."

A fuel puddle near his boot shivered. For a breath, something moved through its reflection, tall, ancient, patient, but nothing stood behind him. The rain erased the shape. Lucien didn't look down.

"Five," Ghost said. The loop ticked in his voice.

"Four."

"Three."

"Two."

"One."

The yard went silent, like a finger pressed to the city's mouth.

Dark, not blackout. The floods were dead. Only rain and suppressed fire.

Two guards dropped. Armor buckled. Bodies hit wet ground.

Helmets tipped. Blood washed thin in the rain.

Rook slid under the first transport and cut the ignition lines with a kiss of steel.

Victor swept the flank, dropped a guard onto his back, and put a round through his forehead.

They advanced, voices clipped.

"Left. Clear."

"Down."

"Fuel first."

A woman's voice cut through the dark, low and controlled. "Hold your lines."

Lucien froze for half a second. *That was not rent-a-cop tone.*

From behind the next carrier, a figure stepped out. Riot armor stripped of insignia. Sidearm clean. Stance square.

Even the rain seemed to hesitate around her.

Ghost's voice tightened in their ears. "Lucien. That's Captain Dane. Lansing's hammer."

Victor exhaled. "Didn't think she got her hands dirty."

"She does tonight," Lucien said.

Dane's radio flared static. She slapped it, scanning the cranes.

"You're trespassing on a restricted site," she called. "Drop your weapons."

Lucien lifted his head just enough for her to see the silhouette, and the calm inside it.

"So are you," he said. "Difference is, I know why I'm here."

For a heartbeat, the rain hung suspended.

Dane's voice broke through the channel. "Identify your,"

Ghost cut in, a click sharp enough to feel.

"Signal folded. Their comms are eating themselves."

Her radio collapsed into a single tone.

Dane slapped it once, hard. Nothing.

Around her, helmets turned. Men touched earpieces that weren't talking back.

Dead air.

For half a heartbeat, no one knew who was in charge.

Then a muzzle flashed off to their right, panic fire from a guard who had already lost the thread. The burst lit the yard for half a heartbeat, painting armor and faces in white shock. For that blink of light, no one knew who belonged where.

Smoke crawled in, heavy with cordite and wet metal. The air tasted of batteries and blood waiting its turn.

"Twenty seconds," Ghost murmured in their ears. A steady countdown, almost gentle.

Victor ghosted a signal from cover, two fingers toward the jeep.

Lucien tapped his comm twice. Now.

Rook moved on cue, one muffled shot, then another. Two bodies folded into the wet gravel like the rain had claimed them early.

The dark inverted the fight. Hunters lost their angles. Patrol became quarry. Quarry became scripture.

Another breath. Another shift.

When the light returned, it came back thin and green, the flood array limping half-alive.

What it showed was a woman on her knees.

Captain Dane lifted her head through the rain, slow but unbroken, like a soldier refusing to disappear before the world acknowledged her.

Her visor was cracked. Rain carved clean tracks down a face built for control. She looked up into the half-light, jaw locked against what she already understood.

"You're on camera," she said. Brave, because some people were born with only one gear.

Her eyes cut to the mast cam above the jeep, blinking red.

"Then let them see."

Lucien stepped into the dripline. The muzzle rose and found the hollow beneath her chin, close enough that their breath met in the space between.

Victor angled a body-cam toward them. Dane's hands didn't shake.

Ghost seized the feed and dragged it into the dark, threading it through channels that never slept and rooms where truth arrived uninvited. Across the city, the underground blinked awake.

Lucien held the lens.

Not a speech. Not a plea.

Just the line that changed weather.

"We're the fucking police now."

He fired.

The shot cracked through the rain and took her voice with it.

Blood struck the lens like a baptism.

Static answered like a hymn that had lost its words.

The yard exhaled. Movement broke all at once. Armor clattered. Boots pounded toward the gates. What was left of the unit scattered into the rain.

Rook's voice came from the truck. "Fuel loaded."

"Radios boxed," Victor grunted as he dumped a crate. He stacked armor plates on rubber mats, smile thin as a blade, eyes on the prize.

Ghost cut in. "Reinforcements rerouting. Ninety seconds until the sky turns red."

Lucien crouched by the third Civic Shield truck and set a palm-sized charge beneath the tank brace, fingers moving with quiet precision. A magnet kissed steel. A red LED winked once, then went dark.

Victor clocked it. "Fireworks?"

"Symbolism," Lucien said.

Rook closed the last latch. "We good?"

"We're good." Lucien stood. "Go."

They rolled out.

Halfway to the gate, the charge bloomed. A flower of pressure. A bloom of fire. Not a warhead. A halo.

The river caught it and made it beautiful against its will. Orange spun across black water, then fractured and ran.

Borrowed glory burned just fine.

They took the east exit like it had been waiting for them.

The gate yawned. The city's throat opened. They slipped through.

Sirens spooled behind them, late and useless.

A drone dipped into smoke and found only heat where prey had stood.

Inside the truck, fire played across glass and skin. In Lucien's eyes, it looked like the future testing itself.

"First blood," Victor said, quiet and not celebratory.

"First breath," Lucien answered.

Ghost's voice threaded through.

"Feed's viral. Lansing's team can't kill it. Your line's on every screen. They're burning their own wires to stop it."

"Then let them pray to the smoke," Lucien said.

Phones buzzed across the city. Screens lit in alleys, stairwells, back rooms, any place a signal could hide. The underground caught the video first: a man in the rain, voice low, eyes bright as signal.

Somewhere, the loudspeakers still mouthed curfew.

No one listened.

The night had already chosen its side.

In control rooms, precinct houses, and glass offices high above the avenues, screens jerked awake, static flaring into motion.

Lucien's face froze mid-line, blurred, then froze again.

Ghost watched three angles like a medic counting heartbeats.

He didn't save the clip. He didn't label it. He let the city take it.

Coalition command stumbled. Security feeds choked and coughed.

A tech whispered, "Cole's people hit the yard."

Another man made a sound that wanted to be a prayer and wasn't.

In the Northgate garage, the van door slid open and Lena stepped down into the concrete light.

Somewhere beyond the open garage doors, sirens moved through the rain.

Lena paused beside the van and looked out through the open doors toward the city she could hear but not see from here.

She didn't blink.

On corners that resisted curfew, phones lifted like fireflies.

A bootleg live feed flickered behind the gate of a closed bodega.

A livery driver replayed the shot and kept driving.

A kid uptown tried the sentence into his sleeve.

"We're the fucking police now."

It fit.

A longshoreman watched a crane swing, saw smoke climbing over the skyline, and understood the city had just changed hands.

He smiled into the rain, a man hearing an old language return.

In a Civic Shield locker room, silence settled hard.

A nameplate was removed from a door.

A duffel bag zipped shut.

A man who once believed the uniform made him righteous sat down and didn't stand again for a long time.

Down the marble corridor at City Hall, a door marked WAR ROOM spilled a thin line of light, as if it had swallowed a sunrise and failed to hide it.

Inside, the weight of the moment found its owner.

Lansing stood alone in the wash of dying screens, the city burning in fractured panes.

His hand hovered over the phone like it feared the answer.

When he spoke, his voice was thin, a man trying not to hear himself.

"Get me the Governor."

The line held.

A long, empty breath.

Then the tone began to rise, sharp and merciless.

Outside, the smoke kept its promise.

It lifted over the skyline in a slow, steady column, the kind cities only grow when something has broken for good.

Chapter Forty-Nine
THE STORM LOSES ITS SKY

City Hall erupted. Phones barked. Radios cracked. Maps blinked red where the Harlem River yards used to be calm. Staff shouted about transmission control and optics.

Mayor Lansing stood in the middle and didn't move.

Somewhere deep in the building, a relay clicked and the lights shifted a shade colder. Backup systems hummed, doors locked, elevators froze where they were. The building was sealing itself, floor by floor, like it knew something had gotten in.

He lifted the secure line.

"Governor." His voice wavered, then steadied. "We need Guard support. Full deployment. My main Civic Shield unit is down, repeat, down. We've lost contact with the team at the Yard. My captain's dead."

Static. Then a voice, low, even, bureaucratic calm.

"I already gave you the curfew," the Governor said. "I signed the emergency authorization. I let your Civic Shield units run off-grid. That was your containment plan.

And now you're asking me to put soldiers on your streets, Mayor. That's a national headline."

"I'm asking for containment."

"Containment means it's already out of control. And if I deploy, I admit your city's lost. That becomes my scandal, not yours."

Lansing's composure slipped.

"The city is lost," he snapped. "I've got lowlifes, scumbags, ex-cons, and gangs running rampant, armed to the teeth, all of them swearing allegiance to a myth. They're hijacking police convoys and broadcasting executions."

"Then use what you have. You run one of the best goddamn police infrastructures in the country. Call your departments. Enforce your lockdowns. Do your job."

"My job is to keep this city breathing!"

"Then keep it breathing. But it's your mess."

"This isn't about politics."

"It's always about politics." A short breath. "Handle your own devil, Lansing."

The line died.

Lansing kept the receiver to his ear long enough for the silence to feel alive. A tremor passed through his hand.

He set the phone down, reached into his coat, and pulled out a cigarette with fingers that didn't look steady anymore.

The lighter flared and the light slid across his face like a confession.

He inhaled.

Didn't taste the smoke.

He flicked the lighter again out of habit.

Click. Nothing.

The tone lingered until it sounded like shame.

He dialed again. The next connection answered on the first ring.

"I was expecting your call," Pennington said.

Her tone was surgical. Silk, no warmth.

"You already know."

"Of course. Every dark channel carried it. I watched Captain Dane die like a fucking headline."

"She was your captain too."

"No. She was a contractor for you, and you work for us. Layers, Mayor. Liability wrapped in hierarchy. And contractors fail."

Lansing's cigarette burned low between his fingers, ash gathering like doubt.

"Fail? He killed a Civic Shield unit and hijacked our transports. There's a force out there building itself around him, and we're losing ground by the hour. We need containment."

"Containment is for diseases, Mayor. You're dealing with belief."

"Don't give me riddles, Pennington. I need resources."

"You need results. We let you build Civic Shield. The staged raids, the cameras, the clean rescues that made you look like a savior. That was your theater. Now it's time you stop pretending to be a hero and fucking be one."

Lansing's restraint finally cracked.

The cigarette trembled.

He crushed it out against the desk.

"You were the ones who tried to kill his mother, and instead leveled the entire oncology floor, sending him on a fucking warpath."

"Yes," she said, calm as glass. "And like a good dog, you let the city believe the lies."

She didn't pause.

"Fix your goddamn city before the Board decides you're the next sermon."

"Was that a threat?"

Her pause was ice cracking.

"No," she said.

"Just a reminder: history keeps receipts on suicides."

A breath, almost kind.

"You made thunder, Mayor. Don't look to us when it rains."

The call dropped.

Lansing stood alone in the wash of failing light.

His city unraveled on every screen, district by district, breath by breath.

He reached for the phone again, stopped halfway, and let it fall.

"Then God help me," he whispered. "I will."

Outside, the city stirred, low, endless, merciless.

It sounded like a god he had stopped believing in, remembering his name.

Steam curled off soaked jackets as the freight elevator rattled open.

In the garage below, the truck still ticked with heat. Rain slid off the roof in thin lines. Lucien, Victor, and Rook hauled crates stamped CIVIC SHIELD out of the back, radios and armor and fuel cells packed tight inside like stolen intent.

Rook's van was already parked by the wall, dark and dripping.

They loaded the freight elevator in silence, crate by crate, boots wet on concrete, breath still carrying smoke.

Northgate came alive above them under flickering light and the grind of generators, a tired machine refusing to die.

When the elevator doors opened into the war room, Logan looked up from the monitor bank.

Imani straightened from the table.

Lena turned at the sound.

Mara leaned back in her chair, eyes on the crates.

"Did we miss a field trip?"

Rook, deadpan. "Souvenir shop was open."

Victor exhaled smoke. "We brought party favors."

Lena stepped forward, hair threaded with stray pins.

"We heard the blast roll up the river."

Imani took in the crates, the smoke, the screens spiking with alerts.

"What did you idiots pull off?"

"Define pulled," Rook muttered.

Laughter cut through the room, short and real.

Lena crossed to Lucien. Her eyes fell to his hand. The gauze was darker now, stiff with dried blood.

"You're hurt."

He looked down as if noticing it for the first time. "Had a moment with a mirror."

"What kind of moment?"

"The kind that leaves glass in my hand."

She tilted her head, smirk faint. "You didn't like what you saw, did you?"

Lucien shook his head, gentle lie. "Just reflection playing tricks."

Her smile lingered a second too long, like she almost believed him.

She studied him, then let it go.

"Did you at least bring back good news?"

Lucien gestured toward the crates. "Depends how you feel about stolen halos."

She smiled. "Wait until you see me in my dress."

His grin flickered, the first in hours. "Then maybe the city can rest for one minute."

Rook slammed a crate lid shut. "Or burn prettier."

Laughter again, louder this time.

Boots dripped onto concrete. In all that noise was the sound of tired people remembering they were alive.

Outside, rain slid across the glass like a curtain. The skyline beyond it stayed bruised with firelight.

Lena's gaze found him again. "You're so exhausted, my love."

He studied her for a moment, rain and blood and smoke still written on his face.

He kissed her ring.

"Then let the city sleep."

They turned down the hall together, shadows slipping into softer dark.

Downtown, in City Hall, the phones started ringing again.

At Northgate, no one heard them.

Chapter Fifty
HEAVEN ON THE HORIZON

Morning came in soft.

Not the usual iron-gray morning, but a wash of blue and gold slipping through the open curtains, laying itself across the bed, across her shoulder, across his back. It made the room look borrowed from another life.

Lena stirred first.

She felt warmth, weight, the slow, steady pull of Lucien's breathing behind her.

Northgate was quiet for once.

No alarms. No boots. No calls.

Just the compound catching its breath after nights that should have killed it.

She rolled, hair spilling over the pillow, and he was already half-awake, watching her like he'd been waiting for her to move.

"Morning," she whispered, voice still torn from sleep.

His smile came slow, private. "Looks like it."

He reached for her and pulled her beneath him in one motion. His body was heavy and warm, the sheet tangling around them. He kissed her mouth slow at first, like time had finally loosened its grip. Then her jaw. Then the soft place beneath her ear.

Sunlight climbed the room, painting his shoulders, catching the raw line across his hand from the broken mirror.

"Lucien," she laughed when his stubble scraped her throat.

"Mm?"

He didn't stop. He kissed down the line of her neck, tasting the salt of sleep, the quiet curve of her collarbone. His hand slid beneath her shirt and pushed it up, baring skin to the morning air. He bent and kissed the flat of her stomach, reverent, like the world hadn't tried a dozen times to take it from him.

Then lower, slow, like he wasn't going anywhere, along her thigh.

She sucked in a breath.

And just as heat began to rise, just as the morning threatened to become something else entirely, she spoke softly, as if saying it too loud might undo it.

"I had a dream."

He stopped.

He rested his forehead against her hip and looked up at her from there, hair a mess, eyes clearer than they had any right to be after last night.

"What kind of dream?"

She glanced toward the window, toward the impossibly blue sky.

"Us."

His mouth curved.

"That's not a dream. That's inventory."

She smiled, but it bent at the edges.

"No war. No blood. No calls. No drones overhead. Just us. Heaven on Fifth open. My name on the glass. Your mother there to see it."

Her breath hitched, not from sorrow, but something gentler.

"And she did, Lucien. She beat it. The doctors called it impossible, but she just smiled and said she'd been through worse."

Her eyes found his again. "We travel. We breathe. We live like we actually survived this time."

A quiet passed between them. "But you said when you came back that the scales were off. That you weren't pulled out of that dark for peace. That you had work to finish."

Silence settled between them.

For a breath, the man who had woken in the Glass Chapel flickered across his face.

Then he was gone.

He pushed himself up over her again, caging her with his arms. The sheet slid down his back. Sunlight hit his eyes and made them gold.

"When I woke in Sanctuary, I believed it. I thought the second I stepped out of what I am, the world snapped back. Maybe it did."

Her hand moved to his chest, over his heartbeat. "It did."

"Yeah." His mouth twitched. "But here's the thing. I'm still here. You're still here. We're still breathing."

He kissed her once, quick and sure, a period on a sentence.

"So maybe I don't answer to the scales."

She watched him, eyes shining now. "What are you saying?"

"I'm saying," he exhaled, shoulders finally letting go, "fuck the war."

Her breath caught.

"Fuck the Coalition," he went on, eyes burning now, not with fever but choice. "Fuck Lansing, fuck their cameras, fuck every boardroom that thinks it can name us. They can circle, they can scream, they can call me a cult or a king or a criminal. I don't care."

He brushed her hair back, thumb gentle.

"We're getting married. We're opening your house. And we're telling the world we breathe anyway."

A tear slipped into her hairline and vanished.

"You mean that?" she whispered.

"I mean it," he said. "I'm done living like I owe blood to exist."

He drew a breath.

"I meant every word I said when I woke up about coming back for you. I still think the scales are off. I still think somebody has to fix them. But I don't have to do it from a grave. I don't have to do it without light."

A grin cut across his mouth, small and dangerous.

"I can break their doctrine and still come home to my wife."

She laughed, bright and wet. "Your wife?"

He kissed her ring. "My wife."

Silence wrapped them.

Not the heavy kind.

The warm kind.

The kind that said for thirty seconds, the city didn't get a vote.

Then he rolled off her, swung his legs out of bed, and the general came back, barefoot but still the man who could silence battlefields.

"Get dressed," he said, glancing back with that look that always made her move. "We're going for a drive."

Her brows rose. "Right now?"

"Right now." He grabbed his watch, his gun, his comm. "Before somebody decides to make today about fear again."

She sat up, sheet falling, hair wild, a slow smile forming. "Where?"

He looked at her like she'd asked something impossible.

"Heaven on Fifth, Lena. We built a future and almost lost it. I'm not letting it sit behind glass one more day."

Her heart slammed.

The dream she'd just whispered.

He had picked it up like a weapon.

She slid out of bed, dressed in leggings, an old shirt, and boots, then twisted her hair into a knot.

He watched her like he always did, like every ordinary motion was proof she was still here.

As they stepped into the hall, Northgate was still mostly dark. Emergency strips glowed low along the floor. Weld seams shone dull and fresh where the siege had bitten into the walls.

The place smelled like coffee and metal. Rain-damp jackets hung along the racks to dry.

Down the corridor, the war room door was open.

Victor sat alone at the table, monitors dimmed to a low-security cycle. He had a mug of coffee in one hand and a cigarette in the other, ash tapped into an empty bolt tray. His hair was a mess; his eyes were clear. Watchman mode.

He clocked them instantly.

"Well, look who survived curfew." His voice was raspy with too-little sleep. "I figured you two were going to hibernate till Lansing repented."

Lucien smirked. "We're heading out."

"At." Victor checked the wall clock. "Seven-thirty in the damn morning?"

Lena smiled. "Daylight is cheaper."

Victor squinted at them, at the way they were dressed, at Lucien's hand resting low on her back.

"Let me guess. Not a weapons run?"

"Heaven on Fifth," Lucien said.

Victor whistled low. "About time you opened the pretty box."

"We're just breathing it in," Lena said. "Planning."

"Uh-huh." Victor dragged on the cigarette, blew the smoke toward the ceiling vents. "Bring back breakfast. I've been up since four making sure we don't get rolled by a bunch of municipal accountants."

Lucien's brow lifted. "What do you want?"

"Anything that used to have a face. And coffee that isn't brewed through a generator."

Lena laughed. "We'll see what Fifth Avenue has the morning after a lockdown."

Victor pointed the cigarette at Lucien. "Comms on. If Civic Shield or the Coalition sneeze, I want to be the first to bless them."

Lucien tilted his head once toward Victor, that soldier acknowledgment they always gave each other, and palmed the door control.

He looked back at Lena.

"You ready to see Cole on Heaven one day?" she asked.

Lucien looked over with a half-smile. "What do you mean?"

She stepped closer, light from the skylight cutting down through the war room and threading through her hair.

"Well, in a few weeks I'm going to be Lena Cole. By the time it's all wrapped up, we'll be opening it under our name, not just mine."

From the table, Victor didn't look up from his coffee.

"Better headline than anything on CityCast," he muttered. "Married crime legends open Heaven on Fifth, film at eleven."

Lucien smirked. "Make sure they spell it right."

He kissed her once, quick, in the doorway of a fortress built for war.

Then Lucien Cole and Lena Hart walked out into the morning, with heaven on the horizon.

CHAPTER FIFTY-ONE

AFTER HEAVEN

Morning made the city look innocent.

Helicopters slid between skyscrapers, slow and indifferent, their rotors scattering morning light across the glass, lazy in the clean spring sky.

Below, the city tried to exhale. Streets half-awake after last night's curfew, delivery trucks rolling, windows yawning open to the morning.

For a rare hour, the war felt like a rumor.

The Rezvani moved through it, quiet.

The windows were tinted, cracked just enough to let the warm air drift through, still high enough to keep them hidden from the city's eyes. Lucien and Lena's hands met over the center console, still and quiet, a small act of peace between the battles they carried.

"Feels fake," she said softly, watching the city pass. "Like we dreamt the last few months."

His mouth tipped. "We didn't."

"I know. My ribs remember."

They eased through a Civic Shield checkpoint not fully awake yet, two guards in reflective vests, one sipping coffee, the other on his phone. No scanners up, no questions asked.

The guards didn't even look up. Morning disarmed them in a way the night never could.

"See?" he said, a half-smile returning. "Daylight still belongs to people."

Beyond the checkpoint, a digital billboard the size of a building loomed through the haze:

CIVIC SHIELD — FOR A BETTER TOMORROW

It showed an armored officer in black-plated riot gear standing on a rain-slick rooftop, the skyline behind him stained with storm clouds and fire. Under his boot, a man was pinned face-down, hands zip-tied behind his back, cheek pressed to concrete hard enough to draw blood.

Not a hero conquering an enemy.

A government enforcer crushing a citizen.

To most, it was another safety poster.

To anyone awake, it was a threat wrapped in patriotism.

And in the corner, half-scrubbed but still visible beneath peeling paint, someone had tagged a message in dripping red:

MERCY DIES HERE

Lucien jerked his chin toward it. "Look at this shit."

Lena looked up at the bright lie, the image glaring down on an empty street.

"The mayor wants a city that forgets what it survived.

A dystopia dressed up as yesterday."

She watched the skyline drift, sunlight breaking across glass.

"The night doesn't even answer to him anymore. He's going to hate that we're doing this."

"He can stand in line," Lucien said.

She smiled at that and lowered the window another inch. The air smelled like wet concrete, bakery, and the early green of spring.

Normal. That was the strangest part.

His phone buzzed in the console.

He checked the screen.

"Mom."

Lena's eyes warmed. "Answer it."

He put it on speaker. "Hey, Mom."

Evelyn's voice came through thin but bright, like the hospital still couldn't touch her.

"I was starting to think you two forgot I'm alive."

"We remember," Lucien said. "How are they treating you?"

"Like royalty. Saint Dymphna's. New floors. Good nurses, better tea. Your father keeps trying to smuggle in croissants."

Lena grinned. "Hi, Evelyn."

"Hello, my girl." Warmth wrapped the words. "Are you keeping him out of trouble?"

"I try," Lena said. "He's difficult."

"I raised him. I know."

Lucien's smile faded. "You resting?"

"I am." Her tone shifted, curious. "Something strange happened this morning."

He stilled. "What?"

"A Bible was left at my bedside. Opened. I didn't ask for it. Your father didn't bring it. Victoria didn't. The nurse swears no one came in."

"Why's that strange?" Lena asked.

"What was it open to?" Lucien asked.

"Revelation. Nineteen, verse two. Someone had underlined it. 'For true and righteous are His judgments; He has avenged the blood of His servants shed by her.'"

Lena looked at him. He didn't look back.

Evelyn's voice steadied. "I don't know why, but I felt like I was supposed to tell you. Like it was meant to be heard."

"You did right," Lucien said. "Telling me. I'll come by today."

"I'd like that. Oh, and Lena." Her voice warmed. "Victoria sent me pictures of you at the atelier last night."

Lena smiled. "She did?"

"She did. And, Lena, you looked like something the world waits its whole life to deserve."

Lena went quiet, Lucien's hand tightening around hers as she balanced between a smile and a tear.

"We'll come see you soon," Lena said.

"Good. Then I'll have a reason to get dressed."

The line went dead.

For a long moment, the only sound was the hum of the engine and the city beneath them.

"What was that?" Lena asked. "You went quiet the second she said Revelation."

He didn't answer.

"Lucien."

He exhaled like it had been sitting in him since the mirror. "Because I've seen it before."

"What do you mean?"

"Before the night of the breach," he said, "before you woke me, I was somewhere else. I was back in that in-between world, but it wasn't how I remembered it. There was this black wolf, smoke and ash, eyes yellow, burning under ice. It led me to a Bible, open to Revelation one-seven."

He paused.

"Behold, He cometh with the clouds, and every eye shall see Him."

Lena watched him, morning light sliding across his face, showing a part of him he'd tried to keep hidden.

"Then after Mercy West, in the tunnel. Flashlights on the walls. Graffiti in red."

She nodded. "I remember."

"And the Wolf was there. I saw it."

She turned to him. "You what?"

"I saw it. I blinked and it was gone."

"Last night I saw it again. In the mirror. Another verse. Same hand. I broke the mirror and thought that would end it."

Her eyes dropped to his wrapped hand.

"So that's what happened to your hand."

"Yeah."

"And now your mom."

"Now my mom," he echoed. "Different verse. Same handwriting. Until now, only Victor knew."

They rolled through the morning light. Even the sky felt like it was watching them.

Lena studied him. "That's too many verses, too many places, to call coincidence."

He said nothing.

"I don't think it's coming for you, Lucien," she said. "But through you. Maybe it's trying to make sure you're still the man who does something when the world starts shaking."

He looked at her. "You think it means something?"

"I think things mean what we decide they mean. That's the part nobody tells you about faith."

The light shifted. She reached for his hand. "We'll face whatever comes, together. Just don't start fighting ghosts while I'm still beside you."

The city opened ahead, alive and indifferent, pulling them forward.

They turned onto Fifth Avenue.

The street opened up, all glass and old stone. Sunlight poured in. And there it was: Heaven on Fifth.

Lena let out a breath.

He killed the engine.

For a second they just sat, looking at it. At what they'd almost lost. At what they had prepared to build before bullets tried to end it.

Then they got out.

Morning washed over them, warm on their faces. The city noise was still low, held down by the night's lockdown, just buses and a few taxis, the distant chop of helicopters above the buildings. Fifth Avenue barely noticed them, two figures in black stepping onto the sidewalk.

They approached the glass doors.

It was exactly as they remembered. Clean. Sleepy. Waiting.

Lucien took the black fob from his pocket, the same one he had shown her in the penthouse when he handed her a future. He touched it to the panel.

A soft beep. A clean click.

He pulled the door open. "After you."

She stepped in.

The air inside was different. Cooler. It smelled like polished stone, new wiring, faint perfume from months ago, and dust no one had disturbed.

The bones had held. Three expansive floors. A sweeping mezzanine. Rooftop glass. The polished black marble that stretched beneath her feet. The warm amber fixtures that hung dark, waiting for power. The steel beams that were left exposed as proof. Reminders they had survived.

Her hand went to her mouth.

"It's real."

"It was always real." Lucien came in behind her, letting the door ease shut on the city. The sound of Fifth faded. "We just had to live long enough to see it again."

She walked the floor like she was afraid to wake it. Fingertips trailing over the wrap desk, the display tables, the mannequins still under white sheets. Sunlight came through the front windows, catching on glass and metal as the building woke around her.

"In my head, I thought maybe I imagined it. That morning. When you showed me. I thought it was just a wish."

He watched her. "We don't wish. We build."

She turned, eyes wet. "Then let's build."

He crossed to the control panel behind the desk and flipped the main. A low hum filled the space. Lights rose floor by floor, warm and expensive, chasing shadow back to the corners. In the daylight, the glow barely showed, just enough for the place to remember itself.

Heaven on Fifth, waking.

It was beautiful.

Not nightclub beautiful. Not sin and champagne. This was clean, purposeful, a house for the woman who had survived him.

He came back to her and slipped an arm around her waist from behind, his chin on her shoulder.

"You see it? The shows, the fittings, the upstairs offices, your name on contracts, models running late, Ghost yelling because he has to scrub their socials before they tag the location."

She laughed, tears spilling.

"I see it."

"Brides. Runway. Editorial. The life you said you wanted before I dragged you into fire."

She leaned back into him. "I walked into fire. On purpose."

He kissed the side of her head. "Then this is your reward."

"No, baby." Her voice softened to a whisper. "You're the reward."

They stood like that for a moment, just listening to the building breathe. Then reality slipped back in.

"We should go see her." Lena's voice stayed quiet. "Before she gets tired."

"Yeah. We lock it up, we go."

He powered the lights back down. They stepped out into the street, the door sealing behind them with a soft click.

He looked up at the brass letters again, memorizing them like he'd said they would.

"Heaven on Fifth. Soon."

"Soon," she echoed.

They got back in the truck and headed north, cutting crosstown through the waking city.

Saint Dymphna's was the opposite of Mercy West. Mercy had once been marble and light, now wrapped in cranes and tarps, its beauty buried under recovery. Dymphna's was untouched, glass and white, gardens in planters, security quiet and polite. Both had been built for healing; only one still remembered how.

They parked underground and came up a service elevator, heads down, hats low. Two nurses recognized Lucien but said nothing. People chose sides, even here.

Evelyn's room was bright.

She sat up in bed, hair wrapped in a soft scarf, eyes clear. The IV hummed softly. A vase of flowers Victoria had brought sat on the sill. And there, on the tray beside her, was a Bible. Open. Waiting.

"My darlings."

She held her arms out.

Lena went first, hugging her carefully. Lucien followed, kissing her forehead.

"You look good."

"I look like I survived my son's enemies." Evelyn's smile carried pride.

"Sit."

They did. The room filled with the quiet pulse of machines and the slow rhythm of breathing. A nurse passed in the hall, then another. Time stretched.

She tapped the Bible. "There."

Lucien looked over.

Something moved through him. Not the jump of battle. Something older. Something that had followed him out of that in-between place the Wolf kept dragging him back to.

"You didn't mark this?" he asked, though he already knew the answer.

Recognition sharpened.

"No, baby. Neither did your father. This wasn't even here before he left. And Victoria was with you last night." Evelyn gestured toward Lena.

Lena glanced at him. She saw it happen, the way his pupils thinned, the way his jaw went from soft morning to cut stone.

"I think it's for you," Evelyn said simply. "However it got here."

They stayed a few more minutes. Small talk about nurses and tea and the garden below her window. The kind of talk people use when they are trying to keep the world gentle.

He bent and kissed her forehead again, longer this time.

"Rest. You need it."

"I will. You two go make something beautiful before the world ruins it again."

"We're trying," Lena said, smiling through it.

They stepped into the hall, and the door closed softly behind them.

Lucien stood there for a second in the white corridor, hands braced at his sides, head down. The sunlight in Heaven on Fifth had been warm. The light here was clinical and steady, the kind that never lied.

Lena touched his arm. "Lucien."

He looked up.

The softness from the morning was still there, but something had layered over it. Not rage. Direction. The look he got when the city drew a line and he decided to cross it.

"They keep sending verses. Different books. Different rooms. Different people."

His mouth flattened.

"If it's them, I'll answer.

If it's Him, I'll answer harder."

Lena watched him, steady. "Then we answer on our terms, not theirs. We do it our way."

"We do." He met her eyes. "But no one else writes the ending."

He took her hand and they walked out.

Downstairs, the city was already changing.

Downtown, in City Hall, Lansing told his staff to send the press away.

The doors stayed closed; the lights stayed on.

He ordered his media team to prepare material, footage, confessions, fear packaged for broadcast.

He told them to make the city afraid again, to put Lucien Cole's face on every sin, to bend the story back into his hands.

The day that started with Heaven was about to end in theater.

CHAPTER FIFTY-TWO

THE ALIGNMENTS

By the time they got back to Northgate, the sun bleached the metal roofs white.

Northgate was louder now, generators steady, radios spilling low chatter, alive again.

Victor hadn't moved far from his post. He had traded the cigarette for anticipation. Fork in hand, plate empty, like he had been waiting for breakfast since the second they left.

He squinted as Lucien and Lena came through the door.

"About time. You two were supposed to bring back breakfast."

Lena tossed him a paper bag. "Don't say I never feed you."

He caught it, tore it open, and looked down. "Cold."

"Then it matches your personality." She smirked as she moved past him toward the monitors.

Victor grinned, worn but awake. "Still the best compliment I've gotten all week."

He unwrapped it like he didn't trust it. "If this has eggs in it, I'm forgiving both of you."

"Miracles happen before noon."

Rook worked the corner console, rewiring a comm line. "You're lucky. He's been growling about that sandwich since sunrise."

Mara leaned against the doorway, arms crossed, watching the room wake up. "Maybe breakfast first, theology second."

Victor took a bite and went still with satisfaction. "I take back every insult I've said today. Except the ones Ghost didn't hear."

Right on cue, Ghost broke over the overhead speakers, dry as static.

"I hear everything, Victor. Eat fast. We've got movement forming."

Lucien leaned a hand on the back of the chair in front of him. "Talk."

"I've got chatter across the dark channels," Ghost said. "The stadium crews are moving again. They want another alignment. Their operations are collapsing; no Coalition money, no routes, no cops looking the other way anymore. They're expecting you to step in and rebuild the routes. They want to know if this rebellion is about control or reconstruction."

Victor blew smoke at the ceiling. "Translation: they're broke and nervous."

Lena folded her arms. "Take away the money and the orders, and all that's left is teeth."

Rook muttered, "Teeth without orders bite whoever's closest."

Lucien's eyes stayed on the central map. "Where are they looking to meet?"

"Down by the harbor," Ghost said. "Word's moving through the dock crews. One of the old Staten Island ferries. Decommissioned, chained up near Battery Park. They've been using the terminal for off-book cargo. It's neutral ground, at least for now."

"Battery Park," Lucien murmured. "That's too close to the Civic Shield perimeter."

"Exactly why they think it's safe," Ghost said. "Shield doesn't watch their own backyard."

Lucien leaned on the table, eyes still locked on the map. "Speaking of Shield, billboards all over the city. They're slapping them up overnight like rot under paint."

Lena's lip curled. "We saw one. 'CIVIC SHIELD FOR A BETTER TOMORROW.' Picture-perfect families, shining streets, not a scar in sight. Same lie, new paint. Bait for the desperate."

Imani looked up from her tablet. "They're flooding the feeds with the same campaign. Hashtags, civic ads, even the kid's channels. It's saturation."

Logan walked in. "Desperation looks good in high-def."

Victor sat forward. "So what's the play? You gonna crown yourself king of the leftovers, or you wanna build something real?"

Lucien didn't answer right away. He looked at Lena, then at the map again, tracing the waterline with a finger.

"Let them talk first. See who still believes in what they bowed to."

The day slipped into late gold.

Plans for tonight. Routes, signals, fallback points.

Everything moved fast.

Lena sat on the edge of the long table, half listening. Lucien was bent over blueprints with Rook, sleeves rolled, moving pieces, aligning edges, measuring twice with his eyes. She knew that look. Soldier. Architect. Believer.

Not a moment to pull him away.

She slipped her phone from her pocket.

The screen lit her palm. Notifications stacked from channels she no longer cared about. Beneath them sat a list of names she had not touched since before everything changed.

Jessica.

Christina.

Her thumb hovered over Jessica's name. She had not meant to look. Had not meant to feel that pull of the girl she used to be. But there it was, sudden and undeniable.

She pressed call.

The screen filled with a photo she had forgotten she still had.

Three girls in a bar bathroom.

Tipsy smiles. Mirror flash. Lipstick too red.

A lifetime ago.

Only months, but another lifetime all the same.

It rang once.

Then,

"Lena?"

Jessica's voice cracked halfway through the name.

Background noise came from a world untouched: ice in a glass, traffic outside, music leaking from a window.

Normal life. The life Lena vanished from.

Lena swallowed. "Hey, Jess."

There was a gasp. Soft, shocked. "Oh my God. Lena, where have you been? We tried everything. Texts, calls, Christina even went to your building. You just... disappeared."

"I know. I should've reached out sooner."

A silence opened between them. Not awkward. Heavy with everything unspoken.

Jessica tried for lightness. "So you're alive. Not kidnapped. Not hiding in witness protection. That alone is a win."

Lena gave a faint smile. "Depends who you ask."

"You sound different," Jessica said. "Not bad. Just... older. Stronger. But also like you're far away from us."

Lena leaned against the table. Across the room Lucien moved his hands across the map, Rook following his logic, Ghost's voice feeding them coordinates from the speakers. The whole place pulsed with intent, danger, and purpose.

With the life she had chosen.

"A lot happened these past few months."

Jessica exhaled like she had been carrying this worry for months. "Listen, can we see you? Please. Me and Christina. Just something normal. Dinner, a drink, anything. I don't care where. I just want my friend back."

Lena's throat tightened at the word friend.

She looked around the room: Victor laughing quietly at something dark, Lucien's eyes flicking toward her just long enough to read her mood before diving back into strategy. Crates stacked. Screens alive. Men sharpening for nightfall.

The war kept breathing.

For once, Lena didn't move with it.

"Yeah. I'd love that."

"You would?" Jessica's voice lifted, bright with relief. "What about tonight? Christina's off. We could go someplace quiet. Early. Before the streets get ugly."

Lena let her eyes rest on Lucien for a long second.

He didn't look up again, but she could feel the pull of him, the storm at rest only for her.

For one hour, the war could breathe without her.

"Tonight's perfect."

Jessica let out a shaky laugh. "Thank God. I'll text you a spot. I cannot wait to see you."

"Me too," Lena murmured.

She ended the call.

The screen went dark.

Her reflection hovered there, older now, steadier, someone rebuilt.

Across the room, Lucien called another order. Rook answered. Victor checked a magazine. Ghost updated a channel. The machine of war kept turning.

Lena slipped her phone into her coat pocket.

For once, she let it.

Northgate was in motion.

Maps cleared. Weapons checked. Engines rumbled in the lower garage like distant thunder.

A rhythm that compressed time, every movement laced with unspoken tension.

Lena lingered near the stairwell, coat half-zipped. She watched Lucien run the briefing with the precision of a man walking a knife's edge. Ghost's voice spilled from the speakers in clipped bursts; coordinates, timings, and the gaps between them.

When the meeting broke apart into quiet departures, Lucien looked up and found her watching him.

"You remember Jessica and Christina?" she asked, her voice cutting through the low static of the room.

His mouth pulled into a faint smile, worn at the edges. "Of course. You three were trouble long before I showed up."

She held his eyes, steady.

"I reached out earlier. They want to see me. I was thinking tonight. Just an hour or two."

Lucien leaned against the table, arms crossed, studying her like he was memorizing the next choice he had to make.

"You're asking if I mind? Lena, I want you to see your friends. I want you to claw back some kind of life from this abyss. You don't owe every breath to me or this war."

Her smile softened. "Then I'm seeing them. I want them at our wedding, you know. Standing with me. Witnesses to whatever's left."

"Then they'll be there. Only thing I insist on is protection."

She lifted a brow. "Meaning?"

"Logan stays nearby. Watching the edges. That's it."

"Lucien." Not angry. Just careful.

"Let me lead tonight without wondering which door I have to kick in. That's all."

Her eyes softened. "Fine. Logan can watch the edges."

He stepped closer, thumb brushing her cheek. "You shouldn't have to live like this. Half in the light, half waiting for it to break."

She placed her hand over his. "Then let's win fast, before it takes everything."

A faint smile touched his mouth. "Working on it."

Logan appeared by the stairwell, keys in hand. "You sure you don't need me behind you?"

Lucien didn't look away from Lena. "Having my back tonight means watching hers."

Logan rolled the keys once in his hand. "Copy that."

Below them, engines turned over, rising like a low call to arms.

Chapter Fifty-Three

FERRY OF KINGS

The city went unnaturally still near the water.

Fog clung low over the piers. Cargo cranes stood frozen against the dim light, hooks swaying faintly in the unseen wind. Even the gulls were gone.

The kind of quiet that meant eyes were already on them.

They moved along the harbor road, tires whispering over cracked asphalt. Victor drove.

Rook rode shotgun, a cigarette tucked behind his ear.

Lucien sat in back, watching the docks through tinted glass.

"Traffic cams are looping," Ghost said. "Fog's too thick for half their lenses to read anything clear."

"Means we've got a window," Rook said.

Victor tapped the wheel. "Means someone wants us to think we do."

Midtown's skyline was distant now, half-obscured in mist. The farther they drove, the more the city fell behind.

Lucien's gaze traced the cranes, the empty freight lanes, the fenced-off ferry terminal ahead.

"How many inside?"

"Ten confirmed on the outer feeds. Visibility's shit. Expect more inside."

Rook checked the mirror. "Neutral ground, my ass. This is every ambush I've walked into. Just wetter."

Lucien cracked a faint smile. "You worry too much."

"I'm still alive, aren't I?"

The ferry came into view.

Municipal orange hull. Sun-faded and chipped. Blue trim peeling in long, tired strips. Rust bloomed along the waterline like old bruises. Its name was half-worn into the side: THE ELLIS. Chained to the pier. Abandoned and left to rot.

Dock lights flickered through the fog.

"Ghost," Lucien said, "you hearing chatter from the crews?"

"Dock talk says they're waiting for you to make it official. Every man with a gun and a debt's on that boat. They think you're about to crown the next decade."

Victor parked beside a stack of shipping containers, engine ticking down.

"If this goes bad, the water's the only exit."

Lucien stared at the ferry. "Then let's keep it clean."

He stepped out.

The air tasted like diesel and salt. Fog shifted around them, swallowing sound. Boots hit metal with a hollow echo.

Rook joined him, scanning the shadows. "If ghosts exist, this is where they hang out."

Lucien didn't answer. His eyes stayed on the ferry, on the silhouettes moving behind its glass.

"Low tide," Victor said behind him. "Good sign. Means the water's holding its breath."

Lucien's mouth curved. "Then we make it count."

He walked toward the gangplank.

The ferry felt like it had already judged them.

Steel walls closed in tight, not with threat but expectation.

A place built for crossings, now turned into something else entirely.

Lucien stepped through the doorway first.

The air carried the sting of rust and something older. Something patient.

It wasn't a smell. It was a warning.

Not a meeting.

A reckoning.

Twenty men filled the main cabin, spread wide, claiming angles and shadows like they owned them.

It showed in the scars and the stance, men shaped by the streets and raised by them.

Gang chiefs marked by a hardness you did not earn without bodies in the ground.

Some faces were familiar, seen a day earlier at the Bronx Stadium, where crews watched the city shift toward a new alliance under a torn sky.

Tonight the leaders came without armies, eyes sharp as switchblades, desperate for a new order before the streets chose one without them.

Lucien strode in and stopped at the center of the scarred table, posture alone claiming the room.

Rook took his left.

Victor took his right.

Ghost's voice settled in their ears, steady and calm, the line between chaos and command.

"Gentlemen," Lucien said.

No theater. No bluff. Only weight.

He planted his palms on the table.

The cabin went quieter.

"You are not here for mercy. You are here because payroll does not care who used to own the ports."

A few jaws tightened. A few eyes flinched and recovered.

"The Coalition cut checks and bought silence. I cut routes and killed the circus. Now you want the flow back, and you want it without raids, without funerals, without a city eating itself alive."

He swept them with a look that did not ask permission. "We carve clean routes. We tax the flow. Seventy stays with the crews running it. Thirty goes into a city fund that keeps the heat off your doors and your people alive."

A tap on the table, once, like a gavel.

"Clinics to keep your runners from dying in alleys. Kitchens to keep neighborhoods from boiling over. Lawyers to keep your families out of cages when the crackdowns come back."

His voice stayed level. "You bow to the code, not my ego."

One of the dock bosses leaned forward, bracelets clinking like small shackles.

"Code's cute, Cole, but code doesn't fill payroll. We ran clean when the Coalition cut the checks. Imports, ports, freight, kickback all the way up. Now you torched their routes, and we're supposed to eat doctrine?"

Another voice slid in, slick with suspicion.

"You killed the system that paid us. Now you want us to tithe. What's the split in risk, prophet?"

A third man grunted, hands flat on the table.

"We built those arteries. You want them to pump again, you tell us who bleeds first and who gets paid after."

Lucien didn't flinch. "You get paid. But not for rot. I don't fund ghosts."

He leaned in a fraction, the smallest movement in the room, and it changed the temperature. "You move right, you eat. You move loud, you vanish."

A laugh cut through the cabin. Sharp. Ugly.

"And who decides what's right," a man said, "you?"

Lucien's eyes hardened. "The city. I just keep score."

Silence took the room.

Not peace. Not agreement. The hush before impact.

Then movement came from the far side of the cabin.

Limping.

Defiant.

Vega.

Gold tooth catching the fluorescents. The same man Lucien had pinned to the pitcher's mound, blade through his hand like scripture. That hand was wrapped in cracked leather now, fingers frozen into a crooked claw.

"Gospel," Vega spat. "That's what you call it now. You want our routes, our muscle, our silence, and you wrap it in mercy."

Lucien met his eyes without blinking. "I want your leash."

A few men shifted. That word hit harder than a threat. It was a claim.

An older voice rasped from the table's edge.

"Coalition's dead to us. Shield's watching everyone. Payrolls dry."

He pointed a finger at Lucien like it was a knife.

"If you're claiming the crown, own it."

"I do not claim a crown," Lucien said. "I claim rules."

He counted them off with his voice, calm as a verdict.

"No kids. No schools. No cameras. No headlines."

His eyes moved across the table. "Move quiet. Pay up. Vanish when I say vanish."

His gaze cut to Vega. "I don't mop up your messes."

A man with a scarred jaw leaned forward, light catching the ridge of old damage.

"And if we tell you to go fuck yourself?"

Victor's reply came low, a growl scraped from steel. "Then go kiss a mayor who scripts his raids and calls it salvation."

Rook spoke, voice steady. "Or follow the man who bleeds for what matters."

Vega shoved his chair back. The screech cut the air like a warning shot.

He stood on his own, shoulders squared, face set like he had a whole army behind him.

"You don't scare me. You got fans. That fades."

Lucien's gaze didn't waver. "They bowed to the names on the grass, not me. That fire does not fade."

Ghost's voice broke through the comms. "Heads up. Three unknowns on the pier, west fence. Utility jackets. Fast hands. Van engine running hot."

Lucien didn't hesitate. "Wrap it."

He swept the table with one last look. Hard. Final. "You want order, take it. You want a throne, sail elsewhere."

He tapped the table twice. Victor and Rook moved. The room exhaled like it had been held underwater.

"Exit in pairs. Two minutes apart. No cowboys."

Vega sneered. "After you, kingpin."

Lucien's voice went ice-cold. "No. After you."

A pause, then the truth, flat and dangerous. "I don't stab backs. I guard them."

Boots thundered down the stairs. The ferry groaned, old hull creaking like it remembered storms.

Lucien, Rook, and Victor held the rear as the crews poured out.

Ghost spoke in their ears. "Van's still purring west. Gangway cam's on loop, but not mine."

Rook's eyes hardened. "Shield's print all over it."

"Tag the plates. Hold the loop."

They stepped onto the deck, the gangway slick underfoot, mist curling around the railings in drifting threads. The pier lay ahead in a pale wash of fog, wide and empty, a kill zone waiting for permission.

Engines coughed to life as crews split toward their vehicles. Vega reached his bike by the fence, the metal slick with fog. He swung on, turned the key, and the engine answered, low and hungry in the quiet.

A white panel van idled near the overpass, its lights dim behind the haze.

"Hold," Lucien said.

They froze. A beat. A breath. The world went too still.

Headlights flared, harsh and blinding.

The van door slid open.

Three shadows spilled out, fast and surgical. No guns. No shouting. Only hands, brutal and precise.

One caught Vega from behind, forearm locking under his throat. Another seized his ruined hand and wrenched, not to break it but to own him. Vega fought, boots scraping across wet concrete, his bike idling beside him like an insult he could not answer.

A hood snapped over his head.

Zips tightened around his wrists.

Five seconds of violence.

Then silence.

The fog swallowed the attackers. The van swallowed Vega. The door slammed, the engine roared, and the van vanished into the white.

The pier stood empty again. Vega's bike still idled, headlight slicing through nothing.

Victor moved first, anger punching through his shoulders. Lucien's arm stopped him cold.

"Not now," Lucien said. "Not under their lens."

Rook spat into the mist. "They'll pin it on us."

"Let them. We will make it cost them."

They left the pier together, heads low, shadows folding back into the dark. Behind them, the old ferry groaned, the sound carrying across the water like a witness refusing to speak.

Chapter Fifty-Four

FALSE GODS

Lena didn't notice the city shift at first.

The restaurant was small, brick walls, old records on the shelves, light that made everything look a little softer than it was. It smelled like basil and wine and normal life. The kind of place that made a person forget curfew was coming.

They sat at a window table, glass still fogged from the rain. Outside, streetlights reflected off wet pavement like melted gold.

Jessica cried when she hugged her. Christina laughed and then cried too. They spoke over each other, voices overlapping the way only old friends ever do.

Questions overlapped.

Are you safe? Is he? Are you happy? Are you eating? Will you tell us later?

Lena answered the way a person answers when love sits on both sides of the table.

"Yes. Yes. Yes."

They ordered pasta, shared wine, talked about haircuts and headlines, about everything except the things she had barely crawled out of. Jessica worked at a design firm now, small team, big accounts, the kind of place that kept her too busy to remember how talented she was. Christina had gone back to school. They laughed about adulthood, about calendars and rent, about anything that did not bleed.

For a moment, Lena almost believed she had just taken a long vacation and came home.

Her phone stayed face down. Logan's voice murmured through the earpiece twice, low enough not to carry past her.

She didn't need the words.

Eyes on the door. Engine running. No surprises.

She allowed herself to relax because he was watching the perimeter.

Outside, fog hung low over the avenue. A Civic Shield billboard flickered above the window, smiling families, perfect streets, the slogan bleeding through static:

PEACE THROUGH VIGILANCE

Christina noticed first. "Those things are everywhere now. Feels like they're watching even when you behave."

Jessica rolled her eyes. "It's just branding. They'll sell safety the same way they sell painkillers, cheap hope on a screen."

Lena didn't answer. The reflection shimmered in her wine until it looked like fire.

Jessica broke the silence with a grin. "So, Lucien Cole, huh?"

Christina nearly choked on her drink. "I can't believe you two made it through all that. Lucien Cole and Lena Hart, still standing."

Lena smiled faintly. "You make it sound like a ghost story."

Jessica leaned in. "Last time we saw you, he was one. You disappeared, Lena. We didn't know if we should call the cops, a priest, or both."

Lena hesitated, then looked down at her glass. "I needed distance. Things got heavy."

Christina nodded, swirling her wine. "Yeah, we know. The media's done a good job filling in the blanks. Half the city thinks they buried him twice."

Her voice softened. "We're just glad you're still breathing."

Jessica's smirk gentled. "And apparently planning a wedding?"

Lena blinked, then laughed. "You beat me to it."

Jessica raised an eyebrow. "To what?"

Lena lifted her glass a little. "I was going to ask you both tonight."

Christina leaned in. "Ask us what?"

Lena looked between them, eyes warm. "To stand with me. As my maids of honor. Both of you."

Christina's hand flew to her mouth. Jessica swore under her breath, eyes going bright. For a second they were all in their mid-twenties again, crowded around mirrors and bad lipstick, arguing over eyeliner like the world had never once tried to kill what she became.

Jessica reached for Lena's hand before she could think twice, thumb brushing the ring like she was checking if it was real. The stone caught the light and threw it back.

"You serious?"

"Dead serious. If I'm walking into that day, I want my girls with me."

The table went quiet, the kind of quiet that let the moment settle in their chests. Even the restaurant noise felt farther away, like it respected what had just been said.

Christina leaned closer, breath catching. "Jesus Christ... it's beautiful, Lena."

Lena smiled faintly. "It's not about the ring. It's about surviving long enough to deserve it."

The words hung there, quiet but charged.

Jessica squeezed her hand. "Then we'll see it through with you."

Christina nodded hard, eyes shining. "No matter what."

They clinked glasses, and the sound was small, but it held.

The conversation loosened after that, laughter finding its rhythm again. Christina threw out ideas for colors and playlists. Jessica fixated on flowers, then candles, then whether Lena needed a walk-in song. Lena watched them build the parts of the night that still belonged to them, and something tight in her ribs finally eased.

"You used to swear your first dance song would be At Last," Christina said.

Lena smiled. "Maybe. But our kind of love doesn't wait that long."

Jessica made a face. "Please tell me he isn't going to pick something dramatic with violins and a body count."

Lena's smile widened. "He's going to try."

Christina laughed. "Of course he is."

Jessica leaned back, studying her like she was trying to read the new version of Lena without losing the old one. "You ever think about what you'd be doing if none of this happened?"

Lena considered it. "Yeah. But then I wake up next to him, and I don't want to change the math."

When the meal was done, they paid the check and stepped into the night.

The door closed, and the normal world stayed inside without her.

Logan waited at the curb, engine idling low, eyes already on the street. He didn't smile, but his gaze softened when he saw Lena safe between them.

Outside, the block had shifted. The fog felt thicker. Sirens sounded somewhere far off, muffled under the city's hum, like the city was clearing its throat.

Jessica hugged her tight. "You look sure of yourself. I haven't seen that in a long time."

Lena smiled. "Maybe I finally caught up to myself."

Christina squeezed her shoulder. "Text us when you get home, okay?"

"Promise."

Across the glass of the restaurant window, her reflection split into two versions of herself, one that used to belong to the city, and one that had chosen Lucien.

Jessica called out as Lena turned toward the van. "You sure you know what you're walking into?"

Lena looked back, half-smile, voice steady.

"I already did. I'm just wearing white this time."

She slid into the van, the door closing like a seal.

Outside, a voice crackled over the city speakers, clipped, official, everywhere at once.

"Attention citizens: one hour until curfew. Please clear the streets and return to your designated zones."

The message looped, sterile and calm, swallowing the street in echo.

Above it, the billboard flickered again, first Civic Shield, then Lucien's face.

The light burned through the fog. His eyes were caught mid-blink, the image too still to be human.

Beside him, new text shimmered through the haze:

WANTED FOR QUESTIONING

$10,000 REWARD

The screen stuttered.

Then it went dark.

In City Hall, Lansing stood in a room with no name on the door.

The kind of room every administration had, and no administration admitted existed.

Staffers watched the frozen frame on the wall.

A ferry deck.

Fog curling around a knot of men.

A silhouette in black that might have been Lucien, caught mid-motion, mid-breath, mid-falsehood.

"Ready," Lansing said.

Communications kept their eyes on the feed. "Ready."

Legal stayed silent.

An aide swallowed, fixed their tie, and tried not to look at the clock.

"Run it," Lansing said.

The edit rolled.

It played like a confession, smooth and damning.

A hard cut from the real ferry interior to a deck dressed to look the same.

The angle was wrong, too high for the camera they had looped.

A muzzle flash bloomed.

A body dropped to steel.

A face they already had on file.

Vega.

A scream that had not existed ten minutes earlier.

The file name said PROOF

The chyron said WARLORD

The crawl at the bottom listed victims who were still alive.

Lansing didn't blink.

"Push."

Across the city, every screen hesitated for a single breath, like the grid itself resisted the lie.

Then the image changed.

The Rezvani hit the ramp hard, engine echoing off concrete as the garage swallowed them whole.

The garage doors rolled down with a metal sigh, locking the night outside.

Rain still clung to the car in a wet sheen.

Fog from the pier rode in on their coats.

Lucien got out first.

Rook came around the front, still watching the docks in his head, eyes measuring distance that wasn't there anymore.

Victor shut his door with the blunt force of frustration held too long.

Upstairs, Northgate was awake to something they had not been told.

Not panic.

Activation.

Imani and Mara moved fast at the screens, reading the city in real time.

The speakers clicked once. Ghost slid in, calm.

"Imani and Mara picked up something after you left the docks. You're going to love what the city thinks you did."

Lucien didn't even stop to peel off his coat. He crossed the floor like he already knew the answer.

"Show it."

Imani tapped a key.

The main screen filled with the ferry deck, fog crawling over metal.

It looked almost real, almost theirs. Men frozen mid-argument.

And at the center, a black silhouette shaped close enough to him to fool anyone who didn't know his shoulders.

Then the cut.

A new angle. Higher. Too clean to be Ghost's.

A muzzle flash, bright. One shot.

A body folding on the deck.

Crawl text burned across the corner of the footage:

VEGA, LOCAL GANG FIGURE, EXECUTED BY COLE

Silence took the room.

Not shock. Calibration.

Victor swore once, slow. "Motherfuckers."

Rook leaned in, almost to the glass. "That's not our camera. That's not our tide."

Mara checked her tablet, fingers moving fast. "Frame says tonight. Metadata says otherwise. They stamped over old footage."

"CityCast push?" Lucien asked.

Ghost came in sharper. "Straight from Lansing's people. Routed through three shells. All friendly. All bought."

Footsteps came from the stairwell.

Logan came in first. Lena followed, eyes finding Lucien before anything else.

She saw the screen and stopped.

Lucien didn't turn. He kept his eyes on the screen. "You're back early."

"Logan drove fast. Curfew's coming. Last place I want to be is on the street without backup."

"Next time, finish the night," Lucien said. "They've taken enough from us. Don't start giving them what's left."

Lena's voice stayed low. "Lucien. The billboards changed."

That pulled his gaze from the monitors. "Changed how?"

"Your face. Every avenue we crossed. It said Wanted. Ten thousand dollars."

The room went still.

Victor looked up from his seat. "They're not wasting time."

Rook rubbed his mouth. "Mayor's cashing in quick. Public bounties turn crowds into weapons."

Lucien's stare set. "Not if I control the story first."

Ghost's voice drifted in again. "Already on it. The feed hit three districts before the loop stabilized. We've got an hour before it cycles again."

"Then we take the hour back."

Imani flicked a corner of the video, isolating a quadrant.

"Here. Waterline's wrong. That's north pier depth. You were south."

She zoomed in.

"And this. That wrist. That's not your watch."

Rook grunted. "Posture's wrong, too. He stands like he's posing."

"Because he is," Ghost said. "They built this to sell, not to remember."

"It was Civic Shield that snatched Vega off the pier," Rook said. "Now they're killing him with your face."

"Not officially," Ghost said. "Not yet. The chyron says executed, but Lansing's copy calls him a violent figure. He's leaving space to confirm it later. That way he gets two news cycles."

Lena frowned at the screen. "So the city sees this and thinks,"

"That I broke my own doctrine in front of every syndicate in the harbor," Lucien finished. "That I say no spotlights and then shoot a man on camera. That I can't be trusted. That I wanted the crown after all."

"It's neat," Mara said quietly. "Too neat."

Lucien exhaled through his nose, slow. It wasn't rage. It was decision.

"Status on Vega."

Imani tapped another key. A map appeared to the side, a trail of three pings, then nothing.

"White panel van. Civic Shield plates, spoofed to sanitation. Bridge ping, then a blackout. Last real location? On-ramp to the FDR. After that, we're guessing truck bay or basement entry."

"So he's breathing," Victor said. "For now."

"Then we get him back before they finish the edit," Lucien said.

He turned from the screen. The atmosphere snapped.

"Victor. Logan. Gear up. We move now."

Victor gripped his rifle, posture locking in. "Where?"

"Every Shield-adjacent bay along the river. Ghost will walk us into whichever one pings first."

Victor looked over. "We pulling Vega back alive or just proving it's staged?"

"Alive. Breathing. I want the man the city thinks I killed to tell the city I didn't. That's cleaner than any file."

"Copy."

Lucien shifted his attention upward.

"Ghost, I want the origin on every upload, every mirror, every account that shared that clip in the first five minutes. Don't just trace it. Name it. I want the Council donors on-screen next to this bullshit before they can say 'misinformation.'"

Ghost's voice curved into something almost like a smile. "Finally a fun assignment."

Lucien turned to Imani. "Two frames. Only two. One with the wrong tide. One with the wrong watch. We show them the lie without teaching them how to fix the next one."

Imani nodded once, decisive. "They'll see the lie."

Lucien looked to Mara. "Line up dockside witnesses. Not gang. Not Shield. Workers. The kind that don't like being used as props."

"Longshoremen. I know who to call."

"Rook. Grab the pier cam Shield forgot to kill. There's always one. If you have to bribe a harbor kid for a phone angle, do it. I want our angle to drown theirs."

Rook snorted. "They always miss one."

He snagged a short-barreled rifle off the rack, slung it over his shoulder, and was gone, boots already pounding down the stairs toward the garage.

Lena was still watching the screen. "The ones who saw the stadium will believe you. They saw who you are."

Lucien looked back at his fake self on the monitor, the one who pulled a trigger he never raised.

"The ones who didn't will believe whatever's loudest."

"False gods need crowds. We have a city."

Lena stepped closer, shoulder almost touching his. "Then show them."

Lucien faced the room. "Gear up. We move when Ghost confirms location."

He turned back to Lena. "Stay here tonight. Work with Imani and Mara."

Her eyes narrowed. "You think I can't handle it?"

He stepped closer, voice low but steady. "I know you can. That's why you stay. Victor and Logan break doors. You read the city. I need that more than another rifle."

She held his stare, something fierce and unspoken between them.

He touched her hand once, brief. "Every war needs an eye that doesn't blink."

Lena exhaled, soft but sure. "Then make it worth watching."

He squeezed her hand once. "Always."

Northgate didn't panic.

It worked.

Outside, the curfew sirens started their first pass, trying to tell the city what hour it was, what it was allowed to be.

Inside, Lucien had already chosen the story.

CHAPTER FIFTY-FIVE

THE HOUR OF FALSE GODS

Their hour had come. The hour of broadcasts, false prophets, and men who mistook a screen for a throne.

Curfew had barely touched the city, and it was already gutted and quiet. Ghost's voice filled the room.

"Everyone listen. Dark chatter just jumped. Street-level syndicates are breaking first, the ones who move fastest and think last. Crews from the harbor are split right down the middle. Half say Cole broke the doctrine. Half are ready to bleed for him. The city's lighting up. Gunfire in Midtown, trucks rolling through the avenues, block by block turning into battlegrounds."

Feeds and maps flared across the screens. Red blooms lit the harbor line.

Lucien stood in the middle of it, coat still on from the pier.

"Who's moving first?"

Ghost's voice thinned. "Vertigo Lords rolling through Chelsea, calling it a correction. Wraiths calling you a liar, saying you staged the ferry for sympathy. Tidal Reapers already answering with gunfire along the East River. It's getting tribal."

Victor swore. "All because Lansing needed a fucking clip."

"It was always going to split like this," Ghost said. "You put twenty heads on a boat and tell them there's a new order, then five minutes later the news says the man calling for order is executing rivals in the fog. Faith does not like being embarrassed."

Lucien didn't hesitate. "Then we embarrass him back."

He looked at Victor and Logan.

"Come on. We're rolling out."

Victor racked his rifle. "We do this fast."

"Fast. And we talk. Shield doesn't get to finish their edit or write my sins."

Every district blinked red on Ghost's wall, static and gunfire where order should have been.

Ghost cut in. "Hurry. The districts are lighting up, and it's spreading."

Lucien paused at the threshold. "We end it before the whole city forgets who lit the match."

He looked to Lena at the monitors, headset on and steady. "Eyes on the feeds, baby. If Shield shifts west, warn me first."

She held his gaze. "Go fix your gospel."

Ghost's voice returned. "You sure you don't want a cleaner night?"

Lucien's reply came almost as a whisper. "I want a true one."

"Then you'll like what I'm about to send you."

Lucien turned for the stairs.

Victor grabbed his rifle, slapped a mag in like punctuation.

Logan met Lena's eyes for a second, a silent promise, then followed them down the stairs.

Outside, thunder broke.

The hour had begun.

FDR SERVICE BAY.

9:54 P.M.

Rain had turned to a fine mist, the kind that made the city look stripped clean.

The van rolled dark under the overpass and killed its lights. Logan kept the engine low, eyes on the bay entrance. Victor sat forward in the passenger seat, rifle across his knees, watching for shadows where headlights should have been.

Lucien sat behind them, silent. His gaze followed the rain crawling down the glass.

Ghost came through their ears. "Two Shield trucks ahead. One generator. One panel van that matches. I count six warm bodies outside, two inside. No patrols running loops. This is a stash, not a fort."

Lucien's voice was quiet. "We keep it that way."

Logan checked the side mirror. "Police?"

"Not yet," Ghost said. "But listen to this."

Static crackled, then another voice bled in, not theirs.

"I saw the video, man. I'm telling you, Cole capped him. You follow him, you fucking die with him."

"You didn't see the stadium. He wouldn't do that. This is City Hall trying to take him off the board."

Someone in the background shouted to reload.

Gunfire in the distance, muffled.

Ghost came back, tired and amused. "That was crosstown. They're quoting you while they shoot at each other."

Lucien watched the dark mouth of the bay. "Then we go before they finish."

Victor checked his rifle. "Call it."

Lucien leaned forward. "We go in sharp. No warnings."

They slid out of the van and into the wet underpass. The service bay was half open, yellow light spilling out. Inside, two Civic Shield officers argued over a tablet. Another smoked near the rear truck. None of them were looking at the panel van.

Victor moved first.

Two shots, suppressed.

The arguing pair didn't drop so much as fold, legs giving out before the sound reached the walls.

Logan broke off toward the third man. One hand clamped over the smoker's mouth, the other drove a knife under the ribs. The body spasmed once. Logan caught the weight and lowered him like luggage.

Lucien followed in their wake, unhurried, stepping over the first corpse without a second glance. His eyes were already on the van.

Victor tore the rear doors open.

Vega stared back at him.

Hood shoved halfway off. Face beaten raw. Both eyes swollen nearly shut.

His hands were not just zip-tied. They were cinched to a steel ring so tight the plastic carved trenches into his wrists.

His mouth was gagged with a filthy strip of towel, duct-taped so brutally it pressed his cheeks inward.

He couldn't turn his head.

He could only stare, wild-eyed and shaking.

Blood smeared the metal floor beneath him. Fresh.

Not all of it his.

Victor ripped the gag out.

Vega sucked air like it owed him his life back.

"Shield took you from the pier."

Vega spat blood. "Yeah. And they're staging it like you pulled the trigger."

Lucien stepped closer, rain still clinging to his coat. "We know. Get up and prove I didn't."

Vega froze, breathing hard, like the voice alone was enough to jolt him back to life.

Logan climbed in, cut the ties. "Can you walk?"

Vega swung his legs out, winced. "Yeah. Yeah, I can walk."

A shout from deeper in the bay. "What's going on out there?"

Lucien turned his head slightly toward Victor. "End it."

Two Shield officers burst through the side door, half-armored, hands going for pistols.

Victor didn't bother with quiet anymore. A three-round burst. Both dropped.

Blood spread fast across the concrete, thin and bright under the bay lights.

Ghost's voice cut in, sharp. "You've got company coming from the south entrance. Two. Maybe three. They're on rotation."

Logan grunted. "Time to go."

Lucien grabbed Vega by the shoulder, pulling him toward the exit. "You're not dying as my headline."

They shoved him into the van. Logan slid behind the wheel.

Victor fired a few covering shots toward the service corridor, then jumped in and slammed the door.

The van lurched forward.

A Shield officer burst from the bay entrance, rifle up, muzzle flashing.

Rounds chewed into the windshield, glass fracturing in white spiderwebs.

Logan muttered, "Hold on."

The officer didn't expect the speed.

The van hit him full-force.

His body snapped onto the hood, rolled across the roof, and vanished behind them as they tore out into the rain.

Bay lights stuttered across the wet pavement as the van shot into the night.

Logan laughed once. "They're awake now."

Victor looked back at Vega, breathing hard, eyes full of rage and humiliation. "You're going to talk tonight."

Vega bared his teeth. "Good. I was getting tired of being the prop."

Lucien watched him for a beat, rain still beading on his collar. "Then stop being one."

CITY HALL.
OPERATIONS SUITE.
10:31 P.M.
Lansing was tired of being told no.

He stood at the front of the room in his shirtsleeves, tie crooked, hair damp at the temples from too much recycled air. Tables glowed with maps, CCTV, and city alert systems. Thirty men and women lined the walls in mixed uniforms: Civic Shield light armor, NYPD blues, plainclothes with badges at their belts.

He looked from one to another.

"You're here because you understand something the city forgets," Lansing said. "It doesn't choose when it behaves. We do. I do. Through you."

No one spoke.

He tapped the screen behind him. Lucien's face filled it, frozen from the ferry edit. Gun up. Muzzle flash. A man falling.

"This is what the city is watching right now. Every screen. Every corner. Your sisters, your kids, the people you swore to protect. They are being told this man is the future. You are here to prove he is not."

A young officer spoke from the wall. "Sir, with respect, why is Civic Shield doing this and not the Bureau or tactical? Half of us were pulled off real posts tonight."

"Because Civic Shield answers to me. And because the Bureau wants a paper trail and a hearing. I want a clean street by morning."

He started pacing, the energy of a man who knew he was losing and didn't know how to admit it.

"Cole is not a gangster. He's a symbol. He's a story. And if you let a narrative run unchecked, it becomes doctrine. You saw what happened at that stadium. That was not a gathering. That was liturgy. He's trying to turn this city into a church where he is the scripture."

Silence. Uneasy. Resentful.

Lansing lowered his voice. "Which is why we will not let him."

He was about to give the next order when the door opened.

No knock.

No announcement.

Lucien Cole walked in.

Outside, the reward billboards still screamed his name, but no one in the building expected the man they were hunting to walk through their own emergency corridors. Lansing's briefing had pulled security inward. Ghost had opened the doors that mattered and lied to the cameras that watched them.

Lucien didn't hurry. He didn't sneak. He walked as if the building belonged to him, as if he had been invited and was right on time.

Victor came in behind him, rifle in hand. Logan followed, eyes on the room, on exits, on hands.

Every gun in the room lifted.

Civic Shield. NYPD. Plainclothes. All of them.

Lucien did not blink.

"Mayor. You have something that belongs to me."

Lansing stared at him as if seeing a ghost he had spent months denying. "You have some nerve."

"I have proof. And a witness."

He lifted his hand.

In it was a small, ugly black recorder. Scuffed. Used.

Logan took one step left. Victor one step right. Their eyes never settled on one threat for long. A moving net.

Lansing tried for composure. "You cannot just walk in here and threaten city officials."

"I can. Because you are lying to the city."

The room was a powder keg. Some of the cops were young and scared. Some of the Shield officers were angry enough to prove something. All of them were watching Lansing to see what he would allow.

Lansing pointed at Lucien. "This man executed a gang lieutenant on a dock tonight."

Lucien didn't blink. "No. You dragged a man into the dark and called it justice. You wrote my name on the sin."

Lansing's anger found footing. "You think this makes you righteous? You murdered Captain Dane and an entire Civic Shield unit on live feed. The whole city saw it."

Lucien didn't deny it. Dane's death was real. What Lansing twisted was the story he wrapped it in.

Lucien met his eyes. "The whole city saw what you wanted it to see."

Lansing sneered. "Shall we roll the footage again?"

Lucien stepped closer, calm and measured. "What, another edit? Another miracle from your media team? You twist proof like scripture, Roland. You burn truth to keep your throne warm."

Lansing faltered. Dane's blood in the rain flickered behind his eyes.

Lucien's voice lowered. "You wanted her death to sanctify your crackdown. It only exposed the hand pulling the strings."

He nodded to Logan.

Logan tossed something across the room. A drive. It clattered across the floor near the console, useless except for the message it carried. The wall screen switched a second later, Ghost already inside their system with the real feed.

Same ferry deck.

Same fog.

But this time wide. This time from the actual pier cam Rook had pulled. Timecode clean. Angle untouched.

Vega walking toward his bike.

The white panel van.

Three Shield officers dragging him inside.

No Lucien. No gun. No execution.

Whispers rippled across the room.

A sergeant muttered, "Jesus Christ."

Lansing's face went pale. "This is doctored."

Lucien's gaze stayed on Lansing. "Here is the difference between you and me. I do not need a lie to make this city listen."

He clicked the recorder.

A voice spilled out.

Pennington.

"Contractors fail. Containment is for diseases, Mayor. You're dealing with belief."

It was the call from the night they returned from the Harlem River yards.

Ghost had pulled it while Lucien was still inbound.

Lansing's face went gray.

"That recording is inadmissible," he snapped. "You're wiretapping city leadership."

"You are staging murders. And now every screen that ran your edit tonight can run this."

He turned to the officers along the walls. "All of you signed up to keep people alive. Not to make snuff films for a mayor drowning in his own headlines."

Some muzzles lowered. Others held.

Ghost's voice cut in, steady. "For the record, the gangs just stopped shooting. They're all watching the leak. You're changing minds in real time. Also, Harlem crews are lighting trashcans at checkpoints. They're daring Shield to come fix it."

Lansing latched onto the nearest lifeline.

"You think humiliating me will fix this? You think the Council,"

He cut himself off.

A young cop frowned. "The what?"

"Nothing," Lansing snapped. "Focus on your job."

Lucien stepped closer. "The Council started this when they burned the floor my mother was on. I'm not fixing it for them. I'm fixing it for the people who watched your video and thought I abandoned them."

The room held the breath of a building about to fall.

No one challenged him again.

No one wanted to ask what lived behind that word.

Lucien kept advancing.

Two Shield rifles tracked him.

Victor's rifle tracked them.

"Here's what happens next.

You'll issue a correction to every outlet you lied to.

You'll open an internal investigation into Civic Shield's edited evidence.

You'll suspend Shield operations until you confirm your people aren't kidnapping civilians.

And you'll do it tonight."

Lansing barked a single brittle laugh.

"Or what? You shoot a mayor on camera?"

Lucien shook his head. "No. I do something worse. I leave you alive with the truth playing on a loop."

The line hit harder than any gun.

Lansing stared, voice cracking. "You cannot win. You don't have the numbers."

Lucien's smile was thin, tired, real.

"You don't understand. I don't need numbers. I have eyes."

He looked at the cameras.

Ghost whispered: "We are live on six dark channels. Your voice is carrying across every district."

Lucien lifted his eyes to the cameras. Then he spoke, and the city heard him.

"This city breathes. It does not perform.

Anyone who tries to turn it into a show again gets named.

And the city remembers its names."

He killed the recorder.

Silence.

Then an older NYPD officer lowered his weapon.

"I signed on to lock up shooters," he said softly. "Not make them."

Another gun followed.

Then another.

Civic Shield hesitated, reading angles, exit points, two rifles, and one man who walked in without blinking.

They lowered.

Lansing's power bled out of the room in real time.

Lucien met his eyes one last time. "You have tonight. Use it to tell the truth."

He turned and walked out.

No shots.

No blood.

Just a mayor sinking inside the ruins of his own lie.

Outside, curfew sirens kept running their script into dead air.

Ghost came through the comm, steady. "Confirmed. Pier feed is gone. Harbor's quiet. Anger turned to signal. Uptown's asking why Shield is kidnapping people. You cracked the illusion. It's bleeding, not dead yet."

Victor exhaled into the night. "Good. I was getting tired of ghosts shooting ghosts in the fog."

Lucien looked up at the billboards still showing his face.

"They wanted a ghost. Now they have one."

And for a moment, the city listened.

CHAPTER FIFTY-SIX

DREAMS OF A SCARLET WOMAN

Lucien opened his eyes to red.

Not light. Reflection.

The air shimmered as if every breath had been steeped in wine. He was standing in a cathedral built from ribs and glass, its windows pulsing with slow, arterial color. The floor bled upward, veins in the stone alive and moving.

At the center stood Lena, or something wearing her shape.

She wore white, but it was not cloth. It was light strained through bone and smoke. In her hands, a golden cup caught the glow from above. When she tilted it, the liquid ran over her fingers like blood and mercy had become the same thing.

A whisper moved through the cathedral, not from her lips, not from his. It came from the walls themselves, and as it spoke, the words appeared in burning script along the stone.

THE WOMAN WAS ARRAYED IN PURPLE AND SCARLET, AND DECKED WITH GOLD, REV. 17:4

The flames etched the verse as the Wolf's shadow stretched across it, swallowing the last word whole.

Her name left him before he could stop it.

"Lena."

Her smile was small, distant, wrong.

"You built the altar," she whispered. "Someone had to drink."

She lifted the cup to her mouth.

Blood traced her throat as she swallowed, slow as confession.

The sound wasn't human. It was prayer without God.

Every drop that touched her lips turned to glass. Each pane showed him kneeling, bleeding, confessing.

He took a step forward, but the floor moved with him, like the world was a lung and he was caught inside its breath.

The stained glass behind her melted. The scenes shifted, Lena's face becoming Evelyn's, Evelyn's dissolving into the Wolf, only an image at first, black fur threaded with light.

Then the glass bulged outward, and the reflection stepped free.

The Wolf stood at the edge of the altar, silent, its eyes yellow as flame through fog.

It didn't growl. It only watched her drink, as if keeping score.

Lucien reached out, but his hands were wet.

Blood to the wrists. Dripping. Unending.

Every drop that hit the floor became another rose, its petals blackening as it bloomed.

His voice came out hoarse.

"Stop. Lena, stop."

She lowered the cup. Her mouth was red and shining.

The voice wearing hers softened.

"You told me to follow you. Now follow me."

Behind her, the Wolf's shadow stretched across the altar, devouring color, swallowing her shape until nightmare made one silhouette of woman and beast, crowned in flame.

The cathedral cracked down the center.

Light poured out like judgment.

Lucien staggered backward as the cup fell, striking the stone and exploding into liquid fire.

It raced toward him in veins of gold and scarlet.

He felt it climb his legs, his chest, his throat, burning and freezing him at once.

The last thing he saw was Lena's eyes, wide and bright, and the Wolf watching from the doorway, patient as eternity.

Then the world folded in on itself.

Lucien woke gasping.

Or thought he did.

The room was dark, the sheets damp with sweat. His pulse hammered through his ribs.

Outside, thunder rolled slow over the city, and for one impossible heartbeat, he thought he heard a voice in it whisper his name.

At the open door, where the shadow from the hall met the floorboards, a shape stood, tall, still, silent.

Two yellow eyes watched him from the dark.

He didn't move. Didn't speak.

The air felt wrong, too heavy, the kind that bends sound.

The eyes blinked once.

The walls shivered.

A low tremor rolled through the floor, then another, closer, deeper.

The lamp by the bed slid an inch, glass humming. The doorframe began to crack.

Lucien tried to stand, but the room tilted, splintering at the edges.

The Wolf stepped forward, its paws silent, its gaze steady as the world began to break around it.

"Lucien."

Not Lena's voice. Something older.

The ceiling bowed, raining dust and shadow.

Then hands were on him. Real ones.

"Baby, hey, wake up!"

He dragged in air, real and cold, his pulse kicking like a trapped animal.

Light struck his eyes.

Not fire. Morning.

The world was whole. The tremor was gone. The room held.

Lena knelt beside him, eyes wide, her palms still pressed to his chest.

Sunlight poured through the curtains, cutting gold across her hair.

"You were yelling." Her voice shook. "I couldn't get you to wake up."

Lucien stared past her, breath shaking, until the shape in the doorway was nothing but daylight.

The light should have felt safe. Instead, it was too still, too bright.

"What day is it?" he asked.

Lena frowned. "What do you mean?"

His eyes stayed on the doorway.

"The last thing that felt real was City Hall."

Her face softened. "Lucien, that was over a month ago."

He sat up, breath catching.

Lena's hand found his arm. "You remember pieces. But you've barely slept since. The mayor made public apologies. Shield's running half-staff now. Ghost says the underworld's quieter than it's been in a while. We did it, Lucien. We all did."

He rubbed a hand across his face, still tasting smoke. "Feels like I just left that room."

"Then maybe it's time you come back to this one." She kept her hand on his arm. "It's our rehearsal dinner tonight, remember?"

Lucien stared at her for a long moment. "Rehearsal dinner?"

"For the wedding."

The faint smile faded.

"Lucien?"

He looked down, then back at her.

"Yeah. Just hard to believe it's already here."

He turned toward the window. The city was alive, normal, too normal.

Beneath that noise, he thought he heard the low echo of paws on stone.

Chapter Fifty-Seven

FOR NOW

The world this morning looked almost domestic.

No sirens.

No sentries on the stairwell.

Only Imani near the table, tapping through three news feeds at once while coffee steamed.

Mara sat with a white binder open, pages covered in Lena's notes and venue diagrams, looking like an intel officer briefing a wedding. "Good, you're up. Do not disappear. We still have details to confirm for tomorrow."

Lucien raised a brow. "Do we?"

Imani turned her tablet. On the screen, Mayor Lansing stood at a podium. Hair neat. Face contrite. Behind him, the Civic Shield logo had been softened with an American flag.

"Another review statement," Imani said. "Same script. 'An internal review is ongoing.' 'Evidence was not properly vetted.' 'We will not allow rogue elements to undermine public trust.' He's been chewing those words for a month and still can't swallow them."

Mara didn't look up from the binder. "Someone made him."

Lucien watched the screen for a moment. Lansing's mouth moved. The words washed over him. Empty. Gesture without teeth. "Anything from Pennington?"

Imani lowered the tablet. "Not directly. She's quiet. The Council's still breathing. They're just doing it softly."

Lena stepped in, barefoot, hair damp, wearing an oversized shirt that belonged to him in another life. "No work. Not today. We are practicing being people."

Lucien moved past them toward the bedroom to change. "Not my best trade."

Inside, empty spaces waited in the dresser where his clothes should have been. Someone, probably Lena, had already laid out his suit for the evening. Dark. Clean. Timeless.

He opened the top drawer for his watch.

Then stopped.

Across the room, on her bedside table, something caught the light.

The little black book.

It wasn't supposed to be there. Yet there it sat, quiet and certain, as if it had been waiting for him.

He crossed to it slowly, every step thick with memory, and picked it up.

The leather was worn along the edges. He opened it carefully, the pages smelling faintly of smoke and old ink. The first page waited under his hand, smudged and warped where tears had dried.

The words stared back at him, lines he had written when he still believed he had a choice in how he died.

At the top of the first page, her name waited: LENA.

And beneath it, the first line he ever wrote to her: I WROTE THIS FOR YOU DURING THE NIGHTS I DIDN'T THINK WE'D MAKE IT

Faint water rings marked the page. Not his. Hers.

He stood there for a long moment, thumb running over the page. His chest tightened in a way violence never could.

Footsteps behind him. He knew them. Hers.

He didn't turn around. "You kept this."

Lena appeared in the doorway. "Of course I did. I'm marrying the man who wrote it."

He closed the book and slipped it into his inside pocket. "I never wrote vows."

She smiled. "Baby, you lived them before you ever put them on paper."

For a moment she only watched him. The light from the window caught the edge of his face, the part of him that still looked half elsewhere.

Lena crossed to him, her voice quiet. "Lucien. Sit down."

He obeyed without protest, the way a man follows the only steady thing left.

She sat beside him, close enough that their knees touched, and brushed her fingers along his jaw like she was reminding him he was real. "It's okay to be tired. It's okay to just live for a minute."

"You've been awake through weeks your body should have slept through. That does something to a man."

He looked at her, unsure if he could.

"You've been fighting for so long. You forgot what peace sounds like."

He exhaled, the kind of breath that had waited years to leave him.

382

Then she walked him through the day, grounding him in details and ordinary life.

"Victor and Logan are your groomsmen. Victor's your best man. You asked him two weeks ago, though you probably don't remember."

Lucien gave a faint, weary smile. "That sounds like something I'd do."

"Imani, Mara, and Rook won't be standing with us, but they'll be there at the dinner. They're family. And Jessica and Christina are with me. You know them, they're loud, they're sweet, and they're terrified of you."

He almost laughed. "Smart women."

Lena's expression softened. "They're just not used to our world. But they're trying. The invitations went out two weeks ago, black and ivory. Victoria handled everything. Barely two weeks' notice, but when a Cole wedding calls, people show up."

Lucien looked down at their hands. The words drifted around him like sunlight he didn't know how to hold onto. It all felt distant, like he was watching someone else's life play out behind glass. "You sound like you've been planning this forever."

Lena reached for his hand, squeezing gently. "We all have. You just needed to catch up. We're doing the rehearsal at The Sanctuary of the Sacred Heart. It's at four."

Lucien turned his head slowly. "Who's officiating?"

"Father Adrian," she started.

"Dimas," Lucien finished, voice low.

Her eyes softened. "Good, you remember. Father Adrian Dimas. He's an old friend of your father."

That hit him, not religion, but memory.

Lucien's gaze dropped to the floor. "Adrian baptized me. When he was still a young priest. He's been in and out of our lives my whole life. Weddings. Funerals. Confessions." His voice lowered. "He's heard most of my sins."

Lena smiled. "Then he'll know what to do with the rest. He'll be doing the ceremony tomorrow too. He's traveling north after the wedding, to the Vale of Saint Arden."

She stood, light returning to her tone. "The church looks a lot like Saint Arden. Same vaulted ceiling. Same light. It'll feel right when we promise each other forever."

She turned toward the door, smiling back at him. "Come on, Mr. Cole. You coming?"

"Something like that."

But when he looked toward the window again, the light had shifted. For a split second, the reflection was not his face. Something watched from behind the glass.

He blinked.

Gone.

The church sat on a quiet corner of the West Village, red brick and white stone trim, the sort of church people walked past without knowing what had survived inside. The doors were propped open. A warm draft carried incense and old wood into the street.

Lucien stepped inside and felt something loosen in him. The vaulted ceiling, the long center aisle, the way the afternoon light bled through the stained glass in slow color.

Father Adrian was already there, sleeves rolled, vestments draped over a pew. Time had traced him gently, fine lines around the eyes, pale spots along the skin, but none of it had touched his calm.

He opened his arms. "Lucien. You look alive."

Lucien stepped into the embrace, brief but real. "Trying to stay that way, Father."

Evelyn sat in the front pew, shawl drawn close, the afternoon light resting soft across her face. Alexander sat beside her, proud and composed, the kind of stillness that held weight. Between them, Victoria leaned forward with a small smile that held both nerves and awe.

When she saw him, she rose, slower than she once would have, but with the same grace. Lucien bent and kissed her forehead. Her hands came up, framing his face for a moment, eyes bright, steady.

"You look tired, my love."

A tired warmth touched his face. "I look like the city."

Her thumb brushed the corner of his jaw, mother and blessing in one touch. "Then let the city learn from you for once."

Alexander stood next, straight-backed, gaze steady. "You've carried the weight long enough, son. Let Lena help you carry the rest."

Lucien's eyes found her. "She already has."

Lena crossed the aisle to greet them. She hugged Evelyn gently, then turned to Victoria.

Their eyes met, the kind of moment that didn't need language, two women bound by the same love, the same fear of losing Evelyn.

Lena's voice lowered. "You've held her up."

Victoria's eyes softened. "So have you."

Evelyn smiled between them, pretending not to hear.

Victor and Logan entered behind, both in clean suits that still managed to look like armor. Victor clapped Lucien's shoulder. "You survive the rehearsal, we drink. Fair trade."

"Ghost will keep eyes on the city while we take a night off," Lena said.

Lucien nodded once. "Good."

The doors opened again. Jessica and Christina entered, dressed for church, eyes wide as they took in the space. They were still civilians. They still whispered to each other when they looked at him.

Christina grinned. "You clean up nice, Cole."

Lucien glanced toward Lena. "Trying to impress someone."

Father Adrian gathered them all at the altar and spoke like he was narrating something sacred and ordinary at once. "Tomorrow you will not be thinking about your feet. So think about them now. We walk, we pause, we honor who brought us here."

He walked them through the procession. Logan first. Then Victor. Jessica and Christina took their places. The line formed in quiet reverence.

Lucien watched Lena cross the aisle in practice and still felt his breath catch. Her hair was simple, pinned back just enough to show the strength in her face. The light through the stained glass washed over her in red and blue, colors shifting across her skin like something remembered.

For a heartbeat, the world blurred.

The cathedral from his dream flickered behind this one, ribs of glass and shadow overlapping the real.

Then the light steadied.

She was only Lena again, laughing softly under her breath as Father Adrian called out the next step.

He blinked. It was gone.

Father Adrian noticed before anyone else. "You are somewhere else."

Lucien shook his head once. "I'm here."

Adrian held his gaze. "Stay here. There are no enemies in this room."

Lucien nodded, but his body still listened for war.

They finished the walk-through. Adrian spoke the blessing they would hear tomorrow, but without the charge, without the eyes, without the finality. He looked at Lena the way a father might. "You chose a hard man."

She smiled. "I chose a true one."

He looked at Lucien. "You chose a brave woman."

"I chose the only one," Lucien said.

Evelyn dabbed at her eyes. Victoria's hand found hers and held it steady.

Outside, through the open doors, the city moved slow. People walked dogs. Delivery bikes cut through traffic. There were no curfew warnings, no billboards flashing his face. Lansing had done what he was told. For now.

The rehearsal dinner was held on the top floor of a Tribeca restaurant overlooking the water.

Alexander had left the church ahead of them, wanting to make sure the night went right. He was already there when they arrived.

He had lived the same storms, fought the same wars, but tonight he was only a father.

Alexander hugged him tight. "My son. You look like a man who's finally breathing again."

Lucien gave a faint smile. He'd heard three versions of himself today, alive, tired, breathing. Everyone saw a different answer. "Still remembering how."

Evelyn kissed his cheek and went to greet Lena. The two women fell into easy talk. There was no division there. They had both steadied him when the world tried to take him apart.

The team filtered in over the next ten minutes.

Rook in a dark shirt, hair still wet from a shower.

Imani in a simple black dress that made half the room look underdressed.

Mara with her hair down for once, a rare thing, eyes softer.

They hugged Lena first, then shook hands with Lucien's parents, polite but wary, soldiers playing guests.

Jessica and Christina sat near Lena, slightly stiff at first, eyes flicking to the men with scars. Then Victor made them laugh. Logan offered them wine. The air loosened.

Plates came. Wine poured. The room warmed. For the first time in months, maybe ever, conversations overlapped without strategy sitting inside them.

Logan watched the lights drag across the Hudson. "City looks different. Too quiet."

Rook set his glass down. "It won't stay. Men like Lansing don't stay humiliated."

"They've been quiet for two weeks," Mara said. "Wounds take time to scab."

The table went still for half a breath, old instincts rising.

Then Imani broke the tension. "Let them scab. We deserve one quiet night. Even God rested."

Lucien listened without fully entering the conversation. His eyes kept drifting to the windows. The river caught the fading light and held it in place. The skyline softened around the edges, like a city pausing long enough for him to breathe.

Evelyn rose slowly, the glass in her hand more for balance than ceremony. "I will not make this long. My son does not like speeches."

Laughter moved through the room, soft, knowing.

Her smile faded. "I lived the night they told me he was gone. I felt the world stop, and then start again without him in it. I heard the words every mother fears, but I waited. I waited because I knew him. I knew he would fight his way back, even from whatever waited on the other side."

She looked at him then, voice low but steady. "I watched this city try to bury him twice. I watched him bury his own anger so he didn't become the man who broke him. And tonight, I'm watching him sit at a table with people he calls family. That is a greater miracle than any doctor ever promised me."

She lifted her glass. "To peace that is earned. To love that stays. To Lena, who brought my son home."

Glasses lifted. "To Lena."

Lena's eyes shone. She mouthed thank you.

Jessica leaned in when they sat again, voice low. "We still can't believe we're here. This is not the life we pictured when we were hopping turnstiles and falling for the wrong men."

Lena laughed. "No, it is better."

"Scarier," Christina said.

"Better," Lena repeated.

Across the table, Victor was telling Lucien's father a heavily edited version of the Harlem River yards assault. Lucien's father listened, eyes narrowing, then finally said, "So when you say 'convoy disruption' you mean 'arson'."

Victor leaned back. "Sometimes."

Laughter rolled across the table.

For a while, it was just that. Laughter. Family. Warmth. Plates cleared. Rook telling a story about bribing dockworkers. Mara arguing over which harbor kid had given the best footage. Imani and Jessica finding common ground in design work and code. Evelyn holding Lena's hands and asking about fabrics.

Lucien let himself lean back.

He looked out at the river again.

The sun was nearly gone. The water was dark. Bridge lights dragged across it in long smears of red and gold.

For a second, he thought that was all he was seeing.

Then he realized one patch of red was not moving with the tide.

A cloud had rolled low across the river, dense and slow, tinted the same dark crimson as the cathedral walls from his dream. As it shifted, the shape gathered, broad shoulders, narrow muzzle, something too much like a wolf leaning over the current.

He blinked.

The shape broke, swallowed by tidewater and passing headlights along the waterfront.

Only the river remained.

Only the city, breathing.

Chapter Fifty-Eight

THE NIGHT BEFORE

They came back from dinner full and smiling, the kind of night that almost passed for normal.

But in a world that only pretended to sleep, no one at Northgate really did.

Lucien didn't go to bed.

The place was awake, warmer than it ever felt during war.

Someone had put music on low, nothing loud, nothing sharp, just enough to let people talk and remember they were human.

The war room table was cluttered with takeout containers from Tribeca, fresh-poured wine in half-empty glasses, somebody's heels kicked off by the couch.

Lena was laughing with Mara and Imani, Victoria pulled into the circle for the night, all of them bent over something on a phone.

Heads bent together like girls again, not women who had rewired a city.

Victoria smiled with them, catching the warmth even without all the history behind it.

Lucien stood in the hallway and just watched her.

Memory moved through him like a slow reel.

The room blurred, the voices went soft, and she stayed in focus.

Everything that had brought them to this night came back in order, like it had been waiting.

La Maison Élite.

She'd been on the floor that first day, neat, small, trying to vanish into the seams, straightening fabric that didn't need it, hiding from a world that had already marked her.

Enigma.

The neon blaze. The endless line. She and her friends stopped cold at the velvet rope, capacity reached, and him already on the other side, watching as if that single moment could rewrite her fate.

The corridor's dim pulse. The man who reached for what was never his. The fear in her eyes when his men tore him away.

Not weakness.

The kind of strength that learns to survive in silence.

The penthouse meeting that bled into dinner, into rooftop confessions, into everything he never knew he craved.

The stalker. The fire's hungry roar. LUCIEN'S WHORE sprayed across the wall in venom.

The car slamming into her like violence had learned her name.

Hospital lights glaring like accusations. Her hand trembling against the sterile sheets, nerves frayed from a chaos she couldn't outrun.

Even half-gone, she fought to piece together a world that kept shattering around her.

His estate, forged in iron and glass, a cage he built to defy the storm outside.

The warehouse abyss. Her body broken. Her spirit nearly taken. Michael torn apart by the kind of cruelty that leaves echoes.

Lucien charging in anyway, a vow made to fire and ruin.

Miami's heat. His father's shadow, nothing inherited, nothing owed.

Betrayal waiting, Ghost in the wires. And Victor Dresnik's twisted choice, sealed in flame.

Atlantic City. Kearny's underbelly. Royce's shadow.

The bounty that turned the night crimson for ten million dollars, and still she stood unbowed.

Her courage disguised as protection, left in Corsini walls meant to shield her while Lucien baited Royce.

But loyalty broke easy there, and they let Royce inside the silence that should've kept her safe.

Stonehaven's ghosts. Isabelle's whisper from the grave.

The cemetery ablaze with every buried sin.

The club's thunder. Shots cracking like fate's whip. The hospital's cold grip.

Him flatlining, heart stilled in the void, her voice pulling him back, reading his black book confession like a lifeline.

Three months in that mountain glass prison, relearning breath while she pressed against the barrier, waiting, unyielding.

The Coalition tightening its grip. Civic Shield marching at Lansing's command.

Lansing calling it peace while the city bled beneath the banners.

All of it had crashed into this: Lena Hart in this fortress, bathed in soft light, laughing with the women who'd become her unbreakable sisters, on the eve she became Lena Cole.

He let himself drown in that sight for an endless, aching minute.

Then the walls closed in. He needed air, or he'd shatter.

He slipped past the room without breaking the moment and took the stairs to the roof access. At the top, he shouldered the door open.

Night met him, cool against his face.

Northgate's roof carried the faint chill of steel. Far off, Manhattan burned in a river of light, the skyline sharp against the darker Hudson. The city looked like it was pretending everything was fine.

He pulled out a cigarette, lit it, cupping the flame with his hand like he always had. The first drag hit easy, familiar. Smoke curled into the night, rising against the skyline, a habit he never shook, only learned to hide better.

He stood at the edge and watched the city breathe.

Boots behind him.

"Figured I'd find you up here," Victor said.

Logan followed, hands in his pockets, jacket open, the kid who'd betrayed him once and earned his way back.

Lucien didn't turn right away.

"Figured you two were down there trying to charm Imani into drinking."

"Imani doesn't get charmed," Victor said. "She audits souls."

Logan smirked. "She said no."

Victor joined him at the edge, eyes on the skyline.

"Nice night. Almost looks honest."

Logan smirked. "Nothing here's honest. Just waiting its turn to burn again."

"Don't ruin it," Lucien said, smoke moving past his mouth. "I'm trying to pretend."

Victor glanced down through the skylight where the women were.

"She looks happy."

"She is," Lucien said. "She deserves to be."

"You do too," Logan said.

Lucien huffed a breath that was almost a laugh.

"I don't know if I was built for happy."

Victor glanced over. "You weren't. You adapted."

They stood like that for a minute. Men who'd walked through too much to fill silence with nothing.

Victor broke it first.

"You were staring downstairs like it was the end of a movie."

"It is. And the start of another."

"Thinking about all of it?" Logan asked.

"All of it." He tapped ash off the end. "How many times she could've walked away. How many times I would've let her. How many times the city tried to take what we built. And somehow we still ended up here."

"Stubborn love," Victor said. "Best kind."

Logan leaned on the vent. "You ever think it was supposed to be like this? Like you were steered?"

Lucien looked at him. "You been talking to my mother?"

"I've been listening. To all of you. Father Adrian. Evelyn. Even Alexander sounds like he believes things line up on purpose."

"Things line up because we force them to. God didn't carry us here. We did."

Victor snorted. "He didn't used to talk like this. He used to just shoot the problem."

Lucien smiled, small. "I still shoot the problem."

"Not tomorrow."

Lucien's eyes went back to the city.

"No. Tomorrow I marry her."

That made the other two quiet.

"Does it feel real yet?" Logan asked.

"Feels undeserved." Lucien was quiet a moment. "Like when I died and came back, something got rewritten. Like I was supposed to stay in oblivion, and someone pushed me back and said, 'No. Finish it.'"

Victor's voice lost its edge for once. "Then finish it."

Lucien flicked ash over the edge. "That's what tomorrow is. Not just a wedding. It's me saying I pick life. With her. Even if the city doesn't. Even if the wolf comes back. Even if Lansing finds his courage again. I'm done letting war be the only thing I'm allowed to be good at."

Victor watched him, brow furrowed. "You still seeing it? The wolf?"

Logan looked between them. "What wolf?"

Victor didn't miss a beat. "The one that visits when you've stared too long into your own sins."

Lucien didn't answer right away.

"Sometimes. In glass. In verses. In the corner of rooms. It's quieter now. But it's not gone."

Victor exhaled through his nose.

"So it's like the rest of them. They lost the right to be loud."

Lucien exhaled smoke. "Something like that."

They stood there, three men looking out across the city they'd bled for.

Victor rolled his shoulders. "So what happens after? You get married. You open Heaven on Fifth. We keep Lansing from crawling back onto a camera. Then what?"

"Then I build. We all do. Empire without rot. Routes without kids. Safe places that don't become cameras for men like Lansing. Heaven and the other ventures making more money than the old life ever did. Northgate running clean. Ghost running wires for daylight, not war."

"And us?" Logan asked.

Lucien looked at them both. "You're part of it, if you want to be. This doesn't work unless it's built by the same hands that tore the old world down."

He paused, softer now.

"You drive until you don't want to. Then I buy you something quieter. Victor pretends he retired and still shoots anyone who looks at me wrong. We raise kids in a world that knows our name for the right reasons."

Victor smirked. "You planning to make kids, boss?"

Lucien flicked ash. "Tomorrow I plan to start trying."

Logan grinned, leaning against the rail. "Except Victor. His swimmers probably show up late and complain about the music."

Victor snorted. "Kid, mine have survived wars yours couldn't spell."

Logan's smile didn't fade. "And somehow you're still the loudest in the room."

Lucien breathed out a thin laugh, the kind that belonged to men who'd finally earned one. The skyline burned gold, and for a moment, life felt almost like peace.

The laughter faded gently.

Victor sobered first. "You know we're still watching. Even after tomorrow. Even if you're playing husband and architect."

"I know."

Logan leaned on the rail. "You saved the city's face, at least for now. Lansing will lick his wounds. The Coalition will listen. But the men who liked chaos are just sleeping."

"I know," Lucien said again. "We stay ready."

He glanced down through the skylight. Lena was looking up now, like she felt him. She smiled at him from below glass and distance.

He smiled back.

Victor jerked his chin toward her. "That right there, that's why all of this made sense."

Lucien's voice softened. "I know. She's the only thing that ever did."

They fell quiet again. The river moved. The city gleamed, red where the lights hit water.

After a while, Victor glanced toward the door. "Get some sleep. Big day tomorrow."

Lucien finished the cigarette, ground it out on the ledge.

"Sleep's never been the hard part."

Victor smirked. "No, it's staying asleep that kills us."

Logan lingered.

"You good?" he asked.

Lucien looked at the skyline one last time. The future was finally something he could see without aiming at it.

"Yeah," he said. "For now."

Logan pushed off the rail and went inside.

A shift in the dark caught the corner of his eye.

Not movement, reflection.

For one breath, the glass of a nearby HVAC panel showed a shape behind him, tall and wrong around the edges.

Then a gust hit the roof and the reflection snapped apart, gone like it had never been.

He let out a slow breath, steadying himself.

His voice barely moved. "Tomorrow. Not tonight."

The city held.

Five quiet minutes passed before Lucien descended the stairs, the cool night air still clinging to his jacket like something that didn't want to let go.

The music had softened, a low murmur around the remnants of the evening.

The women were winding down now, half-curled on couches, shoes off, trading quiet laughs, the glow of wine and warmth lingering in their eyes.

Lena spotted him first, her gaze finding him across the room.

She set her glass down on the cluttered table, a loose half-smile on her lips, radiant from wine and the rare luxury of feeling safe.

She swayed just a touch as she crossed to him, her bare feet silent on the polished floor, dress whispering against her thighs.

"Hey, you." Her voice was a little husky, a little playful.

She tilted her head up, eyes sparkling with that intoxicating mix of mischief and affection. "Hiding from the party?"

He caught her waist, steadying her with hands that knew every curve by heart.

"Just needed a smoke. You look like you've been conspiring."

She laughed, low and warm, pressing closer until her body fit against his.

"Only about how to sneak more wine past Imani. She refuses to let anyone show up hungover tomorrow."

Her fingers traced lazy patterns on his chest, over the fabric of his shirt.

"Missed me up there?"

"Always," he murmured, dipping his head to brush his lips against her forehead.

The scent of her, jasmine, vanilla, and wine, grounded him, pulling him back from the city's endless hum.

From across the room, Victoria waved, her grin bright and easy, the kind only a sister could give.

"Don't get into trouble before the vows," she called. "Or if you do, leave me out of it."

She blew a kiss, cheeks flushed from the wine, already drifting toward the door where Logan waited with the keys.

"Logan's my chauffeur tonight. I've been officially cut off."

Lucien raised a brow.

She smirked. "You'll live. Just don't break her before tomorrow."

"Get home safe, Vic."

"Always." She winked at Lena. "Night, future sis. Keep him in line."

Lena looped her arms around his neck. "Carry me?"

He didn't need asking twice.

He scooped her up in one fluid motion, cradling her against his chest as her legs draped over his arm like silk.

She laughed against his neck, light and unburdened, and it cut through him harder than sorrow as he carried her down the hall and kicked the door shut behind them.

The room was dim, moonlight leaking through the curtains in thin silver strips.

He lowered her onto the bed, but she pulled him down with her, smiling against his mouth before the kiss stole the smile away.

For a while, there was no city.

No Lansing. No Coalition. No wolf in the glass.

Only Lena beneath him, warm and alive, her hands moving over him like she was making sure he was real.

His mouth found her throat, her shoulder, the places where scars and softness lived side by side. He touched her carefully at first, reverent despite the hunger in him, as if some part of him still feared the world would punish him for wanting anything this much.

"You still feel like the world I keep fighting for," he whispered.

Her fingers tightened in his shirt.

"Then stop fighting. Just be here."

Something in him broke open.

He kissed her harder then, and she met him with the same fire, pulling him close until there was no space left between what they had survived and what they still wanted. Clothes gave way. Breath turned uneven. Her laughter vanished into a softer sound that nearly ruined him.

He loved her like a vow before the vow.

Not gently. Not entirely.

But truly.

With every scar. Every sin. Every piece of him that had come back from death because her voice had called him home.

Later, when the room had gone quiet and the world stayed outside the door, she lay with her head on his chest, listening to the heart that had once stopped and started again for her.

Lucien held her like he had finally learned the difference between possession and peace.

Tomorrow, she would become his wife.

Tonight, she was already his life.

CHAPTER FIFTY-NINE
THE DAY GOD WATCHED

Morning came soft, touching corners that rarely saw it.

It ghosted across high windows and cold steel floors, cautious, as if afraid to disturb a place that had lived too long at war.

For the first time in ages, the building held its breath.

No wailing alerts.

No frantic welds sealing breaches.

No whispered plans for who might die next.

Just a house learning how to be quiet.

Just people learning how to live again.

And a man standing at the threshold of something impossibly ordinary.

Marriage.

Lucien sat on the edge of the bed.

No sirens tearing the air.

No metallic tang of gunpowder lingering like regret.

Only faint laughter drifted up from below, women's voices light in a place that had forgotten how to hold them.

Lena's was among them, bright and alive, a sound the city had tried to snuff out but never could.

He rose, drawn to the dresser.

There, beside his cufflinks and the watch that had ticked through too many last stands, sat a single white rose in a slender glass vase.

Next to it, a small note in Lena's handwriting read:

VICTORIA BROUGHT THIS FROM YOUR MOTHER
SAID IT'S YOURS TO WEAR

Evelyn had been leaving him quiet mercies since he was a boy, tokens of love in a world that devoured it.

He lifted the rose carefully and inhaled its clean, fragile scent, a reminder of things that bloomed despite the ash.

He set it down and caught his reflection in the mirror.

Not the shadow of the man who had kicked down doors in the dead of night, hijacked shipments under the city's watch, and buried friends too young.

No hunted eyes.

No hollowed jaw.

Just a man in a crisp white shirt, sleeves loose at his wrists.

A man ready to step into a life he never thought he would earn.

He buttoned slowly, as if committing the moment before fate could rip it away.

On the dresser, beside the watch and the rose, lay a small plastic sleeve, its edges warped from heat.

Inside was the rosary his mother had pressed into his palm the night the oncology floor was blown apart.

He didn't need to remember the fire to feel it.

The weight was enough.

He slipped it into the pocket of his slacks and let the weight ground him as the morning settled around him.

Then he drew a long breath and stood.

A knock cut through the quiet, sharp and familiar.

Victor's voice followed, gravel-rough from decades of smoke and shouts. "You decent, boss?"

Lucien opened the door. Victor stood there in a suit that looked borrowed from a better life, tie half-undone, looking more used to war than ceremony.

"You look like a cop." The words came lighter than he felt.

Victor grunted, eyes crinkling with a warmth that didn't quite reach his scars. "I look like a man who never figured he'd outlive his sins long enough for this. Come on, Logan's been primping his hair for twenty minutes. Told him he ain't the bride."

From down the hall, Logan's voice carried, edged with fake hurt. "I heard that, you old fuck."

Lucien almost smiled, but the weight pressed in, joy tangled with the ghosts of what they'd clawed through, too heavy to let it break free.

They'd turned the makeshift war room into the groom's quarters.

The air still carried the faint scent of sweat and old strategy.

Maps and crates had been cleared away, replaced by a dark cloth draped over the table.

Polished shoes sat ready beneath the table, neat in a room that had never known order.

A tray of cufflinks winked under the light.

Northgate, forged in siege and survival, was pretending to be a family home.

Somehow, it was pulling it off.

Logan fidgeted before a mirrored panel, wrestling his cuffs like they owed him money.

Rook stood beside him, adjusting the knot on his tie with surgical focus. "I prefer operations that don't require formal strangulation."

Victor glanced at Logan. "Relax. You look like you're about to testify."

"I'm not nervous." Which of course meant he was. "Just respecting the occasion."

"The occasion isn't about you." Victor moved past him to grab a tie clip. "It's about that woman finally taming the city's most dangerous stray."

"Stray." Logan grinned despite himself. "You grew up soft, old man."

Rook looked up, deadpan as steel. "You'd be soft too if you'd survived enough endings."

Victor shot him a glare, half-hearted. "I liked you better when you weren't talking."

"Too late for that." Rook smoothed his tie.

The laughter faded, leaving a hush that felt too real. Outside, engines hummed in the yard. Doors closed. Then Alexander stepped in with the quiet authority of a man who had stood at the head of the table for decades. Navy suit, white shirt, no flash, no need. His gaze found Lucien and softened at the edges.

"She's already crying. Your mother. Swore she wouldn't, but here we are."

"Good. Means it's real."

Alexander stepped closer and adjusted Lucien's collar, his fingers lingering a second longer than necessary.

"You look like a man I could trust with my daughter's heart."

His gaze held. "And I don't make that easy on anyone."

Victor snorted. "Ain't that the goddamn truth."

Logan cleared his throat and stepped forward. "Oh, yeah. Lucien, here."

He held out a small velvet box.

Lucien took it.

The shape sat strangely in his hand, too familiar and not familiar enough.

He opened the box. A woman's wedding band caught the light. Simple. Beautiful. Exactly the kind of ring he would have chosen for her.

That was the problem.

He knew that with certainty.

He just couldn't remember choosing it.

Logan's voice pulled him back. "You okay, boss? You gave it to me last week. Told me to hold it till today."

Lucien looked back down at the ring.

Last week.

The words landed wrong, like they belonged to someone else's life.

"Right. Thanks."

But it wasn't right.

A faint vertigo tugged at him. The room tilted, just slightly.

He could remember the wedding.

Wanting this.

Lena's hand in his, the way she looked at him when the world finally went quiet.

But the ring itself sat outside memory, shining like a missing hour.

He couldn't recall handing it to Logan.

He couldn't pin down buying it.

As if one thread of time had unraveled without him noticing.

He closed the box, but the gleam stayed behind his eyes.

He took the ring from the velvet lining and slipped it into his inside pocket, resting it beside the rosary.

Lucien fastened his watch around his wrist, letting the familiar weight settle against his pulse.

Not burdensome.

Earned.

Yet beneath it, a whisper of wrongness lingered, as if the world had shifted when he wasn't looking.

The thought barely settled before the ceiling speaker crackled to life.

"Convoy's clear," Ghost said. "I've got two men running overwatch with me today. Drones are live. Nobody unwelcome gets within two miles of the chapel. Roads are clean, air's quiet, and even the local cops are pretending it's a holiday."

Victor smirked, looking up at the ceiling. "You always did know how to make a love story sound like a perimeter check."

"Habit dies hard." Dry humor threaded through the static. "Build a slice of heaven in this godforsaken city, and someone's always itching to torch it. Not today."

Alexander raised his gaze to the small speaker near the light fixture, his expression softening with old loyalty.

"Still holding the line from the wires, old friend?"

A brief pause hung in the air.

"Always. Your boy learned from you."

Alexander's mouth curved, the barest twitch of pride. "And from the man who kept him alive when I couldn't."

The speaker hissed softly. "We both did what we had to."

The room stilled for a heartbeat, filled only by the faint buzz of the speakers and the rhythmic breaths of men standing on the edge of something sacred.

Then Ghost broke the quiet once more.

"Make it count. Even soldiers deserve a clean day."

The line clicked off. Silence lingered like prayer.

Alexander straightened Lucien's collar one last time, grounding them both.

Lucien glanced toward the window, then back at him. "Where is she?" His voice was steadier than his pulse.

"Downstairs. The women claimed the east room. You're banned. Strict orders, no exceptions."

Lucien exhaled, and a faint smile found him at last.

"Then let's not keep her waiting."

Downstairs, the east room had shed its tactical skin, transforming into something softer, reclaimed from the storm.

For once, it held no strategy, no warnings, no names spoken like casualties.

Today, it was just a room.

The table had been covered in soft linens, repurposed into an improvised vanity. Open makeup kits spread across it, palettes shimmering, pins glinting in the light.

Brushes lay nearby beside folded notes and small keepsakes the women had tucked into their bags, tiny tokens meant to bring luck or calm on a day no one could practice for.

The air held the mingled scents of hairspray, perfume, and borrowed calm, the fragile kind people cling to before forever begins.

Victoria stood behind the stylists, two trusted friends she'd summoned from uptown's polished salons, her arms crossed, eyes sharp. She wasn't handling the brushes; she was protecting the moment. If the city tried to interrupt this day, she looked ready to handle it herself.

"Chin up. I want him utterly dizzy when he lays eyes on you."

Lena sat before the mirror in her silk slip, her hair half-pinned in elegant disarray, the wedding gown suspended from the door like a promise waiting its turn.

Imani and Mara stayed near the windows, their watchfulness hidden in casual glances, fingers quietly scrolling feeds while pretending not to care about the world outside.

Christina and Jessica sorted through jewelry and silk ribbons, whispering over pearls and laughing like they had been there since the beginning.

"The outer cameras are looped," Imani murmured. "Northgate's broadcasting nothing but a lazy Saturday. Ghost says the city's been quiet, like it's holding its breath for us."

"Good. Let it stay boring. Today, we keep the peace we bled for."

Lena turned back toward the mirror, breath steadying. A small wave of sickness turned low in her stomach, sharp enough to make her pause, fingers brushing the edge of the vanity for balance. It passed in a few seconds.

"Wedding jitters." Barely a whisper.

She turned back to her reflection, where the scar along her collarbone caught the light, a pale thread of survival.

For a heartbeat, she considered hiding it. Lace. Foundation. Anything that could make the past less visible. Then she exhaled and let the thought go. The mark was part of her history, not something to hide.

"He'll see it and know I survived," she whispered to the glass.

Victoria caught the words, her reflection softening. "He'll see it and love you fiercer for the story it tells. Now hold still. Let her work on those eyes."

Near the wall, Evelyn sat beneath the soft overhead light.

The oxygen tank beside her hissed softly, there if she needed it, nothing more.

"You can stop tiptoeing around me." Evelyn smiled. "I'm not about to break."

Mara chuckled. "You've earned the throne today, Evelyn. Hell, you forged it from the fires we all walked through."

Evelyn found Lena's gaze in the reflection.

"Don't let him fight the battles alone anymore. Men like him, like my Alexander, will throw themselves into the fire for everyone else before they admit they deserve a life of their own."

Her gaze held.

"Make him live, Lena. Pull him back when he forgets joy belongs to him too."

Lena's throat tightened. "You make it sound so simple."

"It isn't. Marriage isn't shelter from the storm. It's choosing each other inside it. Day after day. Even when surrender sounds easier."

Her smile softened. "But the beauty of that choice is worth every scar."

Imani's thumb paused over her screen. "Alexander mentioned last night you're set for surgery on Monday?"

Evelyn nodded, unflinching. "They're bringing in a specialist from Boston. Top of his field. He likes our odds, so I'm rounding them up and calling it destiny."

Her smile deepened. "I intend to be on my feet when she walks that aisle today. I didn't survive this long to miss the dawn."

The room went quiet, not from dread, but from respect.

Then Victoria clapped her hands. "Enough of that. If we spiral into tears now, her eyeliner's doomed, and I'll have to commit murder in excellent shoes."

Laughter filled the room, nerves and love tangled together.

Mara sat on the arm of the couch, watching Lena in the mirror. "Did you ever really believe you'd get here?"

Lena looked at the woman in the mirror and remembered the girl who used to disappear into corners.

"I hoped. As hard as I could. I just didn't know if the world would let me keep it."

Imani looked up from her screen, mischief glinting in her eyes. "He's pacing upstairs like a caged storm. Ready as he'll ever be. You should make him wait a little longer."

"Oh, I will." Lena's grin finally broke free. "He made me wait through war. Today, he earns every second of it."

They gathered around her to help her into the gown, hands gentle and sure.

It wasn't extravagant. It was made for a woman who had lived too much to need a fairy tale. Clean lines. Soft fall. Nothing wasted.

As the final button fastened and the fabric settled against her skin, the room released a single breath.

"You look like forever," Victoria said, all pride.

Lena exhaled, grounding herself as joy settled over her like a crown.

"Then let's go give him forever. Scarred, standing, and ours to keep."

The cars waited in the yard like a small convoy pretending not to be one. Black paint, dark glass, engines idling low. Northgate's iron gate stood open, still bearing scars from the last time someone tried to take the compound.

The morning was perfect. Late June sunlight poured down clean and forgiving, warm enough to loosen the city's shoulders. The air carried cut grass, oil, and steel cooling after too many nights of fire.

Lucien came down first with Victor, Logan, and Rook behind him, men in suits that couldn't quite hide the soldiers underneath. The breeze caught their jackets. For once, the city wasn't screaming. It was breathing.

He looked out at the skyline, all glass and promise, and felt something in his chest that wasn't rage. Quieter. Harder to name.

From inside came the soft groan of a door, followed by measured footsteps on weathered stone. Evelyn appeared first, her gown pale in the morning light, Alexander beside her, steady and sure.

Lucien stepped forward to meet her midway across the courtyard, time slowing, not from grief, but from something close to it.

"You did the rose."

"Of course I did. I get one moment of sentiment on my son's wedding day."

She reached up, her hand trembling as she cupped his jaw. "You look like the man I always knew was still in there."

He almost smiled, truly this time. "You look like you're poised to eclipse my bride entirely."

Evelyn's laughter escaped softly, more exhale than sound. "She's the sun, Lucien. I'm just grateful I lived long enough to see her rise."

Alexander drew nearer, guiding her the final steps to the car. "Everything's in place. Father Adrian called an hour ago. The chapel's ready, like it's been waiting for this day."

Lucien drew a slow breath, part pride, part disbelief. He held the door for Alexander, then for Evelyn, before stepping back toward the limo.

Behind the doors, laughter drifted, muffled but bright, the sound of women guarding a secret he wasn't allowed to see. He didn't look back; some traditions are worth the wait.

He straightened his cuffs and waited for the convoy to stir to life.

They divided into vehicles with the precision of an operation pretending to be a wedding.

Lucien rode in the lead limo with Victor, Logan, and Rook. Lena followed behind dark glass with Christina, Jessica, Victoria, Imani, and Mara, the bouquet Evelyn had chosen resting somewhere he wasn't allowed to see.

Behind them, Alexander drove Evelyn in his own car, the window cracked just enough for air, his hand never far from hers.

The city receded in their wake, its clamor fading like a storm moving off the horizon.

By the time the first bell rang through the hills, the noise of New York was only a memory.

The Vale of Saint Arden rested where the river curved through the hills.

Sunlight flowed over its stones like grace finding its way home.

The chapel stood tall on the hillside, cedar and glass catching the quiet light.

They had stood here weeks ago, when it was only a plan and a promise.

Now it was real, waiting.

Outside, cars lined the gravel path. Guests gathered under the birch trees, men Lucien had not seen since the world broke open.

Old friends of Alexander's stood among aunts, uncles, and cousins from before the Cole name carried weight.

A few of Lucien's old guard showed up too, drawn out of the dark for this.

Even the nurses from Mercy West came, along with Evelyn's lead nurse from Saint Dymphna's, all of them bending rules just to be there.

Lucien stepped out of the limo and froze.

He had braced for tension, for security, for anything sharp. Instead he found laughter drifting through clean air, the soft scent of river water, people clasping hands instead of gripping guns.

Across the lawn, the annex waited for the reception, tables set beneath linen canopies, glasses catching light like small signals of peace.

At the far edge of the lawn, near the old stone wall that bordered the grounds, a helicopter waited. Its black hull gleamed under the sun, rotors still.

Alexander had arranged it for after the ceremony, a quiet flight north along the coastline, two hours of sky before the world reclaimed them.

When he told them, Lena had teased him for it, said it was too grand, too much like a movie.

Alexander had only smiled. "A man gets to plan his son's escape once. A wedding should end with wings, not wheels."

Lucien looked at it now, the machine built for leaving, and thought how rare it was to see something meant for peace instead of pursuit. He had owned wings before, but none that promised stillness.

"Welcome home," Father Adrian Dimas called from the steps. His robe was simple, his eyes calm. "This day has been a long time in the making."

Lucien took his hand. "You look sharp, Father."

Dimas smiled. "You look even better. Especially for a man who's survived the roads you have."

Lucien drew him into a brief hug. For a moment, Dimas's hand rested strong on his back, bracing a man he had once helped pull from the edge.

When they stepped apart, the old priest looked at him like a man who had seen every dark corner and stayed anyway. "I heard your hardest confessions, Lucien. But I never stopped believing you were meant for more than survival."

Lucien nodded once. Words failed him.

Behind them, the bells rang out again.

The day was here.

Inside, the chapel was all light and warmth, a sanctuary carved out of a world that had seen too much.

Rows of candles flickered along the arched windows, their glow trembling against the glass, the river moving quietly below.

White flowers lined the altar, lilies open, ivy woven along the rail, the scent clean enough to settle something in the room.

Lena stood at the threshold, veil falling soft around her shoulders, her heart thundering in her chest like a storm held at bay.

A young usher from the parish hurried to steady the door behind her, no older than twenty, his hands shaking with the weight of wanting everything to be perfect.

Father Dimas gave him a small nod of approval.

The boy's shoulders straightened like he'd been knighted.

For a fleeting moment, absence clawed at her: her mother, her father, the hollow places where blood should have anchored her.

Yet as her gaze swept the room, warmth flooded in.

Victoria murmured quietly with Imani, their laughter a soft rebellion against sorrow.

Mara adjusted the train of Lena's gown, hands that had mended far more than fabric.

Evelyn stood near the front in pale silk that caught the light, her grace undimmed.

She had family now.

Not the kind written in records, but the kind that stays when everything else burns.

It was enough.

It was everything.

Near the front, the cellist drew the first note, his dark suit neat on narrow shoulders, brow set in focus, too young for hands that steady and too proud of the honor to hide it.

The doors opened wider and the music swelled, strings carrying something soft and human through the room.

Lucien stood at the altar, Victor and Logan at his sides, shaped by everything he'd survived, but standing anyway.

He had faced men with blood in their eyes, stood at the edge of oblivion, and still this moment held him tighter than any of it, something like fear, something like awe.

He did not blink as the congregation rose.

Then he saw her.

For a heartbeat, the world narrowed to her.

His hand found the rosary in his pocket, the beads cool against his skin, steadying him more than any prayer ever would.

Lena moved down the aisle, and the room seemed to fall away.

Everything they had survived led here.

She came to him, draped in white that caught the light, every step steady, earned.

When she reached him, the noise inside him, the violence, the doubt, all of it fell quiet, replaced by something he hadn't felt in a long time.

Father Dimas watched them with a quiet smile, the years in his eyes, the candlelight steady against them.

"Love," he said softly, "is not the absence of ruin. It is the defiant choice to rebuild amid the wreckage, brick by brick, soul by soul. I have watched this family rise from the embers time and again. Today, that resilience becomes covenant, eternal and unbreakable."

He inclined his head, inviting their vows, the air thick with anticipation.

Lena's voice trembled once, then steadied, stronger than it sounded.

"You were chaos incarnate," she said, eyes locked on his, "a whirlwind of shadows and sharp edges that could have torn me apart. Yet I walked toward you anyway, drawn by the light buried beneath the storm.

You taught me that love isn't rescue from the abyss, it's recognition of the shared darkness, the mutual mending of fractures. Every scar we bear, every sin confessed in the dead of night, I would choose again and again if it meant standing here with you, building a future from the fragments we've gathered."

Lena's final words hung in the air like a benediction.

Then she opened her palm and revealed a ring, black and gleaming, its surface dark as night but catching the light in muted flashes of gold beneath the plating.

Lucien blinked, a faint smile tugging at his lips.

"Black?"

Lena's eyes softened. "Gold would've felt wrong," she whispered. "This one's ours. Shadow and shine, same metal underneath."

He exhaled, something between a laugh and a tremor. "I love it."

She slipped it onto his finger, and for a breath, the world seemed to realign, no crowns, no scars, no war, just two souls tethered by choice.

Silence fell, not awkward or fragile, but sacred.

Lucien swallowed hard, his voice raw and reverent.

"You taught me how to live like I wasn't forged only for dying. In your eyes, I saw more than my failures. I saw the man I could still become.

You showed me that mercy isn't weakness, it's defiance of the world's cruelty, that heaven isn't a distant promise but something we build together, with our calloused hands, our spilled blood, and our unyielding hearts.

You turned my solitary path into a shared journey, and for that, I pledge every breath and every beat."

Lucien took her hand, sliding the white-gold band he'd carried all morning onto hers.

Their fingers lingered, the touch both vow and victory.

Evelyn wept quietly, Alexander beside her, both of them watching the boy they raised become a husband.

Even Victor went still, his edge gone for once, while Logan's usual smirk softened into something unguarded.

Father Dimas lifted his voice again, soft and steady.

"Then by the power of God, and by the witness of every soul gathered here, I now pronounce you,"

He never finished.

A sound thundered through the distant hills, low, ominous, inevitable.

The stained glass quivered.

Light shattered into a thousand trembling stars.

Outside, the birds erupted all at once, dark shapes cutting across the sun, fleeing whatever storm had just found them.

And for one final heartbeat, the world held its fragile beauty.

Chapter Sixty

FOREVER FORGED IN FIRE

The sound hit.

It didn't belong in a church, not among vows or whispered prayers. It rolled in from beyond the tree line, low and merciless, the kind of rumble that had already chosen what it would destroy.

The windows trembled; candles flickered and died. Petals scattered from the floor in slow, bewildered swirls.

Then the first window shattered inward.

Glass exploded across the pews in a sharp, deadly cascade.

Heat slammed through the wall like an invisible fist.

The chapel's far corner coughed out dust and jagged splinters.

For a split second, everything drowned in white noise and blinding light. A roar that swallowed screams and names alike.

Lucien reacted on instinct before his mind could catch up.

He threw his arms around Lena, twisting his body to shield her from the blast.

His forearm curved over her head like a barrier.

Shards stung his back, glass and grit tearing at his sleeve.

A fragment sliced his neck, warm blood trickling down, but he barely felt it.

The floor bucked beneath them, throwing them both hard to the ground.

His lips brushed her ear. "Breathe."

Her eyes were wide, tears cutting tracks through the dust on her face, but she was breathing.

She nodded, her hand reaching up to grip his jaw, holding on like the world depended on it.

Stone ground against stone in the rafters overhead.

A beam groaned long and deep, like a dying animal.

Smoke slithered along the aisle, low and gray, clinging to the floor.

Programs scattered on the seats ignited, tiny flames licking at paper edges, hungry and relentless.

Someone screamed.

Another coughed until it broke into sobs.

A child's cry pierced the air once, then hushed in a stranger's protective hold.

The crucifix above the altar tilted, hanging by a thread.

Father Dimas lay crumpled against the steps, his stole coated in gray dust.

He pushed to rise, arms trembling, but collapsed back.

Through the haze, his eyes found Lucien, and he managed a small, weary smile.

"Get them out," he rasped, each word a labored effort. "Go."

Lucien surged to his feet, adrenaline cutting through the ringing in his ears.

He scanned for exits through the smoke, for anyone still moving, still breathing.

He hauled Lena to her feet, pressing her against a sturdy column that hadn't given way yet.

"Help them."

It came out as a command, but inside it was a desperate plea.

She was already in motion, slipping under the arm of a stunned woman in blue, lifting with steady strength.

"Imani, take her; Mara, right side, now."

Voices rose through the coughs, ragged but responding.

Near the altar, Jessica and Christina were thrown off their feet by the blast, ribbons tearing loose from their hair.

The impact hurled them against the marble rail, scattering petals and glass across the steps.

Jessica's arm was bleeding where a shard had cut deep.

She stared at the wound for half a second, then tore a strip from her dress and wrapped it tight.

Instinct. Survival. Nothing delicate left.

Christina dragged herself upright, coughing through the smoke as she steadied a dazed guest and pushed them toward the aisle.

Her hair was streaked white with ash, eyes burning but clear.

When their gazes locked through the haze, neither spoke.

They just nodded once.

The kind of nod shared by people who refuse to die quiet.

Near the front pews, Victoria staggered to one knee, coughing through a storm of dust.

One heel was gone, a pearl earring missing.

The shockwave had thrown her sideways, ribs aching, cheek scraped raw.

She blinked through smoke until she found their parents.

"Mom!" she shouted, stumbling toward them.

Alexander was already on his knees beside Evelyn, his movements frantic but controlled.

Victoria dropped beside him without hesitation, bracing her shoulder against the wreckage, her hands slipping on blood and grit as she tried to help.

Lucien crossed the altar through swirling debris.

He dropped to his knees beside Dimas, pressing a hand to the old man's chest.

That stubborn heart thumped once, defiant, then began to falter.

Dimas clutched Lucien's wrist with a fading grip.

"Keep the light," he whispered, his voice like the close of a lifelong sermon.

His fingers went slack.

His head turned gently toward the river outside.

Death took him then, quiet and final.

Lucien closed his eyes for one raw moment, not in prayer, but in bitter acceptance.

His priest since boyhood. The man who had heard every confession, every doubt, every sin.

Gone in an instant, stolen by cowards who couldn't face him in the light.

"Help," Alexander called, his voice cracking like brittle glass.

Evelyn lay amid the wreckage, her small oxygen tank crushed beneath a fallen beam.

Alexander had pulled her free, blood spreading across the back of his suit where the wood had gouged him.

Her lips were gray, but her eyes held steady.

Lucien pushed through the smoke and dropped to his knees beside her.

Evelyn saw her son and exhaled a faint, almost amused breath.

"I guess forever... never plays fair."

Lucien slid an arm under her shoulders. Lena knelt beside them, her gown streaked with soot, veil torn.

Evelyn reached for them, weaving Lena's fingers through his with the last of her strength.

"Make it mean something," she whispered.

Her chest rose one last time, a shallow heave.

Her eyes fluttered, then stilled.

The faintest smile lingered, like she had recognized a quiet voice calling her home.

Her hand went slack in his. The world seemed to tilt, sound collapsing into silence.

Alexander bowed over her, silent as stone. His shoulders trembled like a man caught in an endless downpour, refusing to seek shelter. Blood trailed down his back, unheeded; pain meant nothing now.

Victoria knelt back beside them, her face streaked with tears.

She pressed a trembling hand to her mother's chest, as if the warmth might still be there.

"Come on, Mom," she whispered, voice breaking, "you promised you'd dance today."

Alexander held her there as the weight of it all settled in.

Together they stayed, a small circle in the ruin, love refusing to scatter.

Lucien placed one hand on his father's neck, the other in his mother's hair, ash falling soft against his skin.

His face went still.

A mask cracking at the edges.

Evelyn Cole, who had fought every battle with grace and steel, had not been taken by flame, but by the quiet betrayal of a body that had simply given all it had left.

Two days from now, she was supposed to meet the doctor flying in from Boston.

He liked her odds.

She had smiled, rounded them up, and called it destiny.

In truth, she just wanted to see her boy get married.

"Help me get her out."

His voice was low, edged with something dangerous.

Victor emerged from the chaos, blood trickling from his temple, eyes burning with wrath. Logan followed, hacking coughs wracking him as he heaved a splintered pew off a trapped man.

"Clear a path," Victor growled.

They forced the doors wide, turning wreckage into an exit.

Victor shoved rubble aside with raw force.

Logan kicked glass clear, his dress shoes crunching shards.

Rook held the threshold, shirt muffling his breaths, eyes darting for threats.

Lucien lifted Evelyn.

She felt so light. Too light.

Her head rested against his arm like when he was a child, seeking comfort in her strength.

He carried her through the choking smoke, past broken light, and out into the harsh, unrelenting day.

Victoria followed close behind, one hand braced against Alexander's back as they cleared the doorway.

Her dress was torn. Her hair filmed with the pale residue of the blast.

But she stayed upright, steadying her father when his knees almost buckled.

Outside, the river gleamed below, silver and indifferent.

Lucien carried Evelyn to the grass where the wind still moved through the leaves.

He laid her gently down.

Alexander sank beside her, clasping her hand, holding on as if he could pull her back.

For a heartbeat, Lucien lifted his eyes. The river kept shining. The trees kept moving. The sky kept its color. Even in the middle of ruin, the world refused to break with them.

The chapel's roof spat sparks; smoke billowed from shattered windows. A stained-glass saint tumbled and broke at the doorway, red and gold fragments scattering like lost hope.

Lena staggered out, a young girl slung over her shoulder, the child coughing, hair glittering with glass. She set her down gently among the survivors, then turned back. Christina was half-carrying Jessica, whose breaths now came shallow and ragged, lungs burning from the smoke. Without thinking, Lena rushed to meet them, throwing one arm under Jessica's shoulders as they dragged her toward the light.

They reached open air. For a heartbeat, the world stilled, fire snapping behind them. Lena met Lucien's eyes through the smoke.

"I'm going back in."

"I know," Lucien replied, his heart twisting with pride and fear.

Lena turned back toward the shattered nave, ready to charge in again, when a sharp pull twisted low in her stomach.

She hissed, one hand pressing briefly to her abdomen.

Lucien caught it, just for a second.

"You good?"

"Adrenaline," she said, forcing breath back into her lungs. "I'm fine. Go."

She vanished into the smoke.

Victor followed.

Logan too.

People stumbled into the daylight, eyes squinting, clothes ripped, discovering their legs could still carry them.

A gardener dragged a hose, water spraying in futile arcs across the stone.

It couldn't quench the flames, but he kept trying.

They pulled out the living.

Covered the dead.

Rook and Imani, who had never known Father Dimas, carried him out with reverent care, as if he were kin.

They placed him under the old oak where Alexander had once shared tales of his own wedding vows.

The priest's hands were crossed, his rosary wound between his fingers.

His face was serene, even in death.

The nave groaned inside.

The roof sagged.

Fire inhaled deep.

The altar cross crashed down with a final, echoing thud, like a story slamming shut.

Logan stumbled back out through the haze, coughing hard, his shirt torn and eyes bloodshot from the smoke.

He came to stand beside Lucien, the fire reflecting in both their faces.

"They did this."

It was cold truth.

Lucien stared into the chapel's gaping wound until his vision blurred with tears he wouldn't let fall.

He turned to Lena as she emerged again, ash-smeared, hair matted with grit, her ring gleaming against a bloodied palm.

She met his gaze, unyielding.

"We finished the vow." Her voice trembled, but the words were ironclad.

He took her hand, their fingers intertwined. The metal between them felt cold, unyielding, right.

"No." His voice softened. "We live it now."

He looked at Logan and Victor, then down the road snaking south toward the city that worshipped its own destruction.

"Lansing's just the weather." His voice sharpened. "The Coalition's the climate. They wanted this rupture."

Victor's fists clenched; Logan's shoulders tensed.

"Then let the sky go dark," Lucien said. "I'll salt the earth they stand on."

Rage rose then, hot and consuming, fed by his mother's still form on the grass, her hand limp in Alexander's, and by Dimas beneath the oak, his rosary wound between his fingers.

They had taken his peace.

His mother.

His priest.

His goddamn wedding day.

Turned joy to ruin.

He wanted to tear the world apart until the Coalition bled out in the streets.

Wind scattered the smoke, embers floating like defiant stars before winking out in the grass.

Alexander pressed Evelyn's hand to his lips, his face etched with quiet despair, holding vigil over the silence she left behind.

Behind them, the Vale of Saint Arden finally crumbled.

Stone held a moment longer as wood surrendered.

The final stained-glass window shattered under the pressure and heat, colors bursting into the air like a fractured blessing.

Lucien didn't flinch.

He closed his fingers around Lena's, the vow still warm between them, smoke and blood binding where rings could not.

"Forever," he vowed, soft for her, thunder for the men behind him. "Forged in fire."

The river flowed on.

The sky held blue.

The smoke cleared.

The day offered no mercy, and neither would he.

CHAPTER SIXTY-ONE

MAKE IT MEAN SOMETHING

For a while, there was only the crackle of burning wood, the cries of the living, and the silence of the dead.

No sirens.

No help.

Only ruin.

The Vale of Saint Arden lay in shambles behind them.

The chapel's roof had collapsed inward with a thunderous crack that reverberated through the valley.

Survivors clustered across the grass, clutching the injured and the unmoving, staring toward the road like help could be dragged closer by will alone.

Lucien stood over Evelyn's body, the breeze moving her pale silk dress like she might still answer it.

Alexander was still down at her side, fingers entwined with hers, the blood running fresh from the beam's vicious graze along his back.

He hadn't uttered a word since they'd carried her out.

His gaze fixed on her face like he was etching it into his soul.

As if letting go would erase the lifetime of quiet strength she'd given him.

Victoria hovered close, her hands shaking as she pressed a folded cloth to the wound, trying to stanch the bleeding.

Her eyes never left Evelyn.

Faint sirens rolled across the valley, but their light hadn't reached here yet.

Victoria looked hollow, already lost somewhere grief had no map for.

Lucien ached to pull Alexander to his feet, to force motion into the numbness, but sorrow like this didn't yield to commands.

It consumed, leaving hollow shells where hope had once lived.

The weight of it all crashed over him then, not in rage this time, but in silence.

The kind that followed when the shouting died and only the truth remained.

The wedding they had fought so hard for, built from the ashes of betrayal and blood, stolen in a heartbeat.

He saw it all again.

The rehearsal dinner the night before, laughter echoing through Northgate like a rare mercy.

The morning calm that had felt almost holy.

Lena's voice, trembling in vows that had promised forever, only for forever to crumble under the weight of violence.

For one day, they had believed love might survive untouched.

Tears finally broke free, carving hot tracks through the ash on his face.

A soundless sob tore up his throat, not weakness, but the kind of grief that hollows a man out and pours fire into the space it leaves behind.

"Dad," Lucien said softly, crouching beside him, his voice cracked from smoke and grief.

He took the rosary from his pocket and placed it gently in Evelyn's hands.

"You held the light for me," he whispered to her. "Rest in it. I'll carry the fire now."

He touched Alexander's shoulder. "We can't stay here."

Alexander looked up, eyes raw and emptied out.

"Go where?" His voice cracked. "Your mother is gone. Dimas is gone. People who came to bless this day are under sheets."

His hand swept weakly toward the priest beneath the oak, then to the few scattered white sheets trembling in the wind.

"We brought them here. And now they're never going home."

Lucien swallowed against the grit in his throat, tasting dust and defeat.

Dimas, his lifelong confessor, the man who had baptized him and believed in him when no one else did.

The voice that carried absolution through sin and war.

The man who had seen his soul's ugliest corners and still offered light.

Gone in a breath of ruin, his last smile a fading ember of faith.

And Evelyn.

His beautiful mother, whose courage shaped the man he became.

Whose gentleness had steadied every storm inside him.

Who had given him roses and pressed rosaries into his hands on his darkest days.

Who had whispered mercy until her last breath.

Now she lay on this cursed grass, her final plea still hanging in the air, refusing to fade:

Make it mean something.

The fury was no longer wild.

It moved through him with purpose, cold and precise.

His pulse slowed, the heat folding inward until it turned to iron.

No shaking.

No tears.

The vow settled inside him like scripture.

They would answer.

Victor approached, face smeared with blood, Logan close behind him.

"Responders are closing in," Victor said. "Feds won't be far behind. We need out before the questions start."

Lucien kept his eyes on Alexander. "Come with us."

Alexander shook his head, slow and resolute.

"I'll handle what's left here. The statements. The dead."

His gaze drifted to the shrouded bodies, blurred shapes he wasn't ready to name.

"Go. Finish what they started."

Leaving felt like severing a lifeline, but Alexander's gaze sharpened now, anguish forging into steel.

"Promise me," he rasped. "For her. For Dimas. Make them fucking regret this."

"I swear it," Lucien said, clasping his father's shoulder.

Behind them, Victoria sank to her knees beside Evelyn's body, her hands settling over her mother's wrist as if still searching for a pulse she already knew was gone.

It was the last mercy she had left, letting herself believe there might still be something to hold onto.

When she looked up, her eyes found Lucien.

There was no accusation in her face.

Only blood, ash, and the same impossible loss.

She stood, brushed the ash from her palms, and reached for him.

He caught her hand, and for a heartbeat she was a child again, reaching for her brother who once chased away her nightmares before the city learned his name.

"She was right about you," Victoria said. "You were built to rise."

His throat tightened. "I keep wishing she'd been wrong."

She smiled through tears, a soundless, shaking thing that echoed their mother's words.

"Then make it mean something."

Lucien pulled her into a rough embrace, her shoulders trembling against him, her voice muffled in his coat.

"Go," she whispered. "Before this place eats you too."

When he stepped back, Victoria didn't shed another tear.

She just knelt back down beside their mother, hands folded, a sentinel carved from grief.

He turned toward Lena. Jessica and Christina were beside her, helping steady the wounded and clear space among the survivors.

They moved with her, unshaken.

Lena's resolve held firm, unbroken.

Their eyes met again, a silent vow passing between them, rage shared, love fortified.

Yet beneath it lived the shared agony of their stolen day, the wedding that should have been their triumph now a scar they would carry forever.

She crossed to him and took his hand, grief and rage braided behind her eyes.

Above them, the sky shifted.

Fast-moving storm clouds rolled over the valley, dark and sudden, swallowing what little light remained.

The wind shifted, sharp and cold, carrying the scent of wet earth rising from the valley.

Lena glanced up, breath unsteady.

"It wasn't supposed to storm today."

Lucien followed her gaze.

"Nothing about today went the way it was meant to."

A low rumble moved across the hills.

Even the sky refused them a clean goodbye.

With first responder lights cresting the ridge, the team pushed through the chaos toward the far edge of the lawn where the helicopter waited.

Its black hull crouched near the old stone wall, rotors idle.

A sleek machine meant for escape.

Alexander's gift.

Arranged for the post-ceremony flight north, a stolen moment of peace in the sky.

Now it stood as their fastest clean exit, untouched by the blast.

Paramedics flooded the scene, shouting orders, but the dead remained silent beneath improvised shrouds, their stillness a cruel reminder of how fragile happiness could be.

Lucien reached the helicopter and pulled the door open.

The metallic click cut through the sirens, wind whipping ash across his face.

The pilot, a stoic veteran Alexander trusted, straightened inside the cockpit.

"Mr. Cole,"

"Get it spinning," Lucien cut in. "We're leaving. Now."

As the rotors whirred to life, drowning the sirens in a steady thrum, Lucien scrolled to Ghost's name and hit call.

The line connected almost instantly.

"Ghost. Status."

"Lucien," Ghost's voice came tight with urgency. "Saw the whole fucking thing on the drones. You all right?"

"Breathing," Lucien said. "My mother isn't."

Ghost drew a rough inhale.

"Understood."

The pause said enough.

"Blast came from the treeline. Shaped charge, high yield. Whoever set it knew the layout and went straight for the supports. Weeks of prep. No movement during the ceremony. I would have seen it.

But get this. Blast pattern points mil-spec. Serbian stock, if the fragments confirm what I'm seeing. Coalition's been fencing that through dock cutouts."

Lucien's grip whitened on the phone.

"They knew about the wedding?"

"Affirmative," Ghost said. "Leak or long-game surveillance. Coalition's web is thick.

Trigger was remote. Dormant until today. One encrypted fire command, then the module burned itself clean.

By the time I caught the echo, the originating phone was already dead, probably sinking to the riverbed. Whoever pressed the button could've been anywhere on the planet. They waited weeks for the moment."

"Feed me everything," Lucien said. "Lock the grid and black out my trail. I'm going in light. Ghost, if you nail the signal's origin, paint it red. I want coordinates before wheels up."

"Copy that. Eyes in the sky are yours. Hunt 'em down."

Victor's head snapped up. "Lucien, don't."

Lucien silenced him with a look.

"Stay here. You and Logan protect Alexander, Victoria, Lena, and whoever can still move. Get them back to Northgate safe."

Lena stepped forward, her hand on his arm, eyes fierce.

"Not alone. We do this together."

He cupped her face, thumb tracing her cheek through the ash.

"We will. But my father won't leave her. Victoria can't carry him alone. I need you here until Victor moves them."

She searched his eyes, then nodded, pulling him into a brief, hard kiss.

"Come back to me."

"Always."

He turned to the team.

"Hold it down. I'll signal when it's time."

Lucien climbed into the helicopter.

He slapped the door shut.

The metal thud vanished beneath the rotors' roar.

A whirlwind of leaves, embers, and debris exploded outward as the chopper surged skyward.

Below, the valley receded.

The smoldering chapel crumbled amid dying flames.

Smoke curled into the day.

Fire crews moved through the wreckage with grim precision.

Medics worked the wounded and the dead.

Radios crackled through the haze.

As the helicopter climbed, the first cold drops began to fall.

Not weather.

Mourning.

The way angels cry when they're forced to watch.

Alexander remained unmoving, an ancient guardian over Evelyn's still form.

He removed his suit jacket and draped it over her chest, shielding her as if rain could still wound her, as if dignity still needed defending.

From this height, Lucien could still see the wound carved across his father's back, the slash of exposed flesh stark and raw.

A brutal reminder of how hard he'd fought to reach her.

Beside him, Victoria huddled in the scorched grass, her fingers clutching the jacket's lapel as if it were the last warm thing left in the world.

Grief clawed at Lucien's chest, but he shoved it down, letting rage sharpen his focus.

The Coalition had orchestrated this horror, whispering destruction into desperate ears.

He would make them confess.

Then he would make them pay.

He lifted the phone back to his ear as the helicopter skimmed the treetops, a shadow knifing through the canopy, rotors thumping like a war drum against the wind.

"Ghost. Talk. Components."

"Trace leads into Coalition channels. Contractor plates, laundered payments, an interior line feeding a donor network. We're seeing the Coalition's architecture. No clean link to the trigger yet, but the signal bounced through one of their towers."

Lucien watched the trees blur beneath them, rain striking the windows hard enough to rattle the frame.

"Then we hit the architecture."

"Already ahead of you. Last month I cracked an encrypted drop during a breach on their shadow servers. Didn't know what it meant at the time, but the same location kept tagging their outbound traffic. Mountain estate. Switchbacks north."

"Looks quiet on paper, but traffic's wrong. Supply drones, encrypted convoys, late-night thermal spikes."

Static crackled.

The sound of a hunter closing in.

"Has to be a command site," Ghost finished. "Maybe Pennington's personal vault. I'm sending the coordinates."

Lucien folded forward in his seat, letting the fire narrow into something precise.

"First stop. Pennington's nest."

He pulled the phone from his ear and held the display up for the pilot to see.

The coordinates pinged through, the screen glowing faintly against the chopper's dim interior.

Latitude and longitude locked in.

A precise waypoint marked on the display.

"Punch these in. It's a secluded clearing one mile out from the coordinates the drop just sent."

The pilot's eyes flicked to the numbers before tapping them into the helicopter's GPS unit mounted on the panel.

"Copy that. Waypoint set, direct-to course plotted. ETA twenty minutes, staying low to skirt radar."

Lucien lifted the phone back to his ear.

"Copy. I need you to do me a favor."

"You name it."

"I'm gonna text you something I want pushed out. Hit every dark channel you can find. Make sure the whole underground, from here to Battery Park, reads it. Make it sound like payday and war at the same time. Let it move like a rumor that burns."

"Give me the text. I'll seed it, and watch it bleed."

Lucien thumbed the message into the phone.

He sent it.

Hung up.

Slid the device back into his pocket.

Twenty minutes later, the chopper banked low, rotors slicing through the mist-shrouded canopy as it descended into a secluded clearing a mile from the target.

Lucien stepped out onto the wet earth, the downdraft whipping pine needles around his dress shoes.

The pilot gave a quick thumbs-up through the cockpit glass before throttling up, the bird lifting off in a roar that vanished into the gathering storm.

Alone in the pines, rain starting to patter like distant gunfire, he felt the Wolf stir. Patient. Lethal.

Evelyn's words rang: *Make it mean something.*

Dimas's: *Keep the light.*

He started walking.

The estate waited like a false sanctuary.

Mercy wasn't coming.

Judgment was, and it carried his name.

Chapter Sixty-Two

THE CHAPEL OF ARCHITECTS

The flight had been silent. Twenty minutes of turbulence and ghosts he wasn't done burying.

The chopper had vanished behind him. The forest closed in, thick with wet pine and the hum of rain on leaves.

Lucien checked his phone. A message from Ghost flashed across the cracked screen.

You're two clicks from target. Move five hundred yards east, and you'll hit a fork. Take the service road with the broken fence. Less exposure

He adjusted course, dress shoes sinking into the mud, breath steady. Another vibration buzzed through his palm.

Storm's cutting my thermal feed. Static north of you. I've only got one heat signature at the gate, probable guard. You packing anything?

Lucien typed back, **Always**

Ghost replied a beat later.

Copy. What you asked for is moving. Dark channels are lit. Word's spreading fast

Lucien stared at the screen for a moment, rain stinging his face, then slid the phone back into his pocket.

He kept walking.

He found the fork Ghost had mentioned, slipped through the broken fence, and took the service road up.

The path wound upward through switchbacks that cut the mountain like scars. Rain slicked the stone, soaking through his shirt, but he kept moving, the Wolf pacing steady in his chest. The pines leaned in close, heavy with water.

The storm thickened fast. Clouds blackened over the ridgelines, dragging daylight out in minutes. Whatever remained of the afternoon vanished, swallowed whole. By the time he reached the outskirts of the estate, the world wore the colors of night, rain turning the floodlights ahead into long, trembling halos.

Headlights flared once through the fog, a patrol car distant, then vanished.

The iron gate emerged from the rain, its lights cold and artificial against the storm.

Beyond it, a black-stone estate rose out of the mist, a chapel that forgot God and learned money.

Lucien slowed, breath steady. The air tasted damp and wild, rain stirring the ground's scent upward.

He moved forward, hand already on the pistol beneath his jacket. Through the rain, the guard's shape came into focus, a dark silhouette caught in the gate's floodlights.

Lucien drew, arm level, the muzzle tracking center mass.

"Easy."

The guard froze. For half a breath he stared like a man watching his own obituary walk toward him, and the rifle sagged before thought could catch him.

Lucien stepped in, stripped it away in one clean motion, and walked past him without a word.

In the courtyard, water spilled from a marble bowl cut with Latin and a nameless crest, carved deep enough to outlast whoever built it.

The estate loomed beyond, a seat of power pretending to be faith.

Inside, it was colder.

Stone corridors stretched long and narrow. Candlelight burned low on purpose, throwing more shadow than comfort.

The air smelled of burnt resin and antiseptic, hospital and cathedral stitched into one skin.

The estate stood on old church land. Consecrated ground. The chapel architecture remained, repurposed into something colder than worship.

They were waiting in the nave.

Shadows clung to the pews like confessions unspoken, secrets pressing down from vaulted ceilings etched with forgotten saints.

Lucien entered without pause. His footsteps echoed through the hollow space. The pistol was still warm in his grip.

Faces turned toward him, pale masks in the flickering glow, eyes once bright with power now fractured by disbelief.

The air thickened with incense and something darker. This was the heart of the conspiracy he had come to end.

They were part of the House's inner council, twenty, maybe thirty in number.

Robes hung heavy, rings flashing when they moved.

A black dais at the far end held a lectern carved from wood too dark to name, lacquered and holy.

Behind it, tall windows framed nothing but mountain and fog.

The room hummed faintly, a frequency in the teeth.

Calming.

Conditioning.

Pennington stood off the dais, unhooded, the only face with the confidence to be seen. Hair pinned clean. A thin chain at her throat. Her palms on the back of a chair like she owned the air itself.

He stopped ten paces short of the platform, close enough to see the tremor in her chain.

"Mr. Cole," she said, voice soft, tired of pretending this wasn't inevitable.

"At last. This moment was always coming."

Lucien tracked exits, arches, the height of the rails. Counted shoulders. He didn't lift the gun.

"You built a church."

"We built a boardroom with better acoustics." Her smile didn't reach honesty. "Please. It's taken so much to bring you here."

He stepped farther in.

Robes shifted in a ripple.

No weapons were drawn. They wanted the myth walking to the altar.

Pennington tapped the chair once.

"Before we do the ugly part, the beautiful part."

"Speak fast."

She took the lectern like a stage she had earned with perfect grades and quiet knives.

"The night you died, the city held its breath. Candles. Prayers. Hashtags. It wasn't grief."

Her head tilted. "It was appetite. For myth. For meaning. For symmetry."

He said nothing.

"We live on symmetry, Mr. Cole. Disease and cure. Sinner and saint. A city breathes easiest when it believes the scales are being touched by more than hands."

She almost smiled, like the outcome had been inevitable. "When your pulse returned in private, we did what responsible administrators do. We stabilized the narrative."

"Get on with it."

"We paid your doctors."

No flinch in the room; a truth rehearsed into policy.

"Neurology. Sleep-response. Sensory-conditioning. Guided comas. Not sorcery. Stimuli. Sound. Smell. If you give a drowning mind a rope, it will climb."

Lucien was quiet for a long second.

Pennington's voice lowered, intimate without warmth.

"We threaded scripture into your sedation. Controlled imagery. Recurring symbols. Auditory anchors. Revelation proved most effective, the language of return, of light breaking through judgment. We didn't build your chapel. We adjusted its echo. Shifted hymns, tuned lighting, buried recordings under frequencies the waking ear ignores. The colorless world, the cracking road, the mountain of stone and paper, all folded beneath the monitor's pulse. Pain needs structure, Mr. Cole. We learned how to use yours."

"The Wolf," he said.

Quiet. A word no one here should've known.

Pennington's brow lifted, and for the first time, she guessed wrong.

"A symbol," she answered, almost fond. "You already had instinct. We gave it shape. We took the patterns your mind leaned toward and fed them back to the streets, murals, sermons, the low current beneath the city's noise. Frequencies you can't quite hear but can't escape."

Her finger touched the lectern; a vibration moved through the stone under his feet.

"That calm you feel now? It's the same signal we threaded through half the city at night. Balance is a frequency before it's a law."

He almost laughed.

"You built lullabies."

"We built rails." Pride showed plain. "We bankrolled Lansing. We wrote his cleansing vows. Then we resurrected you on the other side of that stage. Oppositions with a common wallet, so the wheel couldn't fall off. We own the ports, Civic Shield, the charities, the data feeds, the supply lines that bring both comfort and ruin. We built a Hydra that prays while it eats, a single body made from saints and thieves alike, because mercy photographs better than hunger. And we put you in the middle, a living fulcrum, the axis everything turned on. Half messiah, half monster. The perfect story."

A robed man to her left spoke for the first time, his baritone smooth as wine. "People don't follow power. They follow pattern."

Pennington raised a hand; silence fell back into place.

Lucien looked toward the windows.

Fog folded in on itself.

Lightning flashed once through the glass, gone as quick as breath.

The hum deepened, threading up through his boots, the same pulse from the machine that once sang through his coma. It pressed through the floor, through the walls, into the quiet, a presence that never left.

He thought of the dream, the bone-pale sky, the road, the tide. The world they built in his mind.

But something else had started bleeding through since. The forest. The glass. The Revelation passages.

Now, standing here, he could feel it again, a frequency that made belief feel like memory.

"You programmed my limbo. And carved its symbols into the city's skin."

"We gave you symmetry. You did the rest. You took our scaffolding and built a religion of order. That obsession with balance you quote like a vow? You came by it honestly. We only tuned it to our frequency."

"You mistook a compass for a collar."

She smiled for real now.

"I'm not here to diminish you. Without your will, none of it would have held. That's the genius of our model, you had to believe it was yours. You had to believe you were chosen. That's why you're standing here alone, isn't it? Guns in your lungs, sermon in your blood. We built the altar, you built the faith."

Her eyes softened like a mother praising a son she bought.

"You came for confession."

Lucien's voice broke it.

"Why crown me at all? You could've built a symbol without blood in its veins."

"We crowned you because we needed the public to believe in equilibrium. A myth with a heartbeat is easier to worship than a flag. But when you brought that woman, your wife, into our circle, you rewrote the creed. We designed a solitary god of order, you turned him into a husband. Silas called it evolution. The rest of us called it contamination."

She paused, eyes level.

"He wanted you free. We wanted you functional. He mistook faith for control, and that mistake cost him his head."

Lucien studied her for a long moment.

Candlelight moved across his face like it was searching for a place to settle.

He breathed out, slow.

The Wolf pressed against his spine, patient and black.

He met her eyes.

"You built a god and forgot to fear it."

"God is a word for influence outside your control."

Her hands opened, gentle. "Come into the circle. We'll quiet the streets, temper the storm. You keep your gospel; we keep the order. Balance, as intended."

Low lights marked the perimeter, a perfect ring of control.

"You talk about balance," he said, "but your scales are lined with graves."

He took a step closer.

Pennington didn't flinch. "Intimidation was never the goal. It was the rhythm that kept people still. We wanted calm, not conquest."

Candlelight ran a thin gold line through her chain.

"So you used fear to shepherd me."

"We used circumstances."

Her tone turned candid.

"We didn't expect the leash to snap."

"You didn't expect your creation to bite back. You mistook fear for control, and forgot fear learns teeth."

"No."

Pennington's voice came quieter, almost reverent.

"We expected obedience. Rage we could steer. We didn't account for the other thing in you."

Lucien's voice was quiet, steady.

"What other thing?"

"Love. You kill like you care. That's what made you valuable. That's what made you unpredictable. No matter how deep your cruelty runs, something deeper runs with it, an ache to love, and be loved the same. We tried to rent the blood. We did not buy the devotion."

He let out a small, ugly laugh. "So you bet on my worst half and misread the rest."

"You read the ledger correctly. You read us wrong."

He studied her, roads and losses stacked behind his eyes.

"So that's why you bombed my wedding. If you couldn't stop me, you would make me watch it all burn. If you couldn't control me, you would try and take everyone I love."

Pennington's face folded a degree.

"No, Mr. Cole," she drew a careful breath, choosing precision over apology. "We didn't plant the bomb. We didn't have to. We built the noose and watched him pull it."

She stepped closer to the light.

"Lansing was a man drowning in his own image. We gave him the motive, fear of losing control. We told him to restore order, to prove he could still command a city. And when his approval dropped and your myth grew teeth, he did what desperate men do."

Lucien's eyes hardened.

"He followed your script."

"He improvised. Poorly. The call was his, but every word that led to it was ours. We told him thunder looks like leadership. We just didn't tell him where the lightning would strike."

Pennington slid one hand into the inner pocket of her robe.

Not fast.

Not fearful.

Almost ceremonial.

She drew out a thin black case, no larger than a passport, and set it on the lectern between them.

"You asked why we crowned you. You asked why we let Lansing keep his throne. You deserve to hear his voice explain it."

Lucien didn't touch the case.

Pennington flicked the latch with her thumb. Inside, a small encrypted drive gleamed under the candlelight like a shard of stolen truth.

"He recorded everything. Every strategy call. Every purge order. Every paranoid rehearsal. Lansing believed history would vindicate him if he narrated it himself. The council kept copies, insurance for when the myth outgrew the mayor."

Her eyes lifted to his.

"Consider this the last piece of the ledger. The part you were never meant to see."

Lucien held still, unreadable.

"This isn't mercy," she added. "It's clarity. If you intend to tear down a throne, you should at least hear its king admit what he did."

He closed his hand over the case without looking down.

Something in the room changed.

Even the hum under the floor seemed to pause.

A breath drew in. Fabric whispered as robes adjusted.

Lucien's fingers found his coat, closing on something small and black. He'd carried it for this moment. A slim recorder, no bigger than a matchbox, warmed to his palm. A nest of proof shaped like questions.

He took one step closer, voice steady.

"You talk about balance and order. Fine. But excusing yourself from the wedding doesn't change what you did at Mercy West. You tried to kill my mother first."

Pennington's blink had the measured annoyance of someone who thinks they can still rewrite the scene. "We never ordered her killed. That was not the directive."

Lucien didn't move. He drew the recorder from his coat and thumbed it to life.

"You showed her to me on a monitor and called it leverage. You told me she would keep breathing if I stopped. Then Mercy West burned."

The room inhaled as one. Pennington's face, for the first time, lost its practiced calm.

"We gave Lansing the motive. We opened the window. He chose how to jump."

"Bullshit." Lucien's voice was low and final. "You built the fucking room he jumped from."

Pennington's smile collapsed into a tight, corporate shrug. "We designed the theater. He lit the fuse."

Lucien set the recorder on the lectern and pressed play.

The matchbox clicked on, then filled the nave with their own voices, smooth, confident, merciless.

The donor's voice came first through the recorder: "Declare a truce. Redirect your war. Blame whoever you need to blame. We give you terms."

Then Pennington's followed, cold and final through it: "If you push, the candles die out. The crowns disappear. If you stop, your mother keeps her suite. Your father keeps his breath."

The words rolled through the hall like scripture remembering its author.

No editing. No splice. Just the Coalition's own bargain, mercy traded, death implied, bureaucratic language dressed as mercy and death disguised as collateral.

They all knew what this was. Proof replayed not for evidence but for penance.

No one looked surprised. Only irritated that he'd chosen to resurrect it here, on his terms instead of theirs.

Pennington's face went white. A man in the back clutched a folder until paper whispered.

"You lied," Lucien said simply.

Pennington's gaze swept the table, bankers, fund directors, the men who owned both sides of every law.

"We didn't misjudge," she said, voice like polished steel. "We authorized a pressure strike. Not for spectacle, for leverage. Mercy West was chosen because your mother was there."

Her words didn't slow. "Nothing moves a man like proximity. We meant to wound you into obedience, not try to bury her."

One of the robed figures added, "Fear builds faster than faith."

Pennington's eyes stayed on Lucien. "And you built both. We just gave them fire."

Pennington inclined her head, gracious.

"You're one man in a room of architects. We control the city. The uniforms. The broadcasts. We control the charities that feed the blocks that love you. We are the air around your name. And we are only one chamber in a much larger house."

He didn't raise the pistol. Not yet. He glanced to the high windows. Not fog now, movement. The kind that belongs to an approaching weather no forecast admits.

"You said something true. People follow pattern."

"Yes."

"Then listen."

For a breath, nothing moved.

Pressure shifted. The floor's vibration met something heavier moving through stone. Then came the old sounds, the sounds a city makes when it stands.

Boots on wet granite.

Engines exhaling, then going quiet in rows.

Metal brushing metal in a careful chorus.

Robes turned. The sound moved through the stone, in from the storm, carried through the trees like something waking. Not a rush. Not a charge. A tide.

Pennington's face shifted a degree. "What is this?"

Ghost hadn't summoned them.

Lucien had given the word.

One message dropped into the dark channels and the city emptied into its engines.

Crews rolled out from every block, men who didn't need details, only the name that hit their phones.

They weren't close when the message hit.

They just refused to be late.

By the time he was inside the estate, the ridgelines were beginning to fill with men born for war, answering the name that finally gave them direction.

Lucien stepped from the dais. He didn't need the gun. He didn't need volume.

"You taught them to worship symmetry. I taught them to count."

He lifted his chin toward the doors, blessing a congregation.

"Every head you welded to your Hydra had a neck. We broke the weld."

The streets had answered Lucien's message.

They came to collect their old gods.

The Hydra's lost heads had turned on the hands that once gathered them.

The side doors opened.

Men filled the thresholds. Dock crews who once smuggled guns through Civic Shield checkpoints. Mechanics with stolen radios still whispering police codes. Street lieutenants with ink crawling up their throats. Old enforcers stitched with scar tissue from riots and ports.

Faces Lucien had known as enemies and as sons. The ones who'd bled for the wrong flags, then buried those flags when he rose. The ones who'd watched him carve order out of rot and believed, not because a screen told them to, but because the streets went quiet when he walked.

They came in calm. No shouting. No colors. Safeties off. Eyes forward.

Fog followed them through the doors like breath from a grave.

They poured in from the courtyard, down the stairs, through every corridor. Hundreds, then more. Boots against marble, muffled and slow, the sound of weather deciding where to fall.

Vega was among them, a healing cut stitched tight at his temple, the last yellow shadow of a bruise fading along his jaw.

He didn't break stride. His gaze found Lucien's through the noise and held. One nod. Silent. Absolute.

Pennington didn't step back. Her nails pressed into the lectern's wood and held. The hum was gone now, replaced by the sound of men who had come to stand.

"This is theater." As if naming it could reduce it. "You can slaughter us. The machine remains."

Lucien looked past her to the council, fear under linen and old money. Panic disguised as poise, exit plans multiplying by the second.

"You mistook me," he said. "I don't crave balance. I enforce it."

The Wolf moved at the edge of his sight now, breath at his shoulder, yellow eyes steady in the dark.

He looked back at the council.

"Hoods off."

No one moved.

The men at the thresholds didn't lift their weapons. They didn't need to. The weight of them was enough.

The House had found something it could not command.

Pennington's mouth found a thin line.

For a moment it held something like respect.

"You were never the myth, Mr. Cole. We designed it."

He stepped closer. "And I outgrew your blueprint."

Rain thickened. Silence claimed what control couldn't.

For a breath, nobody moved.

Then the first hood came down. Another followed.

Faces came into the light.

Pennington didn't move. Of course she didn't. She looked at him like she could will a second outcome into being.

They didn't stay there long.

His men moved among them, pulling the council into a broken procession and driving them outside.

"You think you've won," she said.

"I think the city can breathe," he answered.

He let the pistol hang at his side.

Rain worked the windows as boots settled and the lights steadied.

The estate exhaled its last illusions; stone leaned in like witnesses too old to flinch while Lucien's men guided the robed figures from shadow with the slow, sure grace of inevitability.

Pennington walked through them, unbowed, her chain a thin noose of her own making. She met Lucien's gaze as they were drawn into the courtyard where the marble bowl overflowed with rain and its Latin wept into the gravel.

The fog had eased; the switchbacks were veins, and the city's reclaimed blood ran under them.

"Line them."

His voice was low as weather.

They set the robed council into a ragged crescent by the iron gate, twenty-eight faces stripped of hoods and pretense, Pennington at the center, palms open as if to be absolved.

The guard from the arch stood with the crews now, rifle back in his hands, his eyes still carrying the shock of the man he chose to let through.

Some came with rosaries; others came armed, pistols and knives catching the rain, the tools men carry when the city demands a price.

Thirty-four guns rose like accusation. The night thickened with wet pine and gun oil, and the estate's false sanctity dropped away, leaving only cold stone and truth.

Lucien's men took shape, shoulders squared, breaths set to the pulse he'd taught them.

The cadence of consequence.

He stepped before the line. "You built gods. Now kneel to the altar you forged."

Knees met gravel, one by one. Pennington remained last, her stare never leaving him; defiance thinned into recognition.

"Balance demands a counterweight," she whispered.

He nodded once. "Fire."

The volley broke the night open, thunder rolling through the fog, muzzle flashes cutting through the dark.

Bodies folded fast. The ground took them.

The iron gate shuddered, and the floodlights along the walls trembled.

He stood unmoving as the echoes faded.

The rain eased, thinning to mist.

Lucien holstered the pistol and turned from the dead.

Behind him, the estate sagged into silence, stone settling back into itself.

Beyond the walls, the city still breathed, wounded and waiting.

The scales shifted. Not toward order. Toward consequence.

Wind moved through the pines.

The Wolf moved ahead, silent, waiting for him to follow.

Somewhere, a mayor still played savior behind locked doors, rewriting the story while the ink was still wet.

Lucien started walking.

Mercy was done. The ledger wasn't.

CHAPTER SIXTY-THREE

AFTER THE ASHES

By the time Lucien returned, rain had gathered on Northgate's steps like tears.

The compound was too quiet, the kind of stillness left behind by a wound too deep for sound.

The war room stood open, lights low.

It looked nothing like the room where they had planned to survive.

The maps had been packed away early that morning to make room for mirrors and ties and freshly pressed shirts. The table had been cleared for cufflinks and vows. The speaker they had dragged in for the rehearsal dinner still sat against the wall, its cord loosely coiled, the music from the night before now nothing but memory.

The room had been stripped twice. Once for celebration. Now for loss.

Lena stood near the table, still wearing her wedding dress.

The silk was no longer white. Ash clung to it in gray streaks, the bodice smeared with blood from the people she tried to carry and shield before the chapel gave way. The hem was torn, the train frayed where it had dragged through smoke and falling glass. Her veil hung in tatters down her back, a ghost of what it had been earlier that day.

Her hands gripped the edge of the table like it was the only thing keeping her upright.

Her hair was matted with charcoal dust, the kind that settles after beams snap and roofs fail.

Her eyes were red with fatigue.

There were no tears left.

Victoria sat curled in one of the chairs, knees pulled up, a blanket draped around her shoulders. Powdered plaster streaked her hair and cheeks, but she hadn't brushed it away. She stared ahead, unmoving, like the world had quieted around her and she hadn't decided whether to step back into it.

Alexander sat in the shadow near the far wall, shirt cut open, fresh gauze taped across his back. His posture stayed rigid, like if he bent an inch the whole night would split him in two. One hand was clenched in his lap. The other rested empty on his knee, as if it still expected Evelyn's fingers to find it.

Rook stood near the window, shoulders squared, eyes swollen but clear. He wasn't talking. He watched the rain like it might confess something.

Victor and Logan stayed near the stairs, speaking low, even though no one needed quiet. Imani and Mara stood behind them, hands clasped, hollowed out by shock.

Outside, engines rolled down the broken road.

Not one.

Not a pair.

A formation.

Dozens of them climbing Northgate's drive and outer road like a slow-moving tide.

The team stiffened. Victor's hand went straight to his rifle. Logan shifted his stance, one step forward, shoulders squared. Even Rook turned from the window, listening.

The war room screens flickered once.

Ghost's voice came through the overhead speaker, calm as a surgeon.

"Stand down. Identification confirmed. It's him."

The engines cut.

The house held its breath.

When the doors opened, everyone lifted their heads.

Lucien stepped inside.

For a heartbeat, no one breathed.

He looked carved from the storm outside, rain caught in the seams of his collar, eyes dark, jaw set the way a man set it when there were no words left between ribs and throat. Behind him, the men in the courtyard stayed back. Grief had boundaries. Even soldiers knew not to cross them.

Then Lena broke.

She crossed the room in three uneven steps and crashed into his chest, reaching for certainty in a world that had just proven itself cruel. Her fingers clutched his shirt like she needed proof he was real. He wrapped an arm around her, steadying her against everything she had carried alone.

Her voice cracked into his coat. "You came back."

Lucien held her tighter. "I told you I would."

Victor approached. "Boss, did you get your answers?"

Lucien set the black case on the table. "We have a lot of catching up to do."

Logan stepped forward, voice a gravel whisper. "Lansing?"

Lucien didn't blink. "Consider him unfinished."

Imani swallowed. "And the Coalition?"

His gaze stayed flat. "Their council is gone."

The room absorbed it. The weight. The truth. The cost.

Only after it settled did Victor keep going.

"After you lifted off, it got bad."

Lucien didn't move. He didn't blink. "Tell me."

Victor swallowed. "Local responders reached the valley first. County fire. Township medics. They tried, but they were drowning the second they got out of their trucks."

Lena's fingers tightened against Lucien's shirt.

Victor continued, voice low. "The moment their boots hit the grass, they went straight to Evelyn. Alexander never left her side. They saw the blood on his back, thought he'd drop, but he wouldn't move. They had to work around him."

Victoria flinched, her forehead pressing to her knees like she could make herself small enough to hide from grief.

Victor tried again.

"Father Dimas,"

Alexander's voice cut through the room, soft but absolute.

"He did not die alone. That is all that matters."

The room went even quieter.

Victor's voice dropped. "There were others who didn't make it."

Lucien didn't breathe.

"One of the string players. The cellist. He never got up. And the usher helping Father Dimas, the young man from the parish. The blast took him before he even understood what was happening."

Victor hesitated, then forced the next line out.

"There were more. Two men who'd been sitting in the back row. They stepped in to pull someone out before the roof went."

Alexander's eyes opened, tired and hollow.

"Old friends. Family, long before blood ever meant anything."

A tremor rolled through his chest, the kind that came from a wound with no edge to hold onto.

Victor drew a slow breath.

"There's no morgue up there, so the feds set up a recovery line in the field. Floodlights. Tarps. They tagged the bodies gently. They tried to be respectful. Even the county kids. They did their best."

Victor dropped his gaze. "They took Evelyn back to Saint Dymphna's."

"Good."

Victor shook his head. "It wasn't cold. It wasn't careless. The hospital chaplain, Father Keene, met them at the doors. He told the feds he'd sit with her until we came."

Lucien's throat moved like he swallowed fire.

Lena whispered, "Father Keene said the chapel candles are lit. All of them."

Lucien closed his eyes.

That image alone, Evelyn below while the chapel above her burned with a hundred candles she would never see, nearly broke him.

From the corner, Alexander spoke again.

"I watched them lift her."

His voice sounded like a man who knew old wounds too well and had just been handed the worst one yet.

"They wrapped her so gently. Like she might wake if they weren't careful. The medic kept smoothing her hair away from her face. She didn't have to. She just did."

Victoria rose and went to him, slipping her hand into his. His fingers curled over hers, weak but warm.

"She weighed nothing. Monday morning, she was supposed to walk with me to the car. She told me it would be the start of our second life."

Lena's hand lowered from her mouth. Her voice barely held.

"She said the doctor liked her odds. So she rounded them up and called it destiny."

Alexander closed his eyes, breath shuddering.

"She believed in certainty. She was hope."

He lifted his eyes to Lucien. "She saw it happen. The vows, the rings, the way he looked at her. She didn't need the words finished. She believed in moments, not sentences."

Lucien knelt in front of him, voice soft.

"She saw it. She saw forever."

Alexander's voice thinned. "She smiled. Even when the air burned. Even when the beams gave way. She smiled at me."

He looked at Lena, then Lucien. "She smiled at you both. Like she knew she could finally rest."

Then he bowed his head. "She was holding my hand. Not because she needed me. Because she didn't want me alone when she let go."

Victoria pressed her forehead to his shoulder, breaths tightening.

Lucien spoke gently, the words pulled straight from his chest. "I put the rosary she gave me in her hands before I took off. She should have light with her, even in that place."

He exhaled, shaky, carrying years. "I spent the entire ride back thinking about the man I used to be. How many years I stood beside her and still missed what she was giving me."

His eyes lifted to Alexander, to Victoria, to Lena's ruined gown.

"I thought there'd be time. Time to fix things. Time to finally show up."

A bitter breath escaped him. "But time doesn't slow for us. It never did. And now she's gone."

Lena stepped closer. "You saved me a thousand different ways," she whispered. "Let me save you from thinking you're poison."

She lifted a hand to his cheek, brushing rain and the residue of the day's violence from his skin.

"We'll bring her home. Not in a van. Not in a file. We bring her home."

Lucien looked at Victoria. "She deserves a farewell built by hands that knew her."

Victoria lifted her head. "People from everywhere will come. She left light wherever she went."

Lucien brushed a tear from her cheek. "She didn't belong to one place. She belonged to people."

Alexander's voice stayed thin. "I have to make calls," he murmured. "Friends in Miami. Family. I need to tell them. Get them on flights."

He swallowed. "They'll come. Even if it takes days. She deserves a room full of the people she loved."

Silence carried the room again.

Real silence.

The kind that wrapped itself around grief and refused to let go.

Lucien rubbed a hand over his face, slow, almost defeated.

"Dad, after today, I don't think anyone wants to stand within twenty feet of this family."

Alexander looked up, startled.

Lucien's voice cracked, barely. "Not because they didn't love her. Because they'll be terrified of what comes with us now."

The room went still. Not from fear. From truth.

Lena stepped forward. "Then we promise them security like no one has ever seen."

Imani shook her head slightly. "How? After this, how do we promise anything?"

Rook finally turned from the rain-streaked window and walked to the monitors. He hit a button.

The courtyard cameras lit up.

The army was breaking apart in the rain, not abandoning them, just peeling off in disciplined clusters to cars and bikes and blacked-out vans, dispersing to the edges of the city the way soldiers returned to posts after a battle that wasn't finished.

Some walked with heads bowed against the storm. Others lingered under the awning, hands clasped, waiting to see if Lucien would come back out.

Rook pointed at the screens. "There's an entire army dispersing out there. And that's only a fraction of what answered."

He gestured toward Lucien.

"They answered because he called. The streets are our backbone now."

Mara's voice came thin with exhaustion. "They're waiting out there for a reason."

Victor met Lucien's eyes. "Maybe you should talk to them."

Lucien stared at the screens, and for the first time since the blast, something in him wavered.

Not fear. Not doubt.

Just the quiet, unbearable truth that the city crowned him in the same week he lost his mother.

On the screens, engines rolled slow through the rain, loyal and patient, giving him space to grieve before following wherever he pointed next.

He took a slow breath.

"They'll get their orders. Just not tonight."

He rose, heavy with everything he carried.

"We're done spilling pieces of ourselves for the world to gawk at. Tonight, we hold the line. Tomorrow, we start making plans. However long it takes, we do it right."

No one argued.

Outside, the rain fell harder.

Inside, the world grieved.

They didn't pray.

They mourned.

And tomorrow, they prepared to bring Evelyn Cole home like the queen she had always been.

Chapter Sixty-Four

THE DAY THE STREETS STOOD STILL

Mother,

I have stood in fire. I have walked through bullets. I have bled on floors waiting for the world to stop breathing. But nothing, nothing has ever broken me like losing you.

I keep trying to solve the math of it, like some equation that might make sense of the senseless. How Heaven chose you and returned me, like the world needed another weapon more than it needed your warmth. How the light vanishes first, abandoning the shadows to claw through the dark alone. I turn these questions over like jagged stones in my fist, and every one slices deeper, drawing blood I can't staunch.

They say Heaven calls its warriors home early, that the good buckle under the world's weight. But I watched you shoulder burdens that would crush armies; smile through agony that should have dropped you to your knees, hold our fractured family together with nothing but chamomile tea in cracked mugs, whispered prayers, and a love so fierce it turned chaos into sanctuary.

If Heaven needed you, it should have fucking asked. It didn't have to rip you away like this, in a blast of fire and screams at my own wedding.

I keep replaying your smile from the front pew, bright even as the smoke swallowed the aisle. Your eyes locking on mine in the chaos. Your hand finding mine and Lena's, weaving us together even as the world caved in. And I keep hearing that broken sentence from the front pew, soft as breath but sharp enough to carve itself into me:

"I guess forever never plays fair."

I hear it every time I close my eyes. It lands before sleep does. It lands before breath does.

God, I don't know how to live with that. I don't know how to carry a sentence like that knowing it was all you had left, knowing it was meant to hold me together and all it's done is split me open.

You didn't tell me to be strong. You didn't tell me to lead. You just told me the truth, the kind that makes grief honest instead of hollow. Make it mean something.

I am trying. But every step without you feels like walking through fire without skin.

I slipped the rosary into your hands because it felt like blasphemy to send you off without light. You spent your life pouring it out for us; beads worn smooth from your fingers, prayers murmured in the dead of night. You deserved to carry light into the dark. Not empty-handed. Never empty-handed.

The world is wrong without you. Chairs sag even when no one's sitting in them. The walls echo like they're waiting for your voice, and I don't know how to tell them you're gone. Even the rain sounds different, like it's grieving in a language only the broken understand.

I wasted so many days armored in isolation, convinced love was a weakness that dulled the blade. You tried to show me otherwise; that love is the only steel that never rusts, the only fire that warms without burning. I see it now, Mother. Too goddamn late.

There's a gaping wound in me that won't scar over. Not with time's empty promises. Not with vengeance's hollow roar. Not with thrones built on blood and broken bones. The only salve is the truth you etched into my soul: Family is sacred. Love demands its toll. And time? Time is the cruelest thief of all.

I swear this to you: I won't squander what's left. I'll shield what you cherished with my last breath. I'll forge this family into something unbreakable. Your name not a faded echo but a war cry, a light I'll spend the rest of my life trying to live up to, a legacy carved in stone.

You taught me love is the closest we ever get to touching God. If that's true, then losing you feels like being cast out of Heaven, cold, forsaken, adrift.

But I'll claw my way back. Through the fire, the bullets, the endless nights. Because you'd demand it. Because you saw strength in me when all I saw was shadow.

Rest now, in the quiet you earned. I'll carry the storm. Just meet me on the other side when it's done.

Lucien's handwriting blurred for a moment, the ink swimming as he reread the final sentence.

The room around him was silent, too still, the kind of quiet that lets grief breathe. His chest tightened, each word on the page pulling at the raw edges inside him.

Down the hall, her voice rose softly. "Lucien?"

He lifted his head.

A second passed.

The world returned in pieces: her footsteps in the hall, soft and hesitant; the faint rustle of her dress, like a whisper against the wood; the way she said his name, laced with worry, as if she could sense the fracture in him from across the threshold.

Lucien closed the book.

He tore the page free, not with violence, but with reverence.

A clean rip.

A small wound in paper, gentler than the one inside him. His fingers trembled as the edges parted, the sheet still warm from his grip.

He folded it once, slow, like he was folding a memory, and slipped it into the inside pocket of his suit, close to his heart where it burned quietly.

He set the journal on top of the dresser, placing it there with the kind of care people reserve for fragile things that matter.

Outside the door, her footsteps slowed.

A wave of dizziness washed over her without warning, the hallway tilting for a heartbeat. She caught the wall with her fingertips and waited for the world to settle.

She steadied herself, breath shallow. "Come on," she whispered. "Not today."

It passed as quickly as it came.

Then her voice rose softly through the wood.

"Lucien, are you ready?"

He looked at her, eyes rimmed with the weight of everything he'd written, unshed tears making the room shimmer.

"Yeah. Let's go."

When they arrived at the funeral chapel, it was silent, lit only by rows of candles that moved in the still air.

Evelyn Cole lay in the finest black lace dress they could choose for her, the unyielding queen of a fractured empire, beautiful even in stillness.

Her hands were folded as if she were only resting, the rosary Lucien had placed woven gently between her fingers, dark wood against soft skin that would never warm again.

Her face was serene in a way the past months never allowed.

Lucien stepped forward alone. He reached into his suit and pulled out the folded page, the letter he'd written in the quiet hours before dawn, words too raw to speak aloud, the one only the dead and God were meant to read.

He traced the edge of the note with his thumb, the paper creasing beneath his touch. The words echoed in his mind, his own voice whispering them back to him, bone-chilling in their finality.

He smoothed it once between his fingers, then tucked it beneath the lace at her wrist, sliding it just inside the silk. Close to her skin. Close to her.

His voice was barely a whisper, but it carried like scripture.

"You can't take it where you're going, Mother, but this will follow you into the earth, where time buries us all and forgets our names."

A single tear dropped onto her sleeve. He didn't wipe it away.

"It's yours," he whispered. "All of it."

He rested his hand over hers for one final breath. Then he stepped back, and the world felt colder for it.

It was a secret offering for her journey into the dark.

The private family hour was beginning now.

Close friends and relatives filtered in, their footsteps soft on the marble, voices hushed as they gathered to pay their respects before the real wake began.

An hour had passed.

The room felt empty, but not abandoned, like a shore waiting for the tide to return, already bracing for whispered condolences and stifled sobs.

Now, it was just Lucien again, standing sentinel beside the open casket, his hand resting lightly on the polished mahogany edge as if afraid to let go, or afraid to hold on tighter.

Lena had stood with him for a few silent minutes, her hand a steady anchor on his back, her tears running quiet and steady like rain on a windowpane.

She didn't speak.

She didn't need to.

In a room cold with death's chill, she was the only warmth, the only reminder that life persisted beyond this veil of loss.

Eventually, she had slipped away to check on the others, leaving him to his vigil, but her presence lingered like breath in the air.

The double doors creaked open, splitting the silence the way lightning splits a summer sky.

Victor entered first, his breath short and ragged, face tight with something like awe laced with alarm. Rain dripped from his coat onto the marble.

Logan came in right behind him, soaked through.

Rook, Imani, and Mara followed, tense and unsettled, carrying the kind of news that changes a room just by existing.

Victor's voice came low but urgent, cutting through the hush. "Brother. I'm sorry. We could barely make it down the block."

Alexander lifted his head from the front pew, his eyes red-rimmed, hollowed by exhaustion.

"What do you mean you couldn't?"

Logan's gaze didn't waver. "You might wanna go take a look."

Lucien went quiet for a moment.

Then he looked at Lena, who had reappeared at his side like a shadow drawn to light.

Together, they walked out, everyone's eyes following them into the unknown.

They stepped outside into a wall of sound that hit like a physical force, horns blaring in frustration, engines rumbling like distant thunder, boots scraping on wet pavement in a restless rhythm.

The rain had turned the world gray, but it couldn't dim the spectacle unfolding before them.

Not dozens of men.

Hundreds.

Rows of cars lined the block, double-parked in defiant chaos, choking traffic for half a mile in either direction.

Men stood shoulder to shoulder in the downpour, black coats slick with rain, holstered weapons catching the gray light.

Tattoos of every crew in the city marked their skin, rival colors that should have sparked bloodshed now united in a silence that felt like worship.

They all bled for the same queen today.

Every set of eyes turned to Lucien as he emerged.

Every one of them bowed their head, not in hollow ceremony, but in raw respect. In allegiance. In promise.

Lena's breath caught in her throat, her hand tightening on Lucien's arm.

"Lucien," she whispered, her voice a mix of wonder and fear.

He didn't blink.

Didn't speak.

Just took it in, his face a mask of stoic resolve.

The city had shown up armed to guard a wake, his mother's. His.

It was something unforgiving, this sea of hardened souls paying homage to the woman who stood beside a king and raised its prince.

Sadness twisted in his chest, mingling with a fierce pride that burned like fire in the rain.

He leaned closer, voice barely above the storm.

"She'd tell them to go home and eat. And they'd listen."

Lena's hand tightened on his arm. "Not today."

When they stepped back inside, the chapel's warmth felt stifling after the cold fury of the street.

Logan handed out ear comms to the team.

Static popped in their ears, a brief crackle like lightning.

Then Ghost's voice filled the void, calm, commanding, laced with something immovable.

"No one gets inside. Not today. Not on my watch."

Lucien adjusted the earpiece, something in him settling into a new kind of steel, forged in loss and tempered by loyalty.

The sadness lingered, but now it was armored, ready for whatever came next.

Doors opened.

The room began to fill.

Not a rush. Not chaos. Just people moving with the reverence of soldiers entering a sanctuary.

Coats dripping. Heads nodded. Shoes almost silent on marble.

Family. Relatives. Old friends who had known her before the world turned sharp.

They came in from the rain to stand with their dead.

Chairs filled. Every row. Every corner.

The space tightened, not with noise, but with grief that knew exactly how to hold its breath.

The room smelled of lilies and damp coats, the fragrance of sorrow woven into every inch of air.

For twenty minutes, the chaplain moved through the room, offering his rites and soft-spoken comfort, words meant to steady the living more than honor the dead.

When he finally stepped back and the doors closed again, the real wake began, built from breath, heartbreak, and the unbearable work of saying goodbye.

Victoria sat closest, her head bowed, tears slipping silently onto the bouquet she held.

Lucien stood behind her, unmoving, his hand on Lena's back as she leaned into him.

He could feel the weight in her breath, the way her ribs strained with quiet mourning, but she stayed upright.

Stayed strong.

For him. For all of them.

Then Alexander rose.

He walked to the front with a slow, heavy pain that made the room go still.

His back straightened before he spoke.

His hand brushed Evelyn's arm, a brief touch, gentle as a farewell could ever be.

When he faced the chapel, his voice carried a depth that silenced every chair, every sigh.

"My wife did not walk through life quietly. She did not hide. She did not fear. She taught this family to stand in storms with our heads high and our hearts open. She gave us more than love. She gave us reason."

His breath hitched once, a sound he swallowed.

"When Lucien was a boy, she told me he would change the world. I didn't believe her. Not because I doubted him, but because the world is a cruel thing. Today proved her right. This city came here not for a king. Not for a crew. Not for a legend."

He turned, eyes falling back on her.

"They came for a woman who loved everyone, even when they were unlovable."

Silence pressed close. Even the lights seemed to soften.

"She deserved more time. We all know it. But she left nothing undone. She stitched light into every dark place she touched. And she did not leave us empty. Her legacy is sitting in this room. Her strength is standing at the door. Her love is the spine that keeps this family on its feet."

Alexander placed a hand on the casket, gentle, final.

"Rest now, my love. I will walk the rest of this life without you, until we meet again."

He returned to his seat with Victoria guiding him, her hand never leaving his.

Lucien closed his eyes, the words crushing and lifting him at the same time.

The murmurs faded. People shifted. A moment of collective breath held together.

Then Ghost's voice snapped through every earpiece at once.

"Lucien, we have a problem."

Lucien stiffened, eyes opening.

Ghost continued, voice tight.

"You're not gonna like this. The press is outside. Civic Shield is guarding them. They're outside your mother's wake, broadcasting the crowd live. The feed is already everywhere."

Silence hit. Stunned. Appalled.

Ghost's voice sharpened.

"The mayor granted exclusive media clearance and sent Civic Shield to protect the feed. They set up a press perimeter right as the wake began. They wanted the circus."

Outside, on the corner, a Civic Shield van sat angled across the sidewalk like a barricade, its lights flashing blue and red in mockery of the somber day.

A news reporter stood in front of a live camera, flanked by a loose circle of Civic Shield officers, rain darkening their gear, badges gleaming like false promises.

He was smiling.

Like he was reporting on a parade instead of a funeral.

"And today, the city gathers for the controversial funeral of Evelyn Cole, mother of suspected insurgent leader Lucien Cole, the man the mayor's office has repeatedly called a public threat, the so-called king of the streets."

Lucien stepped through the chapel doors, the rain soaking him instantly, but he moved with predatory grace.

He didn't raise his voice.

His presence alone cut through the broadcast like a scalpel.

"Did your mayor tell you who bombed my wedding?"

The reporter froze, his smile cracking like cheap glass.

The camera swiveled toward Lucien, capturing the moment in unforgiving high definition.

Lucien kept walking, his steps measured, rain tracing paths down his face like unshed tears.

"Did he tell you who ordered explosives into a church filled with strangers? With families? With children?"

The reporter sputtered, his composure shattering.

"Cameras off. Cameras off!"

He waved frantically at the crew.

Civic Shield tightened their formation, hands hovering near holsters, eyes darting between Lucien and the growing restlessness in the crowd.

Lucien stopped ten feet away.

His voice was low but carried like an incoming tide.

"Tell me. Did your mayor tell you the truth? Did he?"

Five officers reached for their weapons, fingers twitching with nervous energy.

Behind Lucien, four dozen men stepped forward as one, a wall of muscle and menace closing in.

The reporter panicked, dropping the mic with a clatter that echoed off the buildings.

"Shut it down! Shut it down!"

A shout cut him off, guttural and sharp, lost in the tension.

An officer jerked nervously, his hand fumbling.

A gun went up too fast.

A single shot cracked through the street, sharp and final, piercing the rain-soaked air.

A man behind Lucien dropped to his knees, clutching his side, blood blooming dark through his coat.

His eyes found Lucien's for a split second, wide with shock, then softening into something like acceptance.

Silence held for a heartbeat.

The world suspended in that fragile pause.

Then the entire block detonated.

Hundreds of men surged forward as one, a tidal wave of rage crashing over the Civic Shield line.

Civic Shield tried to stand their ground, guns still drawn, shouts of authority dissolving into chaos.

But they were swallowed whole, arms flailing, boots slipping on wet pavement as the mob engulfed them.

It wasn't a riot.

It was an execution.

A city saying, We saw what you did. We will never forgive it.

Fists flew like hammers, connecting with bone-crunching force.

Weapons, holsters emptied, guns turned to blunt instruments, slammed down in righteous fury.

Officers went down one by one, dragged into the fray, their uniforms torn and bloodied.

The crowd moved as one, bodies lifted overhead and passed hand to hand through the sea of men while the rain washed blood into the gutters.

Civic Shield vanished under the onslaught, no longer officers but targets, their authority stripped away in a storm of vengeance.

One by one, they were passed over the mob and down the block, limp and broken, like offerings to some ancient god of retribution.

The sadness of the day twisted into something darker, something primal.

It broke loose as a bone-chilling release of grief through violence, the city's heart breaking and beating back in unison.

And through it all, a chant rose, raw and rhythmic, building like drums of war.

"No more Shield! No more Lansing! Long live Cole!"

It echoed off the buildings, a brutal symphony blending with the sounds of struggle, grunts, cries, the wet thud of impacts.

The reporter screamed and sprinted away, slipping in puddles, his tailored suit muddied and ruined.

The cameraman tripped over his own feet, crawling desperately as the lens shattered under a boot.

Lucien stood at the edge, rain tracing cold lines down his face, watching the inevitable unfold.

He had not given the order.

He also knew no order would stop it now.

The escalation had been building since the wedding, since the bombing, since the losses that refused to settle.

Today, the city mourned with fists and thunder, guarding the wake of their queen in the only way they knew.

Sirens wailed at the edge of the district, too late to matter.

Too late to stop what had been set in motion.

The bodies were gone, dragged into the rain.

The cameras lay shattered on the pavement.

Lucien stood in the doorway of the chapel, rain and silence settling over the street like smoke after gunfire.

This wasn't rebellion.

This was grief with teeth.

This was judgment.

And in the ruin that followed, the city spoke in the only language it trusted.

We mourned with you.

Now we burn with you.

Chapter Sixty-Five

BETWEEN GOODBYE AND FREEDOM

The rain never quit.

It slid down windows and brick and pooled in gutters already scarred by older storms, turning every street into a mirror that refused to look away.

It did not feel like weather. It felt like a verdict, as if Heaven and whatever watched beside it had agreed that no tear would go unspent.

What happened outside yesterday became legend before the sirens finally reached the block.

By the time the blue-and-whites arrived, Civic Shield was gone, swallowed by the same streets they used to patrol.

Inside the chapel, nothing had crossed the threshold.

No shots inside.

No breach of the wake.

No raised voices.

Men who had killed for less stood in the rain and held their line.

Because there was a casket inside.

Because there was a mother inside.

Because grief came first, and anything else could wait.

That day, the city learned a new rule:

Lucien Cole buried his dead untouched.

Even when the world outside devoured itself.

They laid Evelyn to rest at Saint Brigid's Field, the oldest consecrated land still kept in private hands.

It sat tucked beyond the river, where the city surrendered to wild grass and low fog.

The Cole family had held plots there for generations, though no one had been laid to rest in that earth since Lucien's grandfather.

Evelyn used to call it the last quiet place she trusted.

There were no cameras. No engines. No press lights turning sorrow into content.

Just wind, water, and time.

The burial did not live in Lucien's mind as a clean sequence.

It came back in shards.

Mud pulling at black shoes.

Rope biting into damp palms as the casket started down.

The soft, hollow knock of wood against the rigging, once, twice, then the slow surrender.

Lena's fingers threaded through his, knuckles hard, breath shallow against his sleeve.

Alexander's profile, cut sharp against a sky the color of old steel, eyes locked on the box as if refusing it could change the outcome.

Victoria trying to pray, the words rising half-formed before breaking.

There was no crowd to hold them up.

No wall of men outside to make it feel protected.

Just family, the team, and a handful of relatives who had survived distance and silence and still showed up when it mattered.

Shovels spoke.

Earth struck polished wood, dull and final, the sound of a door closing with no handle on this side.

They did not bury the woman who turned chaos into a kitchen and war into a home.

They buried what was left to bury.

The body.

The part the world could take.

Everything else stayed where it always had.

In the people who loved her.

In the habits she left behind.

In the way they stood there afterward.

Heads bowed under black umbrellas.

Rain running steady.

None of them ready to choose between leaving and staying.

Because both felt like betrayal.

Then life did what it always did.

It moved. Stubborn. Merciless.

And it dragged them with it.

They said goodbye outside Saint Brigid's Field.

The rain had thinned to a soft, steady curtain, light enough to see through, heavy enough to blur the world around them.

The grave was filled.

The casket sealed.

The hearse was gone.

The last of the mourners had drifted toward cars and wet gravel roads, leaving only their circle behind in the hush of the cemetery grounds.

Alexander stood by the curb, the car idling beside him, one hand on the open door and the other around Victoria's shoulders.

Grief had carved him down, but not hollowed him. There was still iron in the set of his jaw.

Lucien stopped in front of him, Lena beside him, her arm hooked through his.

For a heartbeat, no one spoke.

The sky lightened above them, a single blade of brightness cutting through the clouds like it had no right to touch this moment.

Alexander's voice was low, rough from too many words in too little time.

"There's work I need to finish. The ones who couldn't get here will hold their own vigil in Miami. Old friends. People who loved her. I need to stand with them when they do."

"She would want that."

"She would have wanted a lot of things."

No bitterness. Only truth.

He breathed in like a man forcing himself to accept a decision he never wanted to face.

"I'm selling the house down there. Miami was heaven while we had it. But heaven is wherever she is now. And she's here."

His eyes drifted toward the field, toward the fresh earth still dark with rain.

"One day the ground beside hers will take me too. As much as she loved the sun and the heat, I know she wanted her rest here. This is home."

Lucien's chest tightened. "She'd tell you you were stalling."

A faint smile touched Alexander's mouth and vanished.

"She always did have opinions about my pace."

He looked at his son, really looked, like a man measuring what the world had left him.

"The city is not done with you. You are not done with it."

His gaze sharpened. "Listen to me, Lucien. This place took her life. Do not let it take her meaning. Do you understand?"

Lucien held his father's stare. "Yes."

Alexander stepped in and wrapped one arm around him, pulling him into an embrace that was brief but real.

Lucien stiffened, then let himself lean into it, just enough, just this once.

When they parted, Alexander's eyes were wet.

"I'll see you soon."

He turned his head and found Lena.

Something in his expression softened as he moved to her and took her hand in both of his.

"My daughter."

The words landed heavier than any blessing.

Lena's throat tightened.

She squeezed his fingers, answering with a nod because her voice wouldn't hold.

"Take care of him."

"I will," she managed.

"And yourself."

She almost smiled at that.

"I'll try."

He let her go, then opened the passenger door of the waiting car.

Victoria hugged them both, clinging to Lena for a heartbeat longer as she whispered something broken into her ear.

Lena kept her arms around her until she had to let go.

When the car pulled away, Lucien and Lena stayed by the gate.

Saint Brigid's Field lay behind them, the city rose ahead, and the place they'd left her rested in a hush that followed them out.

The clouds had finally broken.

Sunlight spilled across the grass, clean and unbroken. It shone on the wet stone and the pale markers as if Heaven had finally finished crying.

It didn't heal anything. It didn't pretend to.

But it felt like a breath after drowning, the first moment the air no longer hurt.

Victor and Logan were across the street, silhouettes beside the Rezvani.

They didn't wave.

They didn't shout.

They just waited, patient and still, like soldiers holding a silent line.

Lena exhaled slowly.

"Home?"

He nodded once. "Home."

Northgate felt different.

The steel and concrete were the same, but the air inside it was not. The place wasn't a fortress today. It was a vigil.

Grief had settled into the walls like a second architecture. Even the lights seemed quieter.

Mara, Imani, and Rook were waiting in the main hall when they stepped inside.

They didn't rush forward. They stood a few paces back, giving Lucien and Lena space to cross the threshold as if it were sacred.

Victor and Logan entered behind them, closing the door softly, sunlight catching on their damp jackets where the last of the rain still clung.

For a few seconds, no one moved. No one needed words.

Mara broke first. She stepped forward, dark eyes locked on Lucien's face.

Whatever sharpness she usually carried had been tempered into something quieter.

"Your pain is our pain."

No ceremony. No speech. Just that.

"You don't carry this alone," Imani added.

Rook did not reach for words he did not have. He just closed the distance and put his hand on Lucien's shoulder, solid and steady.

Lena's breath stuttered as Victor's hand settled at the small of her back and Logan's palm eased onto her shoulder.

A second later, they were surrounded, not crushed, just held, each touch an anchor, a promise.

They didn't need to say it. The circle said it for them.

We are still here.

Lucien stood in the center of them, eyes closed briefly, letting the weight of their hands and their presence press against the raw places inside him.

Then he opened his eyes.

"No more offerings. We finish."

They stepped back a little, enough to see his face, enough to give him the space he needed to step into the role he had built for himself.

Lucien lifted his eyes to the room.

"Ghost."

The walls answered, Ghost's voice dropping into the room like a familiar current.

"Here."

"Updates."

There was a brief crackle, the sound of keys and feeds rearranging on screens.

"You are not going to like it. But here it is. Lansing thinks he has his miracle tour lined up."

Lucien went still. "Talk."

"City Hall put in a formal permit for a public address this Saturday. Three days from now. Fourth of July. Civic Plaza."

The room tightened around the date.

"They've got an all-day schedule. Speech in the afternoon, fireworks at night. Flags, music, the whole spectacle. They're calling it a 'Day of Freedom' event. Victory over fear. Cleaning up crime. All that garbage."

"Press?" Lucien asked.

"Every major outlet invited. Televised, livestreamed, translated, cut into clips before he even opens his mouth."

Imani frowned. "Security?"

"Thick. Civic Shield in dress uniforms. NYPD on visible detail. Private contractors I don't recognize yet. And a whole lot of unmarked gear that smells like federal eyes without federal names."

Ghost paused.

"They're turning the plaza into a stage and a cage at the same time."

Rook scoffed under his breath. "Fourth of July. He wants fireworks and applause while the dirt on the graves is still wet."

Ghost did not disagree. "He is going to use the word freedom so many times it will not mean anything by the end of the first paragraph."

Lena looked at Lucien. His face had gone still, the way it did when something inside him had already started moving.

"Crowd size?"

"If the weather holds and the propaganda hits, thousands. Half of them will come because they believe him. Half because they hate him. All of them will be watching."

The room felt smaller.

The city was listening.

The mayor meant to use that.

Lucien refocused.

"Record everything between now and then. His calls, his drafts, his rehearsal, his security changes. I want to know who writes his speech. I want to know who approves it. I want to know where every camera in that plaza will be pointed."

"Already in motion."

"Good."

No one else spoke.

The Fourth hung in the air between them, a date and a reckoning.

Lena watched him as his shoulders squared.

Grief didn't turn to rage. It hardened into something colder, sharper. Purpose.

He turned in the circle of his people, looking each of them in the eye. "We buried her."

"Now we make it mean something."

He faced the room again.

"We finish it. On the Fourth."

The room didn't move. Neither did he.

Lena stepped closer, her hand brushing his arm.

The smell of food somewhere down the hall turned her stomach, a sharp twist she forced down.

Stress, she told herself. Nothing more.

CHAPTER SIXTY-SIX

THE SHOT HEARD EVERYWHERE

The Fourth of July hit the city like a lie it was trying hard to believe.

Flags in windows. Grills smoked on rooftops. Kids ran through broken hydrants with sparklers clutched in small fists. Cheap fireworks cracked over alleys that still smelled like old tear gas. News anchors called it a "Day of Freedom" with voices that sounded a little too rehearsed.

Every screen carried the same headline.

FREEDOM RALLY

MAYOR LANSING ADDRESSES THE CITY

They built the stage in Civic Plaza, at the foot of City Hall's glass-and-stone steps, where politicians had promised change for decades and delivered almost none of it. No robed donors now. No quiet men with steel tokens hiding in shadows. Just metal barricades, rows of chairs, cameras on cranes, and a podium drowning in flags.

The city had not forgotten the wedding. It had just been told what to call it.

TERROR AT SAINT ARDEN

The crowd was split before Lansing even opened his mouth.

Front rows in collared shirts and clean jackets.

Back rows in hoodies and work boots, carrying the weight of streets that never got a holiday.

Some clapped when he stepped out.

Some only folded their arms.

A low boo rippled through the crowd, half warning, half promise.

Ghost wasn't in Civic Plaza. He didn't need to be.

Every camera, every CityCast feed, every news van, every hijacked traffic loop ran through the rig he had built, synced to broadcast lines like nerves he could command on instinct.

"Audio lines green," he murmured. "Video feeds green. Civic Plaza, local, national, international. We are officially sitting in everyone's living room."

Static flickered once, then steadied.

"Lucien," Ghost said quietly, "whenever you're ready."

Lucien stood three streets over, in the shadow of a narrow service alley that smelled like hot metal and street food. Black shirt, sleeves rolled to his forearms, collar open. No armor he wasn't willing to lose.

Victor stood on his right. Logan on his left.

He could hear the crowd, even from here. That low animal sound a city makes when you gather too many bodies and give them something to look at.

He closed his eyes once and saw his mother's hands folded around the rosary.

The hundred candles at Saint Dymphna's. Her casket lowering into the earth. Her smile through the smoke as she threaded his fingers through Lena's and told them to make it mean something.

Something inside him answered.

"I'm not going to ask if you're sure," Victor said. "You passed sure a long time ago."

Lucien opened his eyes. "You know what happens when I speak in front of him."

Victor nodded once.

"He will try to shut you down. He will try to spin it. You step on that stage and you make him bleed in front of the city, even if it is only with words."

Logan said nothing for a second. "We can still cut you a way out if this goes sideways. Cars ready. Routes mapped."

"No more shadows," Lucien said. "A city deserves to know the hands that shape it, and the ones that break it."

Victor studied him for a long second.

"Then say what needs saying and walk out. Do not let him drag you into a fall you cannot climb back from."

Lucien didn't answer.

The choice was already written in his silence.

Victor exhaled. "Choose your words carefully. Once they're out, you don't get them back."

Lucien's mouth almost twitched.

"Then I'll take the cost."

He looked up, past the alley mouth, toward the sliver of sky carved between towers. It was clear. Blue with heat. Not a hint of rain.

For the first time since the wedding, the world above him did not look like it was mourning.

"Ghost."

"Here."

"Are we in?"

"We are past in. We are the spine. Every line from that stage runs through my hands now. I can reroute the feed faster than they can kill it. They'll have to shut down the whole plaza to stop me."

Lucien nodded to himself.

"On your word," Ghost said, "history starts."

Lucien stepped out of the alley.

Lansing held the podium with both hands like a man who knew this was not his crowd and still believed it was his city.

"Today, we stand in the light."

His voice rolled across Civic Plaza, thick and practiced.

"For too long, this city has lived under the shadow of violence. Underworld kings. False prophets. Men who made themselves into symbols of fear and called it balance."

The cameras slid over faces. Some nodding. Some hollow. Some hostile.

Lucien moved through the back edge of the crowd with Victor and Logan flanking him, heads down, like three more bodies in a sea of them.

"Crime is down. Drones are grounded. The streets are safer today than they have been in years. We did that together. We did not bow to terror. We did not surrender to those who would play God with our lives."

Ghost's voice was steady in Lucien's ear. "You are clear on route B. Two barricade gaps ahead, aisle between cameras three and four. Security is soft in the middle. They are facing outward. They expect an attack from the fringe, not the heart."

Lucien's steps never broke rhythm.

"For the first time in too long," Lansing continued, "families can stand here without flinching at every noise. Children can look at the sky without wondering who owns it. That is what freedom looks like."

A cheer rose from the front rows.

It faltered as it hit the back.

Lucien reached the first barricade. A Civic Shield officer stood there in half-polished gear, bored and sweating, scanning for trouble he did not understand. Victor moved first, drawing a crumpled flyer from his pocket.

"Sir, I work media soundstage three. I have an issue with the feed list. Our timing got bumped and the coordinator at the tower said to find..."

He let his voice trail, eyes searching like a man looking for a name tag he knew would not be there.

The guard half turned, confused.

Logan's hand brushed his elbow, not rough, not gentle. "Hey. Eyes on me."

The guard did.

Lucien slipped through the gap like it had been designed for him.

Another step. Another gap. Another bored man staring in the wrong direction.

It came too easy.

"You seeing this?" Ghost muttered.

"Focus."

He didn't have room for luck to rattle him now.

"Freedom is not a gift. It is a responsibility. It is the courage to say no to fear and yes to law. Yes to order. Yes to leadership that does not flinch when cowards throw stones from the dark."

The big screens flanking the stage showed his face in close-up, every line of strain tucked behind the politician's smile.

Lucien was in the center aisle now.

No more barricades.

Just people.

They felt him before they saw him.

Heads turned. Conversations died mid-whisper.

A woman in a faded gift shop Mercy West sweatshirt went pale, hand rising to her mouth.

A boy of maybe thirteen with a crooked crown of plastic stars on his head frowned in confusion, like he had seen this man in two different stories and didn't know which one the world believed.

The checkpoints were thin. Too thin for a city that remembered blood.

Lansing had softened the perimeter for the cameras, trading safety for a clean headline.

Lucien did not look left or right.

He walked.

"Security's light," Victor muttered. "PR move. Lansing didn't want riot shields behind him for the big speech."

Ghost's voice came low. "Ten seconds to stage steps. No movement from their command. They still think you're crowd spill."

"Good."

He reached the security line at the base of the steps.

Four men.

New badges. Old habits.

One stepped forward. "Sir, you cannot be... here..."

The last word fell apart in his mouth.

Recognition hit him hard. His stance broke for half a second, like his body knew the name before his mouth could say it.

Lucien held his stare. "You know who I am."

The guard swallowed hard.

"I am going up," Lucien said. "You can try to stop me, or you can let your city hear the truth."

He did not wait for permission.

He moved past.

A hand brushed his jacket, thinking about grabbing. Then it thought better of it.

"Not here," another guard hissed under his breath, terrified of triggering a riot.

Rook's voice came faintly through the comms from the war room.

"Holy shit," he whispered. "He's just walking up there."

Every screen showed Lucien approaching the steps.

Rook stood beside Lena, breath held tight. Mara and Imani hovered behind them, the glow of the monitors washing over faces pulled tight between fear and belief.

Lena gripped the edge of the table the same way she had at the viewing.

White-knuckled. Barely breathing.

"Lucien."

He took the first step.

He rose into their sightline row by row.

Lansing didn't see him until he cleared the final row of seated officials.

The crowd saw first.

A murmur rolled forward like a wave breaking.

Heads turned as one.

The front rows stood up.

On the screens, the camera operator cursed and yanked his frame wide, trying to include both the mayor and the man coming up behind.

Lansing turned.

His face drained, then hardened into something ugly.

"You are trespassing." His words cracked on the edge. "Security, remove this man."

Lucien did not touch him yet.

He stepped to the side, so the cameras could see them both.

Mayor and myth.

Law and outlaw.

The city's chosen face and the one the city had started painting on walls.

Victor and Logan stopped below the steps, close enough to move, far enough to let the city see Lucien alone.

Ghost spoke calmly into the void.

"Audio transfer in three... two..."

Lansing started to speak again.

His voice cut.

The speakers popped once, twice.

Then another voice filled Civic Plaza.

His own.

Lansing's recorded voice came cold and clipped.

"Bomb a wedding if you have to. No one mourns a myth for long. They adjust. They move on. We show them the danger of getting that sentimental."

The plaza froze.

Heads turned. Hands stilled. Breath caught.

Lansing's own voice poured from the speakers, steady and unmasked.

Ghost let the file play in full.

Lansing's recorded voice continued.

"If you strike him at his wedding, the city learns fear again. It learns obedience again. We clean it up with press. We blame the underworld. We bury it before Monday. I want the Cole name erased."

Gasps rippled through the crowd like a shockwave.

A woman clutched her chest. A man shouted something raw and word-less.

A dozen phones went up at once, filming not because they needed proof, but because their minds refused to believe the proof already burning through every speaker in Civic Plaza.

Lansing's live face turned gray. "Audio manipulation! That's fake! It's fabricated!"

Another clip cut him off.

"Plant it underneath the treeline. No cameras face that direction. The blast radius will take the chapel but not the annex. He will die and the city will unify. This is how you control a narrative."

Someone screamed, "Murderer!"

Someone else shouted, "You killed those people!"

"You murdered them!"

And then the last line hit:

"If Lena Cole dies with him, even better. The city gets a martyr it can cry over, and a mayor it can cling to."

The air shifted.

It wasn't anger anymore.

It was something colder.

Older.

Lansing opened his mouth, but no one heard him.

Ghost still kept the mic line dead.

Lucien stepped closer.

Every camera in Civic Plaza found him.

Every news crane, every broadcast rig, every hijacked feed.

Every household watching the Freedom Rally saw both men in the same frame:

Lansing shrinking behind a podium dressed in flags.

Lucien standing in the light like consequence itself.

His voice carried low, like thunder.

"You murdered my mother. You bombed a church. You tried to kill my wife. And then you stood here today and told this city you gave it freedom."

Lansing backed up, one hand fumbling behind the podium.

Security did not move.

Not one of them.

Lucien reached into his jacket.

They shifted too late, too afraid of the crowd to move first.

Ghost's voice sharpened. "Lucien, wait. This is enough. You already exposed him. Pull back."

The crowd sucked in a breath.

Victor cut in right behind him. "Brother, think. Any further and this turns into something you cannot walk back from."

Logan's voice followed, strained in a way Lucien had never heard. "Stop. Say your piece and get out. Don't do this."

Lucien didn't draw immediately.

He let the weight of it hang between them.

"You said we adjust. You said we move on. You said no one mourns a myth."

He went still.

"You were wrong."

In the war room, Lena pushed forward, hands braced on the table, watching him lift his arm.

"Lucien," she breathed. "Please. Don't."

He stepped forward and drew the pistol.

Fourteen cameras framed it at once.

There was no angle hidden.

No blind spot.

No shadow to bury this in.

"Lucien," Lansing whispered, sweat cutting clean lines through his makeup. "Think."

Victor's voice cut in, sharp. "This doesn't end here."

"Boss, stop!" Rook shouted from wherever he was watching.

"Lucien," Ghost said quietly, almost broken.

"If you do this, they will take you."

Lucien raised the pistol anyway.

"Lucien no!" Lena cried.

Lucien fired once.

The round hit Lansing straight through the chest.

The sound cracked across Civic Plaza like the sky itself splitting open.

Lansing crumpled with no grace, no ceremony, no final lie.

His body hit the steps, rolled once, and came to rest at the base of the podium.

For a moment, the whole world stopped.

No shout. No movement.

Just silence so absolute it felt holy.

Security froze.

Hands jumped to earpieces, but all they got was static.

Ghost had cut every comm in Civic Plaza.

No one fired.

They knew one shot would turn the crowd into a stampede.

Lucien exhaled like a man finishing a prayer.

Victor and Logan didn't move.

They knew that breath.

It meant surrender, not escape.

Then Lucien lowered the gun.

He set it on the stage.

He stepped back and raised his hands, wrists together.

He was offering them the cuffs.

Security stared.

No training prepared them for an entire city watching and refusing to call it wrong.

Finally, one of them stepped forward with shaking hands and snapped the metal around Lucien's wrists.

The crowd erupted.

Not screams. Not panic.

A roar, raw and unified and terrifying.

Phones rose like torches. People climbed barriers.

A chant ignited from somewhere deep in the back, rising like a heartbeat catching fire.

"COLE! COLE! COLE!"

Victor and Logan didn't fight.

They didn't move.

They watched, eyes burning with something close to worship.

From the war room at Northgate, Lena's breath hitched.

Tears spilled before she realized she was crying.

On screens across the city, across the country, across oceans, Lucien stood in cuffs.

Calm.

Unbroken.

A man who had walked into the city's staged miracle, ended the lie in front of the entire world, and made good on a vow at his mother's grave.

Ghost's voice cracked softly over the line.

"It's done," he whispered. "You did it."

Lucien didn't answer.

He looked out over the sea of people.

Not with regret.

Not with fear.

With clarity.

The kind of clarity that only comes when a man stops arguing with the cost.

As they led him down the steps, the crowd surged but did not break.

People reached for him as if touching him would bless them.

Others chanted his name until their voices tore.

The cameras stayed on him the whole way.

No cutaways.

No silence.

The world watched as Lucien Cole was placed into the back of an armored transport.

The door slammed shut.

Darkness.

But even inside that darkness, with the hum of the engine vibrating through the walls, one thought burned through him like scripture.

It was only beginning.

CHAPTER SIXTY-SEVEN
THE WORLD ANSWERS

The war room felt too small for what had just happened.

Victor stormed in first, shirt plastered to his back with sweat, breath sharp from the dash through the service route Ghost cleared for them. Logan was right behind him, chest heaving, both of them carrying the heat of a street they'd only just shaken.

Screens burned across the far wall, a patchwork of feeds, each one replaying the same moment from a different angle.

The mayor at the podium.

Lucien standing across from him.

The gun rising.

The shot that hit Lansing square in the chest, turning the Fourth of July into background noise.

Lena stood beside the table like someone holding herself up out of habit, not strength. Her arms hung loose at her sides, fingers barely curled, as if even forming a fist took too much from her. She stared at the central screen without blinking, eyes wide and glassy, the kind of stare people get when their mind has gone somewhere far away to survive. Her breaths came thin and uneven, like her body wasn't sure it wanted to stay upright anymore.

Mara and Imani flanked her, one on each side, close but not touching. Rook hovered behind them, unreadable for once, his face locked down tight.

When Victor and Logan came in, every head snapped toward them like the room needed a new center.

"Tell me that wasn't real," Lena said.

The words came out hoarse, stripped raw. No hello. No how bad is it. Just that.

Victor looked at her. There was a smear of someone else's panic across his sleeve. His eyes were red at the edges, not from tears, but from something still shaking loose inside him.

He couldn't lie to her.

"You saw it. Same as us."

Lena shook her head once, as if she could loosen reality from her skull.

"He was supposed to expose him, Vic. Not..." Her voice broke. "Not that."

Logan scrubbed a hand over his face, as if he could wipe the memory away.

He couldn't. He looked older than he had that morning, the shot still lodged somewhere behind his eyes.

"He wasn't trying to corner him. He killed him. Right there. No way back."

Rook stepped closer to the screens, thumb jabbing at the central remote. The feed jumped from one channel to another, then another, each replaying the same clip with different banners screaming across the bottom.

LIVE: MAYOR LANSING ASSASSINATED DURING FREEDOM RALLY

BREAKING: NOTORIOUS UNDERWORLD FIGURE KILLS MAYOR DURING RALLY

EXCLUSIVE: COLE EXPOSES CITY HALL CONSPIRACY, THEN FIRES

On one network, the commentator's voice shook as she tried to pick a word that fit.

"Assassination. Public execution. Call it what it is."

On another, the host whispered, "Justice," like he was afraid of the word but more afraid not to say it.

Lena stared at all of it at once. "That was not supposed to happen. We had the recordings. We had proof. He could have burned Lansing without killing him. Why would he do this? Why would he walk into that cage on purpose?"

Her voice was rising, frayed and desperate. It made the room flinch.

Imani stepped in, hand hovering near Lena's arm, not sure if touch would help or shatter her.

"Lena, just breathe a second."

"Do not tell me to breathe," Lena snapped. "Do not tell me it is going to be all right. They took him in chains on live television. There is no 'all right' after that."

Silence dropped heavy.

The only sound was the hiss of the air system and the low murmur of a distant newscaster filling dead air with practiced concern.

"Ghost," Victor said finally, voice tight. "Say something."

The ceiling speakers crackled once. Ghost's voice came through rougher than usual.

"There's nothing to spin. He pulled the trigger. The whole city watched him do it."

"Tell us he planned it. Tell us he has some back door out of this."

Ghost did not answer right away. He was already running the math on outcomes none of them wanted.

"I have been in two wars. I have watched men walk into gunfire with a smile because it meant their families would eat. I have watched men throw themselves over grenades with their eyes open because the math said one body was better than five."

The room held its breath.

"I have never seen a man execute a sitting mayor on live global broadcast," he went on. "There is no doctrine for that. There is no playbook."

"That is not helping," Lena whispered.

"I'm not here to make it feel better. I'm here to tell you what I know."

He paused, voice softening by a fraction.

"You asked why he would do this. Why he would not just leak the files and let the city gnaw Lansing alive. Why he would walk into irons and leave you behind."

"Because he is stubborn," Rook muttered.

"Because he is reckless," Mara added, more bitter than playful.

"No," Ghost said. "Because he is a son."

The word landed and stayed.

"When a man looks into the eyes of the one who took the woman who gave him life, you stop measuring him by strategy. You measure him by grief. You measure him by love."

Lena's grip on the table loosened, then tightened again. Her eyes stayed on the screen even as they blurred.

"This was not senseless," Ghost continued. "If he had only wanted blood, he could have killed Lansing in a hallway, in a car, in a hundred blind corners few cameras ever see. He chose the stage for a reason. He chose the mic. He chose the world as his witness."

Victor exhaled slowly, understanding starting to surface through the shock.

"He made sure they all heard Lansing's recorded confession before he pulled the trigger."

Ghost's voice came back, low and certain.

"Confession before judgment. And no edit bay in the world can cut around it. They will replay those words every time they replay the shot. They cannot call him a mad dog without playing the tape that made him bare his teeth."

Lena swallowed hard. "So he traded his life for the truth. Is that what you're telling me?"

Ghost did not hesitate. "He traded his freedom. He is not dead. They have not killed him. Not yet."

"Yet," Lena echoed, hollow.

Logan stepped closer to the screens, saying nothing as the clips cycled.

"The governor will have to act. The state cannot pretend this did not happen. They will throw every charge they can find at him."

"Murder, terrorism, inciting unrest," Imani said quietly. "They are probably inventing new acronyms right now."

Rook shook his head. "And there is nothing we can do. We cannot break him out without turning the whole city into a war zone."

"We're already halfway there," Mara said.

She pointed at one of the screens. "Look."

Rook switched to that feed.

Crowd shots.

Not just Civic Plaza anymore.

Other boroughs. Other neighborhoods. Pockets of the city flaring up like sparks catching wind.

Some chanting his name like it was a prayer.

Some shouting for order.

Some screaming at each other in languages the subtitles failed to soften.

The bottom of the screen crawled with a new line of text.

UNREST ERUPTS ACROSS MULTIPLE DISTRICTS AFTER MAYOR'S DEATH

"Here we go," Victor muttered.

Lena tore her eyes from the screen long enough to check her phone.

The moment she opened the app, a live stream auto-loaded, someone replaying the moment Lucien was taken in cuffs.

The comments fired upward so fast they blurred into a vertical waterfall of noise.

Thousands watching.

Thousands reacting in real time.

Hearts. Flames. Skull emojis.

Lucien's name in every language she recognized and several she didn't.

A wall of comments exploded across the bottom of the feed:

COLE DID NOTHING WRONG

LANSING EXPOSED WTF

THE CITY IS DONE BOWING

LET HIM SPEAK

#ColeTrial
#WhoOwnsTheCity #LansingExposed
No faces she knew. No familiar names.

Just the world, raw, frantic, unfiltered, moving faster than she could breathe.

The numbers climbed in real time.

Millions of views.

Millions of eyes.

"He was a secret once. A rumor. Now he is…"

She let it hang.

A symbol again, only bigger. Only sharper.

"Traffic is spiking on anything with Lucien's name," Ghost reported. "Old news clips. Street footage. Rumors dressed up as fact. They are stitching a narrative together in real time. Different channels, different versions."

"Which one is winning?" Mara asked.

"Depends where you stand," Ghost said. "In the towers, they're calling him a monster. In the blocks, they're calling him the only honest man left."

Rook turned the sound up on one panel.

A reporter stood in front of a precinct, hair whipped by the hot wind, voice raised over the din behind her.

"Officers have abandoned their post outside City Hall after crowds gathered, demanding accountability for the bomb that resulted in several casualties, including Evelyn Cole, mother of the detained crime suspect."

Rook flicked to another.

"The Governor's office has released a preliminary statement condemning the execution and promising a full investigation into the allegations against Mayor Lansing. Sources say National Guard units are on standby in case local law enforcement cannot contain the unrest."

Another.

"In downtown, fireworks have been set off in broad daylight, crowds cheering at every replay of Lansing's confession. Multiple businesses are closing early as rumors of a citywide curfew begin to spread again."

Lena felt the world tilting under her feet.

It wasn't just their city anymore.

It was everyone's.

Her phone buzzed.

The sound cut through her like a blade.

She pulled it from her pocket without thinking, thumb already lifting the screen.

Alexander.

Just the name stopped her breath.

She opened the message.

What happened. I saw it live

Tell me my son is still breathing

The words hit harder than any footage on the screens.

Harder than the chants.

Harder than the headlines.

Her throat closed.

She read the message again, hoping the letters might rearrange into something she could answer without breaking.

They didn't.

Her thumb hovered over the keyboard, useless.

Anything she wrote would either be a lie or too close to the truth to survive saying out loud.

She locked the phone and set it facedown on the table.

Not to ignore him. Not to run.

Just to steady herself long enough to stand.

The war room snapped back into focus.

Screens flickered with violence and prophecy.

The air felt too thin to hold all their fear.

Lena drew in a breath that shook.

"He is out there alone," she whispered. "In a box. In chains. And we are standing here watching strangers argue about his soul like it is a headline."

Victor took a step closer.

"What do you want us to do?" he asked, not as a challenge, as a promise.

"I want to go to him."

Her eyes shone, but nothing fell. It was like grief had burned past tears and left only heat.

"I want to walk through every corridor, every checkpoint, every locked door, and sit across from him and say, 'You are not alone in there.'"

"You will," Ghost said. "They will parade him. They always do. Courts like cameras too."

"It will not be today," Logan added. "Or tomorrow. They will keep him buried until the lawyers build their cage around him."

"Then we start now," Lena said. "We find out where they are taking him. We find out who holds the keys. We meet this head on, not hiding here while the world decides what he is."

Her voice steadied as she spoke.

The panic did not vanish, but it had something to stand beside now.

Purpose.

480

Ghost exhaled, steady and heavy.

"They'll hold him in Central first. But they won't keep him there. Once the paperwork clears, they'll move him federal. High security. Low visibility. I'll track every mile."

He paused.

"Take a breath, Lena. Not to calm down. To strap in."

She drew one in. Shaky. Real.

"Good. Because this is not just his trial. It's the city's."

Victor looked at Lena.

"He stepped into the fire. We hold the line while he burns."

Lena's eyes hardened.

"He is not burning. He is blazing a trail. There is a difference."

No one argued.

The screens stayed lit, silent and restless.

The transport was cold.

Lucien sat on a narrow bench bolted to the wall, hands cuffed in front of him, the chain humming softly each time the vehicle hit a bump.

There were no windows, not really. Just a thin slit in the rear door, a line of unsteady light that swung with every turn, offering brief flashes of sky and buildings and the backs of other cars.

Across from him, two officers sat facing him, rifles between their knees, eyes fixed on the middle distance. Their uniforms were clean, creases still sharp, like they had been pulled out of a press and dropped into armor they did not feel ready to fill.

The older one was in his thirties, mouth tight, a muscle jumping in his cheek. The other looked barely old enough to drink, Adam's apple twitching each time he swallowed.

Neither spoke.

Lucien kept his gaze on his hands, the cuffs catching the light.

The engine droned beneath them, steady and impersonal. Sirens wailed faintly outside, some close, some far, all bleeding together into a single long note of panic stretched over hot streets.

He could still hear Civic Plaza in his mind.

The crowd roaring.

The gasp after the shot.

The chant that rose when the shock burned off and the truth settled in.

He had not asked for the last part. He had never asked for any of the names they gave him, in this life or the one they tried to engineer in his head.

He thought of the stage.

The speakers shaking.

Lansing's voice spilling over the plaza for the very first time without his permission.

The truth had finally been pulled out of the dark and forced into the light where the whole city could see it.

Not edited. Not buried. Not rewritten in some back room by the men who owned the judges and the headlines.

For once, the city had heard Lansing exactly as he was.

He shifted, the cuffs biting his skin, a small reminder that his body had limits his will refused to honor.

The younger officer glanced up at the sound, eyes flicking to Lucien's face, then away again like eye contact itself might count as a mistake.

"You were there?"

The officer's shoulders tensed. "We are not supposed to talk to you."

Lucien tilted his head.

"Were you in Civic Plaza? Or did they pull you from somewhere else?"

The older one answered, voice flat.

"We were perimeter detail. When the shot went off, command reassigned us to the transport. Easier than leaving us in the crowd."

He did not say what he was thinking, but Lucien heard it anyway.

Easier than letting them watch this from the outside.

"You have families?"

The younger officer blinked, caught off guard. "What?"

"You were not drafted into a war today. You were already in it. Today you just saw the front."

The older man's jaw worked. "Save it."

Lucien let the silence settle again.

He leaned his head back against the metal wall and closed his eyes.

He saw his mother.

Not from the altar. Not in the ground.

In the kitchen, steam rising from a chipped mug as she set it down in front of him. Her hand on his hair when he was too young to understand what his father was building. Her fingers on his face at the chapel, her lungs on fire, still smiling for him.

He heard her last words again, the ones that had cut deeper than any bullet.

He had tried to make it mean something.

He had burned the Coalition's council to the ground.

He had watched his mother descend into the earth with his own eyes.

And today, he had walked into the sun and dropped a man in front of the whole world, not for spectacle, for balance.

Lansing had bombed a church and called it order.

Lucien had put a bullet through his story and called it consequence.

He did not regret the shot.

He regretted that it could not bring her back.

The transport slowed.

The engine's pitch changed, dropping as they took an exit. The light through the slit shifted from blue to gray as they passed under concrete.

The younger officer muttered, "Where are they taking him?"

The older one didn't look up. "Central first. Federal after. We're just the handoff."

Lucien opened his eyes.

"I will walk through as many doors as they have. You know that, right?"

The older officer looked at him for the first time, really looked, like a man examining a weapon he had only heard about in rumors.

"You're not walking anywhere," he said. "You're done."

Lucien's mouth curved, not quite a smile.

"You believe that?"

The man hesitated.

The transport slowed.

Then stopped.

"Stay ready," the older officer muttered, more to himself than to Lucien. "They'll be watching."

Not the people.

Not yet.

The agencies.

The cameras.

The chain of command scrambling to look like it still meant something.

Lucien listened.

Through the metal, through the hum of the engine cooling, he heard it.

Distance.

Open air.

Boots.

Radios.

A helicopter somewhere above.

Control pretending it still held.

"You should know something," Lucien said quietly.

Both officers looked at him despite themselves.

"I'm not a miracle. I'm a repercussion. They made this. Your mayor. His council. The ones who fed them power and called it mercy. I am just the bill coming due."

The older officer looked away as if the words had weight.

Boots approached the rear door.

Keys rattled.

The younger officer's fingers tightened on his rifle, knuckles white.

"On your feet."

His voice cracked despite the order.

Lucien rose.

The cuffs clanked.

His shoulders squared.

They think they caged me, he thought.

All they did was build me a new stage.

The bolts slid back.

Light hit him first.

A white wall of heat that burned through the dark of the transport.

Not a roar.

Not a crowd.

Just the stark, unforgiving brightness of Central intake, built to strip everything human from whoever walked inside.

"Prisoner out. Now."

Hands closed on his arms, not rough, not gentle, just practiced, guiding him forward. The cuffs bit as they pulled him toward the ramp.

Lucien stepped down one measured pace at a time, boots finding the edge, then the ramp, then the hard concrete of the intake yard.

Heat shimmered off the ground.

The yard was boxed in on all sides by tall prefab walls and chain-link topped with razor wire.

Watchtowers manned by tactical units in black armor.

Cameras on every corner, lenses tracking him like predators learning a new shape.

No civilians.

No reporters inside the gates.

Just the residue of a city that had not yet figured out how to breathe after what it had watched.

A handful of barred-off media crews stood far beyond the outer fence, their cameras trying and failing to catch angles through the maze of concrete and steel. A news chopper carved a slow loop overhead before being ordered back by air patrol.

No chanting.

No signs.

Only the hum of power and the sound of weapons shifting as every guard on duty tried not to stare at the man walking past them.

Lucien kept his head high, breath steady, shoulders square.

Let them film, he thought.

You lied about me in every shadow you could find.

You do not get to hide my face in the light.

The gate swallowed him.

Steel slid shut behind him with the sound of a jaw locking closed around something it did not understand.

Lucien did not look back.

Back in Northgate, the sound had returned.

Rook brought the volume back in increments, letting it bleed along the edges of the room until it settled at a low roar.

Footage of the transport played on one of the central screens, a shaky shot from a news chopper trying to keep the convoy in frame. The armored van turned off the freeway and disappeared behind high walls topped with razor wire. No address. No labels. No on-screen banner.

Just the anchor's voice saying they were "tracking an unconfirmed secure transfer," though no official destination had been released.

The chopper drifted too close, and the feed glitched once, twice, then stabilized from farther out. Someone had pushed them back.

No crowds. No signs.

Just the empty perimeter of a holding facility built to process men, not myths.

Lena leaned forward as the camera zoomed through the grain. Even from that distance, she saw him the moment he stepped out of the transport, framed by a dozen armed guards.

Head up.

Back straight.

Hands bound, but nothing else confined.

Lena's phone buzzed again.

Victoria.

The notification previews glowed on the screen.

We saw the reports

Dad is beside himself

If you know anything, please tell us

Lena swallowed, eyes flicking between the message and the grainy footage of Lucien stepping out of the van.

For the first time since the shot rang out, she had something she could say without breaking.

She typed slowly.

He's alive

They moved him to Central intake

We're tracking every second. I'll keep you both updated

Three dots appeared.

Disappeared.

Reappeared.

Jesus Christ

Please keep us updated

Love you

Lena stared at the words for a long beat, her thumb trembling above the glass.

She turned the phone facedown again, not to hide, but to breathe.

She lifted her eyes back to the screen.

Lucien disappeared behind the steel doors.

The world held its breath with her.

"They can try to shrink him. He never fits the frame."

Victor stood beside her, arms folded, eyes narrowed.

"They will try harder. Solitary. No cameras. No visitors. They will want him to disappear into procedure."

"Then we drag him back into the light. Every day. Every way."

Imani glanced between them. "You know this means trials. Depositions. Hearings. Dates. Years, maybe. They will slow-walk everything until the city forgets."

Rook pointed at another screen.

"The city will not forget."

He pointed at another screen.

Riots. Marches. Sit-ins. Streets flooded with people. Candles blooming on steps and sidewalks.

People held up printed stills of the moment Lansing confessed.

Others of the moment Lucien fired.

Some wore shirts already. No one knew who had time to print them, but there they were.

A stylized image of Lucien's face. Eyes shadowed.

Below it, in simple letters:

WE HEARD YOU

"It took them long enough to bury his first death. They will not bury this one so easily."

Ghost's voice came through again, tempered steel. "National Guard is mobilizing across the state. Curfew is coming. Officially to stop unrest. Unofficially to make sure your husband's name does not become a permanent bonfire."

"Let them come. Let every camera catch every face that refuses to bow. He gave them the truth. They gave him chains. That is not a story that dies quietly."

Victor looked at her with a mix of grief and respect.

"You sound like him."

She met his eyes. "Good. This city does not just belong to the men they lock up. It belongs to the women who refuse to let them vanish."

Outside, somewhere beyond the concrete and steel, the city burned and chanted and bled and breathed.

Inside Northgate, the war room pulsed with light and purpose.

Lucien had stepped into the cage.

The world had stepped onto the line.

What came next would not just decide his fate.

It would decide what the word freedom meant when spoken without permission.

The night had not fallen yet.

By the time it did, the city would not be the same.

CHAPTER SIXTY-EIGHT

INTAKE

Inside, the noise dulled by half, then half again as they passed through a narrow corridor of concrete and caged fluorescents. The air smelled like disinfectant, sweat, and old fear that never quite washed out of the walls.

"Prisoner Cole, Lucien," someone read from a clipboard. "Central intake. High-risk classification. Special handling protocol."

He watched the words pass between them like they were handling a live grenade.

Two sets of uniforms moved around him.

City blue.

Federal tactical black, the kind worn when D.C. sent people to take over a scene.

The badges on the black ones all said different things, but their faces wore the same tension. The city cops looked hollow and red-eyed, like they had been sprinting all day. The feds looked stiff, like they were offended the mess had spilled into their jurisdiction.

"You get one set of prints, one set of mugshots, and he is ours," a woman in a blazer said. "No interviews, no comments, no grandstanding in the hallway. Do I need to spell it out, or are we still pretending chain of command means something here?"

"We still have a mayor on a slab at the Medical Examiner's," the captain in city blue snapped. "Do not bark orders at me like I am one of your junior analysts."

"Your mayor signed his own warrant on tape," she shot back. "Washington is already looking at transfer flights. Trust me, you do not want this staying under your name."

Lucien let their argument wash past him.

He felt the world through details instead.

A young officer at the far desk, hands shaking as he rolled ink across the pads.

A crack in one of the overhead fluorescents, the light inside buzzing slightly off rhythm.

Old blood on the tile near the door, smeared by a boot, not cleaned yet.

The city had reached even here.

They sat him down in front of a lens.

"Face forward."

He did.

The camera clicked once. Twice. No flash. Only the soft mechanical sound of a memory being taken.

"Turn."

Left profile. Full face. Right profile.

"Hands."

They took his prints, fingers pressed into ink, then onto card stock, then onto a glass scanner.

Each touch felt like a little piece of him being catalogued.

The same hands that had pressed a gun to a mayor's chest after making him confess before the world.

"Eyes."

A pen tapped beneath the lens.

"Look into the red dot."

He stared straight through it.

When they finished, the woman in the blazer stepped closer.

Hair pinned tight. Her mouth a thin line. The small pin at her lapel caught the light.

"I am Assistant Director Harper," she said. "Justice Department. I command the Crisis Bureau task groups for this region. Until Washington decides otherwise, I have custody and oversight. You will be moved again at the earliest safe opportunity."

Her use of the word safe tasted wrong. Not because she meant him harm, but because safe had no fixed point anymore.

"What are you calling me now?"

Harper blinked once.

"You are Lucien Cole. Primary subject of the Federal Crisis Bureau dossier that leaked last winter. Sealed juvenile file exposed. Holdings seized. Shell companies under review. Every club, every account, every mirror that ever hid your money."

Her voice sharpened. "Newark narcotics seizure. The Dade County massacre at the Midnight Club, Victor Dresnik's property. The federal task force that launched the minute you and Dresnik were framed for twenty-two homicides."

She let that sit.

"The Bureau has been digging for eight months. Nothing stays buried forever."

She drew in a breath. "And now you executed a sitting mayor on live global broadcast."

"Executed a liar."

His voice stayed level.

"Different thing."

"You turned a national holiday into a crime scene," Harper answered. "You dropped a man at a podium in front of the entire world."

"Did you listen to the recording?"

Her mouth flattened. "Yes."

"And?"

"It's in evidence. It will be examined for authenticity, for chain of custody, for admissibility. None of that gives you the right to stand in a public plaza and put a bullet in the chest of an elected official."

"Nothing gave him the right to bomb a church full of families and call it protocol. He did it anyway."

Harper stepped closer, voice low enough that the uniforms could not hear. "You think you are a martyr. You are not. You are a symbol. Symbols get carved into whatever shape the people with cameras need. Do not mistake what comes next for anything noble."

"You are one of the people with cameras. So tell me, Assistant Director Harper, how are you going to carve me?"

A flicker crossed her face. "I do not know yet. Washington will decide what you are allowed to be."

"No."

His voice stayed quiet.

"Washington will decide what they are allowed to call me."

Her eyes hardened. "There is no deal waiting for you this time. No Agent Hall. No quiet arrangement. No alternative path out the back door. The Bureau wants a conviction. The Department wants a message. The country wants a villain who bleeds on cue."

She leaned in. "You will never walk free again. You are done moving pieces. You are done making calls. You are done putting your hands on the scale."

Cold.

Final.

"Mr. Cole."

She let the name settle like a sentence.

"You will never see the light of day for the rest of your God-forsaken life."

For a moment, neither of them spoke.

He thought of stained glass and fire and the sound of his mother's lungs filling with poison.

The verse burned behind his eyelids, the same one from the Bible in that other place.

Lena's hand on the glass at Northgate.

Harper straightened. Already turning away. Already filing him as finished.

They re-secured the cuffs and led him down the corridor that smelled like fresh paint laid over old rot. The building had been a logistics hub once, all open bays and steel shelving. Now it was a maze of interior walls and makeshift cells, security systems bolted into places they were never meant to fit.

A siren wailed somewhere deep in the facility. The lights flickered in response.

"Power interruptions," one of the guards muttered. "We aren't even officially open and they're already cutting our grid to patch Midtown. Half the city's infrastructure is bleeding."

"Keep walking," the older guard said. "If we lose doors on this guy, I'm retiring in a body bag."

They turned into a holding block.

Eight cells. Four on each side. Thick glass fronts, concrete and steel behind. Every door had three separate locks visible from the outside, red diodes blinking steady.

Six of the cells were already full.

Fallout arrests. People swept up in the chaos after the shot.

A man in his fifties sat on one bunk, suit soaked in blood, tie hanging loose. Two younger men in street clothes paced another cell, eyes raw, knuckles bruised. A woman in scrubs sat on the floor of another, back to the wall, staring through it.

They went quiet when they saw him.

"Put him in C," the panel guard said. "Nothing else is clean."

The locks on the third door to the right released with three sharp clacks. Lucien stepped inside. The space was barely bigger than the bed along the back wall. Metal shelf, thin mattress. Toilet. Sink. Single bolted shelf. No window. Only a rectangle of glass high in the corridor wall that bled in a faint, jaundiced light.

When the door shut, the cell changed shape. The air felt smaller. The sounds outside dulled, then came back sharper. Keys. Boots. A faraway shout.

He sat on the edge of the bunk. The mattress groaned. The chain between his wrists bit his skin. He lifted his hands and studied the marks. They looked almost like someone had tried to underline his veins.

He raised his bound hands slightly, chains whispering as he turned his palm.

The black ring on his finger sat steady, unmoved, the one piece of his life they couldn't strip away.

Lena.

The only part of him they could not catalog, seize, or sentence.

He felt her in the vows they whispered, a promise carved deeper than blood.

Even when he crossed into places no one should come back from, she reached through and pulled him back to earth.

The cell pressed in around him.

He let the ring ground him.

They could cage his body.

They would never cage what tied him to her.

Chapter Sixty-Nine
THE CITY RISES

I climbed to the roof on the night this country still dares to call freedom.

Fourth of July.

The sky cracked open in celebration while every screen below sold the same lie in high definition.

Tonight it felt like revolution.

They zoomed in on the cuffs as if the metal mattered more than the man.

Up here the air tasted of sulfur and hot tar. Only sirens reached this far out, and the restless growl of a city deciding whether to breathe or scream.

Northgate crouched beneath me. My concrete ark. My hiding place for months. Its lit windows looked like half-healed wounds that never learned how to close. Beyond it, the city was inventing new constellations out of burning police cruisers and overturned dumpsters. Fireworks and Molotovs competing for the same patch of night. Both beautiful if you forgot what they cost.

I liked to believe I would watch these displays with Lucien from the fire escape of a life I pretended was small enough to have. We would drink cheap beer and flinch at the booms, laughing because flinching felt safer than admitting the noise sounded like incoming fire.

Tonight every burst felt personal. Timed, almost. A cosmic joke synced to the exact second they dragged him offstage in irons.

They are calling it an execution.

They are calling it terrorism.

They are calling it the end of civil discourse.

None of those words fit in my mouth.

I was there when the moment opened inside him.

I watched the moment the idea walked into his eyes and sat down like it owned the place. I could have spoken. One sentence, maybe two, and history would have turned left instead of burning straight ahead.

I said nothing.

I let him carry the match because putting it out would have meant denying the system was rotten.

So here is the truth I came up here to choke on:

I am not the witness.

I am the kindling.

All these years I curated silence like it was a virtue. I catalogued the right thoughts, looked away at the right moments, told myself distance was the same as innocence. I built a whole personality out of not being the one who lit the fuse.

Lucien was never one to play that game. He walked up to the lie in front of the entire world and signed the match with his own name.

And I hated him for it.

For three heartbeats I hated him, because he made my old careful life look exactly like what it was: cowardice in good shoes.

Then the hate turned into something hotter and cleaner and I understood his mother's last words weren't instructions for him alone.

Make it mean something.

She was talking to both of us. To anyone still pretending the story ends if we just keep our hands clean.

Somewhere out in the city, someone has painted his name across an entire billboard in dripping red. And right now, someone else is probably trying to erase it with a fire hose and sheer desperation. The city cannot decide whether to canonize him or crucify him, so it is doing both at once.

Good.

Let it tear itself in half trying.

I press my palms to the rough gravel of the roof and feel it bite. Real. Solid. Something that doesn't lie about what it is.

I have spent years floating above consequences, above this city, above my own pulse, telling myself observation was the same as integrity.

No more.

Lucien is in a box tonight because he refused to let the truth stay abstract.

If I stay up here watching the apocalypse I helped schedule, I become the epilogue he never asked for, the wife who watched, who felt everything, who did nothing.

So this is the reckoning the roof demanded:

I am not harmless.

I never was.

My silence had weight. My inaction had address. Every time I looked away, I co-signed.

The blaze isn't coming for me.

It's been inside me the whole time, patient as scar tissue.

I stand up. The wind tastes like gunpowder and future.
My hands are empty, but they remember how to carry.
Tomorrow the cameras will want tears or manifesto or dignified restraint.
They'll get none of it.
I have a promise to keep to the woman who gave him life and gave me a family, and to the man who heard her when I only pretended to listen.
Make it mean something.
Fine.
I will.
I climb down from the roof no longer watching the fire.
I climb down to become it.

Lena lifted her hand from the page. The ink was still drying in thin, steady strokes, her words claiming one more blank space in the black book.

She closed it gently and stood, the night air still clinging to her skin as she stepped back through the stairwell and into the dim halls of Northgate.

Grief had weight.

Purpose gave her balance.

In the bedroom, she set the book back on the dresser.

That was when she noticed it.

A torn edge near the front. A page missing, ripped out clean.

Her chest tightened.

Lucien had written in it again.

Not the old note from months ago, the one on the first page, written so deep it felt permanent.

This was new.

Fresh.

Days ago, maybe less.

His grief pressed into paper the same way hers now was.

She knew it was recent. She had kept this book close for months, tucked in drawers, bags, and bedside tables, beside the first note he ever wrote her. Lucien had only found it again the day of the rehearsal dinner, hours before, touching it like something half remembered and half feared.

The absence of his page felt louder than any words she could have found on it.

Lena ran her thumb along the frayed seam, the two of them suddenly sharing the same silence, the same book, the same wounds.

She placed her hand on the cover.

Not in mourning.

In vow.

Movement found her before thought did.

The city reached her even inside, rising against Northgate's walls, and by the time she noticed, her feet were already carrying her toward the war room.

The second Lena stepped inside, the space felt like it was shaking.

Not from bombs. Not from gunfire.

From human pressure, a thousand angers and griefs grinding together like tectonic plates under a collapsing sky.

The screens glowed like exposed nerves.

The room was already in motion. Weapons out. Radios lit. Eyes locked on the screens.

Mara pointed to the central monitor.

"Look at this, Lena."

She did.

Half a dozen rooftops had turned into makeshift artillery nests, people hurling cinder blocks down onto armored trucks trying to push through. Sparks flew as concrete shattered windshields and dented steel, every impact drawing a roar from above loud enough to shake the block.

Fires were blooming everywhere. Trash cans. Patrol cars. The stone steps of government buildings blackened and smoking.

Kids climbed lampposts and hung fireworks like live charges, then let them rip through the sky in screaming arcs of red and blue and gold, as if the city were trying to outshine its own grief.

A city of almost nine million was tearing itself open under the weight of a truth it didn't know how to carry.

Pressure had been building for weeks, then days, then hours. The wedding bombing. The wake. Lansing's lies. The confession over loudspeakers. All it needed was a spark.

The curfew wasn't broken.

It had been laughed at.

Sirens spiraled through boroughs in overlapping circles, each one swallowed by a roar that wasn't protest, wasn't riot, something older. Something tidal.

This wasn't unrest.

It was fracture.

A chant rolled through the streets.

At first scattered.

Then synchronized.

Then everywhere at once.

"COLE DID NOT LIE!"

"WHO OWNS THE CITY?"

"WE DO!"

Ghost came through the speakers, thinner than usual, like even he couldn't hide the tremor under it.

"We've got National Guard on the freeway. Mounted patrol locking down the Midtown bridges.. Whatever is left of Civic Shield is getting overrun block by block. Half the city is ignoring every order they've been given since sundown."

Logan checked a second feed. "Ignoring? They're dragging Civic Shield vans into the street and setting them on fire. People are calling it history."

Victor muttered, "Good."

Mara didn't bother correcting him.

On another screen:

Times Square.

Fifth Avenue.

Queensbridge.

Hunts Point.

Harlem.

St. George.

Everywhere, the same thing repeating.

A city turning confession into fire.

Lena stepped forward, and the room parted around her.

She wasn't shaking now.

She was focused.

Northgate felt it.

Ghost felt it.

The city outside felt it.

The speaker trembled once before Ghost spoke again, quiet and almost reverent.

"Tonight isn't about politics. Or gangs. Or factions.

Tonight the city is choosing its myth."

Lena whispered, "And they chose him."

No one in the room mistook that for victory.

The sky was supposed to be celebrating.

Fourth of July fireworks cracked somewhere over the river, but they were drowned out instantly by something louder, closer, angrier.

The city wasn't watching fireworks tonight. It was throwing them back.

Above downtown, a news chopper dipped low over the crowds flooding the streets.

It never got the shot.

A streak of red tore up from a tenement roof, some kid, some rebel, someone the cameras would never name, and an illegal mortar shell clipped the tail.

The helicopter bucked, spun once, then twice.

Someone screamed. Someone else cheered.

Lena stood frozen as the camera feed caught the final seconds.

The chopper clipped the side of a corporate tower, the glass panels exploding into a storm of glittering knives. The machine spun out, slamming into a scaffolding rig six stories high. The whole structure folded like wet paper and crashed into the street in a roar that rolled across the city like distant thunder.

The feed cut to static.

Another monitor lit up, this one from Midtown.

Crowds surged past barricades the National Guard barely had time to assemble. Lines broke instantly. Riot shields crashed backward as bodies hit them like waves swallowing rocks. Rubber bullets snapped through the air, some ricocheting off brick, others punching into shoulders, ribs, skulls. People went down, but the mass didn't stop. It surged right over them.

Tear gas canisters arced across the screen. Someone kicked one back into the line of soldiers.

The fog rose, a white chemical ghost curling through the streets. Sirens drowned beneath a million shouts, footfalls, and hearts beating in the same violent rhythm.

On another camera, Bronx.

A crowd on Fordham Road had hijacked a city bus and turned it into a moving barricade, ramming through abandoned cruisers to clear a path.

People clung to the roof, waving shirts and signs, the bus dragging sparks like a comet as it tore down the avenue. Police lines broke before it even reached them.

The Grand Concourse had become a river of bodies, tens of thousands moving as one. People poured over medians, cars, police tape, anything in their path. Mounted officers tried to hold the line and were swallowed instantly, the horses buckling under the crush of bodies surging from every direction.

Queensboro Bridge.

The bridge itself was a battlefield. National Guard armored trucks pushed into the crowd but couldn't make it ten yards before bodies swarmed the tires, ripping open grates, smashing lights with bicycle chains and rocks. A soldier fired into the air. The crowd ducked, then roared back with the kind of fury that didn't care about consequences.

Staten Island. St. George.

Crowds ripped down Civic Shield banners from the ferry terminal and set them ablaze. Someone tied one to a lamppost, and someone else climbed up and lit the edge with a cigarette lighter. People cheered as it burned like a flag from a country no one wanted anymore.

Brooklyn did not wait for orders.

Flatbush Avenue turned into a spine of movement, bodies pouring from side streets in numbers too large to count. Storefront gates rattled like metallic applause as crowds surged past them. Speaker stacks rolled into intersections, block-party towers wired to car batteries, bass lines rattling brick and bone, engines coughing to life under stoops and scaffolds.

It wasn't music.

It was pressure.

It was pulse.

The sound did not ask for permission. It claimed blocks.

In Bed-Stuy, the streetlights began dying in sequence, not all at once, but in waves that moved with the crowd. One corner dark. Then the next. Then the next. Traffic signals blinked red and stayed there. Patrol cars stalled in intersections they suddenly could not see through. Above it all, rooftops bloomed with red flares, a line of fire signals stretching from Crown Heights to Bushwick like the borough was speaking in code.

No single fire.

No single riot.

An entire grid shifting under its own will.

By the time armored units tried to push in from Atlantic Avenue, the streets had already rearranged themselves.

Brooklyn wasn't burning.

Brooklyn was moving.

Every screen turned into a mosaic of collapse, rebellion, and something that looked disturbingly like celebration.

Logan muttered, "This is war."

Imani whispered, "No. War has rules. This doesn't."

Ghost's voice broke in, breathless for the first time since Lucien dragged them all into this story.

"Everyone, listen carefully. The Guard just declared downtown a red zone. Drones grounded. Transit closed. Curfew collapsing. They are losing control in real time. They can't contain it. The numbers are too high. This city,"

Static swallowed the rest.

The line crackled once, then found Ghost's voice again.

"This city isn't fighting them."

The static cleared, and Ghost's voice came through like a prophecy.

"It's rising."

On the farthest screen, the camera caught a wide shot across the East River.

The skyline flickered.

Buildings reflected the flames below like the whole city was wearing war paint.

People climbed fire escapes to rooftops, holding phones, holding flags, holding nothing at all, just screaming into the night like it was finally listening.

The boom of fireworks blended with the thunder of stun grenades.

The pop of rubber bullets with the crack of champagne bottles.

The chanting with the crying, the laughing, the breaking.

Chaos and celebration danced together.

A city in a fever dream.

A city in labor.

Lena stared.

Her pulse matched the flashing lights on every screen.

She felt something raw and enormous rising in her chest, part terror, part awe, part destiny.

Behind her, Mara's voice came almost reverent.

"Lucien didn't light this."

She swallowed. "He only gave it permission."

And Lena whispered what the whole skyline already knew:

"No."

Her eyes didn't leave the burning city.
"They lit it for him."

Chapter Seventy

WHERES THE GUARD?

It was past two in the morning when the floor shuddered.

A deep vibration rolled up through the steel beams, not from footsteps or crowds, but from something detonating miles south, somewhere inside the city's bones.

Rook grabbed the edge of the console as dust drifted from the ceiling tiles.

Another tremor followed, harder.

On the central screens, news feeds flashed red and footage rolled.

Checkpoints buckling under human floods.

Armored patrol trucks overturned, burning in the middle of intersections.

The National Guard line retreating across Midtown, shields cracking under thrown debris and raw numbers.

Victor slammed a fist on the desk. "Where the fuck are the reinforcements? That sector should've been locked down."

Ghost's voice cut in, low and brutal.

"This isn't containment anymore."

Lena didn't look away. "Why?"

"Because this isn't a riot. It's infrastructure failure."

Logan frowned. "In English."

Ghost switched to another feed from his end.

A bridge.

A convoy trapped at the midpoint, hemmed in by abandoned cars.

"The Guard can't drive armor through Manhattan. Too narrow. Too old. Too dense. One wrong turn and they crush thirty civilians on live television."

Rook nodded grimly. "He's right. Tanks weren't made for a city like this. The streets fight back. You try to turn an MRAP on Canal, you take out a deli, two brownstones, and half a grid line."

Ghost continued. "They brought MRAPs. BearCats. Light APCs. But it doesn't matter. The streets are choke points. Cars are blocking intersections. Fires are blocking the rest."

Another feed replaced it.

A guardsman screaming into a radio, drowned out by noise.

"Their units are scattered. No clean lines. No clear sectors. Everything they trained for assumes crowd control."

The map zoomed in.

"This is not crowd control."

Mara stared at the red-spattered city grid. "So what is it?"

Ghost's voice came back without hesitation. "A population revolt. Multi-borough. Simultaneous. Emotional ignition. Zero unified command."

The map tightened on the screen.

"You cannot stop a million people moving at once. Not with tear gas. Not with shields. Not without turning the city into a massacre on every screen in the world. And not with tanks you can't even get between the parked cars."

The room went silent.

Ghost's voice dropped lower. "You want to know why the Guard is retreating? Look at this feed."

He pulled up another camera.

A Humvee was swallowed by bodies. Not a crowd. A frenzy.

Fists hammered the hood. Boots slammed against the doors. A brick exploded across the windshield, glass fracturing into a spiderweb of panic.

Inside, a soldier screamed into his radio while another raised his rifle with hands that could not stop shaking.

Fire or don't fire.

Both were suicide.

The side window shattered. Hands punched through the gap, grabbing, dragging.

A bottle burst against the hood and flame bloomed fast, black smoke climbing the frame.

The crowd didn't retreat. They closed in.

They weren't surrounding the vehicle.

They were tearing it apart.

"They have rules of engagement. And this city just shredded them."

Lena's voice cracked. "So what are you telling us?"

"That the streets have turned into rivers, and the Guard is drowning. This isn't a force. It's a tide. You don't stop tides. You survive them."

Her breath left her.

Rook shook his head. "Holy shit."

"And here's the worst part. These crowds aren't moving because of fear.

They're moving because of belief. Belief is harder than bullets."

The volume spiked on one feed.

A guardsman was crying, mask up, knees shaking, as the crowd surged past him, ignoring him completely.

"When the public stops acknowledging authority, stops fearing uniforms, and stops listening to commands, the Guard isn't an army anymore."

Static cracked across the line.

"They're just people in vests."

The words hit the room hard as the screens flickered and the crowd kept swelling.

The floor shuddered again.

Closer.

One screen changed without anyone touching it.

Central intake.

For a second, no one spoke.

The outer perimeter lights flickered through smoke. Beyond the fence, streets that should have been empty were filling with bodies, blocks away still, but moving in the same direction.

Not scattered.

Not lost.

Converging.

Lena whispered, "Then nothing stops them from finding him and reaching him."

Ghost didn't disagree.

He didn't speak at all.

The city answered for him, a thunder of voices beyond Northgate rising like the tide he warned them about.

The reckoning had begun.

Nothing on earth was going to stop it.

And Lena knew exactly whose cage they were coming to break.

CHAPTER SEVENTY-ONE
TRANSFER ORDER

Lucien had no sense of time.

There was no clock, no window, no shift in the light.

Only the rise and fall of distant noise grinding through concrete, reminding him the world outside was still breaking.

It felt like hours. Six, maybe eight. Long enough for his throat to go dry, for hunger to fade into something dull and distant, for the city to change shape.

His muscles ached from standing still. He sat, stood, then stretched in the narrow gap between the bed and the door, moving through the same patterns that had kept him alive in worse rooms than this.

No water. No food. No phone call.

Somewhere beyond the walls, the intake block shook with noise that had not been there before. Not footsteps or routine movement. Something heavier, angrier, rolled through the building with no visible source.

A television hung near the guard desk.

Lucien couldn't see it from his cell.

Only the voice reached him, polished and practiced, starting to crack.

"Citywide emergency declared earlier tonight. Multiple boroughs reporting full loss of control. National Guard units forced to retreat after sustaining heavy injuries. Fires continue to spread through the districts."

Static swallowed the next few seconds.

"Authorities now confirm over a hundred simultaneous protests, riots, and armed clashes across the five boroughs. Transit is shut down. Bridges are barricaded. Several precincts have been overrun or abandoned entirely."

His own name came through distorted, swallowed by the chaos.

"The alleged catalyst, Lucien Cole, remains in federal custody, though officials have not disclosed his location. Social media streams continue to show crowds chanting his name."

A second reporter cut in, breathless.

"We are receiving confirmation that Civic Shield is no longer functioning as a city agency. Their central command office in Manhattan has been overrun by crowds. Newly issued Civic Shield patrol vehicles have been torched throughout the district, and all dispatch lines tied to the unit have gone silent."

The guard swore under his breath and stabbed the volume down to a murmur.

From deeper in the block, noise surged and broke. A shout. The thud of boots running in the wrong direction. Radios spitting codes no one sounded confident using.

The world was no longer trying to calm anyone.

It was trying to survive itself.

"Secure all outer doors!"

"Repeat, we have activity at the south fence."

"They are not supposed to know we are here. How the fuck did they find out where we took him?"

"Phones," another voice said. "People broadcast faster than we can move."

He caught fragments through the wall like shapes through fog.

"Crowds at the perimeter."

"The Governor's office wants reassurance."

"National Guard is pulling back from the bridges."

"We do not have enough bodies to hold this much concrete."

The shouting outside rose, then fell, then rose again. At first it was only noise. Then the syllables separated.

He heard it.

"HE DID NOT LIE!"

"WHO OWNS THE CITY!"

"WE DO!"

Under that, another layer, lower, like an echo under the chant.

His name.

Called like a question. Answered like a verdict.

Lucien let the sound move through him.

This was not what he had wanted, not exactly. What he had wanted was truth.

He had not wanted the city to bleed itself open like this.

But then, it was already bleeding.

All he had done was hold up a mirror.

The door lock clicked.

Lucien opened his eyes.

A young guard stood in the narrow window slot, a metal cup in his hand. His hair was plastered to his forehead with sweat. He had the look of someone who had been promoted three rungs too fast in one night.

He slid the cup through the opening.

"Water," he said.

Lucien took it. The metal was cool in his hands. The water tasted like chlorine and old pipes, but his body seized it like he had crossed a desert. Not hunger. Not thirst. Just the shock of water after a day that had not stopped moving.

The guard watched him drink with tight fascination, trying to reconcile the man in front of him with the man on the screens. His nameplate caught the light.

ORTIZ

Thin black letters above a trembling hand.

Lucien lowered the cup.

"You have something to say?"

Ortiz shifted his weight. "We are instructed to keep interactions minimal."

"That did not answer the question."

Ortiz hesitated.

Then he exhaled.

"I have never escorted someone the whole world is shouting about. Feels like being inside the story the whole world is watching."

Lucien's eyes stayed on the nameplate.

"You think I lit this?"

Ortiz rubbed his palms against his vest. "I don't know what you lit. I just know they built the fire long before you ever touched a match."

Lucien studied him. The man looked exhausted, strung thin, too young for the weight on his shoulders.

"What do they think I am?"

"The world can't decide. Half of them are scared of what you did. The other half are scared of what it means."

"What do you call me?"

Ortiz's eyes flicked toward the cameras, then back to Lucien. His voice lowered.

"I call you the reason the ground feels like it's shifting under all of us."

The words seemed to surprise him. He flushed immediately, glancing back toward the desk as if honesty carried consequences.

"I shouldn't have said that," he muttered. "Forget it."

"I won't," Lucien said.

Ortiz swallowed.

"They're moving you. Out of the city. Somewhere no one can get near the fences. Somewhere the news can't camp outside and turn you into a campfire story."

"When?"

"Soon. They're trying to find a window where the roads aren't on fire."

Behind him, Harper's voice cut across the block.

"Ortiz. Step away from that door."

He stepped back as if yanked by a leash. The slot slid shut.

Lucien set the cup on the floor beside the bunk and leaned his head against the wall.

They were going to move him. Of course they were.

They would not let him sit in a box on the edge of the city, close enough to hear it chant. Close enough for anyone with a pickup and a dream to try a rescue.

They wanted him quiet, contained, trapped in legal language and closed sessions until his story went flat.

He smiled, just a little, at the ceiling.

"Good luck," he murmured.

You cannot put an idea in solitary.

Outside, the television voice came back in slices.

"Governor urging calm."

"Further deployments under consideration."

"White House has not yet issued an official statement."

"Experts remain divided on whether Cole's actions will inspire copycats or force a reckoning with state power."

Experts.

Always so eager to explain a fire they never helped put out.

He thought of Lena again.

He wondered what she saw tonight.

He did not let himself linger there long.

That way led to panic. Panic had no place here.

The lock clacked again.

This time it was Harper at the window, her blazer slightly crooked now, hair no longer immaculate.

"We are moving you."

His chains clinked softly as he shifted.

"Where?"

"Out of the city. That is all you need to know."

"It is all you will tell me."

She held his stare. "Fair enough."

A beat.

"The Governor called. So did Washington. They want you handled quickly. Quietly. Cleanly."

She let the words settle. "That is not going to happen."

Her eyes flicked toward the concrete beyond him. "The city is already treating you like a fault line. Stand too close, and something gives."

"And you?" Lucien asked.

Her mouth moved, almost a smile, almost a warning.

"Working on it."

She nodded to someone out of sight. "Chain him for transport."

The door opened.

Two guards stepped in, weapons low but ready.

They bound his wrists with thicker cuffs. A second chain looped to a belt at his waist. Another line ran to his ankles.

Layer after layer of metal, not rushed, not sloppy.

Ceremonial.

He rose without being told and let them fit the restraints, let them handle him like unstable ordnance, like something that might detonate if they breathed wrong.

Outside, the chant swelled.

It didn't sound like noise anymore.

It sounded like pressure.

Ortiz stood near the door, staring at a patch of concrete as if it might offer absolution.

Lucien caught his eye anyway.

"Ortiz," he said quietly.

The young guard swallowed. "Yeah."

"Call your mother when you can. If she asks what you did tonight, tell her you told the truth once."

Ortiz's throat tightened. "Yes, sir."

Harper's gaze flicked between them. Calculation first. Then something softer. Something she buried quickly.

"Move out."

They escorted him down the corridor, past the row of cells, past faces pressed to glass.

No one shouted. No one cursed.

Some stared like the sight of him had changed the shape of the room.

An older man Lucien had not seen before stepped forward and placed his palm against the glass.

No threat. No plea. Just acknowledgment.

The intake doors opened, and night hit him like a blow.

The noise had changed.

It was no longer a crowd.

It was a perimeter.

Bodies gathered beyond the outer fence, past floodlights, past razor wire. They packed the service road, spilled into dirt embankments, climbed guardrails and abandoned vehicles.

Not trying to breach.

Trying to witness.

Helicopter beams drifted overhead like searching fingers.

Sirens washed the horizon in red and blue, colors that once meant warning.

Tonight they meant declaration.

No one touched the fence.

Their presence pressed against the facility like water against steel.

Testing.

Waiting.

A convoy idled in the yard, matte black, unmarked, plate numbers obscured, windows blacked into anonymity.

An unmarked helicopter lifted from the far end of the lot before the convoy moved, rotors chopping the smoke apart as it rose into the dark.

Harper stepped closer.

"Federal transfer. You will be briefed on your rights at the next facility. Until then, you remain silent. You do not address the crowd. You do not address the officers. You do not give the cameras anything we have not already taken."

Lucien looked at her.

"The cameras are not yours anymore. They belong to the city."

For the first time that night, she had no immediate reply.

Annoyance flickered across her face. Not at him.

At the truth.

They guided him forward.

Each step echoed off concrete.

The chant pressed closer, vibrating through air, through bone.

He couldn't make out the words anymore.

It was too large.

Rage and hope and grief braided together into one living sound.

He thought of his mother's grave.

Of Lena's hand in his.

Of the Bronx Stadium, empty field stretching under open sky, ready to hold something better than what had always been fed to it.

They are not shouting for me.

They are shouting at the cage.

They reached the armored truck.

The door opened.

Darkness waited inside. Deeper than the cell. Steel bench. Restraint straps. Bolted walls.

A box within a box.

He turned once.

Just enough.

Over the walls. Over floodlights. Over razor wire.

He couldn't see the skyline. Only a smear of gold and ember-red bleeding through smoke that swallowed glass and steel.

For a heartbeat, the haze shifted.

Two yellow points burned in it.

Watching. Still. Patient.

The shape hung at the edge of his vision.

The Wolf.

Not in flesh. Not in shadow.

Still there, watching from the rim of the storm.

You are late.

The shape blinked out.

Maybe it had never been there.

Maybe his mind was stitching meaning into smoke because meaning was the only thing keeping him standing.

Or maybe it was done waiting.

He stepped into the truck.

The door slammed.

Metal swallowed him.

The lock slid home with a final, echoing clack.

Not a period.

A hinge.

The engine rumbled to life beneath him.

The convoy rolled forward.

Outside, the chant didn't fade.

It followed.

They thought they were extracting him from the epicenter, removing the spark, separating the symbol from the ignition.

Lucien leaned back against the cold metal wall and closed his eyes.

You cannot outrun what has already begun.

The truck turned toward the highway, toward bridges, toward water, toward the unlit airfield waiting beyond the city.

Behind them, the city didn't settle.

It rose.

They thought they were driving him away from the fire.

They were only driving him deeper into it.

CHAPTER SEVENTY-TWO

TWO IN THE DARK

It was three in the morning now.

The war room had gone quiet. Not peaceful. Just a silence that pressed against the walls and waited to be broken.

The team stood around Lena, each one hollowed out by the night.

Victor. Logan. Rook. Imani. Mara.

Every face turned toward Lena like she was the last thing holding the building upright.

She didn't cry.

She couldn't.

Her breath was slow, steady, terrifyingly calm.

She placed her hands on the table.

"I have to tell you all something."

The words dropped like a stone.

The room straightened.

Victor stepped forward.

"Lena, whatever it is, we can,"

"I'm pregnant."

Silence cracked open.

Not a gasp.

Not a scream.

Just the kind of silence that changes everything.

Logan went still, like someone had just rewritten the plan.

Mara pressed a hand to her mouth.

Imani whispered something shaped like a prayer or a curse.

Rook froze completely, unreadable for the first time in his life.

Victor shook his head, not in denial. In shock.

"Does he know?"

"No. He doesn't."

The quiet thickened, heavy as smoke.

Rook finally found his voice.

"Lena, the city is collapsing. The Guard is retreating. The whole country is watching him burn. And you're,"

"I know what this means. For him. For us. For everything."

Her hand drifted to her stomach.

Not soft.

Not tender.

A vow.

"This child will grow up in a world their father changed with his bare hands, a world that won't know whether to worship him or punish everyone who carries his name."

Her voice sharpened.

"So listen to me. All of you. I am not running. I am not hiding. I am not letting him face whatever comes next alone. We find him. We stay above the noise. And when the world decides what it thinks of Lucien Cole,"

She lifted her chin.

"I will be standing right beside him."

A tremor rolled through the building, distant thunder shaking a city that had lost its mind.

Everyone stared at her like they were seeing her for the first time.

Not Lucien's shadow.

The woman walking into a burning world with the future inside her.

No applause.

No cheer.

The room went still around her.

Lena held their eyes until they stopped looking at Lucien's shadow and started looking at her.

And that was enough.

The helicopter doors opened and cold air rolled in, sharp and clean, nothing like the city he had left behind.

There was no crowd waiting. No cameras. No skyline pressing at the edges of the night.

Only trees. Miles of them. Black silhouettes standing shoulder to shoulder, swallowing the horizon.

The helicopter blades wound down behind him, their echo dissolving into the forest. Hands guided him forward. His boots sank into wet dirt that swallowed sound.

There were no signs. No marked road. No perimeter fence.

Just a concrete structure half buried in the earth, as if someone had planted a bunker there and waited for it to grow.

No windows. No flag. No number.

Nothing that admitted it existed.

They walked him down a narrow staircase that smelled of rust and cold metal, deeper into a place that did not care about time. The hall was lit by a single dying bulb. The air carried the steady hum of a generator somewhere below, feeding a system that was built to outlast men.

Another door.

Another lock.

His new cell was concrete and shadow.

There was no cot. Only a bench bolted to the wall and a drain set into the floor.

The door shut behind him with the kind of finality reserved for decisions that did not get appealed.

Lucien sat.

Not defeated.

Not afraid.

Waiting.

Time peeled away until the dark became its own world.

Then came a sound.

Soft. Deliberate.

Breathing.

Lucien opened his eyes.

A silhouette stood in the doorway, tall and still, hands in his pockets like the corridor answered to him.

Lucien couldn't see the face. Just the outline. The presence.

Then it spoke, low and calm.

"Mr. Cole. You have made several powerful people very afraid."

Lucien didn't answer.

He stepped closer. The line of his jaw emerged from shadow.

Lucien watched him.

The dying bulb overhead stuttered.

Lucien lifted his chin a fraction.

"I'm listening."

The man smiled.

Only one side of his mouth caught what little light remained.

"Good," he said. "You're going to want to hear this."

He stepped inside.

The door shut.

Locks engaged with a quiet finality.

The lights flickered out.

In the perfect dark, Lucien exhaled once.

The cage had just changed shape.

Thank you for surviving this story.

Lucien's war isn't over.

The city you walked through is still burning on the horizon.

The truth he dragged into the light is still echoing through every street.

The myth he became is still taking shape.

What happened in these pages wasn't an ending.

It was the moment the world learned his name.

Book 1 made him a rumor.

Book 2 made him a revolution.

What comes next is bigger than the city, the Council, the chains they tried to put on him.

The world is widening.

The shadows are deepening.

The war is only beginning.

If you want to keep walking with him,

step inside.

The Lucien Archives are open.

Character files. Hidden recordings. Timelines.

The music behind the myth.

Secrets the pages could not hold.

Enter the archives at:

Anthonyblodgett.com

The sirens will keep screaming.

The streets will keep rising.

And the world will not forget the name it chants now.

This is not the end.

This is the ignition.

About the author

Born and raised in Staten Island, New York, Anthony Blodgett spent years shaping emotion through music before turning to fiction. Writing became more than an outlet, it became survival, a way to turn feeling into fire. His work is driven by grief, longing, love, and the unseen forces that linger at the edges of ordinary life. He writes for the haunted, the heartbroken, and anyone who has ever felt too much. His goal is not to comfort, but to confront, to shake something loose inside you and leave it burning long after the final page.